THE ANCIENT

R. A. Salvatore was born in Massachusetts in 1959. He is the acclaimed author of the DemonWars trilogy: *The Demon Awakens*, *The Demon Spirit* and *The Demon Apostle*, as well as *Mortalis*, *Bastion of Darkness*, *Ascendance* and the *New York Times* bestseller *Star Wars: The New Jedi Order: Vector Prime*. He lives in Massachusetts with his wife, Diane, and their three children.

R. A. Salvatore

The Ancient

TOR

First published 2008 by Tor, Tom Doherty Associates, NY

First published in Great Britain in paperback 2009 by Tor
an imprint of Pan Macmillan Ltd
Pan Macmillan, 20 New Wharf Road, London N1 9RR
Basingstoke and Oxford
Associated companies throughout the world
www.panmacmillan.com

ISBN 978-0-330-45845-0

Copyright © R. A. Salvatore 2008

1 3 5 7 9 8 6 4 2

A CIP catalogue record for this book is available from
the British Library.

Printed and bound in the UK by CPI Mackays, Chatham ME5 8TD

Map illustration by Joseph Mirabello
Chapter opening illustrations by Shelly Wan

Acknowledgments

As with everything I do, this is for Diane and our children. Their support through this long journey has made it wonderful, indeed.

For this book, I also have to give my heartfelt thanks and appreciation to Mary Kirchoff. She found me in a slush pile twenty years ago and gave a (kind of) young writer a chance, and then two decades later found me again and brought me to Tor Books to continue my Demon-Wars work. So to Mary, a dear friend, a fabulous editor (again!) . . . but most of all, a dear friend.

Doing this book gave me something I've wanted for a long, long time—the chance to work with Tom Doherty. Tom is old-school publishing, maybe the last remnant of the days when every decision didn't have to go up one chain of command and down the other. He doesn't talk a good game, he does a good game. All I can say about my expectation compared to my actual experience is: As advertised. I'm proud to be a part of the Tor family now. Top to bottom, I've dealt with nothing but competence, enthusiasm, and a constant reminder that, at the end of the day, this is supposed to be fun.

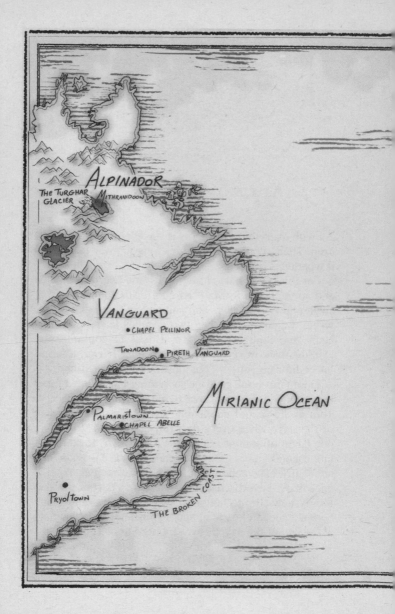

THE ANCIENT

PRELUDE

A Few Years Ago . . .

He walked across the windblown ice of the glacier known as Cold'rin, its frozen surface not causing him the slightest discomfort, not even in his feet, though he wore open-toed sandals.

He was Badden, Ancient Badden, leader of the Samhaists, who knew the magic of the world more intimately than any others in the world. Badden was the greatest of them; no creature alive was more connected to those magics than this man. So while he stood upon hundreds of feet of solid ice, he felt, too, the earth below that freeze, where the hot springs ran. Those very springs had led him to this place, and as he neared the edge of the glacier, the wide expanse of Alpinador opening before him, the old Samhaist trembled with excitement.

He knew.

He knew before he glanced down from the edge of the glacier that he had found it: Mithranidoon, the steamy lake of legend, the place where the god Samhain forsook his mortal coil and melted down into the earth, the source of all magic, the guardian of eternity. Samhain's servant was Death, men like Badden believed, who would bring the souls to the harsh judgment of the god who suffered no fool.

It was a clear morning. When Badden looked down his breath fell away from him, and many heartbeats passed before he could catch it once more. Below him was a fog-shrouded, huge, warm lake, perhaps twenty miles long and half that wide.

Mithranidoon.

The old man smiled at the rarely seen sight. He had found the holiest of Samhaist places and the source of his greatest magic just as his war with the Abellicans in Vanguard to the south had begun to ignite.

"Dame Gwydre," he mouthed, referring to the leader of the men of Vanguard. "You chose poorly in taking an Abellican as your lover." He ended with a chuckle, and no aged wheeze could be detected in the voice of the strong man, however many decades had passed since his birth. Most who knew him—or knew of him, for few actually knew Badden in any real way—believed that eight full decades and part of the ninth were behind him.

Ancient Badden slowly turned about to survey the area. He could feel Mithranidoon's strength keenly now that he had confirmed the location. Mithranidoon had beaten the glacier, and her power permeated the standing ice. He could feel it in his feet.

This place would serve, he thought, continuing his scan. Up here on the glacier he had easy access to the low mountain passes that would get him to the roads leading south into Vanguard. The vantage also afforded him solid defense against any advancing armies, though he recognized that no hostile army would ever get anywhere near to him. Not here, not with Mithranidoon feeding him her power.

"Mithranidoon," the old man said with great reverence, as if merely glimpsing the place from afar was enough to validate his entire existence, his sixty years as a Samhaist priest. But it wasn't enough, he realized suddenly, and he looked up to the heavens.

"You, there!" he said loudly, lifting his hand toward a distant, circling crow.

The bird heard him and could not ignore the call. Immediately it turned and swooped, speeding down, upturning its wings at the last moment to light gently on Ancient Badden's outstretched hand.

"I would see below the mists," the old Samhaist whispered to the bird. Badden stroked his hand over the crow's face and closed his own eyes. "To the scar Samhain rent in the earth."

Suddenly Badden launched the crow with the flick of his hand, his eyes tightly shut for he did not need them anymore. Ancient Badden saw through the eyes of the crow. The bird followed his instructions perfectly, sweeping down from the glacier, soaring vertically the hundreds of feet before it straightened out and rushed across the lake, barely a tall man's height above the water.

Ancient Badden took it all in: the caves of the trolls, lining the bank; the multitude of islands, dozens and dozens, some no more than a few rocks jutting above the steamy waters, others large and forested. One of those, particularly large and tree-covered, was dotted with huts of the general design common to the barbarians of the region, though not nearly as fortified against the elements as those found on the Alpinadoran tundra. Sure enough he spotted the tribesmen, large and strong, decorated with necklaces of claws and teeth, though, as they resided on a warm lake, they wore far less clothing than the average Alpinadoran barbarian.

Badden fell within himself and experienced the warm air coming off the spring-fed lake, warming the wings of his host.

So the barbarians had dared to inhabit this holy place. He nodded, wondering if he could somehow enlist them in his battles against Gwydre. Some tribes had joined him, if only for brief excursions against the Southerners, but none of those occasions had gone as Badden would have hoped. These Northerners, the Alpinadorans, were a stubborn lot, predictable only in their ferocity and wedded to traditions too fully for Badden to hold much sway over them.

The old Ancient chuckled and reminded himself why it was important for him to keep his eyes turned southward, toward the northern Honce province of Vanguard and to Honce proper herself. These were his people, his flock, the civilized men and women who had followed the Samhaist ways for centuries. They had followed unquestioningly until the upstart Abelle had brought them false promises in the days when Badden was but a child.

The Samhaist let those unpleasant thoughts go and basked again in the beauty of Mithranidoon, but he winced soon after as the crow continued its glide over an almost barren lump of rock. Almost barren, but not uninhabited, he saw as the bird sped past. It pained the old man greatly to see powries, red-capped dwarves, settled upon the lake.

But even that could not prepare him for the next sight, and when the bird passed another of the islands, Badden noted a familiar-looking design well under construction. Even here, they had come! Even in this most holy of Samhaist locations, the Abellican heretics had ventured and now seemed as if they meant to stay.

So shocked was Badden that he lost connection to the bird, and he staggered so badly that he nearly toppled from the edge of the glacier.

"This cannot stand," he muttered over and over again.

His mind was already whirling, calculating, searching for how he might cleanse Mithranidoon of this awful infection. All thoughts of enlisting the barbarians on the lake dissipated from him. They were all unclean. They all had to die.

"This will not stand," Ancient Badden declared, and in all his many years as leader of the Samhaists he had never once made such a declaration without seeing it to fruition.

PART ONE

In the Shadow of the Stork

I knew my course. How could I not? I had escaped my infirmities partly through use of the Abellican gemstone known as the hematite or soul stone, but even with that item of focus most of my liberation had come as a result of the training I had received by reading the book penned by my father. The Book of Jhest, the body of knowledge of the Jhesta Tu mystics, an order to which my mother belonged in the southern land known as Behr. If there was more freedom to be found from my affliction, I would find it there.

The road was obvious. All my hopes to free myself from the gemstone and the shadow of the Stork resided in one place to be sure.

That place lay to the south and east, through the port city of Ethelbert dos Entel, around the arm of the mountains and into the desert land of Behr. There I would find the Walk of Clouds and the Jhesta Tu mystics; there I would strengthen my understanding of the ways of Jhest to the point, it was my hope, where I would be free of the Stork.

It wasn't just my hope, but my only hope.

And therein lay my fear, deep and rooted and pervasive to the point of paralyzing.

We left Pryd Town, banished and glad to be. With war raging between the lairds there would be no easy passage, of course, but the ease with which I turned away from the road to Entel to the more hospitable lands surprised me, even as I justified it to Cadayle and her *mother. Pretty words, grounded in logic and honest fears, made the change in course an easy sell to my companions, but no amount of apparent justification could hide the truth from me.*

I changed course, delayed my journey to Ethelbert dos Entel and beyond, because I was afraid.

This is no new epiphany. I knew when I changed paths the true reason for my hesitance; it was not based in the many fierce soldiers Laird Ethelbert has spread across the land. Even as I offered that very reason—"too dangerous"—to Cadayle and Callen, I recognized the lie.

And now I accept it, for what is left to me if I travel all the way through the deserts of Behr to the land of the mystics only to find there that there is no deeper understanding to be gained? What is left to me if I learn that I have progressed as far as I can ever hope to climb, that the shadow of the drooling, gibbering Stork will never be more than a stride behind me?

My condition dominates every aspect of my life. Even with the soul stone strapped to my forehead, focusing my line of chi, I wage constant battles of concentration to keep the Stork at bay. I practice for hours every day, forcing deep-seeded memories into my muscles so that when they are needed they will hopefully heed my call. And yet I know that one slip, one break of concentration, and all of my work will be for naught. I will bumble, and I will fail. And not just in battle. My concerns run far deeper than simple vanity or even the price of my own life. I cannot make love to my wife without fear that she may birth a child of similar disability to my own.

My one great hope is to be free of the Stork, to live a normal existence, to have children and raise them strong and healthy.

And that one great hope lies in the Walk of Clouds and nowhere else.

Is it enough to have the hope, even if it is never realized? Would that be a better existence than discovering ultimate futility, that there is no hope? Perhaps that is the secret—the hope—for me and for all men. I hear the dreams of so many of the folk, their claims that one day they will go and live quietly in a peaceful place, by a stream or a lake or at the edge of the mighty Mirianic. So many claim those dreams throughout their lives, yet never actually find the time to execute their plans.

Are they afraid, I wonder, as I am afraid? Is it better to have the hope of paradise than to pursue it truthfully and find that it is not what you expected?

I laugh at the folly and preposterousness of it all. Despite all of my worries, I am happier than I have ever been. I walk beside Cadayle and her mother Callen and am warm and in love and loved.

My road at present is west and north. Not to Ethelbert dos Entel. Not to Behr. Not to the Walk of Clouds.

—BRANSEN GARIBOND

ONE

The Would-Be King

Small and thin, Bransen nevertheless walked with the stride of a confident man. He wore the simple clothing of a farmer, breeches and shirt and a wide-brimmed hat under which sprouted tufts of black hair. He carried a thick walking stick, too thick, it seemed, for the fit of his fine hands. But it, like the hat—like the man himself—concealed a great secret, for within its burnished wood was a hollow, and within that hollow a sword, a fabulous sword, the greatest sword in all the land north of the Belt-and-Buckle Mountains. Fashioned of wrapped silverel steel, decorated with etchings of vines and flowers and with a handle of silver and ivory that resembled a hooded serpent, the sword would grow sharper with use as the thicker outer layers of wrapping were nicked or worn away.

It was a Jhesta Tu blade, named for the reclusive mystics of the southern nation of Behr. No detail of the sword had been overlooked, not even the prongs of the crosspiece, each resembling smaller snakes poised as if to strike. For to the Jhesta Tu, the making of the sword was a holy thing, a signal of deeper meditation and perfect concentration. This sword had been fashioned by Bransen's mother, Sen Wi, and whenever he held it he could feel in its details and workmanship the spirit of that remarkable woman, long dead.

A simple wagon pulled by two horses and a donkey tethered behind rolled beside him on the cobblestone road, driven by a woman who commanded Bransen's attention so completely that he was caught off his guard when another woman walked up beside him and tucked his silk bandanna up higher under his hat.

Instinctively, Bransen's hand snapped up to catch the wrist of the older woman, Callen Duwornay, his mother-in-law. He turned to her with a smile.

"I like the way you look at her," Callen said to him quietly, motioning with her chin toward her daughter. Oblivious of Bransen's stare, Cadayle sang while she steered the wagon.

"She is the most beautiful woman I have ever seen," Bransen replied quietly enough so that Cadayle couldn't hear. "Every time I look at her she seems more beautiful still."

Callen flashed him a wide smile. "A man looked at me like that once," she said. "Or so I thought."

Though she smiled her voice was filled with wistfulness and a hint of regret. Bransen understood the latter all too well, for he knew Callen's sad tale because it was intricately and intimately entwined with his own.

Callen had been in love once, but not with her husband. She met her soulmate after she had already been given in marriage, without choice and without say, as had been the custom twenty years before in Honce. The revelations of her adulterous affair had brought her a death sentence. As per the brutal Samhaist tradition, young Callen had been "sacked"—placed in a canvas bag with a poisonous snake. After being bitten repeatedly, her veins coursing with deadly poison, she had been staked out at the edge of Pryd Holding and left to die.

Bransen's mother had come upon Callen on the path and intervened, had used her Jhesta Tu magic to draw the poison from Callen and into her own body. But unknown to Sen Wi she was with child, with Bransen, and the poison damaged him severely.

Thus he kept close his second secret, concealed under a bandanna that he wore under his hat. The bandanna held in place a soul stone, a hematite, a magical gemstone enchanted with the Abellican powers of healing. While wearing that stone Bransen could walk normally with confidence. Without it he reverted to the clumsy and awkward creature often derided as "the Stork."

"Your lover betrayed you," Bransen said, but Callen was shaking her head before he ever finished.

"He had no choice. He would have been killed beside me if he had either denied or confirmed the affair."

"That would have been a noble deed."

"A stupid one."

"Speaking the truth is not stupid," Bransen argued.

Callen grinned at him knowingly. "Then throw away your hat and draw your sword out from that log you call a walking stick."

Bransen chuckled, accepting her point. "What was his name?"

Callen shook her head. "I loved him" was all she would say. "And he gave to me my Cadayle." She looked past Bransen then to her daughter. In that moment Bransen saw more clearly than ever the resemblance between Callen and her daughter. They had the same soft, wheat-colored hair, though Callen's was showing gray now, and eyes of similar brown hue, though rare were the times Bransen had seen Callen's eyes sparkle as they did at that moment, as Cadayle's always did.

Bransen followed her gaze to his beloved wife. "Then I forgive him his cowardice, whatever his name," he said. "For he gave me Cadayle, too, I suppose."

"As your mother gave you to her. As your mother

gave life itself to Cadayle by saving mine when I carried Cadayle in my womb."

"When my mother carried me," Bransen said, looking back at his mother-in-law.

Callen sucked in her breath at his words. "I am sorry," she said.

Bransen waved her off. "Tell me true: Would you have stopped Sen Wi if you had known that drawing the poison would so damage me?"

Callen struggled for an answer as she glanced at Cadayle, which made Bransen smile all the wider.

"Nor would I," he said. "I would rather be the Stork with Cadayle beside me than a whole man without her."

"You are a whole man," Callen insisted. She reached up and tucked the hem of his bandanna.

"With the gemstone."

"Or without it," Callen said. "Bransen Garibond is a better man than any I've e'er known."

Bransen laughed again. "And perhaps one day I might walk without the soul stone. Such are the promises of the secrets of the Jhesta Tu."

"What are you discussing with your titters and giggles?" Cadayle asked from the wagon. "Are you stealing my husband then?"

"Oh, but if I could!" Callen replied.

Bransen put his arm about Callen and pulled her close as they walked side by side. It was not hard for him to understand the source of Cadayle's beauty, physical and emotional, and he knew himself to be a lucky man to have such a mother-in-law. To even think that someone would have so viciously tried to kill Callen—Bernivvigar the Samhaist had attempted to do so twice!—confounded him and filled him with outrage. Bernivvigar had also mutilated Garibond, Bransen's adopted father.

And now Bernivvigar was dead, cut down by the very sword in the log, by the very man holding the thick walking stick. Bransen was glad of it.

The conversation was ended by the sound of hooves coming down the road from behind, moving at a fast clip. That could mean only one thing on these roads in this day.

"Stork," Callen whispered to Bransen.

He was far ahead of her warning already. He closed his eyes and severed his connection—one that had become almost automatic at this point—with his soul stone. Immediately, the young man's fluid motions ceased, and he began to walk again in a gangly and awkward manner, literally throwing one hip out before him to swing his leg ahead. Now the walking stick became more than ornamental as Bransen tightened his grip on it and used it as a true crutch.

He heard the horses closing in fast from behind, but he didn't dare turn to observe for fear that the effort would make him fall flat on his face. Callen and Cadayle did look about, though, and Callen whispered, "Laird Delaval's men."

"Make way!" came a gruff command from behind a moment later. The riders pulled their horses to an abrupt stop. "Move this wagon off the road and identify yourselves!"

"He is speaking to you," Callen whispered.

Bransen struggled to turn about, finally managing it, though he nearly tumbled at several points. When he did come around he noted the astonished looks on the faces of the two soldiers, a pair of large, older men.

"What are you about?" asked one of them, a portly giant who sported a thick gray beard.

"I . . . I . . . I . . ." Bransen stammered, and he honestly couldn't get out any words beyond that, for he had grown unused to speaking without the aid of the gemstone. "I . . ."

Both men crinkled their faces with disgust.

"My son," Callen explained, and she moved to support Bransen.

"You admit that," asked the other soldier, younger

and clean-shaven, except for a tremendous mustache that seemed to reach from ear to ear. Both men laughed at Bransen's expense.

"Bah, but go on now and leave him be," said Callen. "Wounded in the war he was. Took a spear in the back saving another man. He's deserving your respect, not your taunts."

The gray beard looked at them both suspiciously. "Where was he wounded?"

"In the back," said Callen, and the man put on a sour expression indeed.

"Good lady, I've not the time for your ignorance nor for your feigned ignorance."

"South o' Pryd Town!" Callen blurted, though she had no idea if there had been any real fighting south of Pryd Town.

That answer seemed to satisfy the pair, however, to Callen's relief—until the younger man fixed his gaze upon Cadayle, his gray eyes immediately lighting up with obvious interest.

"He's not really my son," Callen blurted, drawing his attention. "He's my daughter's husband, so I'm thinking of him as such."

"Daughter's husband?" the younger man echoed, staring at Cadayle. "He's married to you?"

"Aye," said the woman. "My beloved. We're for Delaval to see if any of the monks there might be helping him."

The soldiers shared a look. The younger one slid down from his saddle and moved beside Bransen and Callen.

"What's your name?" he asked, but when Callen started to answer for Bransen, the man held up his hand to hush her.

"Bra . . . Br . . . Brrrran," Bransen sputtered, spraying the man with every forced syllable.

"Bran?"

"Sen," Callen added, and the man hushed her with a scowl and a sharp retort.

"Bran?" he asked again.

"S . . . Sssss . . . Brranssen," said the Stork.

"Bransen?" the soldier asked, walking a circuit about him.

"Y . . . Y . . . Yes."

"Stupid name," said the soldier, brushing into Bransen, which sent the Stork into an exaggerated stumble, one hand flailing, the other desperately trying to get the walking stick under him for support.

The honesty of that awkward gait and those fumbling movements had the soldiers glancing at each other again with a mixture of disgust and sympathy. The younger one grabbed Bransen roughly and helped steady him.

"I'm sorry for your loss," he said to Cadayle.

"He's not dead," the woman replied, obviously trying hard to fight back her anger at the soldier for bumping Bransen.

"Sorry for that, too," said the man with a snicker. "Monks ain't to help this one. Better for him and for yourself if he'd've just died out on the field." He gave a derisive snort and walked away from Bransen, toward the wagon, visually inspecting it as he neared. "You're loyal for bringing him to the monks, I expect. But if he ain't for pleasing you, then you just let me know," he added with a wink and a lewd smile.

Cadayle swallowed hard. Callen moved immediately to Bransen and put her hand on his forearm, fearing that he would leap ahead and cut the fool down for the insult.

Abruptly other sounds could be heard from behind, plodding hooves and the creak of a coach.

"Or maybe she's liking those jerking movements in their lovemaking, eh?" the young soldier asked his older companion, who frowned at him in response.

"Just get the wagon off the road," the gray beard said.

"But the ground is uneven and full of roots," Cadayle complained as the younger man moved around to the side of the horses. "And our wheels are worn and will not—"

"Just shut your pretty mouth and be glad that we've not the time for other things," the younger soldier said to her. "Or the time to take the horses and wagon in the name of Laird Delaval." He gave a disapproving look at the wagon and team and old Doully the donkey tethered behind, adding, "Not that any of 'em're worth stealing."

"Don't, I beg!" said Cadayle, but the man grabbed the nearest horse's bridle and roughly tugged the creature to the side, guiding the wagon down a small embankment, where it rolled fast for a few seconds, coming to rest up tight against a tree.

Up on the road across the way, the gray beard walked his horse at Callen and Bransen, forcing them to move off the other side of the road, pulling his companion's horse beside him as he stepped farther along.

"Bow your heads for Prince Yeslnik, Laird of Pryd!" he instructed, staring at Callen all the while, making sure to keep his horse between the two wanderers and the approaching coach. As it rolled by, all gilded in shiny gold and pulled by a fine and strong team, Bransen noted the drivers, a pair of men he had seen before. He saw, too, the Lady Olym, Prince Yeslnik's annoying and spoiled wife, as she stared out the window.

He smiled as he glanced up at her from his half-bowed head. She regarded him with a start, which seemed a bit of recognition. Bransen winked at her for that, and she fell back, putting her gloved hand to her mouth.

That made Bransen smile all the more, but he kept his face aimed at the ground to make sure the gray-bearded soldier didn't catch on.

"He is a prince, you say?" Callen asked the man. "Or a laird, for you're calling him both."

"Prince Yeslnik of Delaval," the gray beard confirmed, moving his horse onto the cobblestones. Across the way, his younger companion rushed up the embankment to join him and quickly mounted.

"Named Laird of Pryd, soon to be Laird of Delaval," the younger man insisted.

"Aye, and the king of all Honce, don't you doubt," said his companion. "Ethelbert's soon to break, and when we're done with that one, we'll put the other lairds in place in short order."

"Aye," agreed the younger. "Now that we've got the river running free o' wild northmen and goblins, and Palmaristown's joined in Laird Delaval's cause, the ships're moving and it's not to be long. Ethelbert's city of Entel will find herself blockaded by the spring, and without his supplies and warriors flowing in from the southland he won't last long."

The gray beard shot his young and boisterous companion a scolding expression, clearly willing him to silence by showing him that he was wagging his tongue too much.

Bransen caught the nuance and understood that they were speaking of something terribly important.

To him, though, it all seemed meaningless banter, for he cared not at all which side won this fight, or what Honce came to look like thereafter. He had no love for any laird and could only hope that they would all kill each other in the last throes of the seemingly endless war. One thing did strike him, though: the notion that Prince Yeslnik had already been named as the replacement laird for Prydae, a man dead because of Bransen. It amused Bransen to think that Yeslnik was in line to become Laird of Delaval, and even king of Honce. The man was a fool and a coward, Bransen knew all too well. He had come upon the very coach that had just rolled past a long time before, when vicious bloody-cap powries had forced it from the road. Yeslnik, his wife, and their two drivers (one of whom had been seriously wounded) were surely doomed, but Bransen, the Highwayman, had come to save the day.

Of course, he had taken some reward for his efforts—much more than the stingy and ungrateful Prince Yeslnik had offered—and so the tale of his heroics had been buried by the prince's wounded pride.

Bransen closed his eyes and reconnected with the soul stone set under his black silk bandanna, leaving the Stork far behind.

"Laird Yeslnik?" he whispered under his breath as the two soldiers moved off. Cadayle called to the departing men, begging them to help her get her wagon back on the road, but of course they just ignored her.

"King Yeslnik?" Bransen asked quietly, shaking his head as if the possibility was truly incomprehensible. And indeed, to him, it surely was.

Still, given his experience with the nobility of Honce, he was hardly surprised.

"We should have gone straight out for Behr, as we'd planned," Cadayle said to Bransen as he coaxed and tugged the horses to get the wagon back on the road.

"No choice to us," he answered, and not for the first time.

Cadayle sighed and didn't argue. Both of them had wanted to get out of Honce to board a ship in the port of Ethelbert dos Entel and sail around the Belt-and-Buckle Mountains into Behr. Bransen's greatest desire—at least, that which he expressed to his two companions—was to find the Mountains of Fire and the Walk of Clouds, the home of the Jhesta Tu mystics. Their centuries of wisdom had created the tome that Bransen's father had penned. Bransen's mother, Sen Wi, had been of their order. In their midst, Bransen believed, he would find the answers to his dilemma. There, he would attune himself more fully to his *ki-chi-kree*, his line of life energy, and would thus free himself of having to wear the soul stone strapped to his forehead. That soul stone allowed Bransen to keep his line of life energy straight and strong; without it, his energy sputtered and flitted in every different direction, leaving him the crippled Stork.

The Jhesta Tu had his answers, he believed, and he prayed. But he could not go there at that time, as he had hoped, not through Ethelbert dos Entel, at least, for the place was locked down, and any man who entered the holding of Laird Ethelbert without proper authorization would find himself pressed into service or hanged by the neck.

And so the trio had come southwest instead of southeast and now neared Delaval, the principal city of the land, the seat of power for Laird Delaval, the man who would be king of Honce. Rumors along the road said that passage could be gained to Behr from that city, though it would be a roundabout journey indeed, sailing up the great river, the Masur Delaval (recently named for the ruling family), then through the southern expanse of the Gulf of Honce, and down along the broken region of small holdings known as the Mantis Arm.

It would be an expensive journey, no doubt, and perhaps one full of danger, but the roads simply were not an option at this time of intense warfare.

Or perhaps they were, but Bransen wasn't quite ready to make that all-important journey.

They were moving again soon after. Around a bend in the road less than a mile to the west the trio came in sight of the renowned city nestled at the base of southern hills, surrounding three fast-flowing tributaries that swept down through the streets and joined in a deep pool before the city's northern wharves. This was the head of the Masur Delaval, a river whose currents swirled and backed with the varying tides of the northern gulf.

The city itself was everything Bransen, Cadayle, and Callen had imagined, with rows and rows of stone and wooden buildings, many two or even three stories high. A stone wall surrounded much of the town, including all of the central region. Within it sat the most impressive structure that any of the three had ever seen, a castle so imposing and expansive that it dominated the landscape wholly, a series of three connected keeps whose walls towered so high and strong that Laird Delaval's designs on ruling the entirety of Honce as the one king suddenly seemed all too tenable.

By late afternoon, the trio had come to the outskirts, crossing through lanes bordered by trade shops of every type and with a large produce market set in a wide square just outside the city wall. A few peasants moved about the market, old women mostly, trying to get in a last purchase before the vendors closed their kiosks.

"Rotten goods," Callen whispered to the others, for Cadayle had come down from the wagon now to walk beside them, the three of them leading the team slowly. "Kitchen throwaways from the castle, no doubt."

"No different than in Pryd Town," Cadayle said. "The lairds and their closest take all the best, and we get what's left."

"Except the best that we never let go their way in the first place," Callen remarked with a wry grin.

"Or the best that a certain black-clothed highwayman took from them," added Bransen, and all three shared a laugh.

Cadayle was the first to stop, though, as she caught the undercurrent of the statement. She stared at her husband suspiciously until at last he looked her way with a puzzled expression.

"You can't be thinking . . ." she said.

"I often am."

"Of letting him out here," Cadayle finished. "The Highwayman, I mean. You keep yourself in the guise of the Stork while we're in Delaval."

"No guise, I fear," said Bransen as he reached up and popped the soul stone out from under his bandanna, quickly pocketing it. Instantly he felt the first twinges of separation, the first sparks of discord from his line of *ki-chi-kree*. "It is who . . . oo I ammm."

Cadayle winced at the stutter, despite her insistence.

"You hate seeing me like that," Bransen remarked, his

voice relatively strong and steady. Cadayle looked at him in surprise. In response, he merely glanced down at his hand, still in his pocket, still holding the soul stone. He was getting much better at maintaining that connection even when the stone was not strapped to the focal point of his *chi*, up on his forehead.

Cadayle frowned, though, and Bransen immediately began his awkward gait.

"Don't you be thinking of stealing anything in this town," Cadayle whispered. "Laird Delaval frightens me."

Bransen didn't reply, but of course he was thinking precisely that.

They were turned away at the gate, for no wagons and horses were allowed inside other than those owned by the fortunate nobility who lived within the walls and the higher-priced merchants and tradesmen who had to pay dearly for a license to bring a horse or donkey or wagon inside. The guards did point them at a nearby stable outside the wall, however, and assured them that the proprietor was a man of high regard.

His reputation didn't matter much to them anyway. They had little of value in the wagon other than Bransen's silk clothing and the pack they simply would carry away with them. Doully was old and more a friend than a worker, and they had planned to sell the horse team upon their arrival anyway, for the poor beasts had seen too much of ill-groomed roads and broken trails.

"They'll both need shoeing, to be sure," Yenium the stablemaster informed them. He was a tall and very thin man with a dark complexion and darker beard that grew in every day. "Ye been walking a long way."

"Too long," said Callen.

The man stared at Bransen.

"Bringing him to the monks," Cadayle explained. "He was hurt in the war."

Yenium laughed aloud. "But they'll do ye no good," he said, waving his hands in apology even as he spoke the words. "Not unless ye got good gold to pay, and lots of it."

Callen and Cadayle exchanged sour looks, though neither was surprised, of course. It seemed as if some things were constant throughout the land of Honce.

"Our funds run short," Callen said. "We were hoping that you would have need of the horses and the wagon."

"Buy 'em?"

"They've walked too much of the roads," Callen explained.

"True enough," Yenium said. "And the donkey?"

"We'll be keeping that one," said Callen. "We've a long way to go yet."

Knowing their negotiations to be in good hands, Bransen let Cadayle lead him off to the side. Sure enough, Callen joined them shortly after, jiggling a small bag of silver coins and even a single piece of gold. "And he's to board Doully for us free for as long as we're in Delaval," Callen said with a satisfied grin. "A fair price."

"More than," Cadayle agreed and slung the pack over her shoulder. She was about to suggest that they go and see the city proper before the daylight waned but was interrupted by the blare of horns from inside the city wall. Cheers followed, and many of the peasants outside the wall began streaming for the gates, moving eagerly and chattering with obvious excitement.

Callen and Cadayle flanked Bransen and moved him along swiftly to beat the rush. Fortunately, they weren't far from the gate, and with a rather lewd wink at Cadayle, the young guard let them through. Not that the view was any better beyond the wall as thousands had gathered around the grand square, all jumping and shouting, lifting their arms high and waving red towels.

"What is it, then?" Cadayle asked a nearby reveler.

The woman looked at her as if she must be crazy.

"We've just come in," Cadayle explained. "We know nothing of the source of the celebration."

"The laird's come down," the woman explained.

"The king, ye mean!" another corrected.

"Laird Delaval—King Delaval soon enough, by the graces of Abelle and the Ancient Ones," the first said.

Bransen shook his head shakily, continually amazed at the manner in which the peasants always seemed to hedge their bets regarding the afterlife, citing both of the dominant religions.

"He's come down with his lady and all the others," said the woman. "Tonight the brave Prince Yeslnik's to be formally named as Laird of Pryd Holding. That and a host of other honors on the man. Oh, but he's handsome, and so brave! He's killed a hundred of Ethelbert's men, don't ye know?"

Cadayle smiled and nodded, hiding her knowing smirk well as she turned to regard Bransen, who of course knew better than to believe any such supposed heroics attributed to the foppish Prince Yeslnik. But Cadayle's smile disappeared in a blink, for Callen stood there alone with no sign of Bransen. Immediately Cadayle brought a hand up to her pack, realizing as she grasped it that it had been relieved of some of its contents. It was not hard for her to guess which things might have been taken.

She gave an awkward bow and moved away from the peasant woman, catching her mother by the elbow and leading her to a quieter spot.

"What is he thinking?" she asked.

"That with all of them down here . . ." Callen motioned with her chin toward the castle.

Cadayle heaved a great and helpless sigh.

Her husband was a stubborn one, she knew.

And that stubbornness was likely to get him killed.

Bransen didn't change into his black silk suit until he reached the shadows at the base of the stone wall to the castle's highest and most fortified keep. The exotic cloth had held up well through the years, and was still shiny, as if through some magic the dirt could not gain a hold on it. The right sleeve of the shirt had been torn away by Bransen, to make both his mask (for he unrolled the gem-holding headband down to the tip of his nose, with eyeholes cut in appropriately) and a strip of cloth that he tied about his upper right arm to hide an easily identifiable birthmark.

As he had expected, almost all of the soldiers had gone down to watch the pomp and ceremony of the anointing of Laird Yeslnik. The main gates were guarded, he noted as he crossed about the side streets and back alleys, as were all the entry points to the castle proper.

But Bransen was Jhesta Tu, or a close approximation at least, and he didn't need a doorway. So he moved to the back wall, out of view, and donned his black suit.

He glanced around, hearing the distant sounds of the growing celebration. He saw no guards in the area and held confidence that any who were supposed to be here, behind the structure and thus blocked from the merrymaking, were likely away from their posts, watching the happenings in the lower bailey.

He couldn't be sure, though, and that truth gave him pause.

"But you are the Highwayman," he reminded himself, his grin widening beneath the black mask.

Bransen fell within himself. He thought of the gemstones, of the malachite, and used the feelings its touch had inspired to reach that corresponding energy within his *ki-chi-kree*. If he had had the magical gemstone in his possession he could have floated off the ground, he knew, but even without it, even just remembering its powers, Bransen lightened his body greatly. He reached up with one hand and pulled himself up the wall.

Like a spider he scrambled, his hands and feet finding grooves in the stone. So weightless had he become that it mattered not how deep the ledge or how firm his grip. In less than a minute the Highwayman had scaled the seventy-five feet of the highest tower, all the way to the one narrow window on this back side of the structure. He peeked inside, then settled himself securely on the ledge. With a look all around at the wide and glorious rolling countryside south of Delaval, he slipped into the dimly lit room.

This was the tower of royalty, he knew at once from the many valuables—paintings, tapestries, vases, and a plethora of other trinkets and utensils and artworks.

The Highwayman rubbed his hands together and went to work.

It is long overdue, and less than you have earned," Lady Olym called back behind her as she entered her private bedchamber. "Your uncle should have named you Laird of Delaval and been done with it. His only son is not worthy, of course."

A murmur of protest came back to her from Yeslnik's room, too garbled for her to decipher—not that she cared to, anyway.

"Laird of Pryd Town," Olym said. If she was thrilled her voice did not reflect it. "Now I suppose we will have to live in that dreary place."

She pulled off her bulky bejeweled dress and an assortment of accessories. Stripped to her sheer nightdress, she sat down at her vanity, admiring her powdered face in the pretty mirror set atop the small marble table. One by one she pulled off her oversized rings, each set with a fabulous precious stone.

They paled in comparison to the necklace she wore, though, which was set with diamonds, rubies, and emeralds, one after another, three rows thick and from shoulder to shoulder. Olym gently stroked the precious stones, staring at them in the mirror as if in a trance. So fully did they hold her attention that she didn't even notice the black-clothed figure that had moved up to stand directly behind her.

Olym jumped indeed when a hand settled on her own and a soft voice whispered, "Allow me to help you with that, dear lady."

She started to scream, but the hand clapped tightly over her mouth.

"Do not cry out, I beg of you," the Highwayman said. "I will not harm you, dear lady. On my word." He brought his head down to rest his chin on her shoulder so that they could look each other in the eye through the mirror. For a moment Olym seemed to swoon, her chest heaving.

"On my word," the Highwayman said again, and he gave her a plaintive and questioning look and eased his hand away from her mouth just a bit.

Olym nodded her head, and the Highwayman pulled his hand away.

"You have come to ravish me!" Olym wailed.

The bemused Highwayman stared at her, for her tone sounded more hopeful than terrified.

Olym turned on him sharply. "Take me, then," she offered. "But be quick and be gone and know that I shan't enjoy it!"

Without the soul stone Bransen always stuttered badly, but never had he found words harder to find than at that moment, though the soul stone was, of course, strapped securely to his forehead.

Olym turned further about and threw back her head, the back of one hand across her forehead as if in despair. The movement thrust forth her breasts, of course, and the sheer nightdress did little to hide her obvious excitement.

"Take me, then! Ravish me! Have at me with your animal savagery."

"And force you to make little barnyard noises?" the Highwayman asked, trying hard not to laugh.

"Oh, yes, if you must! If that is what I need do to escape murder at the end of your blade!"

The Highwayman didn't quite know how to say, "But

all I want are the jewels," so he stuttered again—until footsteps sounded in the hall, coming their way. "I beg your silence," he whispered, putting a finger over his pursed lips, fading into the shadows so seamlessly behind a tapestry that Olym had to blink and stare stupidly, wondering if he had ever really been there.

"Ah, wife," Yeslnik said, entering the room. "I am randy from the excitement of the day." He paused and looked at her admiringly, at her nearly naked form and obvious state. "Apparently I am not alone in my humor!"

Now it was Olym's turn to stutter. She glanced repeatedly at the shadows where the Highwayman had disappeared.

Yeslnik sidled up to her and pulled her tight against him, his eyes narrowing. "I am the Laird of Pryd Holding," he said, and then again and again. With each proclamation he squeezed Olym tighter to him.

"My laird," Olym said, looking past him as he turned, again to the spot where the Highwayman had gone.

Had gone and returned, she noted, for he stood there, leaning against her vanity, one arm bare and one blanketed in black silk crossed over his chest, a look of utter amusement on his face, his so-handsome face.

Olym took a deep breath and gave a mewling sound.

"Oh, my princess," Yeslnik gasped. "I am the Laird of Pryd Holding!" He shuddered as he squeezed her against him more tightly still.

"So you have mentioned a dozen times," a masculine voice said behind him. Yeslnik froze in place. "If you say it a dozen more, perhaps you will convince yourself you are worthy of the title."

Yeslnik spun about. "You!" he cried.

"I could be no one else," the Highwayman said with a shrug.

"How?"

"Your interrogation techniques leave much to be desired, I fear," the Highwayman said. "More so when one considers that if anyone here is a prisoner, it is not I."

"Not you?" Yeslnik stammered, trying hard to catch up.

"Yes you, not I," said the Highwayman.

"Not I?"

"Yes, you!"

"You?"

"Now you have it!" the Highwayman said, and pointed at Yeslnik and emphatically added, "You."

"Do not harm him!" Olym cried, and she threw herself in front of Yeslnik, her arms wide to hold him back—and also to give the Highwayman a complete viewing. "Take me as you will. Ravish me!"

"Olym!" Yeslnik cried.

"I will do anything for you, my laird," Olym wailed.

"Back to the barnyard, always there," the Highwayman remarked. Yeslnik stared at him incredulously.

"I will suffer his passion for you, my love," Olym said to her husband. "I will save you with my womanly charms."

"With your jewels, you mean," the Highwayman corrected. Faster than either of them could react, he came forward and snatched the necklace from Olym's neck, then, for good measure, scooped the rings from the vanity.

"Not again!" Yeslnik cried. In a moment of uncustomary courage (or more likely it was just his anger overruling his good sense), he threw Olym aside and raised his fists threateningly. He snapped his hand to the near side of the vanity, where Olym kept a sharp knife she used to scrape the dark hairs from her chin. Yeslnik stepped forward, waving the knife out before him.

The Highwayman dropped his hands to his side, sighed, and shook his head.

"You'll not make a fool of me again," Yeslnik declared.

"I fear you reached that marker long before I arrived," the Highwayman replied.

The Laird of Pryd Holding finally sorted that insult

out and stabbed at the man in rage. The Highwayman turned, and the blade slipped past harmlessly.

Yeslnik retracted and stabbed again, and the Highwayman dodged the other way.

Yeslnik slashed across at the man's head, but of course the agile Highwayman easily ducked the awkward strike, then came up again and with even less effort sidestepped the next futile stab.

"Truly, Prince Yeslnik, you are making this more difficult," the Highwayman said. He ducked another slash, sidestepped another stab, then caught the move he had been waiting for, an uppercut thrusting the knife for the bottom of his chin.

It never got close. The Highwayman's left hand caught the prince's forearm, and his right hand clamped over Yeslnik's at just the right angle for the thief to buckle the prince's wrist, bending the hand forward suddenly. The Highwayman pressed, overextending the bend, driving Yeslnik's knuckles down toward his wrist. Under that strain and pain, Yeslnik could not hold his grip on the knife. Even as he realized he had let it go, the Highwayman's left hand shot out and slapped him across the face, backhanded him the other way, and slapped him a third time for good measure.

"Do you insist on making this harder?" the Highwayman asked, presenting the knife out, handle first, toward the prince.

Infuriated beyond reason, Yeslnik grabbed the blade and slashed wildly, again hitting nothing but air. In sheer frustration he threw the knife. His eyes went wide indeed when he noted that the thief had caught it so easily.

Yeslnik turned and cried out, bolting for the door. "Take my wife!" he shrieked.

The Highwayman sprang into a sidelong cartwheel, catching his hand on the edge of the vanity, planting his other hand flat on its top, and springing away to intercept Yeslnik at the door.

"Your knife," he said, tossing the blade into the air.

Yeslnik's eyes followed its ascent as the prince skidded to a stop. To his credit Yeslnik caught the blade, but when he looked back down he found the tip of a fabulous and too-familiar sword an inch from his face. He gave a curious sound, strangely similar to his wife's earlier mewling, and let the knife drop to the floor.

The Highwayman shook his head. "Now what am I to do with you?"

"Oh," Lady Olym wailed, throwing her arm against her forehead and falling back, conveniently onto the room's rather large bed.

Both the Highwayman and Yeslnik sighed.

A noise from somewhere down the hall reminded them that the ceremony had ended and many of the castle's inhabitants were returning from the lower bailey.

"Under the bed," the Highwayman ordered Yeslnik abruptly, prodding the prince with his sword, guiding him around. Finally he stepped up and pushed Yeslnik forward.

"While you ravish my wife above me?"

"Oh," wailed Olym, and her knees drifted apart.

The Highwayman shoved Yeslnik harder for that, putting him down to his knees at the side of the bed. "You with him," he ordered Olym, and all humor had left his tone. "Under the bed!"

"But . . ." Olym protested, as sadly as any bride left at the altar.

"Under the bed. Now! The both of you." He prodded Yeslnik as he spoke, driving the man under with the tip of his sword. Grabbing Olym with his free hand, he yanked her off the bed. She fell heavily at his feet, but nothing other than her pride was hurt, he saw, as she looked up and reached for him desperately.

Yeslnik grabbed her and dragged her under the bed with him.

"In the middle," the Highwayman ordered. He dropped down and prodded at them with his sword, forcing them

back from the edge. He looked all around, thinking to
block the four openings of the bed. But alas, there was
not enough furniture in the room to seal them in.

Sounds from outside the room heightened the Highwayman's urgency. Improvising, he leaped in a roll across
the end of the bed, coming to his feet facing the foot. He
looked from its thin legs to his sword and back. His eyes
scanned the headboard. He could clear it and easily, he realized, as the movements sorted out before him. He had to
be precise; he had to be quick.

But he was Jhesta Tu.

The Highwayman presented his sword before him
and took a deep and steadying breath. Underneath the
bed Yeslnik and Olym chattered but he left their voices
far behind, concentrating on the task before him. Both
hands grasped the hilt of the sword as he lifted it slowly
before his right shoulder, keeping the blade perpendicu-
lar to the floor.

He stepped out with his left foot suddenly, slashing
the blade down low, then reversed the swing so quickly
that it passed over the severed bed leg before the bed
had even dropped. Now he stepped right, finishing the
move as his backhand took out the other leg.

The foot of the bed dropped as the Highwayman
leaped back to the right in a twisting somersault. He
came to his feet beside the bed, his back to it. Halfway
up its length he continued his spin, his blade neatly severing the third leg.

Yeslnik and Olym cried out in protest, but their initial
escape route, anticipated by the Highwayman, had been
lost with the collapse of the bed's right side.

The Highwayman let go of the sword with his right
hand as he came around. As soon as he faced the bed
squarely again his legs twitched, lifting him in a dive
ahead and to the side. He turned his free right hand under and caught the top of the headboard, allowing him
to turn about as he lifted a straight-legged somersault
that ended with a sudden tuck that spun him over and a

more sudden extension that landed him upright facing the bed. But only for a moment, for he dropped and slashed to the right, and the fourth and final leg fell away, dropping the full weight of the bed onto Yeslnik and Olym, mercifully muffling their annoying cries.

The Highwayman stepped back and regarded his handiwork with a nod that reflected both surprise and satisfaction. He looked down at the small sack tied to his belt, bulging with coin and jewels, and nodded again.

"Do remember that I did not kill you, and it would have been an easy thing," he said to Yeslnik, bending low and peering under at the grunting and outraged man. "And do remember that I did not ravish your wife."

Yeslnik cursed and spat at him, but the Highwayman had perplexed himself with his own words. He leaned back to consider them and didn't even notice the feeble insult, verbal or watery.

"You remember that I did not ravish her," the Highwayman clarified, looking back at Yeslnik. "I do hope that dear Lady Olym will forget that fact, for I am certain that my lack of action angers her more than anything else I might have done, murdering you included."

"How dare you?" Yeslnik demanded.

"It is really quite easy," the Highwayman assured him, and with a tap of two fingers to his forehead, he rushed away to the window.

But darkness hadn't fallen yet, and the upper bailey teemed with guards.

Nearly an hour passed before Prince Yeslnik finally managed to squirm out from under the heavy bed. His howls took some time to get the attention of some servants, who at last rushed in and helped him pull the bed up enough to allow Olym to unceremoniously slither out.

"You!" Olym screamed at her husband. She made no

effort to cover herself, though more and more people were charging into the room to see what was the matter. "You fancy yourself the laird of a holding, and you cannot deal with a single thief? You are a hero among men, and yet a single, small man chases you under your wife's bed like a frightened rabbit?" She moved to slap him, but Yeslnik caught her arm then her other one and held her fast.

"Would you be less angry if he had ravished you?" Yeslnik asked, more an accusation than a question. Lady Olym wailed—the first sincere wail she had offered that day—and collapsed onto what was left of her bed.

It seemed as if Yeslnik only then realized that the room was full of people, many of whom were staring at his revealed wife. "Out! Out!" he demanded, chasing them from the room. He gave a last, disgusted look at Olym and followed, ordering the guards to find the Highwayman and not return without the bastard's severed head.

Olym brought her hands to her face and sobbed for a long, long while as the room darkened. She was near sleep when soft lips brushed her forehead.

"Marvelous lady," said the Highwayman, who had never left the room. Olym's eyes popped wide open, and she thrust herself up to her elbows to face him directly.

"I cannot ravish a married woman, by the code of honor that guides me," the thief graciously explained. "But I assure you that the code is sorely tried when I glimpse a creature of such beauty." He reached up and gently stroked her face. Olym closed her eyes and swooned, falling back to the bed, her fingers kneading at the plush blankets.

"Think of me," the Highwayman bade her, "as I travel the wilds of the northland."

And then he was gone, sprinting to the window and

going through so easily and swiftly that he was out before Olym had even glanced his way.

Not to fear," Bransen assured Callen and Cadayle the next day when they walked down the road out of Delaval, leading Doully the donkey. "For I told Lady Olym that I would be in the North."

"But our road is to the north," Callen replied. "And there you will truly be."

"Exactly," said Bransen and he flashed that grin, smug and disarming at the same time.

Sure enough, Laird Delaval's guards, at the request of Prince Yeslnik, streamed out of the city that same morning, heading south in search of the Highwayman as the Lady Olym had directed.

TWO

Feeding the God Well

Samhaist Dantanna crouched low as he moved through the area of knee-deep white caribou moss. The plant could be mashed into a potent salve and made a fine tea, but Dantanna was looking for something even more valuable: dauba bulbs. They only grew among the moss, and never in great number. Even one bulb would make for a fine day's hunting, though, for the Samhaist could then prepare the most wonderful dauba stew, a brew that would take all the pains from his joints for a week and more.

Dantanna didn't like this land, Alpinador, far preferring the milder climate of Vanguard, south of the mountains.

It was not his place to question, though—at least not openly.

He had to keep telling himself that, for there was so much afoot in the world that Dantanna, still young and not completely jaded, did indeed wish to question. He bent low and brushed aside the moss as he quickened his pace. He knew there would be some dauba around this particularly thick strand of caribou moss—there had to be.

"That's a bootlace, not a vine, boy," came a gruff voice, and only then did Dantanna realize that he was not alone in the white field, though how in the world someone else had come in without gaining his attention he couldn't begin to fathom.

Until he looked up to see the weathered face, the thick mustache, and the pointed, feathered cap. Then he knew. The man standing tall and straight before him might have been forty or seventy—he had those ageless features that exude both strength and the wisdom of experience. So much experience.

"Master Sequin," he stammered, sidling back a few feet. The old scout didn't answer other than to stare unblinkingly and witheringly at the Samhaist. "I did not know that you were in the area," Dantanna said.

"Like to state the obvious, do you?"

Dantanna nodded stupidly. "I am Samhaist Dantanna—once we met, in Vanguard and near to where the Abelli . . ."

"Chapel Pellinor," the weathered Jameston Sequin said. Dantanna nodded, trying not to look too pleased that this great man had remembered him.

"I never forget a face," Jameston went on. "Or the name of a man I consider worth remembering."

Dantanna beamed all the more.

"What did you say your name was again?"

The Samhaist slouched. "Dantanna."

"You travel with old Badden?"

"Ancient Badden," Dantanna corrected, and (surprisingly to him) forcefully.

"You're a long way from home, boy."

Dantanna didn't begin to know how to take that. "There is the war . . ."

"The one your Ancient Badden started."

"Not so!" Dantanna protested with a severity that

surprised him given his ambivalence, often disgust, at the fighting over Vanguard. "Dame Gwydre began it all. She chose and chose ill."

"Because she fell in love with a man?"

"Because she fell in love with an Abellican monk!"

Jameston Sequin chuckled and shook his head. "An offense worth all of this?" he asked.

Dantanna half shook his head and half nodded, giving no verbal response, because he knew that if he did he would never get any true resonance or confidence in his voice.

"Well, you fight your battles as you choose them," Jameston said. "I'll let the folk of Vanguard choose which religion, Samhaist or Abellican, suits their needs."

"And which for Jameston?" Dantanna asked, thinking himself sly for the instant it took Jameston to mock him utterly with a laugh.

The old scout brought his arm out in front of him, holding a sack, and still applying that withering gaze over Dantanna, he upended it before the man. More than a dozen pointy troll ears tumbled out onto the ground at Dantanna's feet.

"It's theirs to choose," Jameston said.

"As it is yours," Dantanna replied, still staring down at the multitude of ears—ears of creatures Ancient Badden had enlisted in the fight.

"If my choice is between a man and a troll, it's not a hard one, boy," Jameston said. "I said I didn't much care, and I don't, but you tell your Ancient Badden that I'm not for letting glacial trolls murder families in the name of Samhain or in the name of anyone else."

"Our struggle is . . ."

". . . none of my business," Jameston finished for him, "and none of my care. But when I see a troll, I kill a troll, and I don't ask who it's working for." He snorted derisively and started away.

"Master Sequin," Dantanna called after him. "If we meet again, will you remember my name?"

Jameston didn't stop or look back. "I forgot it already."

From a high perch on the very edge of the great glacier Cold'rin, Ancient Badden stared out across the miles of the southland. In his mind's eye, he looked past the frozen tundra of Alpinador to the thick forests of Vanguard. He envisioned the battles raging there, Honce man against goblin, Honce man against glacial troll, Honce man against the sturdy Alpinadoran barbarians.

His army, battling the men of Honce, punishing them for their growing acceptance of the heretics of Blessed Abelle.

A smile creased Ancient Badden's face, strangely white teeth (for one of his age) standing brightly in the midst of his wild black mustache and beard, a gigantic affair that poked out in a semicircle of sharp points beneath the old Samhaist's weathered face, its ends sharpened by dung and plaited with ribbons black and red. He would teach them.

Word had come that Chapel Pellinor had fallen—sacked as much by angry Honce men as by Ancient Badden's hordes. The few surviving monks were even then being dragged north, to this place, to be sacrificed to Ancient D'no, the worm god of the frozen lands.

Ancient Badden lowered his gaze to the clouds of steam at the base of the glacier's cliff face, where the ice met the hot waters of the lake called Mithranidoon. The mists seemed to him to thicken. An indication, perhaps, that D'no was pleased by the news? Or his imagination, his thrill, at the prospect of feeding the god so well?

Ancient Badden envisioned the hot waters beneath

that cloud, the Holy Lake of Mithranidoon, the Rift of Samhain, the gift of the Ancient Ones to their children as a reward for their wondrous efforts here.

A particularly sharp retort turned the old Samhaist around, to view the crevice some fifty feet north of where he stood. A pair of giants, fifteen feet tall and with shoulders as wide as the wingspan of a great eagle, rolled heavy mallets up into the air, slamming them down concurrently upon the flattened head of a battered log, a sharpened wedge that drove deeper into the glacier with every smash. Once they had driven that one down to the level of the glacier, Ancient Badden would bless the spike and prepare its end with spells and fire, that another could be placed upon it and driven down, pushing the bottom one even deeper.

Over to the right of the giants, where the crevice was much wider and much deeper, several glacial trolls hung by their ankles, suspended beneath crossbeams by thin ropes. Their arms were weighted, forcing them into a diver's stretch, and their wrists had been expertly cut, their thin blood dripping down into the chasm and turning into a fine, coating mist in the windy gorge. Troll blood did not freeze, and the coating of it in the crevice would prevent the melted waters from mitigating the damage to the edge of the glacier. One troll, at least one, was dead and dried out now, Ancient Badden noted, but no worries, for the wretched little beasts were as thick as hares in summer Vanguard.

He scanned farther to the right, to the elaborate ice bridge he had magically constructed: it spanned the widest expanse of the chasm, with enough room on either side so that it would continue to allow crossing even when the rift had become as wide as intended. Ancient Badden couldn't help but smile as his gaze moved farther to the right, to the mountain wall bordering the glacier on the east, for against that dark stone loomed Ancient Badden's greatest work yet: his home, Devongel, a castle of crystalline ice, of elegant, winding spires and thick walls, of defensive and confusing mazes both practical and beautiful.

His smile disappeared when he looked back to the left, over by the working giants, and noted a smaller form, dressed in the telltale light green robes of a Samhaist, though surely nothing as elaborate as Ancient Badden's gown, decorated as it was with claws and teeth from various carnivores, and with leafy designs woven with threads green and yellow so that it looked as if the Samhaist could walk into a strand of brush and simply disappear. About his waist, Ancient Badden wore a thick red sash, tied on his right hip, with its frayed ends nearly reaching the ground. Only one Samhaist, the Ancient himself, could wear this holiest of belts, and Ancient Badden put his hand on that knot now, as the ever-annoying Priest Dantanna approached, to remind himself of that honor.

Wearing a sour expression, Dantanna circled wide of the giants and hopped the crevice, which, ten feet out from the spike, was no more than a crack, and neared Ancient Badden with a determined stride.

He bowed repeatedly as he covered the last dozen strides to his master, though not as quickly or as deeply as Ancient Badden would have liked.

"You have heard of Chapel Pellinor," Ancient Badden began.

"Burned and with its stones scattered," Dantanna replied, cutting off his words as if it pained him to speak them.

"Another victory over the Abellican heretics. Does that not please you?"

"Many men and women who were not Abellicans were killed in the fighting."

Ancient Badden shrugged as if it did not matter, which, of course, in the greater scheme of Samhain's universe, it surely did not.

"Killed by goblins and trolls and the barbarian mercenaries," Dantanna added.

Another shrug. "That is the way of things."

"Because we choose it to be! Once we battled beside the Honce men of Vanguard against the very army we now turn loose upon them."

"Once and not long ago, they knew their place," said Ancient Badden. Dantanna winced and quieted, the implications hanging heavily in the air. War was general south of the Gulf of Corona, laird against laird, with Ethelbert of Entel battling for dominance against the great Delaval. In that struggle, the true emerging winner seemed to be neither of the lairds, but rather, the Abellican Church, for the monks with their magical gemstones, powerful in both healing and destruction, had gained favor with every laird. Though possessed of magic of their own, the Samhaists could not match that Abellican availability of useful tricks.

"They look to the south," Dantanna dared to say after a few moments of uncomfortable silence. "The men of Vanguard see the turning tide amongst their Honce brethren."

"A tide turning away from us and from the Ancient Ones," said Ancient Badden. "It is a temporary thing, you understand."

Dantanna didn't reply, except that his face showed little in the way of concession.

"The Abellican monks dazzle with their baubles," Ancient Badden explained. "And provide comfort and even battle advantage. But they have little understanding of the proper preparations for the greater course. Death is inevitable—to lairds and to peasants. What answers might the foolish boys who follow the distorted memory of that idiot Abelle offer to mortally wounded warriors?"

"Fewer are mortally wounded because of their work."

"Temporary relief! Everyone dies."

Dantanna shook his head. "Then perhaps we have a role to play in complement with the monks," he said, or started to, for his voice trailed off and his eyes widened with fear as Ancient Badden put on the most fearsome scowl he had ever seen, a mask of danger and death, and the great Samhaist seemed to grow, to rise up above Dantanna, mocking him in his impotence.

But the growth proved short-lived, and Ancient Badden settled back easily, wearing a grin—though one that seemed no less dangerous. "You would like that, would you not?" he asked.

Dantanna tilted his head a bit, as if he did not understand.

"If we were to find a place beside the Abellicans," Ancient Badden clarified.

Dantanna began to shake his head, and his eyes darted about as if he was looking for a way to flee.

"How long did you think you could hide your allegiance to Dame Gwydre?" Ancient Badden bluntly asked.

"I know not of what you speak."

"Do not play me for a fool," Ancient Badden warned. "You counseled Gwydre extensively before her association with the Abellicans."

"Ancient, the Abellicans have been in Vanguard Town for years—before I ever came to know Lady Gwydre. Indeed, they were beside Laird Gendron before his death, when Gwydre was but a girl."

"With all their magical baubles, they still did not prevent his untimely death, did they?" Ancient Badden gave a little laugh. Dantanna winced, for it was widely rumored that the Samhaists had played a role in the "accident" that had taken the beloved Laird Gendron from the folk of Vanguard.

"And so Gwydre rose to power in Vanguard Town, a young, impressionable girl."

"Never that," Dantanna interrupted, and Ancient Badden's scowl put him back on his heels.

"And when your master died, Gwydre's ear was

passed to you," Ancient Badden went on. "Your duty was clearly relayed: to keep Gwydre from the Abellican encroachment. Your own assessment if you will, Dantanna. Did you succeed or fail?"

Dantanna began shaking his head. "It was more complicated. . . ."

"Are you couching an admission of failure?"

"No, Ancient. Dame Gwydre has sought a balance from the beginning. She counts me among her trusted advisors as she counts—"

"The monks of Chapel Pellinor?"

"Yes, but . . ."

"One of them in particular," Ancient Badden said.

Dantanna swallowed hard, unable to deny the truth of it. Dame Gwydre had fallen in love with an Abellican monk, and the Church of Abelle had done nothing to dissuade the union—obviously for cynical, political reasons. Chapel Pellinor stood on the outskirts of Vanguard Town, by far the most important town north of the Gulf of Corona; Dame Gwydre commanded the army of the entire Honce province north of the Gulf of Corona, the region known as Vanguard. As her relationship with her lover monk had grown, so had grown the power of the Abellicans in Vanguard Town and across the land. Dantanna had not been able to resist that movement, and had come to believe that playing an amenable role was the only way he and the Samhaists could retain any semblance of influence over the feisty and headstrong dame of Vanguard.

He had improvised. He had taken his own initiative. He had gambled and had thought that he was carving out a suitable role for his Church—until the hordes had descended upon Vanguard from the north at the direction of Ancient Badden.

"You wear your answer on your face, foolish Dantanna. It is true, then."

"Dame Gwydre beds a monk, yes," Dantanna admitted.

"And you allowed it to happen."

Dantanna balked at the words, spoken as they had been as an accusation. "Allowed?"

"Yes, allowed. You saw the relationship budding years ago, and you did not stop it."

"Love takes its own course, Ancient. I tried to dissuade Gwydre. Indeed, I did. But her heart was set and immovable, and—"

"And you did not kill this monk."

That took Dantanna's breath away.

"Is the importance of this lost upon you?" Ancient Badden asked.

"No, Ancient. No."

"Then why did you not recognize your duty and fulfill it long ago? It has been many months since the commencement of the unholy tryst and yet this Abellican still draws breath."

"You ask me to murder a man?"

"Were you not so trained in the magic of poison? Do you think that training no more than an exercise in the hypothetical?"

Dantanna shook his head helplessly, his jaw hanging slack.

"Have you not the power to kill a single young monk?"

"I am no murderer," the younger Samhaist whispered.

"Murderer, bah!" Ancient Badden huffed, and he waved his hand and walked to the lip of the glacier, looking down the thousand feet and more to the mist rising off the lake. "An ugly word for a noble task. How many lives would Dantanna have saved if he had mustered his courage and done as his duty demanded? This entire war could have been avoided, or surely minimized, if Dame Gwydre had not been smitten by a heretic Abellican, you fool!"

"The war was one of choice," Dantanna dared to say.

Ancient Badden turned on him angrily. "Choice?" he

roared. "You would cede the souls of thousands of Vanguardsmen to the heretic Abellicans?"

"We have our place . . ."

"Shut up," Ancient Badden said simply, and he turned back to look out over the southland. "You have failed, in the one task which meant anything, the one action that might have avoided years of strife and carnage. The misery, the death, the rivers of blood are all upon you because you had not the courage to strike a single blow."

"You cannot believe that," Dantanna gasped.

"I suppose, though, that I should thank you," Ancient Badden went on, as if he had not heard the comment. "The Ancient Ones saw fit to fill my divining pool with images of the battle of Chapel Pellinor. And the screams and cries. It was glorious, indeed."

"How can you say that?" Dantanna asked under his breath, despite himself and his fears.

"To hear men weeping like children!" Ancient Badden snickered. "To hear the cries of women who knew they were doomed for their heresy, who knew their children would be torn apart in retribution! Oh, the beauty of justice!

"And do you know the greatest victory of all?" Ancient Badden asked, spinning about and staring wild-eyed and wide-eyed at the stupefied younger Samhaist, who merely shook his head as if he was numb to it all.

"The captives!" Ancient Badden explained. "Lines of them, hundreds of them, perhaps, tethered together and marching for this very place."

Dantanna turned about to regard the giants, lazily pounding home the wedge spikes. He viewed the hanging glacial trolls, their thin blood dripping down into the melt, hindering the refreezing of the glacier. Another platform had been constructed near to them, this one with a crank and a long, long rope, one that would deposit the anticipated sacrifices deep within the chasm, where the white worm waited. When Dantanna turned back to Ancient Badden, the man's smug smile proved very revealing.

"They will feed D'no, and his frenzy and heat will facilitate the Severing," Ancient Badden confirmed, using the sanctifying term he had coined for his work on the edge of the glacier. "As D'no burrows and further melts the ice, we will feed him more. We will make him stronger and swifter, that he will reach to the stones about the ice to join our efforts with the earth magic of the Ancient Ones." He paused and regarded the younger Samhaist with a nod, one that seemed almost of approval. "I will allow you to offer many of them," he said, and turned back to stare out—mostly to hide his grin at Dantanna's horrified expression.

"Offer them?" Dantanna stammered. "You would murder them as food to further your ambitions here?"

"Murder," Ancient Badden said with a dismissive laugh. "A word you use so easily. Their lives are forfeit, by their own actions. They sided with heretics and so we—you—will exact proper punishment. Perhaps if I teach you to better wield that knife you were awarded, you will be less likely to fail us in the future when you are called upon by all that is holy to put it to proper use."

As he spoke, Ancient Badden summoned his magic to enhance his senses, and he clearly heard Dantanna's approach. Thus, he was not surprised when the man, standing right behind him, gave a shout and shoved him hard. Nor did Ancient Badden resist that push, lifting his arms gloriously wide as he went off the edge of the glacier, plummeting toward the mist below.

Dantanna gave a gasp and even offered a contrite wail as the supreme master, the Ancient of the Samhaist religion, tumbled toward certain doom.

Ancient Badden heard it and smiled all the wider, knowing that he had pushed the young fool to abject desperation. He closed his eyes and felt the wind thrumming about his falling form, his robes flapping noisily.

He used that sensation of freedom from mortal boundaries to fall deeper into his magic.

Back up on the ledge Dantanna sobbed, his head in his hands, and so he did not immediately see the transformation as Ancient Badden assumed the most ancient form of all. His arms became leathery wings, his eyes turned yellow with a single line of black in the middle, and his face elongated into a snout, filled with fangs, and spearlike horns sprouted atop his head.

His shriek, the keen of a dragon, startled the sobbing Samhaist and those giants and other workers behind him—even one of the hanging glacial trolls, near death, looked up in horror. Dantanna sucked in his breath when he scanned far below to see a dragon swooping out from the mist, rising suddenly on the updrafts from the hot waters of the mystical Mithranidoon.

Dantanna scrambled to his feet and turned about, stumbling as he tried to flee. He got up but slipped again when he heard the sharp screech of the dragon. Seconds seemed to pass as minutes, every step became a chore—and most steps left him prostrate on the ice, trying to rise yet again.

Dantanna felt a thunderous slam against his back. He didn't fly forward, though he surely would have, had not a large talon-tipped foot closed about him to hold him fast. Flailing and screaming, he went up into the air a dozen feet and more.

Then he was falling, landing hard against the ice.

Again he was scooped in dragon claws. Again Ancient Badden lifted him into the air. And again Ancient Badden dropped him, though higher up this time.

Dantanna screamed in pain when he hit, his leg snapping under his weight, ligaments tearing, bones breaking. He tried to curl to grasp the wound tightly.

But the dragon grabbed him again, carrying him even higher.

Down he fell, landing with a crunching impact, his breath blown away. He tried to crawl but his bones were shattered and he was too far from consciousness to begin to coordinate his movements, foolishly flailing about. Somewhere in the back of his rapidly fleeing thoughts, Dantanna expected to be hoisted again. But it didn't happen, and he settled down into the deep, cold, gloomy recesses of darkness.

Sharp, agonizing stabs of pain in his shattered limbs awakened him some time later. He was hanging by his ankles from the very rope he had noted on the new platform suspended over the chasm. His hands were securely and tightly bound behind him.

"You failed," he heard, distantly it seemed, though when Dantanna managed to turn his head, he saw that Ancient Badden was standing on the edge of the platform only a couple of feet to the side and above. At the man's feet lay a sack, its contents of troll ears spilled. "A pity. I had thought to educate you. I had thought to build your resolve and your understanding."

As he spoke, the Ancient lifted his arm and signaled behind him.

Dantanna's eyes went wide, and he thrashed about painfully, pitifully. Ancient Badden watched passively as Dantanna was slowly lowered into the gorge, the younger man sputtering desperate pleas. The agony in his shattered legs did not even register any longer through the thickening wall of sheer terror. He screamed his repentance to Ancient Badden, but the old and wicked Samhaist had taken up an ancient song of praise to the great D'no, the white worm god.

Dantanna tried to settle his thoughts. He bent a bit at the waist to get a glance at the rope bound to his ankle, noting that it was the same one that bound his hands. He growled and tried to curl up to get near to that rope. He wanted to free himself, to fall the remaining distance and kill himself outright!

Better that!

But Dantanna's executioner was no novice, and the young priest could get nowhere near the binding cord, nor could he hope to free his hands. In the dimming light he could see the myriad tunnels along the sides of the chasm. The ice was wet down here, as the pieces melted by D'no, blended as they were with the mist of glacial trolls' blood, could not fully refreeze. The web of tunnels. The burrowing of D'no.

From somewhere deep within the ice of the gorge's northern side came a guttural rumble, the growl of a monstrous beast.

Dantanna touched down on the wet ice, a trickle of water running past him. Now he scrambled more furiously, tugging his hands from side to side. Somehow he managed to pull one free, and the other slipped out of the noose. He rolled over and sat up, grimacing against the waves of pain emanating from his legs.

"Crawl, crawl," he gasped, working desperately at the ties about his ankle. His hands were numb and cold, though, and he couldn't get a proper grip on the rope. He cursed and fought harder. He heard a rumbling growl. Right behind him.

Dantanna's heart pounded in his chest. The growl became a hiss. He could feel the intense heat of D'no. He turned to face his doom just as the giant worm lashed at him.

From the platform above the crevice, Ancient Badden could see nothing of the feast. But he heard the screams. Indeed, he heard the horrified, delicious screams.

The rope tugged and jerked a couple of times.

The screaming stopped.

Ancient Badden motioned behind him, and the trolls operating the crank began turning it furiously, working with the frenzy of creatures who knew that they might be the next down the rope if they disappointed their mighty master.

Ancient Badden chuckled when the rope came up, to

see the bottom half of Dantanna's leg still attached, the skin of the upper calf blackened by the heat of D'no.

Ancient Badden casually freed the limb from the rope and tossed it back into the gorge. Then, with a look of disgust at Dantanna's betrayal, he used his foot to sweep the troll ears into the chasm, as well.

"Eat well, Ancient One," he said.

THREE

Rocks, Always Rocks

Rocks, rocks, it's always rocks!" the young and strong man complained, his muscular bare arms glistening with sweat. He was tall, more than halfway between six and seven feet, and though he had lost considerable weight on this multiyear journey, he did not appear skinny and he was certainly not frail, his lean muscles standing taut and strong. A mop of blond hair covered his head, bespeaking his Vanguard heritage, and he wore a scraggly beard, for even though his superiors disapproved of it, they would not enforce their rules against facial hair when they possessed no implement to easily be rid of it. He stood on a slope of brown dirt and gray stones—fewer near him now, since he had already tossed scores over the ridge so that they would roll and bounce down near to the wall the man and his companions were repairing. He hoisted another one, brought it near his shoulder, and heaved it out. It didn't quite make the lip and began to roll back his way. He intercepted it with a few fast strides, planting his foot against it and holding it in place before it could gain any real momentum.

"Catch your breath, Brother Cormack," said an older monk, middle-aged and with more skin than hair atop his head. "The air is particularly warm this day."

Cormack did take a deep breath, then gathered up his heavy woolen robes and pulled them over his head, leaving him naked other than a bulky white cloth loincloth.

"Brother Cormack!" the other monk, Giavno by name, scolded.

"Always rocks," Cormack argued, his bright green eyes flaring with intensity. He made no move to retrieve his heavy robe. "Ever since we came to this cursed island we have done nothing more than pile rocks."

"Cursed?" Giavno said, shaking his head and wearing an expression of utter disappointment. "We were sent north to frozen Alpinador to begin a chapel, Brother. For the glory of Blessed Abelle. You would call that cursed?" He swept his arm to his left, beyond the ridge and to the small stone church the brothers had constructed. They had placed it on the highest point on the island; it dominated the view though the square structure was no more than thirty feet on any side.

Cormack put his hands on his hips, laughed, and shook his head helplessly. They had departed Chapel Pellinor in Vanguard more than three years before, all full of excitement and a sense of great purpose. They were to travel to the fierce mountainous northland of Alpinador, home of the pagan barbarians, and spread the word of Blessed Abelle. They would save souls with their gemstone magic and the truth and beauty of their message.

But they had found only battle and outrage and their every word had sounded as insult to the proud and strong northmen. Running for their lives more than proselytizing, the band had become lost in short order and had stumbled and bumbled their way along for weeks with the freezing winter closing in all around them. Surely the nearly two score monks and their like number of servants would have found a cold and empty death, but they had happened upon this place, a huge lake of warm waters and perpetual steam, a place of islands small and large. Father De Guilbe, who led their expedition, proclaimed it a miracle and decided that here, on these waters, they would fulfill their mission and build their chapel.

Here, Cormack mused, on a lump of rock in the middle of the water.

"Rocks," Cormack grumbled, and he bent low and picked up the heavy stone again, this time heaving it far over the ridgeline.

"The lake teems with fish and food. Have you ever tasted water so fine?" said Giavno, his voice wistful. "The heat of the water saved us from the Alpinadoran winter. You should be more grateful, Brother."

"We were sent here for a reason beyond our simple survival."

Giavno launched into another long sermon about the duties of a monk of Abelle, the sacrifices expected and the reward awaiting them all when they had slipped the bonds of their mortal coils. He recited from the great books at length. But Cormack heard none of it, for he had his own litany against the despair, an unsought but surely found reprieve, one that he hoped would bring him the greater answers of this muddling road called life. . . .

She glided from the boat as the boat glided ashore and with equal grace, her movements as fluid as the gently lapping waves. The moon, Sheila, was almost full this night and hung in the sky behind and above Milkeila, softening her image further. She wore few clothes, as was normal for everyone on the hot lake of Mithranidoon, other than the monks and their heavy woolen robes.

Cormack felt his heavy robe about him now, and he became almost self-conscious of it, for it felt inappropriate in the soft, warm, misty breeze.

Milkeila's hand went to her hip as she moved toward him, and she untied her short skirt and let it fall aside. Still walking, she pulled her top over her head. She was not embarrassed, not uncomfortable, just beautiful and nude, other than the necklaces of trinkets—shells and claws and teeth—strung about her neck and a bracelet and anklet of the same design. A large feather was braided into her hair.

It was the first time Cormack had seen her naked, but it felt no more intimate to him than the last time they had been together, at the great meeting between the shamans of Milkeila's tribe, Yan Ossum, and a few select brothers of Chapel Isle. That's when he had known and when she had known. That's when Cormack had found a witness to his life, a justification of his heart and mind, a spirit kindred, a heart equally wide. All of the bantering, all of the posturing, between the shamans and the monks had played out like a sorry game to him, a juggling of positions with each side trying to gain the better ground.

None of it had impressed him and none of it had impressed Milkeila, and both had recognized the truth of it, the truth of it all, in each other's eyes.

So now she walked toward him with confidence, and all that she had revealed since stepping from her boat paled against that which she had already shown him. He looked at her eyes, at the sense of purpose on her face, at the trust that had already grown between them.

He fumbled with his robe. He wished he could have been as graceful as Milkeila, but sensations overwhelmed him now, and a sense of urgency came over him. They fell together on the sandbar and said not a word as they made love under the stars and moon.

Each had seen the potential of something greater in joining their religions, a wider and more perfect truth, and so it was physically between them, where their union seemed a more perfect form than either alone.

D o you not agree, Brother Cormack?" Brother Giavno said, and loudly, and Cormack realized that it wasn't the first time Giavno had asked him that. He stared at the older man stupidly.

"The glories of Blessed Abelle when the tribes of this lake are brought into our love," Giavno prompted.

"Their traditions are centuries old," said Cormack.

"Patience," Giavno argued, a predictable answer and oft given, but something about the last inflection as Giavno spoke the word gave Cormack pause. He looked over at his Abellican brother, then followed the older monk's wide-eyed stare to the water behind them.

Cormack saw the powries—bandy-legged, bandy-armed, barrel-chested dwarves—floating in on their flat raft just an instant before they began springing into the water near the shore, bursting into a wild charge, brandishing their weapons.

Cormack whirled about, took a few running strides and leaped high into the air, crashing into a pair of dwarves before they cleared the surf. One went down, the other staggered back, and Cormack set himself quickly and launched a circle-kick that caught the standing dwarf on the side of its chin before it could fully recover from the unexpected assault. Its dull red beret, the item that defined the powries, who were also known as "bloody caps," went flying away and that dwarf, too, tumbled under the water.

"Out, or they'll be sure to drown you!" Giavno cried, and he accentuated his point by thrusting forth his hand and loosing the power of the stone he clutched: graphite, the stone of lightning. A bright blue bolt sizzled past Cormack to strike the raft, sending powries tumbling, but as the bolt dispersed into the water, Cormack felt a nasty sting about his legs.

Behind Giavno and beyond the ridge, another pair of monks cried out the warning.

Cormack sloshed toward the rocky shore with all the strength he could muster. He pivoted as he went and managed to somewhat deflect the barrage of clubs that came spinning his way. More than one hit home, though, and by the time he got out of the water, he sported a large welt on one arm and a bruise on the side of his face that threatened to swell his right eye closed.

"To me!" Giavno called, to Cormack and the other pair, and just ahead of the dwarves the young monk ran. When he reached his companion, he skidded low, grabbed up a stone, and turned as he rose, launching it at the nearest pursuer. It hit the dwarf squarely in the chest, briefly interrupting its howl. But only briefly, for the tough creature slogged through the strike and closed fast, smacking wildly with its club.

Cormack didn't retreat; in fact, he surprised the dwarf by coming forward, within the weight of the club, rolling as he went to further absorb the blow. It still blew his breath out, but Cormack fought through that and caught the club as he turned, then turned further, taking the club with him and yanking it from the surprised dwarf's hands. He snapped off a quick smack against the dwarf's head, then pivoted the club fast and sent it out spearlike at the next powrie in line.

That one waved its arm to deflect the missile, but misjudged and whipped his hand past too quickly. The red-bearded dwarf did block the throw, however—with his face, or more specifically his nose—and his head snapped back.

"Yach, ye mutt," the powrie growled, reaching up to grab its busted proboscis, and taking away a palmful of blood. The dwarf sneered and growled louder and started for Cormack with more purpose.

But he stopped suddenly, looking confused, and staggered down to one knee.

Cormack had the time neither to acknowledge his

luck nor to pat himself on the back for a perfect throw, for powries were made of tough stuff and such a strike wouldn't normally bring one down, temporarily though it might prove. As soon as he had let fly the missile, he retracted his throwing arm and drove it down to the side, slugging the initial target in the head.

The dwarf wrapped his strong arms about Cormack's waist and drove him to the side, intent upon bearing him to the ground. The monk worked his legs frantically, trying to stay upright, and repeatedly hit the creature with his pumping right hand. Blood flew, but from his knuckles and not the dwarf, for surely Cormack felt as if he was punching stone instead of flesh!

The monk didn't relent, though, nor did the powrie, taking him far from Brother Giavno and the other two monks and the group of a half-dozen powries bearing down on them. Another lightning bolt shook the ground, and the lead powrie began to dance wildly, arms and lips flapping, his thick red hair and beard straightening to full length and shivering in the air. He danced and hopped, managing another step forward, but then fell over.

The other five rumbled past, ignoring the rock missiles, and the club-fight began in earnest.

Cormack continued to work his legs frantically, continued to punch at the dwarf, but on one slug, the stubborn little creature turned about, purposely putting his face in line with the man's flying fist. Cormack scored a solid, stunning hit, but square dwarf teeth clamped upon the side of his hand and bit down hard.

Cormack thrashed and tore free his hand, breaking out of the dwarf's vise grip in the process. Even as he jumped backward, with the powrie coming in immediate pursuit, the monk launched a heavy left hook that snapped the dwarf's head to the side.

A right cross staggered the powrie even more, and gave Cormack the opportunity to square up against the dwarf.

"Yach, but I'm to scrape the skin from yer pretty face!" the stubborn powrie promised, and came on.

A trio of stinging left jabs put the dwarf back on his heels.

Cormack retreated a bit more; his reach was his advantage, he knew, and when he looked at his opponent, who seemed like a walking block of rock, he figured it might be his only advantage.

Giavno swung hard with his makeshift wooden mace. He scored a solid hit, but the powrie pressed him relentlessly. How the monk wished that he still had the mace he had carried when he had left Chapel Pellinor, a spiked weapon of wonderful balance and weight. But alas, that mace and all of their other metallic items were lost to them, corroded by the constant steam that floated about the islands of this hot lake.

Giavno hit the powrie again, cracking the block head of the weapon against the back of the turning dwarf's shoulder. The monk rolled his shoulders, thrusting forth his free hand in time to deflect the dwarf's smashing response. And as that powrie staff slipped by, the monk wrapped his arm over the dwarf's hands and bore in hard against his enemy.

Big mistake, Giavno realized as soon as he slammed against the dwarf, who didn't budge an inch. For now his advantage, the length of his arms, was lost, and the powrie fast squirmed and twisted free its hands, clamping them about Giavno's waist and tugging him along as it fell into a roll.

Another powrie closed on the wrestling pair, whacking away at Giavno with a weighted stick, raising welts under the monk's heavy brown robes.

Giavno grimaced through the pain and managed to turn about to see the two companions nearest him, both fighting valiantly and fiercely against a trio of dwarves, trading punch for swat. At one point in the roll, the dwarf loosened its grip, and Giavno quickly set his feet and thrust forward, scrambling toward his friends. As he had hoped, one of the powries broke away to intercept, launching a flying tackle at the monk and bearing him back to the two pursuing dwarves.

Still clutching his graphite stone, Giavno fell into its depths. He got smacked with a staff and punched on the side of his head. The dwarf who had tackled him twisted him about as if to break him apart. But Giavno held his concentration and sent his energy into the stone and through the stone, and jolting sparks of electricity fired out in all directions around him.

The powries fell back, were thrown back, and Giavno sprinted for his companions. He glanced over at Cormack with sincere, almost fatherly, concern, but reminded himself that Cormack had secured his position on this mission to Alpinador precisely because he had shown himself to be the finest young fighter at Chapel Pellinor.

Cormack would get back to the three brothers, Giavno told himself, and prayed.

"Ah, ye're that one," the dwarf said, nodding and smiling, and spitting a line of blood at Cormack's feet. "Yer blood'll make me beret shine all the brighter, then."

He howled and brought his staff up above his head, leaping forward.

But Cormack had anticipated the move and was moving as well, diving down to the side and lashing out with his top leg. He didn't hit the dwarf, but slid the kicking foot past him, then bent his knee and brought the leg back in at the back of the dwarf's knees. The powrie halted his swing and overbalanced backward for a second, as Cormack's calf drove in hard against the back of his knees.

That was naught but a ruse, though, as the unfortunate dwarf soon learned. For Cormack rolled out farther to the side, then reversed his flow, throwing his hips over and locking his scissors' grip on the dwarf. The powrie tried to fight the inevitable pull, but had no leverage against the prostrate and rolling man, and Cormack's trailing leg drove the dwarf forward and to the ground. The staff went flying and the powrie hit hard, just getting his hand under him in time to stop his face from smashing against the stones.

Cormack continued the roll to his back, extracting his legs on the last turn. He arched, put his feet under him, and snapped his muscles, lifting him to a standing position over the prone dwarf. He moved fast into position, where he could stomp the powrie's face into the stone, and even lifted his foot over the back of the still-stunned dwarf's head.

He hesitated.

He heard the splashing and turned in time to see the charge of the first dwarf he had decked, out in the water. It came out with fury—no, not fury, Cormack realized, but with terror.

For behind it emerged another creature, its smooth, bluish, almost translucent skin gleaming in the dull and hazy light, its black eyes peering at its prey intently under a protruding brow. A glacial troll, Cormack realized at once, and so too had the powrie, judging from the look of terror on his face!

No taller than the dwarves and far lighter, the glacial trolls were nevertheless the bane of all the island societies. Their thin limbs were deceptively strong, and their teeth pointed like little knives. And where came one troll, inevitably, came many, and Cormack saw that clearly now, the long waggling ears of the ugly goblinoid creatures poking from the surf all about the rocky beach.

The dwarf at Cormack's feet grabbed him by the ankle and tugged hard, and he didn't resist, but let himself fall backward into a roll, one that took him right over and back to his feet.

"Trolls! Trolls!" he cried, and he started toward the beach, yelling at the dwarf, "Faster!"

The dwarf threw his head back as he broke free of the surf and seemed to come on more quickly. Momentarily, though, for when the powrie jerked again, Cormack saw the truth of it.

The dwarf staggered forward, slowing, then slumped down to his knees and gave a great exhale.

"Yach!" cried the powrie on the ground before Cormack, and that one leaped to his feet. "Bikelbrin, me friend!"

That call had all the powries pausing and turning, as the truth of their predicament fell fully on man and dwarf alike. Ten of them stood against more than a dozen of the trolls, who were armed with spears tipped with sharpened, barbed shells and not the relatively benign sticks that the island inhabitants generally used to batter each other about the skulls.

The trolls closed on the kneeling Bikelbrin but so did Cormack, leaping down across the stones in full charge. He heard Brother Giavno shout, "To the abbey!" and understood that his three brethren would take that route, but he could not ignore the wounded powrie.

The glacial trolls neared, reaching for their embedded spears. Cormack put on a burst of speed, closing ground, and leaped, turning himself sidelong in midair as he cleared the dwarf. He was over the spears before the trolls could fully retract them. One let go of the shaft and threw its hands up to block, while the other stubbornly, and with a sickening wet sound, drew free its spear. That one took the brunt of the flying body-block as Cormack bowled both of the trolls over.

He landed atop them hard, smacking his hand painfully against a stone, and his forehead painfully against the back of that hand. A wave of dizziness washed over him, but he knew better than to succumb to it in the midst of vicious trolls! He rolled sidelong, right off the two, who scrambled and bit at him, one catching a tooth on his bare forearm.

Cormack tugged that arm free immediately and managed to slam it down hard on the troll's face for good measure as he regained his balance.

No faster than the other troll, however, which lowered its spear for Cormack's belly and thrust it forward.

The trained monk dodged aside and slapped the spear out wider with the flat of his hand. He started for the opening to strike at the creature, but instinct stopped him and turned him about.

Just in time to deflect the thrown spear of another troll.

Cormack jumped back, three on him now and a fourth coming in. To his left came a sharp retort, and one of the trolls he had bowled over stumbled forward and to the ground. Behind it came the furious powrie, running headlong and empty-handed, for he had thrown his staff, spearlike, into the back of the fallen troll's head. He called for Bikelbrin, but ran right past his wounded friend, leaping onto the second of the trolls Cormack had tackled, bearing it down under his thrashing and kicking form.

Cormack stomped hard on the back of the neck of the first fallen troll, ending its squirming. No mercy for glacial trolls, for everyone on that beach, human and powrie alike, knew that the trolls would show none. Up on the ridge, all of the powries had disengaged from Cormack's Abellican brethren and were charging down, and to the monk's relief, he saw Brother Giavno extending his clenched fist.

"To the abbey!" Giavno yelled again, and Cormack understood that it was for his benefit alone, a warning to him that his three friends would desert him here. A lightning bolt followed that warning, off to the side where it sent a trio of trolls hopping wildly and weirdly, the residual jolts waggling their spindly limbs in a frenetic dance.

A troll leaped at Cormack, and another went for the

powrie and its wrestling companion. The young monk dodged a spear thrust, then a second. He turned sidelong, bent back and down as the third thrust angled high, past his head. Cormack's left hand, his inside hand, grabbed the shaft and he wrapped his right arm over it, just below the seashell tip, as he brought it down. He turned to face the troll and thrust his right forearm, now under the shaft, upward at the same time he drove his left hand down. The sudden movement and Cormack's redistribution of his weight snapped the spear at midshaft, and as soon as he heard the break, Cormack tugged the remaining troll weapon aside and crashed against the troll, grabbing a firm hold on the broken piece of the spear as he went. He felt that sharp piece drive into the troll's torso, and he wrapped his left hand about the creature, boring in harder.

The troll went into a frenzy and tried to bite at him, but Cormack stayed too low for that. The frantic creature wasn't done, though, and it used yet another of its many weapons, its long and pointed chin, and repeatedly drove the bony feature hard against the side of Cormack's head.

Both fell to the ground, Cormack on top, and he shoved up immediately to his knees, his movement pulling free the spear shaft. He flipped it in his hands as he went, and came right back at the troll, this time with the seashell head leading.

The troll scrambled and thrashed, slapped and squirmed, but to no avail, and Cormack fell atop it again, pushing the spear right through its chest. He tugged left and right, ensuring that the wound would be mortal, and finally he fell aside—to see the other troll, the one hit in the back of the head by the thrown powrie staff, standing over him, a rock in hand.

An explosion of bright white light filled Cormack's head as that troll struck. He covered and rolled and somehow even managed to get back to his feet without being hit again too badly.

But the troll was there, punching and biting at him, and all the world was spinning.

Cormack found his sensibilities just enough to punch out, a stunning right cross that through good fortune alone connected solidly on the troll's jaw, snapping its head aside and sending it back and to the ground.

Cormack tried to straighten, staggering left and right. He saw the powries and the trolls, one big pile of confusion and fury.

Then he saw the ground, rushing up to swallow him. He thought of Milkeila, his secret lover, and was sad to know that he would not rendezvous with her that night at their special place on the sandbar to the north, as they had planned. He thought it silly that he thought of that at all, for he didn't know why that image of the beautiful barbarian had flooded his thoughts at this critical time.

He knew then the reason. The thoughts, the image, were a blessing, a moment of peace in a roiling storm. He tried to say her name, Milkeila, but he could not.

The sounds receded, the light disappeared in a blink, taking her beautiful form with it, and Cormack drowned in a cold and empty darkness.

FOUR

The Crutch

Bransen rolled off Cadayle and onto his back. He threw his arm up over his face and even miscalculated that action, thumping himself hard on the forehead. Tears of frustration welled in his eyes, and with much trembling and shaking, he managed to guide his arm down to cover them. Cadayle came up to her side on one elbow to look over him.

Down below, Bransen's foot twitched and shot out to the side, smacking against the front support of their tent, nearly caving in the entrance. In ultimate frustration, the man managed to clasp the soul stone which lay at his side.

Cadayle gently stroked her husband's bare chest and whispered soft assurances to him.

Bransen didn't move his arm, didn't look at her.

"I love you," Cadayle said to him.

Despite his stubborn pride, Bransen reached over and clasped the soul stone that he had placed at his side. "You would have to, to suffer my . . . my clumsiness."

Cadayle laughed, but bit the chuckle off short, realizing that it wasn't being taken in the manner in which she was offering it. "We knew that it would take time," she said.

"It will take forever!" Bransen retorted. "And I do not improve! I dared believe that by now I would be free of the soul stone. I dared hope . . ."

"It takes time," Cadayle interrupted. "I remember the Stork, who could hardly walk. You can walk now without the stone tied to your head. You have improved."

"Old news," Bransen replied, and he finally did lower his arm so that he could look at his wonderful and understanding wife. "My improvements were dramatic and I dared to hold hope. But they have stopped now. Without the stone I am a clumsy oaf!"

"No!"

"Without the stone I cannot even make love to my wife! I am no man!"

Cadayle pulled away from him and sat up, shaking her head. As Bransen rambled on she began to laugh.

"What?" he asked at length, growing very irritated.

"I am unused to the Highwayman so full of self-pity," she said.

Bransen stammered and could not even give voice to his anger.

"You have brought down a laird and robbed the prince of Delaval—twice!" Cadayle said. "You are a hero of the folk—"

"Who cannot make love to my wife!"

Cadayle kissed him. "You make love to me all the time."

"With a gemstone bound to my forehead. Without it I am too clumsy."

"Then be glad that you have it!"

Bransen looked at her blankly. "I want—"

"And you will find it," she cut him off. "In time. But if you do not, then so be it. Be glad that we have the soul stone. Indeed, I am." She frowned. "But even if we didn't have it, even if you could not make love to me with any grace, do you believe that it would affect the way I feel about you? Do you think it would diminish my love and adoration for you?"

Bransen stared at her.

"If I could not make love to you," she challenged him, "would you throw me from your life to find a 'whole' woman?"

Bransen's stammer was powered by more than his physical infirmities.

"Of course you would not," Cadayle pronounced firmly. "If I believed you could, I would never have agreed to marry you."

Cadayle's expression softened. "I love you, Bransen," she said, her small hand stroking his chest. "The physical act of making love is sweet to me with or without the gemstone upon your head. There is no more to be said, and no more of your self-pity, if you please. I cannot suffer it from my beloved, who could kill a dragon protecting me. You have stepped yourself so far above the common man that self-pity from you is worse than irony. It is foolhardy and laughably ridiculous. You are the Highwayman. You are the best man I have ever known. A better does not exist. You are my husband, and every day I awaken and thank God and the Ancient Ones that Bransen Garibond found his way into my life."

Bransen tried to answer, tried to respond that it was he who should fall to his knees in thanks, but Cadayle silenced him by putting her finger over his lips, then bringing her own lips in to brush his softly. She moved atop him, then, straddling him and kissing him all over his face, whispering assurances all the while.

Bransen knew that he was the fortunate one here, but he let it go and lost himself in the softness and beauty of his beloved Cadayle.

She's not to like this," the scraggly-faced old man said through his two remaining teeth.

Dawson McKeege shot the hunched old grump an incredulous look. "They're all dead," he said, sweeping his arms out to the smoking ruins that had been a thriving town only a few days before, and raising his voice so that the others of the troupe could hear him well— before the arrival of Dame Gwydre, who was said to be only a few hundred yards away. "How could anyone like this, old fool? Men and women and children of Vanguard, our brethren, our fellows, slaughtered before us by the monstrous plague."

"Goblins and them wretched blue trolls!" someone shouted from the side.

"Aye, and with Alpinadoran backing, not to doubt!" a third chimed in.

Dawson could only nod. The war had grown all about the northern frontier of Vanguard, and now, if this was any indication, it had snuck in around the edges. For this burned and broken town, Tethmawle by name, sat closer to the Gulf of Corona than to the battlefields in the north.

The sound of approaching horses ended all the chatter, and the fifteen men of the expedition turned as one to regard the procession galloping down the road. The elite guards of Castle Pellinor led the way and took up the rear, sandwiching a trio of monks dressed in their brown robes, a pair of advisors lightly armored and armed, and two women who both seemed at ease on their respective mounts, riding hard and not in the sidesaddle manner, which had become fashionable among the courtesans of the holdings south of the Gulf of Corona. One of those women, the taller of the two, with hair going silver, but her shoulders still tall and straight, held the attention of the onlookers most of all.

"She should not be out of the castle," Dawson muttered under his breath, and he rubbed his weary eyes and tried to be at ease. He could not, though, and he found himself glancing around nervously, as if expecting a host of goblins and trolls and other monstrosities to swarm down from the tree line and score the ultimate kill in this wretched war.

The procession rambled up to the edge of the town, the soldiers fanning out into defensive positions while the seven dignitaries trotted up to Dawson and the others.

"Milady Gwydre," Dawson said with a bow to his ruler, his friend.

Gwydre rolled her leg easily over her mount and dropped to the ground, handing the reins to one of the nearby men without a thought. She spent a moment surveying the area, the smoking ruins, the charred bodies and the bloated and stinking corpses of small gray-green goblins and blue-green trolls littered all about the area.

"They fought well," the old coot near Dawson dared to remark.

Gwydre shot him a glare. "They are all dead?"

"We've found none alive," Dawson confirmed.

"Then it was no small force that came against them," said Gwydre. "How? How was such a sizable group able to sneak so far south?"

"Samhaist magic," one of the monks whispered from behind, and all three of the brown-robed brothers launched into quiet prayers to their Blessed Abelle.

Gwydre seemed more annoyed than impressed, and Dawson agreed with her completely.

"It is a wild land, milady," Dawson said. "We are not populous. Our roads are hardly guarded, and even if they were, a short trek through a forest would bypass any sentries."

"And their determination is aggravating," replied Gwydre. She walked past Dawson and motioned for him to follow, then held up her own advisors, even the Lady Darlia, her dearest friend, so that she and Dawson could move off alone.

As always, Dawson was impressed by how in control and command Dame Gwydre remained. She carried an aura of competence around her, one that had initially surprised many of Castle Pellinor's court. For Gwydre had been just a young girl that quarter of a century before when her father, Laird Gendron, already a widower, had been killed unexpectedly in a fall from his horse while hunting. Gendron, revered by the folk of this northern wilderness known as Vanguard, had held the scattered and disparate communities together with a "warm fist," as the saying had gone—a saying applied to Gendron, to his father before him, and to his great uncle who had been Laird of Pellinor before that.

"I cannot tolerate this," Gwydre said, her lips tight, her voice strained. "Chapel Pellinor's fall has created unrest, and the folk will be all the more unnerved when news of Tethmawle's fate spreads through forest trails."

"You fear they will question the fortitude of their dame?" Dawson asked, and Gwydre sucked in her breath and snapped an angry glare at him. But it did not hold, of course, for Dawson McKeege was perhaps the only person in all of Vanguard who could have spoken to Gwydre with that necessary candor.

"Do you remember when Laird Gendron died?" Gwydre asked somberly.

"I was with you when we received the news."

Gwydre nodded.

"Aye," said Dawson, taking the cue. "And so began the whispers, the laments of 'why hadn't the laird sired a son?'"

"The lower their voices, the louder they sounded," Gwydre assured him. "Those voices were part of the reason I so abruptly agreed to marry Peiter."

The admission didn't startle Dawson. "He was my friend as he was your husband. I suspect that he, too, heard those whispers, and couldn't suffer to see his beloved Gwydre so pained."

"I was a young woman, barely more than a girl," Gwydre admitted. "And never in my life had I done anything that would have, or should have, inspired their confidence. Even those years later when Peiter died, their doubts about me rightfully lingered."

"That was fifteen years ago, milady," Dawson reminded her. "And before your thirtieth birthday. Do you fear that they still doubt you?"

"We are in a desperate war."

"It is Vanguard! We are always at one war or another. The woods are full of goblins, the coast crawling with powries, the northland thick with trolls, and never in my life have I met a more disagreeable bunch than those Alpinadoran barbarians."

"This is different, Dawson," Gwydre said. Her tone quieted the man more than her words. For there lay a truth there that neither could deny. Dame Gwydre had taken a lover, an Abellican brother, and in the two years of her tryst, that particular Church's stature had grown considerably throughout her holding and by extension, throughout Vanguard—much to the dismay and open anger of the dangerous and powerful Samhaists.

"You fell in love," Dawson said to her.

"Foolishly. I placed my heart above my responsibilities, and all the land suffers for it."

"Those same Churches were going to fight, with or without your actions," Dawson argued. "As they fight a proxy war through the lairds in the South, where, it is said, three hundred men die every day."

Dame Gwydre nodded and couldn't deny the truth of Dawson's claims, for indeed, this same battle for religious supremacy over the folk of Honce was playing out throughout the Holdings of Honce Proper. There, the fight between Abellican and Samhaist was shielded from view behind the façade of the warring lairds Delaval and Ethelbert, but it was no less real and no less fierce.

In the South, the Abellicans were clearly winning, for their gemstone magic, both healing and destructive powers, was coveted by the many lairds feuding for dominance. In the quieter North, where few Abellicans and fewer gemstones haunted the wild land, the Samhaists had found refuge, so they had believed. Tied to the seasons and the world and the animals great and small through wise and ancient traditions, Samhaist wisdom served Vanguardsmen well indeed.

But then Dame Gwydre had fallen in love with an Abellican brother.

"There will be more Tethmawles," Dame Gwydre said solemnly. "One community after another will be sacked."

"I beg you not to tell that to your subjects, milady."

Gwydre shook her head to deny the dryness of Dawson's remark, and that action conferred to Dawson that she wasn't being melodramatic. She knew that she was losing to the hordes from the North, the legions of Ancient Badden.

"My council with Chief Danamarga did not go well," Gwydre admitted, referring to the powerful leader of one particularly friendly Alpinadoran tribe, with whom the men of Vanguard often traded, and who many times had graced Gwydre's table at Castle Pellinor. "He will likely keep his clan out of the fighting."

"That is good news," Dawson said. "His warriors are fierce."

"But he will not intervene on our behalf with the other tribes."

"The Samhaist influence is great among the Alpinadorans. But great enough to keep them allied with ugly goblins and the light-skinned trolls?"

Dame Gwydre shrugged and scanned the burned-out village. "We are losing, and Danamarga is a pragmatic man. If Vanguard is to be sectioned by the victors, then he would not serve his clan well to be left out of that gain."

"Vanguard is land. Without us it is empty land," Dawson argued. "What good will it alone bring to the Alpinadorans? What point is this war?"

Gwydre nodded her complete understanding. The Samhaists, so they believed, were egging on the monsters and the barbarians, but the underlying logic told Gwydre and her advisors that Ancient Badden didn't really want to wipe the Vanguardsmen from the region and chase refugees back across the Gulf of Corona.

"Ancient Badden and his disciples do not wish to minister to goblins and trolls," Dawson said. "Nor to the barbarians of Alpinador who loyally follow their own gods."

"Gods not far removed from the Samhaist deities," Gwydre reminded.

"True enough, but would you expect Danamarga and the other chiefs to relinquish their control to Badden's miserable priests? Of course they will not."

"Then this whole war is to teach me a lesson," said Gwydre.

Dawson shrugged, for he could not disagree. "It is to drive the Abellicans back across the waters and secure Vanguard for the Samhaists," he added. "We, all of us— indeed, even Dame Gwydre—are caught in the middle of a war of religions. And it won't end with Vanguard if Badden drives the Abellicans south. He knows that Laird Ethelbert and Laird Delaval have thrown in fully with the Abellicans, and it's not to his liking. He will chase the monks from Vanguard, then use us to cross the gulf and assail Chapel Abelle itself. Begging your pardon, dear woman, but that's no fight I'm wanting."

His dramatic tone brought a much-needed smile to Dame Gwydre's angular features, an impish grin that reminded Dawson of the beauty of the woman. Even now in middle age she retained much of that beauty, but the last year had weighed heavily on her, and too rare flashed that smile, reassuring and warm, superior but not condescending, and surely disarming.

So disarming.

It said much about Ancient Badden's hold on the land, and even more about the current state of the war, that Dame Gwydre's smile had not brought Chief Danamarga to their side.

"We must force upon Ancient Badden that wider fight

you believe he desires, and before the battleground is
his for the choosing," Gwydre said, and her eyes turned
from Dawson to the south.

"An immigrant army," Dawson muttered.

"It is a fine season for the folk of Honce to turn their
eyes to the open and beautiful North, I think," Gwydre
confirmed. "Palmaristown, from all reports, has become
the haven of rats and foul odors, and there are rumors
that the refugees of the war collect en masse at Chapel
Abelle, where there is little excess shelter and supplies.
And yet, we have villages already built and ready to
house those who would seek a better life, and a land as
bountiful as any in Corona."

"Villages empty because all the men are fighting the
war, or are already planted in the ground," Dawson reminded her, but he stole none of her momentum.

"It is the way of things," she said. "A man who comes
here to fight for Gwydre is fighting, too, for his future. If
he remains in the South, he will be swept into Delaval's
army, or Ethelbert's, into a war whose outcome will have
no bearing on the prosperity or security of his family.
What will change for the folk of Palmaristown, or any
other town, if Ethelbert wins? If Delaval wins? They are
two lairds of the same cloth—their fight is one for personal gain and not over any manner of governance. But
up here, the battle has more meaning. Up here, my warriors strike hard at the flesh of goblins and glacial trolls."

"And men," Dawson pointed out.

"Barbarians," Gwydre corrected. "Not the brethren of
the men of Honce as we see in the South. Not a brother,
perhaps, who through mere circumstance moved to a
town now serving the other side."

Finally it seemed as if Dawson had run out of answers,
and so Gwydre looked at him directly, flashed him that
commanding grin, and said, "The gulf is calm, and the
ships are waiting."

"Chapel Abelle?"

"That would be a fine place to start," said Gwydre.

"The brothers there know of our desperation, and they do not wish to have a powerful Badden ruling Vanguard unopposed. Let them direct you to towns not yet emptied by Delaval's press crews."

"If Laird Delaval learns of my actions in stealing his potential soldiers . . ." Dawson warned.

"Do not let him know."

Dawson smiled hopelessly. When Dame Gwydre made up her mind it was not to be easily changed.

"They will come," Gwydre assured him. "You will convince them."

Dawson McKeege knew the meaning of Gwydre's "convince," and while it left a sour taste in his mouth, in looking around at the ruins of Tethmawle, it was not hard for him to weigh one evil against the other. Without hardy reinforcements, this wretched sight before him would soon become all too common.

H e fell down for the fourth time.
   Cadayle ran toward him, but Bransen stubbornly waved her off. Trembling every inch of the way he managed to get over onto his belly and up to his knees. He did well to hide his grimace as he noted the sympathetic and concerned look that passed between Cadayle and Callen.

They were on the road north of Delaval, heading north-northwest along the bank of the majestic waterway that had recently been named the Masur Delaval. Though this northeastern bank was considered the "civilized" side of the river, the road, or trail actually, hardly showed any such signs. They were only three days out from Delaval Town, in a region untouched by the war, yet it was hard to call their path a road. Uneven, muddy, and littered with the large roots of the great willows that lined the river, the trail could trip up any but the most careful traveler. Every step proved a test of courage for Bransen, who stubbornly carried his soul stone in his pouch and not even in his hand, let alone strapped to his forehead.

Resting on his hands and knees to reorient and catch his breath, Bransen fought the urge to slip his hand into his pouch and produce the gemstone. He noticed a pool of red liquid and only then realized that he had slammed his nose on that last fall, splitting his lip as well. He spat a few times, red spray flying from his mouth.

He felt Cadayle's hand on his back and reminded himself that she loved him, that she was concerned for him, and rightly so.

"Don't you think that's enough for the day?" she asked quietly.

"W . . . W . . ." Bransen stopped and spat again, then reached for his pouch. He would have fallen over with the movement except that Cadayle caught him and held him steady. She grabbed his flailing hand and gently guided it to the pouch and the gemstone, then helped him bring the stone to his forehead.

"We've barely covered two miles," he protested in a voice clear and strong. Indeed, the sudden change shocked even Bransen.

"We should try to cross another five before dusk," said Cadayle. "We'll not go another single mile at our pace, and if you truly injure yourself . . ."

Bransen turned his head to eye her hard.

"I understand," she whispered to him, "and I know your reasoning. I wouldn't dare pretend that I have the right to disagree. But I beg of you to measure your pace, my love. You are tormenting your body more than it can take. You'll need more than the soul stone if you break your knee, and where will that leave me and my ma?"

"My patience is long gone with this creature known as the Stork," said Bransen.

"But mine is not."

Still holding the gemstone tight against his forehead, Bransen leaped up to his feet, catching himself surely and with incredible agility. He was the Highwayman now, the rogue who could scale a castle wall of tightly fit weather-worn stones. He was the Highwayman, who could challenge a laird's champion in battle and win.

Bransen pulled the gemstone away. Immediately, he swayed. He caught himself, though, and kept Cadayle at bay with an upraised hand. Then he stubbornly put his gemstone back in his pouch and let it go.

He took a step, awkward and unsteady. He nearly fell over, but he did not, and he even managed to glance back at Cadayle to see her and her concerned mother exchanging frowns.

Hand shaking, arm flailing, Bransen managed to get his fingers back around the precious gemstone. He brought it forth and collected, too, the black silk bandanna he used to secure it to his forehead.

"I did not wish to end with a stumble," he explained, securing it in place. He managed a strained smile, one that undeniably showed Cadayle and Callen that he was surrendering for the day for their benefit and not his own.

"I will be as patient as I can," he promised his wife. Despite his frustration his words were sincere.

"I love you," Cadayle said.

"With or without the gemstone," Callen added.

Bransen licked a bit of blood from his lip.

How could he be so fortunate and miserable all at the same time?

And how, he wondered as he brought his hand up to check on the security of the gemstone, could he both appreciate and resent its healing magic? The soul stone freed him from his infirmities, made him whole—heroic, even. And yet at the same time it trapped him and held him dependent to its powers.

He wanted to be free of it, but he could not tolerate the reality of that freedom.

"You are better than you were before you found the soul stone," Cadayle said. She waved her hand at the rough and root-strewn trail. "This ground trips you up, perhaps, but in your youth the flat grass of the monastery courtyard often left you on your face."

"*Ki-chi-kree*," Bransen said.

"The promise of the Jhesta Tu," Cadayle agreed. "You will overcome this infirmity.

"You already have," she added. Bransen eyed her curiously. "You defeated it with your spirit long before you found any real control of your limbs. To others you were the Stork, some in jest and some in earnest sympathy. But you have always been Bransen. And you will always be Bransen, with or without the soul stone, whether or not you need the soul stone to walk a broken trail."

Bransen Garibond closed his eyes and took a deep breath, blowing out all of his frustration in one great exhale. "I never knew my real father," he said, and Cadayle and Callen nodded, for they knew well the tale. "He studied the Jhesta Tu. He has been to the Walk of Clouds. He copied their book—the same book that Garibond taught to me when I was young. He will have answers."

"Or he will show you where to look for them."

Bransen nodded, his smile genuine, and genuinely hopeful. "Garibond told me that he went to Chapel Abelle in the North. If I can find him . . ."

"Bran Dynard was a good man," Callen said, stepping up beside her daughter. "I owe him my life as surely as I owe it to Sen Wi. He knew why I was put out on the road to die, and why I carried the bites of the serpent. He knew that his superiors in his Church had witnessed my execution and had, with their silence, condoned it. And still he fought for me against the vicious powries, and he hid me away at great personal peril. You are much like him, Bransen. You carry his integrity and his sense of justice. Physical strength is nothing when weighed against that."

"I will find my physical strength," Bransen replied. "It is there—the soul stone shows it to me. I will overcome this infirmity."

Callen nodded. "I would never doubt you, and double

blessed am I to have been saved by your father and again by you, the Highwayman."

Cadayle walked over and took Bransen's arm. "Five miles?" she asked.

"That would make seven for the day," said Bransen. "And we will do seven tomorrow."

Cadayle tilted her head back to get a better look into her stubborn husband's eyes.

"Two without the gemstone?" she asked.

"Two and a half," he replied flatly.

Callen's laugh turned them both to regard her, standing with Doully's reins in hand. "And they say that my walking companion brings a reputation for stubbornness," Callen remarked, shaking the donkey's lead.

All three were laughing, then, and even old Doully gave a snort and a whinny.

FIVE

Foul Chaps We'd Be

It called to him from the far corner of the darkness, a continual growl, a rolling "r." Finally it broke and rewound in its timbre like a wave flowing over itself just offshore.

It grew again in resonance and filled Cormack with its mournful vibration, beckoned him forward in the darkness. He followed, a purely instinctive and unthinking move. He knew not if the sound would take him from the abyss, nor, locked as he was in a state of near emptiness, if he even wanted to come forth from the darkness.

At that moment Cormack didn't want anything. He just was. A moment of pure existence or of nothingness, he couldn't tell. But the rolling "r" pulled him forward as if walking him to the edge of a cliff. He stepped off and fell through the blackness. His eye cracked open, and crystalline brilliance stung him. Sensations returned, and with them consciousness.

The light was the sun, sparkling off the water. The taste in his mouth was sand, for he was facedown on the beach. The sound was a song, a powrie chant.

With great effort Cormack rolled his head to the side.

The bloody-capped dwarves were huddled in a circle, their arms locked over the shoulders of the next dwarf in the ring. They turned their living wheel in perfect cadence, a few steps left, a few back to the right, all the while singing:

Put me deep in the groun' so cold
I'll be dead, 'fore I e'er get old
Done me fights and shined me cap
Now's me time for th'endless nap
Spill no tear and put me deep
Dun want no noise for me endless sleep
Done me part and stood me groun'
But th'other one won and knocked me down

Put me deep in the groun' so cold
I'll be dead 'fore I e'er get old
Spill no tear and put me deep
Dun want no noise for me endless sleep

Cormack tried to lift his head to get a better perspective, and only then did the monk realize that he had been tightly bound, his hands painfully drawn up against his back, the rough weeds tight into his wrists. More than those shackles, though, loomed the noose of pain shooting through his head. As soon as Cormack got his chin off the sand, he dropped it back, grimacing all the way, as hot fires erupted in the back of his skull.

He closed his eyes tight and tasted the sand and tried hard to growl through the burning agony. He wanted to reach up and grab at the spot, but he couldn't wriggle free his hands.

Gradually it passed, and the powrie song continued, and their huddle circled left and right, just off the beach. This time Cormack slowly rolled his entire body instead of trying to lift his head alone, and he managed to gain a better perspective on the powrie dance. He realized only then that the dwarves were circling a particular spot, a particular thing. As he considered the words of their ditty he solved the riddle.

Cormack held his tongue, not wanting to risk interrupting the solemn ceremony. It went on for a long while until finally the ring of dwarves opened, revealing a cairn of piled stones. Still singing, the cadence marking their every movement, the dwarves turned as one so that they were no longer shoulder-to-shoulder, but formed instead a single file as they marched around and then away from the grave of their fallen comrade.

"So, are ye awake then?" the leading dwarf asked when they reached the beach and began to disperse. "Was thinking ye meant to sleep the whole o' the day."

"Better for him if he did, what?" the second dwarf added in a sinister voice indeed. "Better for him if he'd listened to his fellows and done run to their home o' rocks."

"More fun for us that he didn't," another put in, stepping out of the line and pulling his red beret from his hairy head. In the same movement the dwarf drew out a curved, serrated knife, its gleaming blade already marred by blood, and Cormack knew that he was doomed. Powries—bloody caps, as they were known—wore their most prized possession on their heads, and those red berets, through some magic that no race other than the dwarves understood, shined more brightly with the blood of fallen enemies. The intensity of a beret's hue constituted the powrie badge of honor, of rank and respect.

The dwarf with the knife approached. Cormack tried to hold steady his breathing, tried not to be afraid, as he glanced all around for his Abellican brethren.

But they were not to be seen. They were in the rock chapel, as the dwarf had proclaimed, and Cormack couldn't even free his arms to defend himself.

The tall and willowy woman burst from the forest, the wide leaves of the many ferns and low plants slapping against her bare legs as she rushed along the sketchy path. She had hurried from her village, intending to perform the midday service, the Fishermen Blessing, as her station demanded of her. As soon as Milkeila cleared the last brush and viewed the rocky expanse to the beach she knew that her service would be delayed, however, for none of the fishermen were in the water. They stood upon the high rocks, staring out over the calm lake to the southeast. Moving out onto the beach and toward those rocks Milkeila understood the distraction, for the sounds of battle, the sharp crack of sticks, the occasional cry of rage or pain, drifted across the flat water to her ears.

"Chapel Isle," one of her kinsmen said to her. She knew that already from the direction of the sounds, referring to the small and rocky island upon which the Abellican foreigners had built their simple monastery.

"The monks are longing for their homeland again," another fisherman said with a derisive snort, and others snickered at the thought.

Milkeila brushed from her face her thick hair, a rich brown hue that highlighted red before the sunrise and sunset, to peer intently into the fog, though she knew that she would see nothing definitive at this distance across the misty lake. Only on breezy days, when the perpetual fog was blown clear at various intervals, could the people of Yossunfier, this island, catch the slightest glimpse of the monks' home, and even then, it was nothing more than an indistinct blur in the distance.

There was simply too much mist this day, as almost every day.

"Better the powries than the monks," another of Milkeila's kinsmen remarked. The others grumbled their agreement.

Milkeila remained silent and did well to hide her discontent, for she hardly agreed. Nor had it always been this way between her people of Yan Ossum, Clan Snow-fall, and curious southern Vanguardsmen who called themselves Brothers of Abelle. When the monks had first appeared at the lake they had befriended the barbarians, particularly the shaman class, to which Milkeila belonged (though back then, she had been merely a young and eager student). Many of her kin had quickly become disenchanted with the Abellicans because of their insistence that their way was the only way, that their religion was the true religion, and their demand of adherence to that strict order and rituals.

Milkeila's hand moved up to brush the necklace concealed under her more traditional one of claws and teeth and bright feathers. Under her smock the young woman kept a ring of gems, stones of varying color and type and magical property, given to her by one of the younger monks. She glanced around guiltily, knowing that her people would judge her harshly if they ever discovered her secret—and the other secret: that she was privately meeting with that young monk, being tutored in the general ways of Abellican gemstone magic. And much more than that.

The sounds of battle increased across the water.

"Looks like they have a good row going," one of the barbarians said. "We should prepare the boats and paddle in behind the fight. The pickings will be easy. Perhaps we could even go right to their stone church and throw the foolish Abellicans from the lake once and for all."

Others mumbled their agreement, but all present knew the impracticality of the suggestion. No raids could be executed without the proper blessings of the shamans and the careful planning of the elders, and none of that could happen in short enough order for this impromptu mission to occur. Still, the eager nods reminded Milkeila that she and her few rebellious cohorts were playing with danger here in their secret relationship with the Southerners, particularly Milkeila; she was shaman and had dared to take Cormack as her lover.

"Maybe the powries will do our work for us," the same man said after a few heartbeats, when enough time had passed for all of them to recognize the impracticality of his previous suggestion.

To hear her people cheering for powries over fellow humans left Milkeila cold. The Abellican monks had crossed a dangerous threshold early on, one they had stepped over by choice and not heritage. In insisting that the barbarians elevate the teachings of Abelle over their long-standing, traditional beliefs, the monks had, in effect, openly declared themselves heretics and had been branded as such by the elders and the shamans.

Milkeila recalled the day when she had warned the Abellicans about their unacceptable path and winced in her mind's eye to remember Brother Giavno's angry retort. "What do we care if our ways offend you?" he had roared. "Your place is in hellfire while heaven awaits the followers of Blessed Abelle!"

Milkeila hadn't known what "hellfire" might mean, but when Giavno had assured her that she and her people were doomed to sit in eternity beside the likes of the dactyl demons, she had fathomed the point of his rant quite clearly.

Fortunately not all the Abellicans were of similar temperament as that unpleasant one. Some of the younger brothers, one in particular, were quite open to the possibilities that there were other explanations and traditions worth exploring in sorting through the mysteries of life. Of like mind to Milkeila and her small group of friends, who often wondered about the world beyond the borders of the mist-covered lake, a world upon which they were forbidden to venture.

"Be safe, Cormack," the shaman whispered under her breath, her hand brushing her shirt above the necklace

of magical stones, and in an even lower voice, she added,
"My love."

The serrated blade was barely an inch from Cormack's throat when another dwarf grabbed the arm
holding it.

"Nah," that second powrie said, tugging the first
dwarf back from the bound human.

"I won't cut him wrong that his blood's spillin' too
fast!" the first assured the others. "Let him die slow, and
we'll all get our caps in the puddle, what?"

"Nah, ye're not for cuttin' him at all," said the other,
and he moved in between the knife-holder and poor Cormack. He glanced back at Cormack as he did. Cormack
realized from the dwarf's recently busted nose, blood
caked on his thick mustache, that this had been one of
his opponents before the glacial trolls had arrived on the
scene.

"What're ye jabberin', then?" the knife-holder argued. "I come here to wet me cap, and wetting me cap's
what I'm to do!"

"Ye got a dozen dead trolls for cutting."

"Bah, but troll blood's not much for brightening me
cap, and ye're knowing it, ye danged fool, Mcwigik!"

"Best ye're to get, unless some o' them other monks
come out o' their rock house, and that ain't for hap-
pening!"

One of the other powries added a complaint of his
own, and another chimed in, but a second dwarf stepped
forward in support of Mcwigik. Cormack recognized
this one as the wounded Bikelbrin, whom Cormack had
circle-kicked under the surf and had later leaped over
when he had gone to intercept the ice trolls.

"Let him go, Pragganag," Bikelbrin said to the knife-
holder. "If me thoughts're sorting out right, then this
one saved me hairy bum."

"Trolls had ye dead," Mcwigik agreed. "We'd've put ye under a stone pile like we done to Regwegno there."

"Aye," agreed another, and to Cormack's horror, that one held up a heart—Regwegno's heart, apparently.

"But if there'd been no trolls it was us and them monks," Pragganag argued, though even he seemed to be losing steam here and let his knife's tip slip down toward the ground, enough so that Cormack was beginning to think he might indeed survive this ordeal. "Got me a crop o' burned beard," he added, tugging at the left half of his fiery red beard—or at least, the right side remained fiery red, for the clump in his hand had been blackened by one of Giavno's bolts of lightning. "And now ye're telling me that I lost half me beard for nothing? And when there's bright human blood right there, laid out and tied and ready for the taking?"

"Foul chaps we'd be to kill one what saved our hairy bums," Mcwigik growled back at him.

"Flattened yer own fat nose!" Pragganag shouted.

"Aye," said Mcwigik, and he glanced back and nodded—appreciatively!—at Cormack. "Got a wicked punch to him."

"And a wicked kick," added Bikelbrin.

"Then a good kill he'll be!" Pragganag reasoned. "And a brighter cap I'll wear!"

"But ye weren't the one to drop him, was ye?" Mcwigik asked. "Trolls bringed him down, and only because he leaped into the lot o' them to save Bikelbrin. The least ye can do is knock him down yerself afore ye're for taking his bright blood, don't ye think?"

Pragganag stood straighter, the knife slipping down to his side as he eyed Mcwigik and Bikelbrin suspiciously. "What're ye saying?"

Mcwigik grinned, his teeth shining white between the bushy black hair of his beard. He drew out his own knife and stepped fast behind Cormack. With a sudden swipe he took the bindings from the fallen man's wrists.

He reached down and grabbed the man by the arm and roughly hoisted him to his feet.

A wave of dizziness buckled poor Cormack's legs as a ball of fire seemed to erupt within his battered skull. He couldn't focus his eyes and would have fallen back to the sand had not Bikelbrin rushed over to help Mcwigik keep him upright.

"Well, alrighty then," Pragganag laughed. He lifted his knife and advanced, grinning from ear to ear.

Mcwigik didn't even have to intercept, though, as a pair of dwarves behind Pragganag grabbed him by the shoulders.

"Not now, ye dolt," one said. "Fool monk can't even stand."

"Where's yer honor?" the other agreed.

"It's staining me beret!" Pragganag argued, pulling away, but he did indeed lower his knife.

"Now for yerself," Mcwigik said, turning Cormack to face him, hoisting the man again as he slumped back toward the sand. "New moon tonight—ol' Sheila's not to be found. Are ye hearin' me, boy?" He gave Cormack a little shake, which elicited a pronounced groan.

"Next time Sheila's not to be found ye get yerself back to the beach, and we'll come ashore so that ye can fight Pragganag here straight up," Mcwigik explained.

"Yach, but the human dog's not to come out to fight!" Pragganag argued.

Mcwigik tossed his fellow dwarf a dismissive glance and muttered, "It's the best ye're getting," before turning his attention back to Cormack. "Ye come alone and come ready to fight. And if Pragganag's beating ye, then know yer blood's forfeit."

"And what if this one wins?" Bikelbrin asked, giving Cormack another shake, which brought forth another groan. Across the way Pragganag snorted as if that notion was absurd.

"We'll get him something for his trouble, then," said Mcwigik.

"Yach, but ye're giving him his life now!" one of the dwarves behind Pragganag reminded. "Ain't that to be enough?"

"Aye, that's enough," said another.

"Nah," Mcwigik bellowed back, waving his free hand at them. "Making it more interestin'. If this skinny human's to win, then we'll give him Pragganag's cap," he added suddenly, on impulse.

"Aye!" Bikelbrin said, seeing all the faces except for Pragganag's, of course, brightening around him.

"To the dactyl's bum ye are!" Pragganag frothed.

But Mcwigik was quick to reply, "Are ye saying that ye can't take a skinny human one-to-one?"

"Yach!" Pragganag protested and threw up his arms, whirling away.

"Ye heared it all, boy?" Mcwigik asked Cormack, turning the monk's face to look at him directly. "Next time Sheila's not to be seen. Gives ye a month to get yer head put back together. Ye come out and ye come out alone."

Surely the world was spinning, and Cormack hardly registered any of it. But he managed a nod.

Mcwigik and Bikelbrin laid him back down on the sand, and Cormack's thoughts fell far, far away.

Onlookers ignorant of the shamanistic ways would have thought it a dance, though a pretty one to be sure. Milkeila's bare feet scraped across the sand, drawing lines in a prescribed pattern about her as she turned and swayed and sang softly. She crossed her right foot over her left, stepped down with her heel, then gracefully rolled her ankle to lift the heel from the sand and point her toe in. She went up onto the ball of her other foot and slowly twirled all the way around.

This was the circle of power.

Milkeila's hands moved in unison a foot apart out to her left. She chanted more loudly and dug her toe into the sand, connecting her to the power of the earth below her. Then she turned her palms up and lifted her hands to the sky, drawing that power up behind her movement. Her hands came gracefully down before her in a slow arc, and she repeated the process to her right side.

The energy lifted more easily this time, she felt in her soul, so when her hands were high in the sky, she turned about the other way, altered her chant to the god of the wind, and slowly turned her palms over as she found a stance of symmetry. She felt the wind gathered in her palms, so she slowly lowered them down by her sides, her thumbs tapping her hips and then moving lower to brush her bare legs below the hem of her short skirt. They pressed down past the outside of her knees and the sides of her shins as she dropped into a crouch, so low that her hands soon rested flat on the ground.

The shaman pressed the power of the wind into the soil, fanning the flames of the lava she had coaxed from far, far below. The ground around her, within her drawn circle, began to steam and to bubble. Despite what she had told herself before beginning the ceremony Milkeila couldn't resist sending her thoughts into the ruby that hung on the gemstone necklace. She felt the power there, teeming with strength, and sent it, too, into the ground.

One vent popped clear, shooting hot mist several feet into the air to the approving nods of the gathered clansmen and women. Several grabbed their pails of fish, knowing that the cooking circle was near completion.

Milkeila felt the warmth beneath her bare feet and knew that she had done well. But when her mentor, Toniquay, called to her as *"permid a'shaman yut,"* she felt more guilt than pride. For that was her title, the Prime Shaman of Youth, the most promising priest of her generation. She had earned that honor honestly, she knew, and was well on her way to the accolade before the Southern monks had ever come to Mithranidoon. But the fact that she had dared use an Abellican gemstone in this sacred ritual, or that she wore the necklace at all, or that she had given her heart to a man not of Yan Ossum, made Toni-quay's prideful remark sting.

Lost in the swirl of thoughts, Milkeila realized that she should step out of the cooking circle when her feet grew very, very hot. She came out facing the water and walked through the gathering down to the surf.

"Always this beach," Toniquay said behind her. "This is Milkeila's special beach."

She didn't turn to face him, for she knew that she was blushing fiercely. This particular beach faced Chapel Isle and also faced the secret sandbar where she met with her lover.

"The magic is strong here, do you think?" Toniquay asked.

"Yes, shaman," she answered.

"It is the magic of the old gods that draws you to this spot ever again, is it not?"

She felt her cheeks grow even hotter at that double-edged question.

"I see it, too, *permid a'shaman yut,*" Toniquay said, his voice dipped in the syrup of sarcasm as he was so wont to do.

What did he see? Milkeila wondered. How much of the truth lay open to the wise and severe old man?

Despite herself, she lifted her gaze toward Chapel Isle, but only for the briefest moment before turning to face Toniquay. His knowing smile reminded her of her own whenever she chanced to catch some of the younger boys staring at her legs or breasts.

"A place of magic," old Toniquay remarked, and walked away.

Milkeila felt her cheeks flush hot again. She glanced over to see the fishermen and their wives preparing the meal, cooking the catch in the circle she had magically prepared by calling to the old gods of Yan Ossum.

And by extracting the power of the Abellican ruby.

S I X

Keys to Debtor's Prison

The settlement on the mouth of the river where it spilled into the Gulf of Corona was called Palmaristown. It seemed to Bransen, Cadayle, and Callen that this was really two distinct cities and not one. Indeed, a solid wooden fence ran the length of the town, separating the ramshackle hovels in the region of the docks and the great river from the larger and more comfortable homes of the town's eastern section. That secure fence surrounded the inner town completely, with an open gate accepting the southern road from Delaval and a second one in the northeast, running inland just south of the gulf.

Guards walked their stations along a parapet built within that fence, with most concentrated in the west, looking out over the town's poor section and the bustling docks.

And they were indeed bustling, Bransen and his companions noted as they neared the southern gate. Ferries moved continually across the wide river, and so many sailing ships, including many of Laird Delaval's warships, were in port that several had to be moored out from the fully occupied wharves. Teams of dirty men moved to and fro, heavy ropes out behind them as they hauled skids laden with supplies, or thick trunks of trees brought in from across the river to the west, the region appropriately known as the Timberlane.

Drivers cracked whips on the heels of those poor laborers. The trio of visitors at the gate watched in astonished horror as one man fell to the docks beneath the weight of a heavy punch. He hit the ground, and the dockmaster began kicking him and stomping on him, despite his pleas, and none of the other laborers dared do anything more than look on.

"You haven't the stomach for it, then?" one of the guards at the gate asked the trio, obviously noting their horrified expressions. He looked at Bransen mostly, who moved without the soul stone this day in full Stork disguise. The guard crinkled his face at the sight and turned his stare to Cadayle. A rather lewd smile spread across his face.

"My husband," Cadayle said, stepping near to Bransen and taking his arm with her own. "Wounded in the war in the land south of Delaval."

"Fighting for?" the guard prompted. Across from him a pair of other sentries took note of the conversation and watched with sudden interest. They looked at Doully the donkey, too, particularly at the bulging saddlebags slung over her back.

"Laird Delaval, of course," Cadayle replied. "We are of Pryd Town, and Laird Prydae threw in with Delaval against Ethelbert, as has his successor, Laird Delaval's own nephew."

"Welcome, then," said the first. "You have nothing the Abellican monks cannot fix?"

"I . . . I . . . I," Bransen stammered and stuttered and drooled, and the sentry winced in obvious disgust.

"None have helped," Cadayle interjected. "Though many have tried. Perhaps here we will find our answers."

"Father Malskinner is mighty with the stones," one of the guards to the side remarked.

"Come through, then, and find your way," the first said, and waved the trio and their donkey through. "And don't you worry," he said to Bransen as the man staggered by him. "Those fools down there under the whip were brought from Ethelbert's lines."

"They are prisoners?" Callen asked with surprise.

"Until they die from their efforts, aye," the guard explained. He didn't seem bothered in the least by that eventuality. He glanced down at the docks and the bedraggled slaves. "I lost my brother in a ship fight in the gulf. I'd go down there and put the sword to the lot of them if it was my choice to make. But I'll take my satisfaction in knowing that these fools are helping Laird Delaval put an end to Ethelbert's claims. Every log they bring in from across the river, every crate of food or weapons sailing up from Delaval Town, works against the Beast of Entel. When Ethelbert falls, and fall he will, I'll take my satisfaction in knowing that Palmaristown played her part in his demise!"

"I only wish that my husband had not been so badly wounded that he might still aid in the effort," Cadayle said.

"Could be that his wife would offer comfort to guards loyal to Delaval," one of the pair across the way remarked, and his companion chuckled.

Cadayle took care to keep her response muted, neither too insulting in rebuff nor too accepting of the slight that it could coax the man on in his carnal quest. She clutched Bransen's arm tighter and led him through the gate, Callen and Doully coming up behind them.

Of all the towns they had traveled through none possessed the energy of Palmaristown. The city was not on the front lines of the fighting like so many of the settlements from Pryd to Delaval, and few wounded came through. Yet, Palmaristown remained in the very center of it all, for through here came many of Laird Delaval's soldiers, boarding ships to be carried across the Gulf of Corona to the distant eastern reaches known as the Mantis Arm. Here in Palmaristown the war was very real but very distant, an exciting event to be discussed in every tavern and on every street corner but without the torn bodies and missing limbs that cast the pall of harsh reality.

That sanitized reality reflected in the eagerness and excitement of the townsfolk. As word spread down the lanes before the trio many salutes and bows came at Bransen from afar.

They secured a tavern room quite easily, offered at half the normal price to the wounded soldier, and set out to find a stable and buyer for Doully, for the old donkey had seen too much of the road. Whispers preceded them, however, and before they even had the time to walk from the inn to the hitching post to retrieve Doully, they were met by a smiling young Abellican monk.

"Greetings, my friends," he said lightheartedly—so much so that Callen and Cadayle exchanged suspicious looks, for they were hardly used to helpful and cheery Abellicans.

"I am told that this poor man here has suffered terribly in service to Laird Delaval, may Blessed Abelle guide him to kingship," the monk went on.

"He was wounded south of Delaval against the men of Ethelbert, yes," Callen said, the hesitation in her voice reflecting her growing trepidation that Cadayle's lie was soon to be uncovered.

"I am Brother Fatuus of the Chapel of Precious Memories," the monk explained with a respectful bow. "Father Malskinner bade me to come forth and find this hero who walks among us, and to offer—" He paused and reached into a belt pouch, producing a quartet of gray soul stones.

"You would bestow healing to my poor son-in-law?" Callen asked, nodding appreciatively and coming forth to take Bransen's arm. "His wounds are grievous."

"As I see," said Fatuus. He turned a bit to the side and leaned forward in an attempt to view Bransen's back. "From the manner of his walk, I mean, as I have not witnessed any wound as of yet."

"The wound itself is long healed," Cadayle answered. "But the damage remains."

"A spear?"

"No."

"Sword?"

"No," Cadayle answered, and the monk crinkled his face with clear suspicion.

"Dagger?" he asked.

"A club," Cadayle decided. "He was smashed across the back, he told me, and he's had little control of his legs and feet since. And even his voice is lost to us, stuttering as he does."

The monk nodded and put on a pensive pose, as if he had any understanding at all.

Cadayle looked to her mother, who bit back a snicker.

"May I?" Brother Fatuus asked, extending his hand and the soul stones.

"Please, Brother," said Cadayle. She kissed Bransen's cheek and stepped away.

Fatuus began chanting to Blessed Abelle for guidance and strength. He closed his hand over the gemstones and gripped them so tightly that his knuckles whitened. He put his other hand up to Bransen's forehead and began to channel the soothing power of the gemstones into the wounded young man.

Bransen closed his eyes and steadied immediately, basking in the warmth of the wonderful enchantment. This monk was strong, he recognized immediately— more so than any of the brothers at Chapel Pryd. The healing energy flowed pure and direct, and Bransen felt as if he had his own stone strapped across his forehead. Using his Jhesta Tu training, Bransen opened up to the sensation and even dared hope, albeit fleetingly, that Brother Fatuus might offer some permanent benefit.

Bransen knew in his heart, though, that it would not be so.

A few heartbeats later, Fatuus relented and removed his warm and trembling palm.

Bransen opened his eyes, looked the man in the eye and said, "Than . . . Th . . . Th . . . Tha . . . k you." And he smiled and nodded, standing straighter, for indeed he felt much better (although he knew already it would be a very temporary sensation).

Cadayle came back to his side and said, "It is a fine thing you did this day," breaking Fatuus from his apparent trance.

He blinked repeatedly as he looked at the woman and her husband. "The wound is . . . is profound," he said.

"As many of your brethren have told us," said Cadayle. She looked at Bransen, and her smile came wide and sincere. "You performed very well, Brother. I have not seen him so straight since before the wound."

Already, though, Bransen began to bend, a bit of drool dripping from his mouth.

"It will not hold," Fatuus observed, and Cadayle offered a shrug and a forgiving smile in response.

"You must bring him to the Chapel of Precious Memories," Fatuus insisted. "I will beg Father Malskinner to allow others to participate. Our combined powers will lengthen the healing, I am certain."

"Of course," said Cadayle.

"Before Parvespers tomorrow," Fatuus bade them, referring to the ceremony of twilight. "We will be out all the day offering our services to the brave men on the docks."

"The slaves of war?" Cadayle asked. "Indeed, we saw them at their labors, being beaten like dogs."

"The filth of Ethelbert?" Fatuus replied, his eyes wide with horror. "Nay, not them, surely! Nay, nay, good lady, I speak of the privateers." As he finished he pointed to a pair of ships moored out in the open river to the north of the wharves, and sailing under no flag at all, none that Cadayle could see, at least.

"Privateers?"

"Free men," Fatuus explained. "Beholden to neither Ethelbert nor good Laird Delaval. They have sailed in at the behest of Laird Panlamaris the Bold, leader of Palmaristown, who seeks to enlist them in the united effort against foul Ethelbert and his swarthy minions."

"To bribe them, you mean," Cadayle reasoned.

"They will be compensated in coin, yes," said Fatuus. "And through the work of the Brothers of the Chapel of Precious Memories. God-given magic to heal their blistered feet and the many wounds brought back from weeks of toil at sea. It is the least we can offer to goodly Laird Delaval in his struggles against the Southern filth that is Laird Ethelbert."

Cadayle turned her look to Bransen, who, even through his Stork visage, wore a mischievous smirk. They were both well aware, after all, that the southeastern Abellican chapels served Ethelbert as these in the west and north served Delaval—and all in harmony and pragmatism.

Callen had barely closed the door to the room the three rented at a Palmaristown inn when Bransen grabbed up his gemstone and strapped it to his forehead under his black silken mask.

"Privateers," he said, not a hint of the Stork in his strong and steady voice. "Mercenaries."

"What are you thinking?" asked Callen.

"My guess is that my husband has decided that our load of booty is too dangerous to keep saddlebagged over poor old Doully," Cadayle replied, and Bransen nodded.

"I had thought to spread the wealth to the common-folk about the region but feared that some of the jewels would be recognized," Bransen explained. "I've no de-

sire to bring that pain to anyone—the same pain that
both of you felt at the hands of Laird Prydae when I
passed the stolen necklace to Cadayle."

"You need not remind me of that," Callen assured
him. "Did I not bid you to throw the stolen coins and
jewels into the river and be done with them?"

"And now I intend to do something along those very
lines."

"By taking the treasures to the privateers and bidding
them to double-cross Laird Delaval," Callen reasoned.
"So you'd throw in with Ethelbert?"

"I care not if they all kill each other," said Bransen.
"But there is a delicious irony in using that fool Yeslnik's
treasures to buy off Laird Delaval's intended allies."

"As delicious as the Stork becoming a hero of the
land against the interests of the lairds?" Cadayle asked.
Bransen stopped putting on his black shirt and stared
hard at her.

Cadayle merely shrugged, though, and offered him
a warm smile. Her statement had been blunt, of course,
but she, and perhaps she alone, had earned the right to
talk to him in such a manner and many times over.
Bransen could never be wounded by Cadayle's honest
reference to the Stork, since Cadayle alone had stood
by him before the creation of the Highwayman, when
he had found the gemstone magic to allow him to free
himself of the crippling bonds of his physical infirmities.

Bransen finished dressing in the black outfit his
mother had brought from Behr, finishing by tying the
torn strip of fabric over the distinctive birthmark on his
one bare arm.

Bransen took up the fabulous sword, holding it rever-
ently before his eyes as he studied the intricate vine and
flower designs etched into its gleaming blade. The weapon
had no equal north of the Belt-and-Buckle Mountains, and
few swords even of the Jhesta Tu mystics in Behr could
match its quality. Staring at the marvelous blade, Bransen

was reminded that he would one day go there, to the Walk of Clouds, to learn from the masters.

He slid the sword into its sheath and slung it across his back, then took up the saddlebags full of Yeslnik's treasure and tossed them over his shoulder. He moved to the room's small window and peeked around the heavy curtain, considering the setting sun.

"The privateer captains might be ashore," Cadayle said.

"I will find them," Bransen promised, and Cadayle and Callen nodded, neither about to doubt this man who had delivered them from a life of misery beneath the boot of Laird Prydae.

He went out in the dark of night, hand-walking down the side of the two-story inn so fluidly that anyone looking on would have thought he was using a ladder.

The Highwayman didn't need a ladder.

He didn't bother with the bustle he heard emanating from the many taverns along the wall separating the two city levels, reasoning that if the privateer captains were in one of those establishments, they would return to their ships in any case.

He found the docks nearly deserted, with only a couple of slaves swabbing the planks halfheartedly, and with no dockmasters to put whips to their backs. Bransen paid them little heed as he moved through the shadows along the wharves to the smaller docks and the tiny boats. He secured one without incident and floated out from the wharf, gently paddling as the current caught him and dragged him along. That current took him toward the moored privateers, for the tide was receding in the gulf, which meant that he merely needed his oars to steer the craft, and not noisily row it.

He kept glancing back over his shoulders, locating the dark silhouette of a mast protruding into the night sky, and appropriately angled his oars, drifting slowly, slowly, and in no hurry whatsoever. He brought the rowboat up against a mooring line and tied it off there, then gathered up his bags and, with a quick check to ensure that his precious sword remained secure in its sheath, the Highwayman began his climb.

A few moments later he came over the rail, silent as death, dark as night, and carefully paced about the deck, seeking sentries and the general lay of the ship. He'd never before been on a ship and had never even seen one up close. It took a lot of his concentration to resist losing himself in the experience, for truly this craft was a work of art, so sleek and beautiful and ultimately functional. He studied the many ropes, climbing and disappearing into the mass of rigging. Many generations of sailors had perfected this design one rope at a time, he understood immediately, recognizing in general fashion the evolution that had led from simple, single-mast boats to this intricate and wondrous three-sail design.

He found a raised cabin aft and quickly discerned, from the shouting within, that the man inside carried great authority, and was likely the captain of the vessel himself.

Or herself, Bransen realized as he sidled up to a small window beside the forward-facing door and peeked in.

She stormed about a decorated desk, a rolled parchment in hand, a red bandanna tight about her head, with dark brown tresses flowing out behind and halfway down her back. She wore a puffy white blouse gathered about her slim waist and unbuttoned far enough down to be quite revealing with her every sudden turn. Black breeches and high boots completed her outfit, along with a dirk on her right hip, a curved sword on her left. She was not an unattractive woman, surely, and carried about her an aura of competence and danger.

He had come in late in her tirade, and she seemed too upset to speak in complete sentences, apparently, but it wasn't hard for the Highwayman to fathom the gist of her rant: the nature of the deal offered by Laird Panlamaris, representative of Laird Delaval.

"Five months o' sailing!" she cried. "Five! And feedin' a full crew and a hundred hungry soldiers to boot. And that through a gulf full o' powries! E'er ye seen a powrie, boy? Nasty little redcap hungry to open yer belly and tug out yer guts! Might that he'll eat 'em right there while ye're watch . . ."

She stopped and stared, mouth agape.

"Do go on," the Highwayman bade. "I admit that my own experiences with the wretched powries are rather limited, but from what I've seen, I'll not contra . . ."

The woman drew out her sword and leaped for him, thrusting for his throat.

But his own sword appeared in his hand, as fast as a blink, and he easily and gently guided her stabbing blade aside so that it poked into the jamb of the open door. She kept coming, and reached for her dirk, but there, too, he beat her to the quick, and the sailor grasped at an empty sheath!

The Highwayman held her stolen dagger up before her astonished eyes. He edged the privateer back at the point of her own dirk.

"Good lady, you have no fight with me," he said, and he flipped the dagger, catching it by its tip and presenting it back to the sailor.

She stared at him for many heartbeats before grabbing the presented hilt and yanking the dirk back from the intruder. She presented both her blades in a defensive stance as she continued to size up the stranger, clearly unsettled.

The Highwayman calmly replaced his sword in its sheath across his back, and the privateer seemed all the more frazzled.

"Who ye be?" she demanded.

"An independent rogue," he replied. "Much akin to yourself, I would expect."

"Ye're to lead with insults?"

"Hardly, milady. I hold my head with pride and would expect no less from you and the worthy sailors of these fine ships—ships flying under the flag of neither Ethelbert nor Delaval."

"We're in Palmaristown, which has thrown in with Laird Delaval."

"No doubt because Laird Delaval has shown the deeper pockets."

The woman tilted her head back and narrowed her eyes.

"Or because you believe that he will win out in the end and see a brighter future for those who do not oppose him," the Highwayman bluntly added. "In either event, I salute you. I hold nothing but respect for any who can thrive in these dark times. I hope you will come to see me equally worthy of your respect." As he finished, he pulled the saddlebags off his shoulder and tossed them at the privateer's feet.

The woman glanced down at them, but immediately lifted her gaze back to the surprising man in the black mask.

He shrugged.

The woman hooked her saber under the flap of the nearest bag and with a deft flick of her wrist, severed the tie and pulled open the flap in a single, fluid movement. A few coins rolled out, and several jewels showed, and despite her best efforts, the woman's eyes flashed with obvious interest.

"If you came to bargain, what a fool ye be to lay out the ante openly, and with yerself surrounded by potential enemies," she said.

Again he shrugged, so confidently, and the smile showing under his black mask clearly said that he believed he could rather easily retrieve his treasure.

"What army serves ye?" the woman demanded.

"I am independent, and I offer no threat to accompany my gift to you, good lady. I came here to present you with these coins and jewels, stolen from the castle of the Laird of Delaval himself."

The woman glanced at her crewman, who, throughout

this entire ordeal, hadn't even moved. Nor did he notice his captain's look, fixated as he was on the marvelous and surprising intruder.

"You would be wise to keep them hidden while you remain on the river, or even in the gulf," the Highwayman said. "Delaval has sent word far and wide to find these, no doubt."

"Ye mean to push the burden o' them onto me?"

"If you do not want them, lady . . ."

"I said no such thing."

The Highwayman smiled wider.

"And what're ye asking in return for this . . . gift?"

"Nothing," he replied. "They are indeed a burden to me, as I remain in Delaval's lands."

"You would have us sail you to the reaches of Laird Ethelbert?"

The Highwayman paused, and almost agreed to that, thinking that he could then get around the spurs of the Belt-and-Buckle and into the famed city of Jacintha, in Behr, which would allow him an open road to the Walk of Clouds. Black wings of doubt fluttered up all about him, though, forcing him to admit to himself, yet again, that he was not ready for that ultimate journey.

"At another time, perhaps," he said. "I have business remaining here, though I do hope to reach Entel and beyond, all the way to Behr, in the near future. Should we meet again when my business is complete, I would beg of you to consider providing such passage."

"And for now?" the woman asked, looking down at the open satchel.

"I would beg you to hoist your sails and be gone from this place."

The woman looked at him suspiciously. "Ye be an agent of Ethelbert indeed, then."

"Independent," the Highwayman reiterated. "Truly so. I care for neither of the feuding lairds, nor for any of their lackey lessers. If all the nobles of all of Honce are murdered in their sleep tomorrow, I will raise a glass in celebration. But of now, it is Laird Delaval who has most aggravated me, and it does me pleasure indeed to stick pins into his sides, first by robbing his treasury, and then . . ."

"By buying off three ships he has employed for his efforts," the privateer reasoned.

The Highwayman shrugged. "The treasure is an offer of truce from another independent. Perhaps a prepayment for services needed some time hence. But I hold you to nothing at all. I come in salute—better that one such as you possess the coins and jewels than have me bury them in a hole. How should I ever live with myself if these treasures find their way into the hands of an innocent and oblivious peasant, who is then hanged by Delaval's people for possessing them? Here, I know, they are in competent hands of men and women wise enough to keep them safe and secret. So yes, I beg you to relieve me of my burden."

The privateer looked down at the bags again, licking her lips as she imagined the treasures within. If the hints showing on the open edge were any indication, she knew that this might well be the most profitable day of her life. With a sigh, she slid her weapons away and lifted her eyes to regard the Highwayman.

But he was already gone from her cabin.

I t is an amazing transformation," Callen said early the next morning. Bransen had just awakened and was still rubbing the sleep from his eyes when Callen walked through the door of their rented room. Beside him on the small bed Cadayle hardly stirred other than to bury her face in her pillow against the intrusion of daylight.

"I did not know that you had been here before," Bransen replied, his voice steady, for he had slept with the soul stone firmly strapped in place on his forehead.

"Of course I have not," said Callen. "I'm only echoing the words of the townsfolk. Palmaristown has seen a great shift in the last few months. No Samhaists remain in the city, and there are few in the surrounding countryside by all accounts. And even the people here fast abandon the ways of the Ancient Ones."

"The Abellicans have the gemstones and the favor of the lairds across all of Honce," Bransen said.

"But the change is coming more quickly here than elsewhere—even than in Delaval itself from what I could see. I had no such expectation, since Palmaristown is on the border of the wilderness. Across the river is land untouched by the Abellicans by all accounts."

"And land unwanted by the Samhaists, likely," Bransen reasoned.

"Or perhaps the Samhaists are out there, just across the river, watching and biding their time."

Bransen shrugged, as he hardly cared. As he studied Callen more carefully, though, he recognized that she was more than a little unsettled by the sweeping changes, which surprised him given her unpleasant history with the brutal Samhaists.

"Perhaps the world will become a better place as the Samhaists recede into the shadows," he offered. "Not that I expect much better from the Abellicans."

"If they're not killing people it will be an improvement," Callen said, and Bransen smiled at her, glad that his words had apparently eased her troubled soul. He sympathized, and understood her inner turmoil, for indeed the changes sweeping the land were vast and profound, and Bransen recognized that few of the people had come to terms with them as of yet. Looking at it all from a removed point of view, it was more amusing than unsettling. He figured he really couldn't lose, for anything would be better than the present state!

"Did your tryst go well?" Callen asked.

"I believe it did."

"Those ships are from Bergenbel, the one holding south of the gulf that hasn't thrown in for either Ethelbert or Delaval. Both sides value that port, I am told, and so they pay dearly for the services of the privateers who have taken up the mercenary cause."

"Each believes that to be the path toward securing the holding, likely."

Callen nodded her agreement with the assessment.

"Then my visit with the flagship captain last night might prove more irritating to Delaval than I intended," Bransen said, his smile wide.

That smile grew all the wider later in the day when the trio started out of town. On a hill on the northeastern section they watched the Bergenbel privateers raise their sails and glide away from Palmaristown, heading north toward the open waters of the Gulf of Corona. At a nearby smithy, where they sold old Doully (for they could not bear to force the aching donkey to continue the journey), they found confirmation that the departure of the ships was the talk of the town, with many whispering that it would prove a harbinger for disaster.

"Ethelbert's bought them," explained the blacksmith, a hulking giant of a man with a red face and hair black and matted. "Word's out that they might have been spies from the dog, come here to survey Palmaristown's defenses."

"You are expecting an attack?" Cadayle asked.

"Preparing for it," the smith replied. "Who's to know what the dog Ethelbert will do? King Delaval's got him squeezed to the Mirianic."

They let it go at that, with Cadayle handing Bransen, in Stork guise, over to Callen and saying her farewells to Doully. They were some distance from the smithy, on an open stretch of ground reserved for visiting caravans, before any of them dared broach the subject.

"Just as you had hoped," Cadayle said.

Bransen grabbed the soul stone in his pouch and clutched it tightly. "If there were only a way for me to let Delaval know that it was the idiot Yeslnik's coin that bought off his privateers, my satisfaction would be complete."

"It's early in the day," said Callen. "You will think of something."

That brought a shared laugh from the three, but Bransen cut his short, and stuttered it and twisted it around, when he noted the approach of a city guardsman. With help from his two companions, the Stork staggered out through Palmaristown's northeastern gate, and down the open road toward Chapel Abelle, the seat of Abellican power.

A strange and unexpected feeling washed over Bransen at that moment. Suddenly it seemed real to him, this search for Brother Bran Dynard, his father—no, not his father, he decided, for that honor remained with Garibond. To this point, Bransen had considered this journey north a diversion as much as anything else, a delay against facing the hard truth of his road south. He had latched on to the idea of finding his father as much so that he wouldn't yet have to face the Jhesta Tu mystics and their answers (or more pointedly, their possible lack of answers) as out of any real desire to find and know the man who had sired him.

Now, though, with the road straight and clear before him and the last real city left behind, the idea of finding Brother Dynard suddenly seemed very real—and Bransen wasn't even sure what that meant. Would the man acknowledge him? Would the man crush him tight in a hug and be overcome with joy that his son had found him?

Did Bransen even want that? What might such a joyful reunion mean to the memory of his beloved Garibond?

So many questions swirled in Bransen's thoughts the moment that road came clear to him, the moment the idea of finding Brother Dynard became real to him. Questions of how he might react to the man, of how the man might react to him, and most of all, as time and wobbly steps passed, of why.

Why hadn't Brother Dynard returned for him?

Callen had many times called Bran Dynard a good man; Bransen could only hope that the answer to his most pressing question would bear that out.

Brother Honig Brisebolis rambled through the streets of the lower city, huffing and puffing and warning everyone to get out of his way. Wide-eyed and obviously in great distress as he was, few would pause to argue those commands from the three-hundred-pound rotund monk. Nor did the guards at the city's higher, closed gate hesitate at the monk's approach, rushing to swing wide one of those double doors to let the important Brother Honig ramble through without slowing.

Honig did pause just past the gates, however, as he stood on the crossroad. To the right, the south, lay the road that would bring him to Laird Panlamaris's palace, while the left road led straight to the square before the Chapel of Precious Memories. Honig's news would prove important, critical even, to both Laird Panlamaris and Father Malskinner.

"Laird Panlamaris might swiftly dispatch warships to intercept," he said aloud, trying to sort through his jumbled thoughts.

He turned left anyway, realizing that his first duties were to the Church and not the laird. He gathered up a head of steam, gasping for breath but not daring to slow.

"What is it, Brother Honig?" Father Malskinner bade him a few moments later when he burst into the man's spacious private chambers.

Honig tried to answer, but couldn't find his voice for his gasping, and wound up leaning on the father's desk for support.

"Did you meet with Captain Shivanne?"

Brother Honig nodded emphatically, but still couldn't quite reach his voice.

"Brother Honig?"

"They raise sail!" he blurted at last.

A perplexed Father Malskinner stared at him for a moment before rising from his desk and moving to a window that overlooked the river. As soon as he glanced out, he saw the truth of it, as all three privateers had their sails up and engaged. The father turned fast on Honig. "What is the meaning?"

"Shivanne makes for the gulf and beyond," he said.

"But Laird Delaval's soldiers and supplies have not even yet arrived."

Honig shook his head. "She will not wait. She laughed at my protests!"

"Laughed?"

"She was paid, Father. Well paid. 'A better offer,' she said."

"Ethelbert? Here?"

Again Honig wagged his head in the negative. "Captain Shivanne teased and would not say, other than to assure me that it was not Ethelbert, nor any agent of the foul Laird of Entel. A privateer, she called him, this man who brought her a treasure beyond Laird Delaval's offerings."

Malskinner stared at him pensively. "A third party in the mix of this war?" It sounded even more improbable— to both of them—as he spoke the words aloud.

"A thorn, more likely," Brother Honig said. "She said he wore a mask and suit of black, exotic material."

Malskinner's eyes went wide.

"She said that he moved as a shadow, and worked his blade with the skill of a master. A most magnificent blade, she assured me. A blade unlike any she had ever seen, and one, she promised, that would lay low a laird or would-be king."

"The man from Pryd Holding," Malskinner said with a nod of recognition. He moved swiftly for the shelving behind his desk, where he kept all the correspondences of the last months. In a matter of moments, he held the ones that had filtered up from Pryd Town, and the related messages sent out by Prince Yeslnik of Delaval, warning of a most notorious and dangerous figure known as the Highwayman.

Malskinner drew a deep breath as he read the last of those notes, the one informing him that Laird Prydae had been killed by this desperate fellow, who had then set out on the open road, destination unknown.

Flipping through some of the back parchments, the father of the Chapel of Precious Memories found the letter of detail sent by Brother Reandu on behalf of Father Jerak of Chapel Pryd.

"Bransen Garibond," he said to Honig as he digested the letter. He looked at the portly brother. "Of Pryd Town. It is rumored that he was connected to Brother Dynard and an exotic woman of Behr."

"Dynard?" Brother Honig echoed, shrugging and shaking his head.

"An insignificant brother," Malskinner explained. "He traveled to Behr and was there corrupted by the seductive ways of the beastly barbarians. Father Jerak properly dispatched him to Chapel Abelle, to see if his soul could be salvaged."

"Yes, yes," Honig said. "Killed on the road, if I recall."

"That was the rumor. I know not if Chapel Abelle ever confirmed it or not."

"We must tell Laird Panlamaris of this."

"At once," Father Malskinner agreed. "Have him send word far and wide to beware of this creature." He glanced back at the note. "And tell them to look for a damaged and small man."

"Damaged?"

Malskinner shrugged as he read through the description of Bransen, of his storklike gait and his drooling and stuttering. "An alter ego, a disguise of weakness, it would seem," he said.

"Your pardon, Father," came a voice from the doorway. Father Malskinner looked over to see Brother Fatuus poking his head in. "I could not help but overhear."

"Come in, Brother Fatuus," Father Malskinner said. "We are discussing a potential problem that has come to Palmaristown. You have noticed the privateers lifting their sails to the wind?"

"That is why I have come, Father. What did I hear regarding a disguise?"

Father Malskinner bade him approach, and handed over the letter of detail from Brother Reandu.

"Go to Laird Panlamaris," Malskinner ordered Honig. "Tell him everything and warn him to alert his guards to this storklike person."

"I have seen him," Fatuus said suddenly, and both of his brethren spun about to regard him as he stood there, mouth agape, holding Reandu's letter. "This man, Bransen. I saw him only yesterday. I tended him with a soul stone, though to little effect, and bade him come to us this very night before Parvespers."

"The creature described in that letter?"

"Perfectly described. He was named as a hero of the war, and so I went to him generously, as per your commandments on this regard."

Father Malskinner leaned back, then sat on the edge of his desk and nodded slowly. "It is true, then. The Highwayman has come to Palmaristown."

"The Highwayman?"

"A rogue of unusual talent and troublesome ways, it would seem," Malskinner explained. "It was he who paid the privateers to sail from us, by their own admission."

"Why would they divulge such information?" asked Brother Fatuus.

"Captain Shivanne freely told me," Honig interjected. "I went out to her this morning, as arranged, to tend to her crew. They were already readying for sail, and when I inquired, she told me. Indeed, I would say that she was rather proud of her gain—proud enough to rattle a bag of coins and jewels before me, and to tell me of her unexpected benefactor."

"Let us hope that this Bransen, this Highwayman, feels secure enough in his disguise to take you up on your offer of appearing before us," Malskinner said to Fatuus. "If so, we will take him quickly and with as little excitement as possible."

"Brother Reandu, speaking for Father Jerak of Chapel Pryd, takes pains to find kind words for this rogue," Fatuus said as he perused the remainder of the long letter.

"Laird Delaval would not likely see things in that manner," said Malskinner, and he waved Honig away. "Nor will Laird Panlamaris, who will face the wrath of Laird Delaval for allowing the ships of Bergenbel to sail unladen with Delaval's men and supplies. Find this man if he remains within Palmaristown, and if he does not, find out where he went. Perhaps if we offer him to Laird Panlamaris, that he might offer him to Laird Delaval, our failures will be forgiven."

Bransen didn't show up at the Chapel of Precious Memories before Parvespers that night, of course, and indeed, word came back to Father Malskinner even before the twilight ceremony that the man and his two female companions had exited the city through the northern gate, on the road to the central highlands.

Where lay Chapel Abelle.

The next morning, Brother Fatuus rode out that same gate, spurring his horse to the east with all speed to deliver Father Malskinner's warning to the brothers of Chapel Abelle.

So hasty was Fatuus's ride that he didn't stop to inquire about the curious Highwayman at the scattered farmhouses he passed, and so it was on his second morning out that as he rode hard down the lane past a small barn, three sets of eyes stared out at him.

"The one who tried to heal you with the gemstones," Cadayle said.

"He rides as if powries are chasing him," Callen added.

"Powries? Or the Highwayman?" asked Bransen.

SEVEN

Tedium Undone

"Every day's one and the same," Mcwigik lamented, dipping his paddle silently into the water beside the small craft. "Weren't for the changes in the damned moon we'd not know that time's passing."

"Yach but she's passin'," said Bikelbrin, sitting opposite him. "Feeling it in me bones, I be."

"And meself in me broken nose," Mcwigik agreed and brought his hand up to touch his flat, wide nose, a bit flatter and wider still from the smash he'd been dealt twenty-eight days earlier. He had put a piece of white, gummy sap from the small, wide-leafed trees common to the islands across the bridge of his nose to secure it while it healed. He hadn't worn that gum bandage for a few days, but had put it back on just before the scheduled return to Chapel Isle. Pragganag and the others understood the reminder to be for Pragganag's benefit.

"Are ye to babble all then way, then?" said an irritated Pragganag, who was sitting in the back, testing the balance of his wooden-handled metal-bladed hatchet— one of the very few implements of metal still left intact after a century on the steamy lake. "Ye're to let the

whole o' Mithranidoon know we're about, and won't it
be the kitten's mewl to be chased by a fleet o' barbarian
longboats?"

"All with sense've gone to bed," Bikelbrin replied.

"Which is saying what for ourselves?" asked Mcwigik,
and Bikelbrin and three of the others in the small and
stout craft laughed, the fourth being Pragganag, who
narrowed his eyes so much so that his bushy eyebrows
pretty much stole them from view as he glowered at
Mcwigik.

Mcwigik took no note of him, and reached up to grab
his bandaged snout.

"Yach, but that monk smashed ye good, what?" said
Bikelbrin, and he and the others turned to Pragganag.

"Aye, and me nose's still for hurting when I'm laughing," Mcwigik said.

"Good thing yerself's the one what's telling the jokes
then," Pragganag deadpanned, and the laughter began
anew, Mcwigik joining in most heartily. As fierce a race
as walked the world, powries typically relished these
moments of ribbing, even if the best jabs came at their
own personal expense.

The boat quieted then as the powries went back to
paddling.

"We should build ourselves a barrelboat," Mcwigik
said after a short pause, referring to the open-sea powrie
craft, which resembled huge casks and kept most of
their bulk beneath the surface. The interior of a barrelboat consisted of a series of benches set before pedals,
and the tireless dwarves propelled their craft by pumping
legs, with the pedals geared to turn an aft screw. Many a
ship's captain had blanched white upon spotting a barrelboat, or even flotsam resembling such a craft, whose primary attack mode was, with typical powrie finesse, the
ram. "Put her out on the lake, and wouldn't that make all
the men shiver?"

"Ye can't be thinking it," Bikelbrin replied. "Ye might

be making the trolls happy, but ye'd be startin' a war for winning, and not just for playing, don't ye doubt."

"Aye," one of the others chimed in, "ye send a barbarian boat to the bottom and give her crew to the trolls, and all the islands'd join against us and come a-calling. Our rock of Red Cap ain't that big."

Mcwigik offered an exaggerated nod to show that he wasn't being serious. He knew as well as any the agreed-upon protocols of the islands, and primary among those was the edict that no combatant, not powrie nor Alpinadoran nor Abellican alike, would be dropped under deep water. For Mithranidoon's opaque gray waters hid terrible things indeed behind her constant wall of tiny bubbles. Great fish and serpents had been spotted often, and the glacial trolls seemed to know immediately whenever someone went under.

No one survived Mithranidoon's deep waters for long, and the civilized "warfare" between the islands demanded certain rules of engagement.

"It'd be good to feel the screw beneath me feet again, is all," Mcwigik replied with a tone of concession.

"Aye," Bikelbrin and one other agreed, for only they and Mcwigik among the six on the boat had ever experienced such a thing, or had ever seen the world beyond the banks of this lake. The bloody caps had been on Mithranidoon for more than a century now, and though their numbers had dwindled a bit, from eighty to seventy-six, they had been fortunate to recover the hearts of almost all of the more than forty who had been killed—fallen to trolls and storms and barbarians—in the early days, before the silently agreed-upon protocols. The heart was key to an untraditional and magical form of powrie reproduction. Using it, an appropriate mass of stone (and the plentiful lava rock of Mithranidoon was perfect for the task), and a month of ancient magic in the form of sacred songs, the powries could create life itself, giving "birth" to the fallen dwarf's successor. Not often practiced on the Weathered Isles, where female powries were plentiful, Sepulcher, as this magical rebirth was called, had kept the strength of the community of powries on the lake, though they had but three females remaining among the lot of them—for Sepulcher, for some reason that no dwarf had ever figured out, almost always led to a male child, whether the hosting heart had come from a male or female.

Returning from their last trip to Chapel Isle, they had prepared and buried Regwegno's heart and some rock and begun the process. This very afternoon, right before they had departed, they had felt the first rumblings from the Sepulcher (the term also was used to describe the physical grave-womb). Regwegno's son would climb free five months hence, and judging from those initial trembles all expected this one would prove a scrapper to make his sire proud.

"I'm hardly for remembering it," Mcwigik admitted, "for I been a hundred five of me hundred thirty right here on the lake."

The dwarf behind him, the only one other than Bikel-brin who had come to Mithranidoon beside Mcwigik, gazed wistfully out to the northwest, toward the towering glacier wall, and lamented, "I make me brother Heycal-nuck paddle out to the ice, just so I can feel the feel o' cold water. Never thinked I'd miss the dark chill of the Mirianic, did I."

"Aye," Bikelbrin agreed.

"And I'll be finding it again's me hope," said Mcwigik, and even the wistful dwarf behind him stared at him in-credulously for that comment!

"Mcwigik the fool," Pragganag said from the back. "The land's to be freezing yer blood solid inside ye, ye dope. Ye thinking ye're a glacier troll, are ye? Well, ye're thinking's to get yerself dead."

"Yach and aye!" said the dwarf behind Mcwigik. "We're not even for knowing where lies the damned

Mirianic. East, say some, but west for others. How many hundreds fell on the march inland, the one the priests called glorious? Weren't for Mithranidoon and we'd've all been killed to death."

"By the cold, if not the barbarians, if not the monsters," Bikelbrin agreed, but there was a noticeably different timbre in his voice compared to the consternation of his fellow traveler.

Bikelbrin and Mcwigik exchanged a silent thought, then, a slight nod and resigned grin, for they often mused about leaving Mithranidoon, and of late had openly wondered how much worse death, even death without Sepulcher, could be compared to the tedium of life on the foggy lake.

One of the dwarves behind them began to sing, "When the stars come out to shine."

"Twenty boys, side-to-side in a line," another intoned, picking up the solemn chant of an old powrie war song, one that ended, as had the battle it described, badly.

"Yach, but not that one!" another cried. "Tonight's the night for fun, ye fools. We're not for war, but for sport!"

"Sport that's to get Prag's face broken," said the first singer, and all the dwarves began to laugh—except for Pragganag, of course. He stared hard at the others and slid his hatchet's metal head along a sharpening stone, the screech of it lost in their continuing laughter.

The night was dark, so they could hardly see the darker silhouette of Chapel Isle through the mist. They were quite familiar with their approach, though, and few could navigate as well as powries, even when Mithranidoon's mist was high enough to almost constantly obscure the stars.

"Ha, but it's lookin' like the monk's ready for a fight," Bikelbrin said after a long period in which only the quiet dipping of paddles in the warm lake water accompanied the ride. The dwarf lifted his paddle and pointed it ahead, where through the drifting mist a single torch could be seen.

"He's there with fifty o' his friends in wait, not to doubt," Pragganag grumbled.

"Then it's open hunting and me beret's sure to shine all the brighter," said Mcwigik. "Steady and straight to the beach, in either case, and if there's a bunch to be found, ye be quick in passing that axe, Prag, so we can open them up wide and fast."

Cormack never heard the craft's approach, for the wind was up this night and off the water, and the sound of the lapping waves against the rocky beach filled his ears. He had been out of the chapel for several hours by then; his second torch burned low, and his attention had long since left the unseen water. He sat in the sand, his back against a stone, staring up at the stars, which peeked out every now and then through the gray swirl. He worked two gemstones, a soul stone and a lodestone, through his fingers, tapping them together at intervals. The lodestone's power lay in magnetism, and Cormack had often come out with it, using its magical properties to look through it at the beach and shallows surrounding Chapel Isle. He had found many coins, and old weapons and tools, for with the lodestone he could sense metal—he could even use the power of the stone to telekinese small metallic objects to his waiting hand.

He hadn't found anything this night, but he hadn't really looked, using the lodestone as a pretense for getting out of the chapel without drawing suspicion. Once out here, the sun setting, he lost any interest in even pretending to search, as one question dominated his every thought: Would the powries come?

Even the pressing thought of impending battle had been lost to him soon after that, as the stars began to shine and before the mists climbed high enough to obscure them so greatly. Cormack often lost himself among the celestial lights, letting his mind drift back to his days in Vanguard at Chapel Pellinor and across the gulf in Chapel Abelle, the mother abbey of his Church. Those had been good and heady days those years ago. Full of purpose and meaning, Cormack had charged into Chapel Abelle with his eyes wide and his heart open, soaking in every detail, every premise, every tenet and every hope of Blessed Abelle's homily.

Did those ravenous and hopeful fires remain? the monk asked himself. He often found himself melancholy these long and arduous days, his love for Chapel Isle and this lake called Mithranidoon long lost. He did not cheer when the next level of the rock abbey had been completed, for it was a place that no one other than the brothers and their servants ever attended. He did not feel joy at the sermons of Brother Giavno or Father De Guilbe, even when they read from his favorite of Blessed Abelle's teachings. The messengers, he knew, could not inspire him, for while Cormack hated neither man (in fact, he was quite fond of Giavno), he knew in his heart that they had misinterpreted their purpose here in Alpinador. They had been sent to proselytize, to teach and to convert. Out here, the early hopes for their mission had not come to fruition. The barbarians would not hear their words any longer, and the rift would not mend. To Cormack's thinking, and he knew their neighbors on the lake better than anyone else at Chapel Isle, their failure would never reverse.

The fighting would not stop.

The barbarian souls would not be saved.

"Ah, Milkeila, alas, for you were my last hope," Cormack whispered, and his voice thinned even more as he moved to toss a pebble out toward the water, for there, coming at him through the uneven mist, loomed the hairy and wrinkled faces of the bloody-cap dwarves.

Cormack scrambled to his feet, brushing the sand from his pants.

"So ye came out," Mcwigik greeted him. The dwarf stepped closer and glanced all about, and Cormack retreated a step. "Alone?"

Cormack nodded, his eyes scanning the small band, then locking on the one in the back of the bunch, his planned opponent, who stood grinning wickedly and slapping a wooden club across his open palm. For a moment, panic set in, and the monk felt his knees go weak, his brain screaming at him to turn and flee with all speed!

"Alone?" Mcwigik said again, and he slapped the monk on the hip.

Cormack instinctively hopped aside, and all the dwarves bristled, and the man thought he would be overrun immediately. But the attack never came.

"Well?" Mcwigik demanded.

"Yes, alone," Cormack stammered. "I gave you my word."

"Ye did no such thing, but ye didn't argue," said Mcwigik. "Not that ye could've argued and still kept yer blood in yer body."

That brought laughter from the gathering, and Cormack swallowed hard.

"But that ye thinked it yer word, or counted it as such, says good about ye—for a human, I mean," said Mcwigik.

"Says ye got honor, or says ye got no wits about ye," Bikelbrin added, drawing another laugh. "Most with humans, we're thinking the second."

The laughing heightened, but Mcwigik cut it short. "Get it done," he said, nodding toward Pragganag, who came forward, weapon waving at the ready.

"Ye know the rules?" Mcwigik asked Cormack.

"No."

"Then ye do," snickered Mcwigik, and the other dwarves laughed again, except for Pragganag, who wore as fierce a scowl as poor Cormack had ever seen. "Pragganag's looking to finish ye, so if ye lose, expect to lose a lot o' yer blood. For yerself, ye beat him down as much as ye're wanting. Not a one of us'll get in the way. Kill him or bash his head in, or whatever ye're thinking to do—once ye've won, Prag's cap is yer own to claim."

"I ain't for liking that!" Pragganag grumbled.

"Ye're meaning to kill him, but we're just for giving him yer cap," Mcwigik argued.

"Me cap's worth more than his life!"

"Well then he can just kill ye and take the damned thing!" Mcwigik shot back.

"Only way the dog's getting it!"

Mcwigik started to respond, but then just offered a smile to Cormack and stepped out of the way. Cormack was about to ask a question, seeking assurances that he wouldn't get gang-tackled if he did indeed gain the upper hand, but he didn't even get the first word out of his mouth before Pragganag roared and charged in, smashing left and right with his club.

Cormack swung to his right, then again farther to the right, and a third time, which put him facing away from the furious powrie. He dove into a headlong roll, coming to his feet and springing forward immediately into a second dive and roll, for he felt the press of the charging dwarf. His third leap put him over some piled stones and gave him time to turn about on the far side, so that when Pragganag came roaring around the tumble, Cormack was ready and waiting.

"Are ye fightin' or runnin'?" the dwarf just asked before Cormack rushed forward, inside the reach of his club, and smacked him with a left, right combination that abruptly stole his momentum. The monk leaped straight back, and threw his head back farther to avoid a short swipe of the club. He slapped the back of it as it flashed past, driving it out and down, and managed a quick left jab to the powrie's hairy face before leaping back out of reach of the heavy backhand.

"Three hits for him," Mcwigik laughed.

But Pragganag just snorted, and if he had even felt any of Cormack's punches, it didn't show. He roared ahead, swiping wildly and repeatedly, and Cormack could only dodge and dart back.

"How long can ye run?" Pragganag teased, and came forward in a sudden rush and launched a mighty overhead chop.

Far enough to avoid that strike, the dwarf realized, and his eyes went wide as his club descended past his field of vision, to see that Cormack had already reversed course and was coming straight for him. The man leaped and lay straight out, feet first, and caught Pragganag with a double kick about the face and shoulders that sent the dwarf flying back and to the ground.

Pragganag rolled to his belly and started up, but he had barely made it to his knees before Cormack fell over him, driving a knee hard into the side of his head. Pragganag turned to face that knee directly as Cormack pumped his leg, but it took three smashes before the dwarf managed to bite the man, and even then, Cormack was able to quickly retract his leg so that Pragganag had hardly broken the skin.

Cormack fell over the dwarf and rolled about, looping his hands up under the kneeling powrie's arms and up behind the dwarf's neck. Normally this move would ensure victory, for the victim could be rendered helpless from the waist up, but normally Cormack wouldn't put the double vise hold, as it was called, onto a powrie dwarf.

Pragganag balled his legs under him and with tremendous strength lifted himself to a standing position, driving the human up behind him. Cormack tried to jerk and twist to keep his opponent off-balance, but Pragganag went into a sudden frenzy, spinning about left, then back fast to the right, then back and back again, stomping his heavy boots all the while.

Cormack felt as if he were riding a bull. His feet were off the ground more than on, and so he could do little to interrupt Pragganag when the dwarf took up a sudden run. Cormack fell lower on the dwarf's back, letting his legs drag, trying to halt the growing momentum, but Pragganag roared ahead, then bent low at the waist, lifting Cormack back up. At the last instant, Cormack understood the intent, and saw the cluster of large rocks fast approaching, but Pragganag slapped his arms in a cross up high on his chest, reaching back behind his shoulders to grab Cormack's wrists and hold him fast. Then with sheer powrie power, Pragganag ducked again and launched himself into a somersault, bringing poor Cormack right over the top.

Cormack hit the side of the largest rock, and Pragganag sandwiched into Cormack. They hung there for a moment, like a splattered tomato, before both rolled down to the sand.

"Get up," Cormack told himself, trying to untwist, trying to get air back into his lungs. He hardly knew where he was, with bloody-cap dwarves howling all about him, but he kept his wits just enough to realize that it wasn't a good place, and that if he didn't get up soon, he'd be murdered where he lay.

He just started to his knees when the club flashed in. Purely on instinct, purely through the long hours of training he had received in the arts martial, Cormack snapped his left forearm up vertically to intercept that blow. The crack sent a wave of nauseating agony ripping through him, but his trained muscles continued the practiced move. He dropped his arm straight down, catching the shaft of the club in his left hand as he twisted about sidelong to his attacker, his right hand knifing up to catch the club right at the powrie's hand. Tugging down with his left and shoving upward with his right, Cormack gained the angle and tore the club from the dwarf's grasp. He kept the club turning, bringing his right hand right over his left; then he let go with his left as the club came back to horizontal, now directly across his chest.

Cormack gave a grunt and drove his right hand back, stabbing the fat end of the club right into Pragganag's eye with a thunderous crack. The dwarf's head snapped back and he stumbled several steps.

Cormack pursued, spinning the club out far to his right and then driving it hard against the side of the stunned dwarf. Still backpedaling, Pragganag tried to twist and block the blows, but wound up falling right over—to the appreciative howls of Mcwigik and the others.

Cormack went in for the win, thinking to drive the dwarf prostrate and pin him helplessly until he surrendered. Pragganag rolled his shoulder in tight, then burst back out, launching a backhand, and one that Cormack would willingly accept. The man curled only a little, bringing his left arm up to again absorb most of the blow, thinking to come in right behind it with another smash of the club.

But he didn't absorb it.

An explosion of fire ripped through Cormack's arm. He staggered backward, dropping the club and grabbing at his torn skin. He hardly understood what had happened until the dwarf leaped to his feet and faced him directly, the bloody axe swinging easily at the end of his left arm.

"What?" Cormack said, still backing until he fell to his bum in the sand.

Pragganag laughed at him and approached, and Cormack dropped his hands and all pretense of defense— for how with his flesh might he stop the swing of a metal-bladed axe?

"I'm wetting me own cap first!" Pragganag insisted to his fellows, closing the last few steps. He brought his axe up high and stepped in behind the descending blow, driving it down with enough force to sever the man's arm if he had lifted it to block.

And indeed, Cormack did lift his right hand, for when he had dropped his arms down beside him, he had brushed against his small belt pouch. Now he held the lodestone, and he saw the metallic axe head through its magic as clearly as if he were looking at the noontime sun on a cloudless and mistless day. Desperation drove the monk more than any actual thought, and he sent his energy into the gemstone, bringing its magic to an immediate crescendo.

He thought to call the axe head down toward the stone, but instead, again purely on instinct, he let the stone go to its target again. When Cormack opened his hand, the charged lodestone bulleted out with tremendous speed, firing true to the call of the metal axe head.

The sharp report echoed off the stones of Chapel Isle and rolled out to all corners of Mithranidoon. Good fortune was with Cormack, for the gemstone hit the axe as it descended past Pragganag's head, and the force of the blow broke the head from the handle so cleanly that it flew back into the dwarf's ugly face.

The stone flew away—far, far away—and Pragganag staggered back, a crease of blood showing about his cheeks and nose. He tried to stand straighter, growled against the pain and the numbness that was spreading across his stout form.

He was kneeling and didn't know it.

He was lying in the sand and didn't know it.

Cormack grasped his torn arm again and stumbled over to straddle the dwarf. He reached down and pulled the dwarf's beret free, then grabbed a clump of Pragganag's hair and tugged his head up out of the dirt.

"I'm not for knowin' what just happened," Mcwigik said, and he and the others crowded in a bit and seemed none too happy with the sudden reversal of fortune.

"You said I knew the rules," Cormack reminded.

Mcwigik thought it over for a moment, then turned to his fellows and gave a hearty laugh, one that echoed through the dwarf ranks.

And still Pragganag showed no signs of resistance or consciousness, prompting Mcwigik to say in all seriousness, "Do ye mean to kill him to death, then?"

Cormack looked down at the mass of hair and blood, then simply let go, Pragganag's face thumping back into the sand. The man stepped away and a pair of powries went to their fallen comrade, unceremoniously hoisting him to his feet. They gave him a couple of rough shakes and one spat in his face.

"Yach, but what in the dark waters . . . ?" Pragganag sputtered, his words hardly decipherable through his fast-swelling lips.

"What, what?" said Mcwigik. "He popped ye good in the head, ye dope. Put ye down good."

"I'll be paying him back."

"Nah, ye'll be shutting yer mouth and"—Mcwigik paused and moved to the side, scooping Pragganag's beret from the sand—"making yerself another cap."

Pragganag yanked one arm free from the dwarf holding him, and when that fellow tried to grab him again, Pragganag slammed the back of his fist into the dwarf's eye. "No, ye don't!" Pragganag yelled at Mcwigik as the dwarf moved toward Cormack, cap in hand.

"Ye got yer bum beat, and yer cap's the price," said Mcwigik.

"It is all right." Cormack tried to intervene, for what was he to do with a powrie's bloody cap anyway? But Mcwigik wasn't listening.

"The dactyl demon it is!" Pragganag protested, and he tore himself free of the other dwarf holding him, then held that one back with a hateful scowl before advancing on Mcwigik.

"The human kept his word in coming out, but yerself's not got that honor?" Mcwigik asked.

"Ye ain't to give him me cap!"

"It is all right," said Cormack, but no one was listening. Mcwigik turned sidelong to the advancing Pragganag and lifted his right arm up high and back, holding the cap away. He brought his left arm in against his torso, defensively, it seemed.

"Ye give it!" Pragganag demanded, and when Mcwigik kept the cap away from his reach, he slugged the dwarf in the face.

His mistake.

For Mcwigik had retrieved something else when he had grabbed up the cap, and his left arm shot across, neck height to Pragganag.

Pragganag started to shout something, but all that came out was a bubbling bloody gurgle, for that sharpened axe head, quietly retrieved by Mcwigik as he walked over, had cut a neat line indeed across poor Prag's throat.

Mcwigik stepped back and calmly presented the beret to Cormack, while Pragganag slumped down to his knees, choking and grasping at his torn windpipe and artery, his blood spraying high.

Cormack went for his pouch and his remaining stone. "I can heal him," he declared, rushing past Mcwigik— or trying to, for the powerful powrie stopped him dead in his tracks with an outstretched arm.

"No, ye can't. Ye can take yer damned cap and dip it in his blood. Then ye can put it on yer head and get ye gone from here. We're done playing, boy, and the next blood what's spilling'll be yer own." He thrust the beret into Cormack's hand. "Dip it!" he ordered in a voice that brooked no argument.

As he stumbled off the beach a few thumping heartbeats later, wet cap in hand, Cormack heard Mcwigik instruct the others—to their relief, apparently, judging from their responses—to take Pragganag's heart.

By the time he reached the small stone archway that led to the main door of the chapel, Cormack heard the now-familiar powrie burial song carried up by the breeze, its strange and somehow gentle intonations and harmony (given the gravelly voices of the singers) mingling with the sound of the waves so that Cormack would not even have known it to be a song had he not heard it before.

EIGHT

To Prove a Point

The five-man craft drifted through the mist with hardly a sound other than the occasional flutter of the single sail in the slight breeze or the splash of water. Androosis sat forward, his long legs hanging over either side of the prow, which angled up high enough so that Androosis's feet remained comfortably high above the water. At eighteen, he was more than ten years younger than the other Alpinadorans on the boat, three weathered helmsmen and the oldest of the group, the shaman Toniquay. No hair remained on Toniquay's head, and his light skin was stretched thin with age and dotted with many brown spots, presenting an imposing appearance indeed, as if he had already gone into the grave and returned. The few teeth remaining in his mouth stuck at awkward angles and shined yellow, and the thin mustache he wore seemed no more than a shadow, depending on the light.

Another man curled against the aft rail, working the rudder and the sails, and the other two sailors sat in the middle of the fifteen-foot craft, just ahead of Toniquay.

Each held a paddle across his lap, ready to assist at the command of the navigator.

Long lines stretched out behind the boat, each set with a multitude of hooks. The catch had been thin thus far, with only two rather small silver trout thrashing about in the many buckets in the flat hold between Androosis and the paddlers.

"Too calm a day," said Canrak, the gnarled man working the rudder. Though he was not an old man—in fact, he was the youngest other than Androosis—his face was so wrinkled that it seemed as if someone had piled separate slabs of skin one atop the other in the shape of a head. Add to that a thick black beard that grew in places where it shouldn't and didn't grow in other places where it normally would, and Androosis thought the lean and gangly Canrak possibly the ugliest human being he had ever seen. Quite the opposite of Androosis, who, with his fair skin and yellow hair, had caught the eye of almost every young woman of Yossunfier. Tall and strong, with wide shoulders and a solid frame, Androosis also stood out as one of the more promising young warriors among the tribe, and that fact, he knew, had played no small part in Toniquay's decision to carry him along on these long fishing excursions.

"She is calm and flat this day, but never too much so," Toniquay replied. "Mithranidoon is a blessing, storm or still."

He was replying to Canrak, but Androosis knew that the nasty old shaman had aimed those words his way. Toniquay knew well of Androosis's friendship with Milkeila, and he had led the outrage against her those weeks before when she had dared suggest an expedition to the shores beyond Mithranidoon. Subsequent to Milkeila's bold suggestion, it was no secret that the tribal elders had purposely carved up the tasks to keep the suspected conspirators apart. In fact some of those elders, like Toniquay, had been boasting of their wisdom quite openly. When the five had boarded the boat this morning, Toniquay had whispered to Androosis that "this is where you will learn the truth. Not in the wandering hopes of a young woman frustrated because she has found no willing lover among her peers."

Androosis had let the ridiculous insult to Milkeila pass without response, something that still weighed on his proud shoulders. But he didn't want a fight with Toniquay—certainly not! Because on Yossunfier, there could be no such fight. The structure of Androosis's people, Yan Ossum, was akin to that of all the Alpinado-ran tribes. Elders carried great weight and respect, with the older shamans being the top of the hierarchy, second only to the Pennervike, the Great Leader of Yan Ossum, himself.

"Do you believe that we are wasting our time out here, friend Androosis?" Toniquay asked, catching the young man off-guard. He turned to view the smug shaman, and found four sets of eyes staring hard at him.

"A time on Mithranidoon is never wasted, master," Androosis obediently replied, and turned away.

"Well spoken!" Toniquay congratulated, and then in more solemn and dire tones he added, "Do you truly be-lieve that?"

She felt the roiling lava far below her bare feet, but she did not summon it to her this day. For Milkeila had no duties to attend at that time and was utilizing her magical bond with the earth for no better reason than to remind herself of her powers—magical energy considered quite proficient among her shaman peers and elders. The woman needed that reassurance at this time, for she had seen Androosis board the boat with Toniquay that morn-ing. Milkeila was no fool; she understood the significance of Toniquay's unusual trip out to Mithranidoon.

A handful of Milkeila's friends had joined her in

shared fantasies of leaving Mithranidoon, a wanderlust sparked by the arrival of the Abellican monks three years earlier. To that point, none of them had even known that a wider world existed beyond the shores of Mithranidoon, not one inhabited by other men, at least.

It had mostly been idle chatter, of course, teenage restlessness. To Milkeila, though, there had run a string of honesty in that chatter. She wanted to see the wider world! Her relationship with Cormack had only strengthened that desire, of course, since it could never be an open marriage here on Mithranidoon—the elders, particularly surly Toniquay, would never allow such a thing!

The six conspirators had let the matter drop for more than a year and had relegated the plan to a far-distant place when Milkeila had surprised them all by reviving it only a couple of months previous.

The young shaman had recognized her mistake almost immediately. She and her friends were all coming of age now, soon to be celebrated as full adult members of Yan Ossum, and youthful fancies had been lost to more serious responsibilities. Milkeila held no doubts that at least one of the six, Pennerdar, had run to the elders with the news, and while the elders had not confronted her directly, she had noticed the extra glances, none favorable, Toniquay often tossed her way. Oh, but he had given her a fine glower that very morning, right before he had summoned Androosis to join him in the fishing.

"Androosis," Milkeila mused aloud. The sound of her own voice broke her concentration and connection to the earth power far below. Of course it was Androosis singled out for Toniquay's special trip onto Mithranidoon, for he alone had shown some interest when Milkeila had suggested a journey to the world beyond the lake.

Milkeila took a deep breath and unconsciously glanced to the southeast, toward Chapel Isle, fully obscured by the mists. With renewed focus the shaman reached deep into the hot powers flowing below the lake. She lifted her hand to fondle the secret gemstone necklace, seeking the added power there. A sense of urgency gripped her; if she could unlock the secrets of the stones, if she could find a way to blend their powers with her own, then perhaps she would find some answers to the questions she knew Toniquay would eventually throw her way.

The power tickled her but would not come true. She could not join the magic as she had joined her soul to Cormack. She spent many minutes straining until she felt the shaman magic flowing through her powerfully, begging for release as if it would simply consume her flesh and blood. At that moment of magical climax, Milkeila reached into the gemstones. . . .

Nothing.

Earth magic burst from her form, a sudden and flashing gout of flame rushing out in a small circle around her. Several leaves curled and crisped, and wisps of smoke rose from the ground in the aftermath.

Milkeila stood there gasping, both physically and emotionally drained. She looked around at the circle of destruction and shook her head, recognizing that it was no more than she could summon at any time. She brought the gemstone necklace to her lips and kissed it, thinking of Cormack, of the promises they had shared. She knew in her heart that they were not so different, these religions of earth and gemstone. And she believed, as Cormack believed, that the greater answers lay in the joining, in the whole.

If ever they could get there.

Milkeila looked back out at the lake, in the direction where Toniquay and Androosis had gone, and her stomach churned with doubts and fear.

Androosis turned back to regard the man and started to respond but bit it back, seeing that there was no compromise here, that Toniquay was goading him into open admissions that could be used to further split apart the group of young conspirators. If Androosis answered correctly here, then no doubt Milkeila would feel the weight of that response. If he did not, Toniquay would use it as further proof that the young adults of Yan Ossum were running wild and contrary to the traditions that had kept the people thriving for generations untold.

So Androosis said nothing.

"Tend the lines," Toniquay ordered him, not blinking an eye.

"They've nothing on them," Canrak said from the back, but Toniquay still did not blink.

"Bring them in, then," the old shaman said. "Let us learn if we can waste our time more productively."

Androosis studied Toniquay for a long moment, and still the old and withered man did not blink. Did Toniquay ever blink? Would he die with his eyes wide, and remain like that through eternity under the cold ground?

Androosis moved deliberately, finally, past the sloshing trout and between the oarsmen. He purposely focused on the back of the boat as he passed Toniquay, for he could feel the shaman's eyes boring into him, every step.

Canrak quietly laughed at him, but he ignored the fool—everyone on Yossunfier thought that one a fool—and methodically began hauling in the long lines.

Before they were even aboard, Toniquay motioned for the two men before him to dip their paddles. "Bring us right, half a turn," the shaman ordered Canrak.

Canrak nodded and grabbed the rudder, but paused and looked at Toniquay curiously. "Half right?"

"Half right."

"Yossunfier's left and back."

"Do you think me too stupid to know that?"

"No, elder, but . . ." Canrak stopped and licked his lips. "Half right," he said, and turned the rudder appropriately, which presented an obstacle for Androosis as he hauled the long line to Canrak's right. The young man moved outside the angle of the turned rudder, looking intently at the obviously disturbed Canrak all the while.

"Half right and bring us straight, and open the sail wide to the breeze," Toniquay ordered. "And paddle, the both of you. Strong and straight."

"We are not that deep," Canrak dared say, but if Toniquay even heard him, he didn't show it.

Canrak turned directly to Androosis then and gave a concerned look, but the young man, not nearly as experienced with the ways of Mithranidoon, had no response. He kept hauling, and tossed one or two sour looks back at Toniquay, who had his back to him and paid him no heed at all. This wasn't about fishing, Androosis now fully understood. Toniquay hadn't come out here to secure the day's catch. This trip was about Androosis, wholly, and about the conspiracy of the young adults who so desperately wanted to get off this smothering lake.

Even so, the boat's turn had Androosis surprised, as it had obviously unnerved the other three. Beside Androosis, Canrak licked his lips repeatedly and kept his hand tight on the tiller, obviously anticipating, and hoping for, Toniquay's command to change course yet again.

But the shaman didn't make a move or utter a sound, and the small craft glided through the mist. Canrak's warning that they were "not that deep" echoed in Androosis's thoughts.

A dark form loomed in the water, ahead and to port, a rock, prodding up like a signpost warning intruders.

"Holy Toniquay," Canrak started to say, but was interrupted when the shaman said, "Androosis, to the front."

"The line . . ." Androosis started to reply.

"Leave it, and go forward to watch our depth."

Androosis scrambled past the old shaman and the two paddlers. He stumbled and knocked over one of the buckets, spilling water and a trout onto the flat hold. He started for the fish, but met the disapproving glare of Toniquay as he bent and thought better of it, practically falling all over himself to get back to the prow.

He leaned far over, putting his face near the water, trying to get an angle in the light that would give him the best view to gauge the depth. They weren't that shallow at all, he realized to his relief, though another rock showed off to port, protruding several feet into the air above the water level.

He turned back to report such to Toniquay, and met the shaman's bemused expression, the man pointing past Androosis, dead ahead.

When he looked forward again, Androosis understood—everything. Less than fifty running strides away loomed a dark and foreboding beach, sharply inclined and covered with black, sharp-edged lava rock. Just a short distance up and away from the steaming water, the rock mingled with fingers of ice and snow, creating a stark contrast of white and black, each segment of the mix appearing as hardened as the other. A few scraggly tree skeletons showed among the stones, but they hardly constituted a sign of life, seeming more like a warning, warding away any living thing.

The mist blew across Androosis's field of vision, alternately thick and thin, and in a moment of clarity, he picked out among that desolate landscape a series of caves.

He knew this place for what it was, then, and he spun on Toniquay as if to scream an accusation.

"This is the destination of your dreams," the shaman said. "This is the promise of foolish Milkeila. Look well upon the desolation."

"This is one spot," Androosis sputtered.

"Too close to the trolls," the man paddling to Toniquay's left quietly, almost inaudibly, remarked, and he lifted his paddle from the water and brought it across his lap. His companion did likewise, and both stared at the shaman eagerly, as if in anticipation of an order that would get them fast away from this dangerous place.

"There are many such spots," the shaman retorted, ignoring the paddlers' words, actions, and expressions. "And you would need to stumble upon just one to be slaughtered. Nay, you would not even have to find one to arrive swiftly at your grave, fool. We are not like our mainland kin. We have lost their ways of survival, as our blood has lost its thickness. As it has thinned from the warmth of Blessed Mithranidoon. I warn you now, with this fate clear before you, our patience . . ."

A splash in the water just to the north of their position interrupted Toniquay's rant.

"Glacial troll," Canrak warned, his knuckles white on the tiller, and the two paddlers stared hard at the shaman.

Another splash sounded. As he glanced fast over his shoulder, Androosis thought he caught some motion near the caves.

"Do you understand now, young one?" said Toniquay, trying hard to keep himself calm and collected, obviously. "You think this all a game, a play for excitement."

"Holy Toniquay, we must be gone," Canrak dared say, and the shaman spun about and glowered at him, even lifted a hand as if he meant to strike at the man.

But the paddlers weren't waiting for the order any longer, and by the time the shaman turned back forward, they had already splashed their paddles into the water, the man to the right pulling hard, the one to the left reversing his motion, so that even without Canrak's work on the tiller, they set the boat into a standing turn.

And Canrak did work the tiller to aid them, despite the look from Toniquay. Another splash sounded, then two more in rapid succession. It wasn't about decorum or who was officially in charge. It was about simple survival.

Even the stubborn shaman seemed to understand that, for when he turned back fully, he did not berate the three, but kept his focus squarely on Androosis. "Mark you well the lesson of this day," he warned, waggling a long and bony finger at the man.

The square sail fell limp for a long while as frantic Canrak finished the turn, then went to work on the ropes, but the paddlers fell into a swift and efficient rhythm, and the small boat began to move away from the shore into the safety of the mist. After a few moments they all began to breathe easier.

But then both paddlers jerked suddenly. One nearly went over the side before falling back into the boat, his hands empty, while the other put up a brief tug-of-war, hauling his paddle in with all his strength, so much so that he lifted the top half of the troll clutching the other end right out of the water. The Alpinadoran sailor screamed, but to his credit, he did not let go of the paddle—the precious and vital paddle!

Of course, that didn't help any of them a moment later when a second troll speared out of the water, rising high into the air like a fish leaping for an insect. With tremendous momentum, it climbed up higher than the sailor holding the paddle, and as it descended, it grabbed him by the collar. Before the others in the boat could react, the sailor, the two trolls, and the paddle went over the side.

Androosis started for the spot, but stopped and spun about as another troll lifted into the air before the boat, angled to land on the prow. Androosis timed his heavy punch perfectly, catching the aqua-colored creature square on the jaw as it landed, and before it could gain any traction. The troll's head snapped to the side as the young barbarian followed through with all his weight, driving the creature over the rail and back into the water. It thrashed about on the surface for a heartbeat, then dived down, and Androosis knew it would be back, leaping high once more.

He couldn't wait for that. Behind him, the boat

erupted in fighting as one troll after another flew up into the air and crashed down inside the hold.

Canrak and the other sailor flanked Toniquay, who held his hands up before him, his eyes closed as he issued an ancient chant to the barbarian gods. A trio of trolls pressed them hard, clawed hands changing strikes against the small knife of the paddler, and the gaff hook Canrak had collected before coming forward.

Androosis rushed back to join his companions, scooping up a water-filled bucket as he passed. He threw that bucket into the face of the nearest troll, who stumbled backward, and then Androosis closed fast to hit the beast with a left hook, smashing his hand against its chest and driving it over the rail. The creature grabbed at him desperately as it fell back, and caught Androosis's strong arm with both its hands. It couldn't get enough of a grip to resist the throw, but it did manage to hook its clawlike fingernails under the skin of Androosis's outer forearm, and that skin peeled down as the troll fell away.

Androosis clutched at his bleeding forearm, but only momentarily as another troll leaped aboard. He met it with a heavy punch, but this one swung as well, and it carried a club. Fist and weapon came together hard, the barbarian's knuckles shattering under the weight of the blow. He howled and retracted the hand, but went forward instinctively, lowering his shoulder to bowl into the creature before it could strike again with the club.

He and the troll tumbled to the deck, Androosis rolling fully atop the diminutive creature, freeing up his left hand for punch after punch, trying to get his hand past the troll's flailing arms.

Toniquay tried hard to shut out the tumult around him and concentrate on his spellcasting. He called upon the ancient gods of his people, upon Drawmir of the North Wind, gathering the offered power in his hands as he put them up over his head and began moving them harmoniously in a circle. He opened his eyes when Canrak cried out in pain, and saw a spear stabbing through the navigator's shoulder—and saw, too, yet another troll leaping high out of the water to the side of the boat. Its trajectory would have brought it crashing against Toniquay, but he reacted by thrusting his hands out in the troll's direction, throwing forth the gathered wind.

The flying troll looked like it had been flung by a sling, suddenly reversing direction and spinning back out over the water. It landed awkwardly, with a great splash. Toniquay paid it no more heed, turning his attention to the more immediate fighting, and to the sail.

The sail.

The shaman worked his hands again, more quickly and less powerfully this time, and filled the sail with a conjured gust of wind, swiftly driving the boat out toward the deeper water.

He did it again, and a third time, but then he went flying forward as a troll sprang onto his back, clawing at his face and bearing him down to the deck.

Androosis finally got a punch cleanly through, smashing the troll's face, and the back of its head cracked hard against the wooden deck. Clearly dazed, the creature slowed momentarily, enough for Androosis to set his broken hand below him and lift himself up. He reached back behind him with his free left hand, then let himself fall as he thrust out below him, throwing all of his weight behind the punch.

The troll's long and crooked nose shattered under the weight of the blow, and the creature again cracked its skull against the boat's decking.

Androosis rolled off, seeing that the creature was finished, and, now nursing two injured hands, stubbornly regained his footing.

Canrak was down, the troll above him stabbing repeatedly with its crude spear. The poor tiller flailed and blocked, both his arms torn and shredded, blood covering him. More blood than Androosis had ever seen. More blood than Androosis would have ever believed possible from one skinny man.

He shook off the shock and charged back, kicking the troll off of Toniquay as he passed. He stumbled as he went under the sail, but didn't let that slow him as he threw himself at the spear-wielder.

Forgetting his more serious wound, he slapped a backhand with his right, trying to grab the weapon's shaft, but a wave of agony assailed him and he couldn't hang on. That cost him dearly as he came against the creature in his successful tackle, for it managed to extract the spear and angle it so that it caught Androosis on the right hip and drove down.

Fires of pain exploded all along that hip and down his leg, but again he ignored them, forcing himself to understand the consequences of failure here. He bore the troll to the deck and went into a frenzy, battering it with his hands and arms, driving his knee against it hard. He took as many hits as he gave, and the troll even lurched upward, trying to bite him.

Androosis merely tucked his chin in low and drove his forehead right at that biting mouth. He cut himself open on the troll's sharp teeth, but he smashed the creature into oblivion in the process.

Toniquay's cry startled him and turned him shakily about, just in time to see the troll he had kicked leap up against the sail, thrashing at it with clawed hands. Toniquay came in fast behind.

Too fast, for as he collided against the troll, it thrust forward and the shaman could not halt his momentum. Both he and the troll went through the sail, tearing the fabric as they went. They hit the deck hard and rolled apart, and the troll sprang up and rushed to the side, right over the side, taking with it the bulk of the sail!

Androosis and Toniquay exchanged horrified looks, and both started for the side rail, until the cry of the remaining paddler turned them back toward the prow, where the poor man was being hauled by a pair of trolls.

Toniquay turned fast and began waving his arms to summon his magic. But then he lurched and doubled over and grasped at the spear that had hit him in the gut.

Androosis staggered past him, but knew he would not get to his companion in time, and he could only gasp and look on helplessly as the two trolls and the Alpinadoran rolled over the prow and disappeared under the water.

Behind Androosis came another splash, and he turned to see that the troll he had smashed had also gone over. He slumped down next to Toniquay, saw the spear embedded in the shaman's gut, and had no idea of how he might help the man.

A sudden jerk on the boat had him back to his knees, looking aft with concern at the long line he hadn't completely brought in. He crawled to it and peered out, to see the paddler bobbing along behind them, apparently caught in the hooks. Androosis grabbed the line and began hauling the man toward him, but he knew before he got the poor man against the taffrail of the boat that he was too late. He grabbed the man by the shirt and half hauled him over, but as the man's head lolled back, Androosis stared into wide-open, lifeless eyes.

Horrified and gagging on bile, Androosis dragged the man up higher on the rail. But he lost his grip and fell backward onto the deck and lay staring up at the sky. Beside him, Canrak whimpered pitifully, and amidships, near the mast and torn scraps of sail, Toniquay growled and grunted.

Androosis felt consciousness slipping away. He fought against it and lifted his head to regard the man half hanging over the back of the battered boat. He tried to reach out and grab the man, but he found that he could not, found that he was inexorably sinking backward to the deck.

He stared up at the sky, but he saw only blackness.

PART TWO

THE LONG ROAD UNBIDDEN

Perhaps it is because in order to simply survive I had to remain so much more in tune with the workings of my body, or perhaps it was my Jhesta Tu training, but whatever the reason, I find that I am more apt than the average person to understand the subtle clues offered to me by my unconscious soul. So many things we reveal to ourselves without ever realizing them!

The lightness of my step when I departed Palmaristown, for example, whether in the guise of the Stork or in that of the Highwayman, buoyed me; I felt as if I could leap a hundred feet off the ground. With the road straight before me to Chapel Abelle, the hopes of seeing this man, my father, Bran Dynard, filtered throughout my being and lifted my spirit.

Consciously, I wasn't even thinking about such things. Consciously, I told myself, berated myself, that this entire journey was no more than procrastination. The real road was south and east, but I was—deliberately—a long way from there.

But despite my pangs of guilt, I felt that buoyancy clearly and acutely, a sense of excitement, and not just because I had successfully deflected and delayed facing my deepest fears. Nay, on this road to the mother church of the Abellican Order, I felt as if I was moving forward on my journey, as if I was taking a very important and exciting stride.

I wondered if I was betraying Garibond, my beloved father-in-practice, who had raised me and tolerated my infirmities without complaint, who had loved me without condition and without embarrassment. My road seemed to be leading me to the man who had sired me, and my road was walked with eagerness, so what did that reflect upon Garibond and his sacrifices?

And what did I really expect from this man, Bran Dynard?

And why hadn't he come back for me? More than two decades had transpired since his departure from Pryd Town, and he had not returned for Sen Wi or for his child.

As I ponder these many angles, my mind jumbles and shakes and darts in directions unasked for. And to all of them, I have no true answers, I recognize, for I will not know how I feel about Bran Dynard until I have met him. I will not know his answers to my concerns until he has explained them. I will not know the effect upon the legacy of Garibond until long has passed, I am sure.

Indeed, that is the most unanswerable question of all, because the truth is clear and yet clouded by guilt, that most opaque of veils. I loved and still love Garibond with all my heart and soul. I would throw myself upon a pyre of flames to save him, without hesitation! I would do anything, anything at all, to have him back.

Of my sire, I am less certain. Of Bran Dynard, I have only expectations with which to guide my preconceptions.

Well, only those and the Book of Jhest, the tome he penned—or copied, at least. For the contents were such that no one without understanding of the book could properly relay its subtle shades. Perhaps that book remains the paradox of my inner conflict, the source of both excitement and trepidation.

For I would desperately desire to meet the man who penned that book, that marvelous tome which freed me from my abject helplessness, even if he had no connection to me in blood or otherwise, other than the connection I feel in my heart to that which he wrote. On this level alone, I am truly comfortable with my journey.

How could it be otherwise? I desire to meet the man

who penned the wondrous book as I desire to meet the mystics of Behr who live the lessons of that book in their daily existence. And this journey is even safer than that, for whatever the outcome of my meeting with Bran Dynard, the Walk of Clouds remains. Hope remains.

Is this then a comfortable step for me? For all of my other fears regarding this stranger, I hold few or no familial expectations, so I suspect that I cannot be disappointed in that manner, and whatever philosophy Bran Dynard may express now, or whatever he might offer or not offer to further my recovery, he has already given so much to me that I cannot hold any anger against him.

Or maybe I do. Perhaps my anger at his refusal or inability to return to Sen Wi and to me will prove a stronger angst than I anticipate, a thorn more deeply embedded in my heart than I now understand.

And so with a resigned sigh, I must admit it may be that the only real comfort of this journey is that it allows me to put off the even more terrifying march to the Walk of Clouds.

— BRANSEN GARIBOND

N I N E

Work Brings Freedom

Dawson McKeege stood at the prow of his two-masted coast-runner, *Lady Dreamer*, taking in the grand oceanic and coastline view that never grew old for him. For before the craft loomed a three-hundred-foot cliff facing, mighty stone all brown and gray, and atop it, as if growing right out of the rock, stood Chapel Abelle, the heart of the growing, influential Church.

This was the spot where Blessed Abelle had first demonstrated the power of the god-given gemstones. This was the spot where—on guidance from God, it was said—he had learned to make permanent the magical properties of those rocks he had found after being shipwrecked on a distant island in the deep southern Mirianic Ocean. Alone and as removed from civilization as any man had ever been, Abelle had had little expectation of surviving, and seemingly no chance of ever returning to Honce.

But the magical stones had showered down from the heavens, the gifts of God to him, and as he had sorted through their magical properties, this young philosopher had come to understand them fully.

With those stones, Abelle had walked hundreds of miles across the ocean, so it was said, and through the power and potential of the gemstone magic, he had changed the world.

Dawson wasn't yet formally confirmed as an Abellican. He had been raised in Vanguard among a thriving farming and hunting community dominated by the Samhaists, and the old ways died hard. Still, he couldn't deny the spirituality he felt whenever this sight, Chapel Abelle, so impressive and growing grander by the day, came into view.

Hidden among the cliffs was a dock facility, with tunnels that climbed through the stone all the way to the chapel above—tunnels reputedly cut by Abelle himself utilizing a variety of potent gemstones.

"Hail to the flag of Dame Gwydre!" came a shout from the docks as *Lady Dreamer* edged in around the jagged rocks. A pair of monks stood in open view, waving at the approaching ship. Dawson recognized one as Brother Pinower and returned the wave with a familiarity and heartiness reminding him that the relationship between Gwydre and this Church had grown so very strong.

Of course, that very fact had led to the current war in Vanguard, and Dawson couldn't help but grimace as he considered his former spiritual leaders, the Samhaists, now striking so violently and with such vile foot soldiers as goblins and glacial trolls. Never had the man imagined that the supposedly wise priests who had guided his people, as brutal as their customs often were, could so betray their people as to enlist the aid of such wretched creatures.

"Weapons, metals, or foodstuffs?" Brother Pinower asked as McKeege's ship pulled up alongside the longest of the three wharves and tenders hopped to the dock to begin securing her. "You will be hard pressed to get any, of course, in this dastardly time."

"Lairds Ethelbert and Delaval continue their war, then?" Dawson asked, hopping down easily to the planks beside the Abellicans.

" 'Escalate' would be a better word," Pinower replied. "Laird Delaval believed he'd gained an advantage, and so he strengthened his line across the breadth of it, thinking to push Ethelbert right into the sea."

"But it wasn't to be," said the second monk. "Ethelbert's got a few tricks left."

"Aye, and a few allies from Behr," Brother Pinower agreed.

"A laird of Honce is using the desert savages?" Dawson McKeege asked, shaking his head, feeling at that moment pretty much the same about Ethelbert as he felt about the Vanguard Samhaists.

"Desperate folk take desperate measures," Brother Pinower added, and all three nodded.

"I've a hold full of caribou moss," Dawson explained, referring to the white moss that climbed knee-deep in regions of Vanguard and was favored for packing open wounds, among its many other uses. In a time of war that particular purpose of the fungus would take precedence, obviously, but extract of dried caribou moss could also be brewed into a medicinal tea, and sheets of the moss often sold at exorbitant prices as roofing or siding material, both practical and decorative, for the fancy homes of wealthy merchants. Vanguard had many profitable trading goods to offer Honce proper, but in this time of war, none was more sought after than the caribou moss.

"The lairds will pay well for it," Brother Pinower admitted.

"They will pay Chapel Abelle well, then," Dawson explained. "For I've no time to cart my wares southeast or southwest, and my boat's back to Vanguard when she puts out from your dock, presently, unless I am forced to make a detour to Palmaristown."

"We have some goods, of course," said Brother Pinower. "And some coin."

"Some? The whispers say that your Church grows wealthy on the tributes of warring lords."

"Whispers," Brother Pinower replied with an exaggerated sigh. He ended with a smile as wide as the one Dawson offered in response.

"Come," Brother Pinower bade him, leading him off the wharf and to the gated entrance and the winding tunnels that would carry them up to the cliff top and the mother chapel of the Abellican Church.

As soon as he exited that dock tunnel into the courtyard of the abbey, McKeege understood those whispers of growing wealth to be understated. For Chapel Abelle was more than twice the size it had been on his last visit only a year before. Scores of laborers worked the grounds, extending and thickening the already impressive outer wall and constructing new stone structures— barracks and rectories and all manner of buildings. Chapel Abelle had become a town unto itself, McKeege realized, and when he thought about it, it made sense. Once Chapel Abelle had been a small church set on a hill above the medium-sized town of Weatherguard, but in this time of pressing danger, it had become a fortress, a welcomed one for the beleaguered folk of the region.

Dawson looked to the main church, which was now surrounded by scaffolding, monks swarming every region of it with tools and materials. No laymen worked this all-important building, he noted. Its construction remained for the brothers alone.

"Father Artolivan will be pleased to greet you this day," Brother Pinower assured him, hustling him toward the church entrance. "It would help if I could introduce you with your intent."

Dawson looked from the church to the eager brother, who was at least fifteen years his junior, with skin too soft and white and eyes tired already from endless hours spent huddled over parchments. Dawson figured that Pinower rarely ventured outside of Chapel Abelle, other than when he was stationed at the docks, or at work on the abbey, perhaps. The Vanguardsman wished that he had more time, then, so that he could sneak the young man away from his stuffy brethren and put on a good drunk and a better woman.

"Tell the good father that I come with value and leave with purpose, for Vanguard's in need of . . ." He paused there and let the thought hang in the air between them. Indeed, it seemed as if poor Brother Pinower would fall right over from leaning so obviously toward McKeege.

Dawson merely grinned, intensifying the tease.

Soon after, Dawson stood before Father Artolivan, an old friend of Dame Gwydre, who had secretly offered his blessing to her union with Brother Alandrais.

"I've come under full sail," the Vanguardsman said, "and will leave the same way."

"Always in a hurry," the old father of the Abellican Church replied, his voice a bit slurred as if he had partaken too liberally of the bottle.

It was just age, though, and indeed, Artolivan looked every day of his eighty years. Skin sagged about his face, and his eyes had sunk deeply, circled by darkness. He could still sit straight, but not without great effort, Dawson noted, and there remained little sparkle and sharpness in his gaze. The Abellicans wouldn't easily replace him, though. Artolivan, it was whispered, had once glimpsed Blessed Abelle (though he would have been but a young boy), and had been trained by men who had learned directly from the great man. He was the last of his generation in the Church, the last man alive known to hold direct ties to Blessed Abelle and the momentous events of that magical and inspiring time.

"That is the way of the world, I fear," the old priest went on. "None have time to give pause. Patient consideration is a thing of the lost past."

"War breeds urgency, Father," said Dawson.

"And what is your urgency?"

"I've a hold of caribou moss and no time to barter."

"So I've been told—of both situations. You seek coin, then, so name your initial offer."

"I seek coin only to use it for another good," Dawson

explained, and that piqued Artolivan's curiosity, it seemed, as the old man cocked his head to the side. "I will use the coin—and have brought much of my own, as well—to bribe."

"You have come for able bodies?"

Dawson nodded.

"To harvest? To log? As wives or as laborers?"

"Yes," Dawson replied. "All of that. Vanguard is sorely pressed by the Samhaists. Dame Gwydre has victory at hand," he quickly added and lied when he saw old Artolivan's face crinkle with doubt.

"We are all sorely pressed, friend Dawson. War rages the breadth of Honce."

"Yet I see Chapel Abelle swarmed by laborers, many young men who have apparently escaped the fighting."

"Many who were captured and thus put out of the fight on honor," Father Artolivan explained.

"From both camps, no doubt," said Dawson, and Artolivan nodded and smiled. It made sense, of course, for neither Laird Ethelbert nor Laird Delaval had the time or resources to expend on prisoners of the conflict. Neither wanted to enrage the populace by summarily executing captives (many of whom were likely related to constituents and soldiers on both sides of the conflict). So the respective lairds would demand a vow of honorable capitulation, effectively ensuring that the captured soldiers would not return to their former ranks, and then send them here to the Abellicans, to gain the favor of the priests who held the sacred stones. Of course, both leaders, for fear of making honorable capitulation attractive, required the Abellicans to work their laborers brutally, and reward them not at all.

Perhaps there was a winner to be found in the war, after all, Dawson thought as he looked upon the grinning father.

Dawson's own smile didn't hold, though, as he considered the differences in the struggle that faced Dame Gwydre in the North, as he considered the scene of Tethmawle. Ethelbert and Delaval, both posturing to rule the holdings of Honce, offered quarter to the unfortunate soldiers of the other side.

That was not the case in Vanguard's war.

"I had not heard that the Samhaists were near defeat in Vanguard," the wily old Abellican father remarked. "Quite the opposite."

"They have called upon goblins and trolls to strengthen their lines," Dawson replied. "We are sorely pressed. Yet victory is at hand."

"That seems a rather strange interpretation. Three sentences, spoken one following the other as if the logic of them flowed as such."

"Their line cannot hold," Dawson explained. "If Dame Gwydre can counter their latest excursions with a forcible strike, the mishmash of warriors our enemies the Samhaists have assembled will turn upon each other. We have seen it in several regions already. Dame Gwydre is certain that a sudden and—"

Father Artolivan held up his hand to stop the man. "The details of war bore me," he said. "From this church, you will be paid in coin alone—at fair value, given the need for caribou moss at this time."

"Both armies will value it greatly," said Dawson.

Artolivan didn't even try to argue. "What you do with that coin is for you to decide," the priest went on. "The workers here are not free men, but they are many—indeed, perhaps too many. If some choose to sail with you back to Vanguard, you and I, nay, you and Brother Pinower, will reach a proper sale price."

Dawson grinned and nodded and dared to hope that he could fill his hold with able bodies in short order.

Aw, but he come through with a parade and all," exclaimed the excited middle-aged woman who looked much older than that. "Was as grand a spectacle as Oi've e'er seen, do you not think?"

Cadayle nodded politely and let her continue, and she did, for more than an hour, recounting the celebration on the day that Brother Bran Dynard passed through this unremarkable hamlet of Winterstorm.

Bransen and Callen leaned against the front wall of the single-room cottage. Despite his reservations, Bransen continued to listen, but Callen had long ago obviously dismissed the woman's rambling as a desperate attempt to garner some reward—even if it was just the satisfaction of having an audience for her chatter and gossip.

"Was the last we seen o' him, that brother, do you not think?" the old woman said, offering a dramatic upturn in her inflection that startled even the daydreaming Callen. "And so he went, and so goes the world."

"To Chapel Abelle?" Cadayle asked.

The woman shrugged, and when that resulted in a disappointed responding expression, the woman brightened suddenly and nodded too eagerly.

"You'll be staying to break the bread?" she asked. "I've a bit o' porridge, too, and stew from a lamb killed only a week ago and not yet holed by the worms."

Cadayle turned to her companions, who offered postures and expressions perfectly indifferent.

"Yes, a meal would do us well as we continue on our way," she said to the woman, who beamed a toothless smile back at her, then hustled out of the house to gather ingredients and utensils.

"She had no idea that such a man as Bran Dynard ever existed," Callen said when she had gone.

"Do not underestimate the memories of villagers," Bransen cautioned.

"The imagination, you mean," Callen replied. "Their life is tedium, year to year to year. We've brought them something they sorely need: excitement."

"A war rages within a few days' march," Bransen reminded.

"Diversion, then," said Callen.

Bransen looked to Cadayle for some support here, but

all she could offer was a shrug. He accepted that as he had to accept the simple truth of it all. They had covered many miles from Palmaristown, walking a road strewn with hamlets very much the same as Winterstorm, a cluster of farmhouses and perhaps a tradesman's shop or two encircling a common hall. Now with more than half the distance between Palmaristown and Chapel Abelle behind them, Bransen had hoped that the answers to questions about lost Bran Dynard would become more relevant and with answers beginning to flow more openly, but alas, the song remained the same. While some, like this woman, would weave elaborate tales, the quantity of words did little to enhance the quality. Hope had turned to dust in the first few minutes of an hour-long, creative recollection that was at least ten parts poetic license to one part memory. In truth, for all of their inquiries, the trio had garnered nothing at all about Bran Dynard's journey to Chapel Abelle those twenty years ago.

But Bransen wouldn't let his hopes die, for when he considered the truth of his quest he recognized that he should have expected nothing more than that which he had found. Indeed, the hospitality the trio had been granted along this road had made the journey not so unpleasant. His answers, if they were to be found, would almost certainly come from Chapel Abelle itself.

"Chapel Abelle," he said to Callen. She smiled and put a gentle hand on his shoulder. "Soon."

Three," a disgruntled Dawson told Pinower. "They are slaves here, and yet they view what I have to offer as less than even that!"

"I might have expected a few more," the brother replied. "But truly, they have seen the battlefield—many have felt the bite of cold iron. We work them hard, but here they know they will outlive the war. You offer them more war."

"I offer them freedom!"

Brother Pinower chuckled at that. "Vanguard is at war. Everyone here knows that truth."

"The path I offer leads to freedom with land and standing."

"Or to the belly of a goblin. They have been known to eat their captives and enemy dead."

Dawson gave a sigh of surrender.

"Three?" Brother Pinower asked, his tone becoming suddenly hopeful. "Three more than when you arrived. And you can rest easy that Father Artolivan will not allow you to return with only that."

"He will send monks?"

"No, no, of course not, for we have none to spare," Brother Pinower answered. "Not in these times. But there are gemstones that might serve the brothers of Chapel Pellinor . . ."

"Chapel Pellinor has fallen," said Dawson.

"A temporary situation, we are confident. Already the newest rumors from the northland speak of cleanup and rebuilding, with renewed vigor and determination. And many of the brothers of Pellinor remain alive. We will bolster their ranks—your ranks—with gemstones and other supplies. I have already spoken to Father Artolivan about this, and he has given me all assurances."

Dawson nodded. "Dame Gwydre will appreciate such support. But I've a hold to fill with able men, and only three have thus far agreed—and agreed for more coin than I intended to offer. I need fifty, Brother, to make my journey here worth the time and expense of Dame Gwydre, even with your generous offer of gemstones and other supplies. We are in short supply of bodies only."

"Patience, then," said Brother Pinower. "The battles across Honce rage, and more workers come in every week. Perhaps I can speak to Brother Shinnigord, who directs the workers, to more freely use the whip, that your offer sounds a bit more enticing."

"That would be appreciated," Dawson said, and gave a bow.

Brother Pinower shrugged as if it was nothing. "We have too many workers at present," he said. "And more arriving, an endless stream. Perhaps Father Artolivan can be persuaded to address your concerns to Lairds Ethelbert and Delaval, to enact an agreement that would allow us to sail any excess direct to Dame Gwydre."

"Now that, Brother, would serve Vanguard well, indeed," Dawson replied, and nearly choked, so fast did he try to get the words out of his mouth.

It was an offer he dearly wanted to pursue, but some commotion to the side turned the both of them toward the door to the chapel proper, where a young brother came forth along with a pair of the more senior monks of Chapel Abelle.

"Brother Fatuus of Palmaristown," Brother Pinower explained to Dawson. "He rode in hard this day with urgent news for Father Artolivan."

"News that would interest me and my cause?"

Brother Pinower shrugged and promised to return presently, and Dawson went back to the work groups to continue his offers. "Three," he muttered as he walked across the open courtyard, and he shuddered to think of the tongue-lashing Dame Gwydre would give him if he returned with such meager reinforcements as that!

TEN

Gaoler's Price

R ow harder!" Giavno prompted the two monks in the small boat—one of only a handful remaining in Chapel Isle's "fleet."

"Are we chasing ghosts?" one of the men dared ask.

"I saw it, I tell you!" Giavno insisted. "In the mist, drifting."

"Drifting? Or laying in wait?" asked the oarsman.

"Her mast was down," Giavno insisted. "Is down!" he cried, pointing ahead through the filmy gray steam. They all saw the boat, then, bobbing, mainsail torn down and with the craft apparently abandoned. "A prize for us to take back to Chapel Isle."

He looked back at the other two, grinning from ear to ear and certain that Father De Guilbe and the rest of his brethren would be quite pleased with today's catch, particularly since the monks had been forced to take men from their work on the chapel that they could construct more boats. When he turned forward again, though, his smile disappeared, for as they neared, the angle allowed him to see over the side of the craft, and it was anything but abandoned.

Giavno tried to tell the oarsmen to move more quickly, but all that came out of him was a gurgle. He did manage to wave his hand, at least, urging them on, and the paddling men brought the boat in swiftly.

Then they, too, gasped.

Three Alpinadoran tribesmen lay on the deck—the blood-soaked deck. Covered in blood, obviously much of it their own, the three did not react at all as the boats bumped, leading Giavno and his companions to believe that they were already dead.

"They must have ventured too near the glacial trolls," one of the oarsmen said. "We aren't far from the north-western bank." He stood up as he spoke and stretched to grab the other boat with both hands, hooking his feet as he did to serve as a living grapnel. The other oarsman helped Giavno get across.

"Alive," the senior brother said as he bent low over the nearest Alpinadoran, a blond-haired and sturdy gi-ant of a man. He fumbled with his pouch, producing a soul stone, and began praying over the man immedi-ately.

A second monk came over as well, moving to the other injured Alpinadorans. "Alive, both of them," he announced in short order. "But not for long had we not found them, and might not be for long in any case!"

Giavno shortened his healing on the youngest man and moved to the others in turn, casting a minimal amount of healing energy into each to stabilize them and at least stop the more obvious bleeding. He didn't even have to tell his companions their role here as they tied off the drifting Alpinadoran craft to their own and went back to their paddles. They pulled with all speed, towing Giavno and the captured boat straight back to Chapel Isle.

The sound of voices gradually brought Androosis back to the world of the living.

"We are not animals," he heard Toniquay say from somewhere to the side—which side he couldn't be sure.

"Nor do we consider you such," came the reply in the accent of a Southerner whose first language was not Errchuk, the predominant tongue of Alpinador.

Androosis heard a rattle, maybe of bones, maybe of chains.

"There are practical considerations," said the Southerner.

Androosis opened his eyes. It took a long while for the grayness to slip aside and let light into his aching head. He saw a monk standing before him—of course, it had to be a monk. He was in a small room, a dungeon of sorts, smelling of torch smoke and lit only in the sporadic shadows of dancing flames. He was lying down on his side on a hard and damp bed of dirt, and a blanket covered him from waist to feet. He tried to turn onto his back to better view the monk and Toniquay, but the movement shot stabbing pains into him, and he grimaced and settled back onto his side.

"I am chained like a dog!" Toniquay said with a growl.

"It is our only means of securing you for our sake and your own," replied the monk, whom Androosis now recognized as Brother Giavno. Hope rose in the miserable barbarian when he noted another form behind Giavno and recognized it as Cormack.

Cormack would free him, he believed. Cormack was a secret friend.

"Rest and heal," Brother Giavno said. "Be at ease. We will negotiate with your clan to get you out of here as soon as possible."

"At once!" Toniquay retorted. "You have no right—"

"If I had not found you on the lake you would be dead," Giavno shot right back. "As would your companions. I could have left you there for the trolls, yes?"

Androosis couldn't see Toniquay from his angle, but he could well picture the man exhaling.

"I do not ask for your gratitude," Giavno went on. "But I will have your obedience. You—all three—remain in need of our healing stones."

"Do not use them on me!" Toniquay cried.

"If we had not then you would be dead."

"Better that!"

Giavno backed away a step and produced a rather wicked smile that seemed all the more nefarious because of the flickering orange light. "Very well," he agreed.

"Or on them," said Toniquay.

"Without the gemstones the man you call Canrak will die," said Giavno.

"If that is the will of our gods," Toniquay replied, seeming not at all concerned.

How Androosis wished that he could roll over and slap the prideful shaman!

Giavno gave a little chuckle.

"If you would unshackle my hand I could tend him," Toniquay said.

"But we will not."

Androosis gulped at the finality of that statement, made all the more clear as Giavno turned away and stooped to get under the low arch exiting the room, sweeping Cormack up in his wake.

"Hold firm, kin and clan," Toniquay said, reciting the mantra of Clan Snowfall. "We go with certainty."

Androosis heard a weak reply that seemed more of a whimper from farther across the way. His own grunt might have satisfied Toniquay's needs, but it was hardly one of assent.

There was nothing shy and retiring about Father De Guilbe. The road had been hard on him, harder still when he had to come to terms with the failure, or at least the sidetrack, of his important mission to proselytize the northland. But he had been chosen—indeed, had been

promoted to father—as much because of his powerful
temperament and physical attributes as any of his work
on the tomes of Abelle or the philosophy of the church.
Cambelian De Guilbe stood well over six feet tall, and
even with the sparse diet of fish and plants the brothers
realized on Mithranidoon he had retained much of his
three-hundred-pound frame. It was said that he couldn't
sing like an angel but surely could roar like a dragon. It
was in precisely that voice that he ordered the bickering
brothers Giavno and Cormack into his quarters, which
encompassed the entirety of the highest finished floor of
the chapel.

De Guilbe came out around his desk as the pair entered, motioning for them to shut the door. "Your doubts
incite trepidation and fear in your brethren," he said,
leaning forward as he spoke, a movement that wilted
many a strong man.

"All respect, Father," said Giavno, "but there is no
doubt. Brother Cormack is wrong and out of place."

Father De Guilbe's heavy eyes swayed to take in the
younger brother.

"I object," Cormack said, trying hard to keep the
tremor out of his voice.

"To?"

"His heart is too meek for the obvious and important
task before us," Brother Giavno insisted, but Father De
Guilbe held up his hand to silence the man and never
took his scrutinizing gaze off Cormack.

"They are in the damp mud," Cormack said, and the
way he blurted it showed that he was scrambling here to
put his discordant emotions into substance and complaint.

"We live on a damp and dirty island, Brother," Father
De Guilbe reminded.

"The dungeon is the least hospitable room."

"And the only secure one."

Cormack sighed and lowered his gaze.

"He would accept their repaired boat as a proper

chamber for our guests," said Giavno. "Push them off the beach and send them on their way."

"Morality demands—" Cormack began.

"We healed them!" Giavno sternly cut in. Both he and Cormack looked to Father De Guilbe, noting that the man wasn't about to intervene this time, and indeed, was through that very silence inviting Giavno to continue with the scolding.

"The powers of God, through the gemstones, through the wisdom of Blessed Abelle, are the only reason the three barbarians continue to draw breath. We did that, working tirelessly from the moment I tied their broken boat to my own."

"A charitable act worthy of the Church of Blessed Abelle," Cormack interjected, and Brother Giavno glowered at him.

"He forgets why we were sent to Alpinador," Giavno said to Father De Guilbe. "He has lost purpose of our mission under the fondness he has developed for our barbarian neighbors." He paused and stared even harder at Cormack. "And our powrie neighbors," he added.

Cormack snapped a look at the man.

"Place it on your head, Brother," Giavno bade him. Cormack's expression shifted from anger to outright fear as he looked back to Father De Guilbe.

"Oh, do," said Giavno. "Everyone knows you have it with you, that you wear it whenever you believe no one is watching."

When Cormack studied Father De Guilbe he saw no concession there, just full agreement with Giavno's observations, and indeed, with his request. Hand trembling, the young brother reached behind and into the small pouch he kept on his back, secured to his robe's rope belt. He brought forth the powrie beret, the bloody cap.

Father De Guilbe motioned for him to continue, to put it on.

Cormack did, shifting it so that its band was tilted

just a bit across his forehead, down to the right, where the top bulge of the beret flopped over.

Father De Guilbe chuckled, but it seemed more in pity than amusement.

"Why would you wear such a thing, fairly won or not?" Giavno asked.

"There is magic about it," said Cormack, and both of his listeners widened their eyes in surprise, and horror.

"When I wear it upon my head, I feel a greater sturdiness within my body," Cormack tried to explain. "This cap might show us why powries can accept such a beating and continue to fight."

"You wear it to understand our enemies," said Father De Guilbe.

Cormack started to agree and for a moment was truly relieved to be able to. But he stopped himself short, not willing to go so far in accepting that description of the powries—not after they had treated him so fairly and honorably.

"I wear it to expand my understanding of our neighbors," Cormack conceded, but he breathed easier when that seemed to satisfy Father De Guilbe.

"Keep wearing it, then," the father ordered. "In fact, you will face consequences if I see you without it."

Beside Cormack, Giavno snickered, and only then did Cormack realize that these two saw De Guilbe's order as a form of punishment in and of itself, a way to brand and isolate Cormack in the eyes of all the men on Chapel Isle.

"Let us return to the issue at hand," said De Guilbe. "These three barbarians owe their lives to us, would you not agree, Brother Cormack?"

Cormack searched about frantically for a way to dodge the obvious answer, but had to concede simply, "Yes."

"And they were healed through the powers shown to us by Blessed Abelle?"

"Yes, Father."

"Then their debt is beyond our magnanimity, of course."

Cormack replied with a puzzled expression.

"Their debt is not to Brother Giavno—or perhaps it is to a smaller extent," Father De Guilbe explained. "The gaoler's price—and we are not the gaoler, but merely the guards, is owed to Blessed Abelle and to God above him."

Cormack didn't like the way Father De Guilbe was framing the issue, but of course there was no way for him to disagree with the simple logic. "Yes, Father."

"Then the charity you desire is not ours to give," reasoned De Guilbe. "It is for God to determine, and fortunately, we are shown in the teachings of Blessed Abelle how such charity is to be bestowed. These three are prisoners of a higher power, who demands of them fealty. Absent that fealty, God would never have given us the blessed power to heal their mortal wounds—wounds, I remind you, which were wrought of no actions on our part."

"The price was not known to them," Cormack weakly argued.

"They were in no position to negotiate," Father De Guilbe replied. "And there was none to be had in any case. We were sent to Alpinador to show the light of God, and no man beyond Blessed Abelle himself has ever seen it more intimately than the three barbarians for whom you advocate. The truth has been shown to them, the light shines before their eyes."

"But—"

"If they refuse to see it, then they shall remain in the dark, Brother Cormack," Father De Guilbe said with complete finality. "Figuratively and literally."

Cormack could feel Giavno glowing smugly beside him.

"We will not mistreat them," De Guilbe said, turning to Giavno.

"Of course not, Father," the senior brother assured him.

"But our security demands their location, and there they will stay."

"For how long?" Cormack dared to ask.

"Until they dare to stare at the light, or until they are called to the afterlife, where they will see with it the folly of their stubbornness. We are agreed on that, I am sure."

Cormack lowered his gaze again. "Yes, Father De Guilbe," he said.

De Guilbe released them with a wave. Cormack instinctively reached up to the powrie beret.

"Wear it!" Father De Guilbe snapped at him ferociously, and Cormack nearly stumbled away in surprise.

"Wear it now and wear it always, Brother Cormack," De Guilbe demanded. "And never forget why."

Cormack again wore a puzzled expression.

"Why we came here," Father De Guilbe clarified sternly.

Cormack bowed and turned to leave, feeling moisture gathering in his bright green eyes. Brother Giavno's face was creased by a satisfied smile, but he did put a supportive hand gently and sincerely on Cormack's shoulder as they turned together for the door.

He ran his old fingers across the ice wall as he walked in the darkness. The moisture he felt there pleased him greatly, for it represented the fruition of his vision, the beauteous simplicity of his grand plan that would have seemed so complicated to any looking from afar.

The trolls' blood was performing as he had foreseen, coating the chasm carved by Ancient D'no (who was burrowing along the route proscribed by the giants and their mallets). The white worm's godly heat melted the ice; the trolls' blood prevented it from refreezing.

Soon Mithranidoon would be washed free of its infection.

Ancient Badden paused when he happened upon a torn head, its lower half bitten away and most of the skin pulled from the skull bone. Enough skin and hair remained for the old Samhaist to recognize it, though, and he bent and retrieved it, lifting it so that he could again look Dantanna in the eye.

"Ah, my old friend, do you understand now?" the Ancient asked with a chuckle. "Did the Abellican promises grant you immortality? Are the Ancient Ones impressed with your tolerance of the upstart heretics?"

Ancient Badden's features darkened into a fierce scowl. "Were you prepared for your death, fool Dantanna?" He let his fingers curl under the rim of the skull as he spoke, and squeezed tightly against the remaining brain and the ice-fly maggots.

"For centuries we have stood as the guardians of folly," he said, as if lecturing the man. "We have warned the folk and prepared the folk. We taught them to survive, to reap and sow, to treat their maladies, and mostly, you fool—and mostly!—we prepared them for the darkness of eternity. They must know the Ancient Ones to understand the paths they will walk when the specter of Death visits them. They must recognize their insignificance beside the gods that they will accept their dark fate as servants.

"But the followers of the fool Abelle come along and promise the mercy and benevolence of a forgiving god!" Ancient Badden roared, squeezing so hard that a bit of brain seeped out and slipped to the icy floor. "They tease with baubles and extrapolate from them what they consider infinite wisdom and wisdom of the infinite. But they did not know, did they, Dantanna? Empty promises and joy-filled fancies to tempt and cajole. Did the wretch Abelle greet you when Ancient D'no's teeth tore you from your mortal body?"

As if in answer he heard a rumble as he finished the

question. Badden slowly lowered the skull and turned about to glance over his shoulder.

The white worm, a gigantic centipede-like monster, its back glowing fiercely with heat that could melt the flesh of a man to a puddle on simple contact, reared and clicked its formidable mandibles together. Small wing-like appendages appeared just a few feet below its head, flapping and turning to hold it steady and upright.

Ancient Badden realized that this must have been the last sight Dantanna had known.

He laughed, then bowed. "God of the ice who denies the cold," he praised, and bowed again very low.

D'no gave a clicking sound, half hiss and half growl, and began to sway back and forth hypnotically.

Ancient Badden began to chant the oldest of Samhaist songs. No other man in the world would have survived that moment, but Badden knew the secrets, all the secrets, and his tone and cadence and inflection reflected centuries of knowledge and understanding of the wide world, of the great beast, the gods, and of this god, D'no, in particular.

The white worm gradually receded, backing for many feet before rolling over itself and scuttling away down a side tunnel.

Ancient Badden nodded at the confirmation of his powers and the truth of his beliefs. He held Dantanna's skull up before him one last time. "Blessed Abelle would have been devoured," he laughed, tossing Dantanna aside.

Cormack instinctively stiffened when he heard the soft paddling not far away. He stood on a sandbar some distance out to the northeast of Chapel Isle, a quiet and remote location that he had found soon after the brothers had arrived on Mithranidoon.

He listened carefully for further paddling, trying to determine the angle of approach. Was it his brothers following him? If so, he mused, he hoped they would see the powrie beret first, think him a dwarf, and kill him from afar.

That would be easier than explaining to Father De Guilbe why he had come out here.

He heard the paddling again, faint but close, and he knew it could not be the brothers handling a boat that deftly and quietly. No, only the barbarians born and raised on Mithranidoon could so gently navigate the waves, so Cormack was not surprised when the longboat slid in against the sandbar a few heartbeats later and Milkeila climbed out.

She moved right to him, not saying a word, and wrapped him in a tight hug. "Too long," she whispered.

He detected sadness and anxiety in her voice and felt in her hug that she needed comfort. Cormack kissed her and crushed her tight.

"A powrie cap?" she asked, obviously taken aback. She moved back to arm's length and looked up at the man, for though Milkeila was a tall woman, Cormack stood a full head above her.

"A long and complicated tale."

"Then we haven't the time," said Milkeila, and she flashed a coy smile. "I was surprised by your signal but happy to see the light through the mist."

"There is magic in this cap, I will say," said Cormack. "When I don it, I feel . . . thickened. Strengthened. Not armored, perhaps, but as if I could withstand a heavier blow."

"Perhaps that is why the powries can withstand such a beating before relenting in battle."

"That and their temperament, which is akin to that of a cornered animal."

Milkeila smiled and nodded at that apt description. Having spent the entirety of her life on Mithranidoon, she had enjoyed many fights with the ferocious dwarfs.

"You lost three men," Cormack said, startling her and stealing her mirth.

Milkeila stepped back, sliding her arms so that she ended up holding Cormack by the forearms. "Five," she corrected. "How did you know?"

"We have three," said Cormack. Milkeila leaned forward eagerly, and Cormack added, "Androosis among them."

"You did battle?"

"We found them floating in a ruined boat. Trolls hit them and hard. Brother Giavno believes they were fishing in the northwestern waters too near the caves."

"Who are the others?"

Cormack shook his head. "They say little. One is a shaman, and by his dress high-ranking—"

"Toniquay," Milkeila interrupted.

"Stubborn," said Cormack.

"More than you would ever understand. They are alive, then, all three?"

"Healed in the dungeon of Chapel Isle."

A strange expression came over Milkeila's face, one that Cormack could not decipher other than to know it did not bode well.

"Dungeon?" she said, clarifying it all for him.

Cormack stepped back and shrugged helplessly. "Brother Giavno found them adrift. Had he not towed them to Chapel Isle they would have all died."

"Or my people would have found them," Milkeila interjected, her tone sharpening just a bit.

"They would have died even then," said Cormack, and how he wished he could have taken back those words the moment they passed his lips!

Milkeila furrowed her brow.

"They were very near to death," Cormack stammered, trying to climb out of the deepening ditch. "It took the efforts of several brothers working tirelessly with the gemstones . . . their wounds were grave."

"Too grave for the pretend gods of Yan Ossum barbarians, no doubt," the woman said dryly.

"I did not mean . . ."

"You did not have to," Milkeila said.

Cormack paused to draw a steadying breath. "The gemstones—the soul stones—are the most focused healing magic in the world. The lairds of Honce recognize this, truly. I do not diminish your gods." He grabbed her by the hands and pulled her close—or tried to, but she resisted. "You know I never would! But there are practical truths about the sacred stones and their related magic."

"My people are not without resources," Milkeila replied. "Our shamans are not useless fools sputtering meaningless chants to false gods."

"I did not mean . . ." he repeated helplessly.

"You did not have to," Milkeila said again, with a frown. "It is said among the islands that the monks see two ways to the world: their way and the wrong way."

"You do not believe that about me."

"Do not or did not?"

The two stared at each other for a few uncomfortable heartbeats until Cormack added, "Is that statement not true of every clan on Mithranidoon's steaming waters? Could anything less be said of the powries? Of Yossunfier? Of Clan Pierjyk or Tunundar or any of the other tribes of your barbarian kin? The Alpinadoran clans cannot even agree amongst themselves—on anything, it seems!"

If Milkeila was impressed, she didn't show it.

"When will Androosis and the others be set free?" the woman asked.

Cormack swallowed hard—all the answer she needed.

"Then I am bound to tell my leaders that they are on Chapel Isle."

Cormack felt panic welling up inside. "You cannot," he begged. "I told you only because . . ."

"You cannot ask of me that I hold this secret. My kin are out upon the lake, every day, in search of the lost five. They travel to dangerous corners of Mithranidoon. Am I to hold quiet while some are lost to the trolls?"

"I would not have told you."

"Then you should not have told me! Not on that condition! You cannot ask that I pretend ignorance while my people sail into danger. And you cannot ask that I do nothing while my friend—your friend!—sits in your Abellican prison."

"You have to believe me," said Cormack. "I am trying to get them released. As soon as the healing is complete."

"Healing that sickens the heart of Toniquay, no doubt."

"He will allow no more now that his thoughts are back in the world of the living," Cormack admitted. "But he mends. They all do, and they are well fed. And I will press for their release, of course."

Milkeila's posture and the fact that she allowed Cormack to take her hands again revealed that she did not doubt him. But in the end she shook her head, unsatisfied with the promised resolution. "I cannot lie to my leaders. Not about this. I will not explain to them how I know, but they will be told that our lost brethren are on Chapel Isle. You cannot ask anything else of me."

"Their boat is beached on our shore," said Cormack, his tone noticeably short of enthusiasm. "Tell them you spied it from afar."

"My people will come for them," the woman promised ominously.

"I pray that a bargain will be struck," said Cormack. "Perhaps this is an opportunity for a better understanding between Chapel Isle and Yossunfier."

But Milkeila was shaking her head with every word. "There is no bargain to be found," she explained, her tone even and full of certainty. "My people will go to Chapel Isle in full force to demand the release. Anything less will incite war."

Cormack stuttered around a couple of insufficient responses before settling upon "What will Milkeila do?"

She stepped back and stood staring at him in the moonlight for a long while, obviously waging an inner struggle. "I am Yan Ossum," she said, and reached up to her neck to separate her second, secret necklace from her more traditional shamanistic attire. She pulled the gemstone necklace over her head and held it out to Cormack, who widened his eyes, too stunned to respond.

"I am Yan Ossum," Milkeila said again. "If there is to be war, I battle on the side of Yossunfier." She tossed the necklace to him, and he caught it. "It would be wrong of me to use your gemstones against you in that event. I would not so betray your trust."

"As you perceive I am betraying yours?"

Milkeila shook her head and managed a thin smile. "I am Yan Ossum, and you are Abellican. We both battle the limitations of our heritage—I am no more in Toniquay's favor than you are in the eyes of Father De Guilbe. But we cannot escape the truth of who we are, not in the event we both fear. My people will come for our lost brethren, and your brothers will not likely release them. And so we are left in the most awful place where our hopes collide with our realities."

Cormack stood there on the sand, staring at this extraordinary barbarian lass, a woman he had come to love, and he had no answers to her simple and straightforward logic. His shoulders slumped, his arms fell limp by his sides, and he smiled meekly, almost apologetically, back at her. He didn't know whether he should go to her and hug her again or kiss her to assure her that everything would be all right. It was a moot point anyway, for there was no strength in his legs at that moment, powrie beret notwithstanding, to propel him.

Her waning smile carried Milkeila back to her small boat, and she pushed it away from the sandbar and hopped aboard it with the grace only one of her heritage might know.

In moments, the mist enveloped her, and Cormack stood alone.

And never in his life had he been more aware of exactly that.

ELEVEN

Two Birds

It is a lie," Brother Pinower remarked as Dawson, stepping lightly as if the weight of the world had been removed from his shoulders, started out of Father Artolivan's audience hall.

Dawson stopped with a small hop and turned to face the younger monk, but Artolivan spoke before he could reply.

"A tale of mutual benefit," the old priest said.

"A tale untrue," said Brother Pinower. "We know the fate of Brother Dynard."

"Do we?" asked Artolivan.

Pinower licked his lips and glanced over at Dawson. "We know at least that Dawson's concoction has no basis in any known facts, Father."

"Vanguard is a large and untamed place," said Artolivan.

"We make a leap of circumstance based on less than compelling reasoning, Father. To spin such a claim, without cause, seems the very definition of . . ."

"Prudence," Father Artolivan interrupted. "Play it out

to logical conclusion in your thoughts, young Brother, absent this 'concoction,' as you deem it. The benefactors of your veracity would be?"

Pinower's gaze went from Artolivan to Dawson and back again, and again. After a few moments, he could only sigh, having no practical response.

With an appreciative nod to Father Artolivan, Dawson McKeege took his leave.

"Go with him," Father Artolivan instructed Pinower. "Supply to his tale the imprimatur of the Abellican Church."

Brother Pinower's expression showed his ultimate dismay, but he did not argue and did not respond, other than to bow politely and rush away in pursuit of the Vanguardsman.

Named because she sat below the peak of the northern cliffs and thus offered protection from the cold winds that howled down from the gulf, Weatherguard nevertheless still afforded her residents and visitors a magnificent view of Chapel Abelle, so strong and solemn and crisp against the steel-gray sky beyond the high rise.

Bransen, Callen, and Cadayle stood and enjoyed that view for a few moments when they first came in sight of the renowned abbey, with the two women flanking Bransen and holding him relatively straight, as he had been for most of their journey, particularly those parts when they neared more populated areas. Today he walked in genuine Stork form.

"Built by the hand of God, so they say," Callen whispered, awe evident in her voice. For how could it not have been? Many of Honce's traveling bards named this the most impressive structure in all the land, even above the magnificent palace of Laird Delaval.

Bransen slipped a hand into his belt pouch and clutched a soul stone. He had become quite adept at making this movement unobtrusive and even more so at accessing the power of the stone, almost instantly transforming himself. "We know the Abellicans far too well to make the mistake of listening to 'they,' " he reminded. "How might Chapel Abelle measure against the Walk of Clouds of the Jhesta Tu?"

"One day we will know, my love," Cadayle whispered to him. She nudged him gently to make sure he was aware of people walking by.

Anytime Cadayle rubbed his upper arm and said "my love," it meant that he should revert to his disguise. Bransen took the cue and let go of the gemstone. Any hint that he was faking his malady would surely land him on the front lines of the vicious war as both sides scrambled for more and more fodder to feed their kingly designs.

Cadayle and Callen helped Bransen to Weatherguard's long inn, a ramshackle old structure so warped and aged that the floor showed stains of the water that easily crept through whenever it rained or snowed. Still, the common room's hearth was enormous and well stocked. The fire, seeming like three separate conflagrations, worked its way through the jumble of logs piled high behind an iron grate, their flickering ends sometimes joining, sometimes flaring in opposite directions so that they resembled a trio of dancers acting out the tragedy of a failing love triangle.

The patrons in the room showed no such intrigue. Old men and women young and old littered the many small round tables set about the generous floor. Glances both scornful and bitter came at Bransen immediately as he entered. Only as he staggered storklike, drool wetting the corners of his mouth, did many of the patrons nod their understanding and let go of that resentment. Few men of Bransen's age remained in Weatherguard, and everyone in the room had suffered the loss of a husband or son or brother in the seemingly endless war between Ethelbert and Delaval.

"Wounded in the South," Cadayle explained to a

gaggle of old women who stared incredulously as Bransen staggered into a seat.

"Ah," they all said together.

"A pity he weren't killed outright, then, ye poor girl," one dared offer.

Cadayle merely nodded, accepting their misplaced pity. She'd heard that one often enough.

Cadayle noticed then that one middle-aged man in the tavern seemed quite out of place. Sitting in a back corner, his weathered boots up on the table, he was surely of age and fitness to be at the front. He cradled a mug of mead in one hand, absently running the index finger of his other hand about its thick rim. And all the while he stared at her and at Bransen with more than a passing interest. Too much so!

Cadayle told herself that she was being ridiculous, that the man, like everyone else, was simply intrigued by the abnormality of the Stork. She settled into her chair beside Bransen, facing Callen.

Callen's glance over her shoulder was Cadyle's first warning. Before she even turned, a strong hand patted her shoulder.

"Well seen and well to drink," the man greeted, sliding up beside Cadayle near to the fourth chair at the table. He looked to her and then to it as if asking permission to sit down.

Cadayle glanced at her mother, who gave a quick nod.

"Do join us," the younger woman said.

The man settled in heavily, staring at Bransen all the while. "You look as if you've a long road behind you." He motioned to the bartender to bring a round of drinks.

"My husband cannot indulge," Cadayle said quietly.

"Make him unsteady on his feet, will it?" the man asked, and Cadayle glowered at him.

"Apologies, good lady," he said unconvincingly. He half stood and bowed toward Bransen. "Wounded in the war?" he asked, again too intently.

"In the South," said Cadayle.

"A pity, that. The towns are full of torn men. Arms and legs missing. Brains all scattered so that they can hardly speak. An ugly business is this war."

"One you seem to be avoiding," Callen said across the table, and Cadayle was glad indeed for the diversion.

The man gave what seemed to be a helpless chuckle. "I've come from Vanguard to the north across the gulf." He stood and tipped his heavy cap. "Dawson McKeege at your service, good ladies and yourself, good sir. Here on a brief—too brief!—respite. War's no less up there, I tell you."

"So you fled?" Cadayle asked.

The man laughed harder. "Nay, that wouldn't do. I've sailed under Dame Gwydre's banner to Chapel Abelle for supplies, you see? The gemstones of the Abellicans have proven well worth the journey. We're taming a land as vast and great as Honce herself."

"The brothers help you, then."

"Oh, indeed!" Dawson replied. "We've several working our chapels. Good men, one and all, though I've no doubt that more than a few found themselves in the northland for reasons of discipline and not choice."

Cadayle gave a pleasant and polite smile.

"Whenever the Church has one out of line, the road turns north, is my guess of it," the clever Dawson went on. "And don't be misunderstanding me! Pray no! We're all too glad to have them."

"Surely," said Cadayle, sharing a glance with Callen.

"And why might you be at Chapel Abelle?" Dawson asked. "Seeking help for your man, there, from their gemstone magic?"

Cadayle nodded.

Dawson returned it. "If they've the time, perhaps you'll find what you seek, though your man will likely find himself on a wagon heading back for the fighting if they manage the task."

Cadayle clutched Bransen's hand tightly. "He does not fear any battle," she said.

"Surely," Dawson replied. "Have you come far, then?"

"All the way from Pryd Hol . . ." Callen started.

"South of Pryd Holding," Cadayle quickly corrected. "Closer to Entel, even."

Dawson's eyes widened. "A long and trying journey, to be sure, with one so impaired." He paused as the barmaid came over and delivered a pair of pale ales.

"Don't ye let Dawson here bother ye," she said, exactly as Dawson had paid her to remark. "He's the lout of the North, so goes his reputation." She gave him a playful slap on the shoulder as she finished to diminish any real warning in her words, again, exactly as he had paid her to do. There was nothing like a charming rake to calm a stranger's fears, Dawson knew.

"But he's just harmless," the barmaid said in Cadayle's ear. "Always looking for a warm bed for his spike, don't ye know? And he's looking to yer friend there—yer ma, she is, I'm guessing, or yer older sister—and don't she look so pretty? My, but ye'll be a long time with yer charms following that one!"

Cadayle snickered despite herself. She lifted the ale to her lips and took a long and welcomed draw.

"Don't you be showing my dice, Tauny Dentsen!" Dawson complained as the barmaid whirled away, giggling. He looked back at Cadayle to find a warm smile waiting for him.

"How long are you to stay, then?" Dawson asked.

Cadayle and Callen exchanged uncertain looks.

"If you're to wait on the brothers, then some time, of course," Dawson reasoned. "Chapel Abelle is full of activity, readying for the new class of brothers who will enter her gates in but a few days. I doubt you will get Father Artolivan or Brother Pinower to even hear your request before the week is through."

"You know them?" Callen asked before Cadayle could.

"All of them, of course," said Dawson. "I told you

that my Dame Gwydre is on fine terms with the brothers of Blessed Abelle. They've eyes on Vanguard, to be sure, as would any far-seeing man."

"And they have brothers up there," Cadayle added. "As you said."

"Aye, many have come for more than twenty years now."

Cadayle glanced at Bransen, a perfectly natural movement, and one that would not have been telling to Dawson had he not already known the true reason the trio had ventured to Chapel Abelle.

"So you're to seek the work of the brothers with their gemstones," Dawson said. "A reasonable request, and one that would likely be met with some sympathy were it not for these times."

Cadayle furrowed her brow. "What do you mean?"

"The brothers are exhausted," Dawson explained. "Overworked, particularly with the gemstones, as they tend constantly to the wounded of both the warring lairds. As long as you have a writ, you have a chance, I expect." He addressed Bransen directly. "You fought under Delaval's flag, yes? And his commander offered you a Writ of Plea for the Brothers of Chapel Abelle? The higher his rank, the better your chances, of course. A Writ of Plea from Laird Delaval himself would likely get you into their healing chambers."

"A Writ of Plea?" Cadayle asked, shaking her head.

"To be sure! A letter from a laird, or his commanders, begging special attention to a valiant warrior's wounds. Without it, you'll not get near to the leaders at Chapel Abelle, and they are the most powerful ones with the gemstones. They are not so—" Dawson stopped in a hush and sat staring sympathetically at Cadayle, then at Bransen. "So you do not possess a writ?"

A horrified expression came over the woman, and she looked to an equally surprised and upset Callen.

"All hope is not lost," Dawson was quick to add. "Have you a friend or relative among the brothers, anything to elevate your needs above the maladies of so many other poor souls? Was your man there particularly valorous?"

Cadayle stared at him incredulously.

"I recant!" said Dawson. "Dear lady, forgive my foolishness. Of course he was, but what I mean is . . . well, is there a witness to his bravery? A letter of honor if not a Writ of Plea?"

Cadayle's expression answered that clearly in the negative.

"Then a relative among the brothers?" asked Dawson. "Think hard, I pray you. A friend? An acquaintance, even? Anyone who can speak for your poor man there to elevate him from the throngs of wounded."

"We have come in hopes of healing, to be sure," Callen said, drawing the attention of both Cadayle and the man, and both looked equally surprised. "But also in search of one who might well speak for us."

"A brother?"

Callen nodded. "From Chapel Pryd, far to the south. He traveled to Chapel Abelle many years ago, so it is rumored, and we came here specifically in the hopes that he would help my daughter's poor husband."

"Your daughter?" said Dawson, and he seemed as if his breath had flown. "Surely I thought her your sister!"

Callen blushed and smiled, despite the obvious ploy.

"Well, if this brother is here, then you shan't have wasted your time, I expect," said Dawson. "I know all the brothers presently at chapel. What is his name?"

After another quick glance at her mother Cadayle said, "Brother Dynard. Brother Bran Dynard."

Dawson furrowed his brow and fell back in his chair, a look of knowing his expression.

"You know him?"

"No," the Vanguardsman replied. "But I know of him."

"He is at Chapel Abelle?" asked Callen.

Dawson managed a glance at Bransen as he looked to the older woman, and he recognized the sure signs of interest there, how the swaying man was actually managing to lean forward a bit.

"No," Dawson answered, and out of the corner of his eye he saw the clear signs of disappointment on the debilitated man's face. "Not here. Not for a decade and more at least."

Cadayle rubbed her face.

"He is in Vanguard, of course," Dawson said. Both women sucked in their breath, and Bransen turned sharply toward him—so much so that he nearly tumbled out of his seat.

"Aye, across the Gulf of Corona to the north," said Dawson. "Serving Dame Gwydre's flock."

"Then he is alive," Cadayle breathed, words she hadn't meant to utter aloud.

"Last I heard, indeed," said Dawson. "Would you go there, then? To Vanguard to find him?"

Neither woman had an answer to that, as was obvious from their respective, and equally overwhelmed, expressions.

"You cannot walk to Vanguard, of course," Dawson offered. "A month and more by land and through wild lands. The only way to Vanguard is by boat across the dark waters."

"And they sail from where? Palmaristown?" asked Cadayle.

"And the price of passage?" Callen added.

Dawson offered a warm smile. "Sometimes they do, yes, and I know not that there is ever a set price. No passenger boats make the crossing, you see. Trade ships, one and all, like my own *Lady Dreamer.*"

"What price then?" asked Cadayle.

"For the three of you? Why, if I've room I'll gladly have you aboard. The price will be fine company and stories of the South. I can see by the looks of you that you've many interesting tales to tell."

"If you have room," Callen said.

"And I will, though the brothers have bade me to

carry many of the war-weary prisoners," said Dawson.
"Oh, they are not dangerous," he added, seeing a bit of
alarm on Cadayle's sweet face. "Just poor souls fighting
for one laird or another who got hurt or caught and by
agreement of honor and convenience were put out of the
war for its duration. The brothers take them in, both
sides treated equally, but the ferocity of the battle has
given them more than they can handle. Still, I expect I'll
have room for three extras on *Lady Dreamer.*"

Cadayle looked to Bransen and Callen for an answer,
and Callen had one. "You are too kind," she said. "And
we will surely consider your most generous offer. When
do you plan to sail?"

"Tomorrow," said Dawson. "And I will hold three
open seats. You will find Vanguard most accommodat-
ing. We've wood aplenty, and thus, Dame Gwydre has
built entire towns in anticipation of emigration from the
war-ravaged mainland. Most welcomed, I assure you,
particularly with two so beautiful ladies among your
trio."

He stood up then and motioned to the barmaid again,
flashing a piece of silver and setting it on the table for
her.

"I must see to my other arrangements," he said to the
three. "A strong wind to fill your canvas, and moving
seas to you."

He bowed and took his leave. Cadayle and Callen sat
there, stunned, for many moments, each trying to digest
all that had just happened.

"Can it be?" Bransen mouthed quietly to both of them,
closing his hand on his soul stone once more. "Alive?"
Even with the magical aid, the young man seemed to have
a hard time sitting still and sitting straight.

Y ou confirmed my tale to them, of course?" Dawson
McKeege asked Brother Pinower the next day,

soon after he had noted Cadayle, Callen, and the man known as the Highwayman moving through the courtyard of Chapel Abelle and into the tunnels leading down to the dock where *Lady Dreamer* waited.

"As Father Artolivan demanded of me, yes," the monk confirmed.

Dawson grinned as he turned to regard him. "You disapprove?"

"I pride myself on telling the truth."

Dawson looked back out over the wall to the dark waters of the gulf. "In this instance the tale was better for all. Would this Highwayman be better off if he did not sail with me? Or would Father Artolivan be compelled to arrest him, surely to be hanged by the neck? You may have saved a life, good Brother. Isn't that worth a lie?"

"If the man is a criminal then it is not my province to deny justice."

"Criminal. Justice," Dawson echoed. "Strange words in this time, when men slaughter their own kin to further the aspirations of greedy lairds. Would you not agree?"

Brother Pinower sighed and looked out to sea.

"This is an easier course for Father Artolivan and for all of you. Perhaps you saved more lives than the Highwayman's, if it had come to blows. His reputation is impressive. If he is half the warrior Father Artolivan believes, he will serve Dame Gwydre well."

Now Pinower did look directly at the sea-worn man. "He goes to Vanguard under false pretenses. His anger will rise when he learns of the deception. You do not know that he will serve Dame Gwydre at all."

"Oh, he will," said a smiling Dawson. "For he goes not alone, and they, all three, will find themselves alone and vulnerable in a land they do not understand. Consider it his sentence for the crimes of which he has been accused. We will be your gaolers—it seems the way of things."

"If you say," said Pinower, staring out at the dark waters.

Dawson similarly turned. "Oh, he will," the man mumbled.

T W E L V E

Cold Seat of Power

Tinnikkikkik recognized the sense of dread emanating from his hundred glacial troll forces, and indeed felt it himself, for this place was surely unnerving. It was more than the cold air. This temperature hardly bothered the trolls, who swam in the icy waters of melting glaciers and ran about naked on Alpinadoran ice and snow even in the nights of deep winter. The warm waters of the lake below this glacier made them more uncomfortable than the cold, even this high up on the river of ice.

It wasn't the almost preternatural cold, it was the aura of the place. Tinnikkikkik had been in many houses sculpted of ice in his five decades but certainly never before in anything remotely like this one. Great crystalline corridors wound about each other in confusing twists and turns, some climbing higher, some lower, and ice or not, this was easily the largest man-made structure Tinnikkikkik or any of his tribe had ever seen, let alone entered. And it looked all the larger for its sweeping stairs, winding up to side towers that seemed grand indeed though they might only contain a couple of rather smallish rooms.

In addition to the size and grandeur of the palace, the simple truth of its construction only added to its imposing aura. For no picks and flat-blades had built Devongel, as it was called, and no strong arms, human, giant, or otherwise, had lifted the blocks into place to form the thick walls. Devongel had been pulled from the glacier upon which it stood through magic.

And no torches lit it, though it was not dark inside. It wasn't bright, but neither was it as dark as it should have been, even on a clear and sunny day, which this was not. A deep blue light glowed from the structure's ice, only enhancing the cold and empty feel of the palace.

Ancient magic had built this place and lit this place, earth magic, the power of the Samhaists. A different manifestation of the same magic that had compelled Tinnikkikkik to lead his people here, he knew deep in his heart, and though he might recoil at being so magically manipulated, even that realization had not stopped him from coming. He tried to tell himself that he followed the call despite his reservations because he was the bravest of his people—and indeed he had shown that to be the truth through many, many battles. His rank as boss confirmed that, for it was not an inherited title among his tribe, or any of the troll tribes.

Mumbling and shifting all around Tinnikkikkik, particularly the shuffling feet, warned him that the nervousness was threatening to overwhelm his forces. He stood straight—at over five feet, he was taller than most glacial trolls—and let his scrutinizing, roving gaze sweep in the entirety of the band, holding them with its intensity, though they surely wanted to flee.

The troll boss lifted his hand, palm up, before his chest and face, signaling his charges to stand straighter.

"Where do we go, boss?" the troll next to him dared ask, its tinny voice echoing off the cold and sheer walls and other flat facings. Perhaps it was design, perhaps magic, but the echoes seemed to grow in both volume and intensity above the original for a short while before diminishing to a long hissing whisper of sound.

Tinnikkikkik and all the others hopped every which way, trying to get a handle on the cacophony, and finally, in frustration, the troll boss just turned and slapped the speaker hard.

Strangely, that sharp slap did not echo.

But a single set of footfalls did, suddenly though not seeming so, as if they had been around the band all along but the trolls were only now noticing them. They drummed out a steady and slow cadence, and they seemed to be coming nearer, though from which direction was any troll's guess. The band huddled together more closely, every bloodshot eye turning intermittently to Tinnikkikkik, their leader, their boss.

He knew that, and so he stood as tall as he could manage, and did not flinch when Ancient Badden at last came into view, walking along a descending and curved ramp. He wore his trademark light green robes, his great beard spiked with dung, and though his footfalls sounded sharply, he wasn't shod in hard-soled boots, but in his usual open-toed sandals.

He moved slowly but somehow seemed to cover an enormous amount of ground, cleverly stopping just before Tinnikkikkik and the others, which left him higher on the rise. Since Ancient Badden was well over a foot taller than the largest of the trolls, he now towered over them even more, looking like an adult in the process of supervising a band of unruly children.

He spoke to the boss, using the troll language and inflection perfectly (for of course, it was magic that gave him the language more so than practice). "You long in come to me. I call to you long ago. Too long."

Tinnikkikkik shook his head obstinately. "Long walk."

"Long time."

"Only twenty suns."

"Twenty suns," Ancient Badden echoed with a sigh and a shake of his head. "In twenty suns I march my army all the way to the big water."

"Not with fight."

"With fight. Twenty suns? I call you. You should be here in five!" Ancient Badden found the troll language, with its minimal use of tense, thoroughly exasperating. It made sense to him, though, for the trolls never seemed to quite grasp the concept of passing time and rarely seemed to think farther ahead than their next step.

"No, long walk," the stubborn boss replied.

It seemed to Ancient Badden that the ugly little creature was gaining confidence with every word. That wouldn't do.

"Too long," the Samhaist said slowly and deliberately.

"No, long walk," the troll replied.

Ancient Badden stood very straight, even seemed to lean back just a bit. His eyes rolled up so that only the white was showing, and he whispered something Tinnikkikkik couldn't make out.

"What?" the troll boss started to ask, but as the ice floor beneath him melted suddenly to water, it came out as "Wha-aaaaaaaaaa!"

Trolls jumped back at the splash, and Tinnikkikkik went right under—which wouldn't have been a serious problem for a glacial troll except that the floor almost immediately refroze as soon as he was fully immersed.

The doomed troll did manage to thrust one hand up, the tip of his longest finger just prodding through the solid floor. And there he hung, stuck in the ice, encapsulated by the magic of Ancient Badden.

The other trolls shrank back, talking excitedly as one, and all terrified more than angry.

"Too long," Ancient Badden said to them, and when he got no response, he said it again, louder.

A hundred troll heads, all pointy ears and thin lips and sharp yellow teeth, began wagging their agreement.

Ancient Badden herded them before him. He would have to appoint a new boss, he knew, and send this force off at once, for there was a town he wanted overrun before the turn to winter, a last excursion by trolls exclusively to let Dame Gwydre and her Abellican playthings understand that there would be no rest through the cold months.

There would be no rest for the folk of Vanguard until they expelled the Abellicans and gave themselves back to the Samhaists.

It was as simple as that, as simple as a troll frozen in ice.

M y coat's not even for fitting me anymore," Bikelbrin grumbled. He shook his shoulders, emphasizing the looseness of his heavy furred overcoat. "Gone all skinny living on that damned lake, I did."

"Too much fish and berries," agreed another of the party of four, a young and muscular dwarf named Ruggirs. "I hate fish and berries."

"All we e'er known," agreed Pergwick, who had been birthed from the heart of the brother of the powrie who had served as the donor for Ruggirs's own Sepulcher— which made Pergwick and Ruggirs true brothers in powrie tradition.

"Ye'll be feasting on good and bloody meat soon enough," Mcwigik assured them. "Enough o' the lake for me. Too much o' the damned lake for me!"

"Aye, but the season's later than ye thinked," Bikelbrin noted. "Long past midsummer and moving to cold fall." He finished with a shiver to accentuate his point, and to remind them all once again that they were ill equipped to handle the cold of the turning season. Mcwigik and Bikelbrin had the coats they had worn in that long-ago expedition that had brought them to Mithranidoon and had rustled up a pair for their two companions. But though the dwarfs had taken great pains to preserve those original garments, the material had frayed and the fur flattened. They were still in sight of Mithranidoon, moving generally south and east, and already the wind nipped at them through the holes in their coats.

They had wrapped their feet in layers of rags but that hardly helped. Toes were tingling, and night had not even fully fallen.

"We'll be needing a fire," Mcwigik remarked, but he ended with a sigh as he considered his words and looked all around, for the landscape, though in full summer bloom, showed little that could be used for such an endeavor. There were a few bushes to be found, though no trees readily available, so the dwarfs broke their march early and began gathering brush. When night came in full, moonless and dark, Mcwigik finally managed to get a fire going. Knowing it wouldn't last long, they piled rocks about the brush. The flames winked out soon after, consuming the meager fuel; warmed stones would have to do. They huddled about the stones and each other, and it wasn't so bad.

But the howling started soon after.

"Wolves," Mcwigik explained to the two younger powries, who had no experience with such creatures.

"They saw our fire," Bikelbrin reasoned. Pergwick and Ruggirs glanced at each other with obvious concern, something the other two didn't miss.

On Mcwigik's orders, they made a cairn of the heated stones and each sat against it facing in a different direction.

"Ye hold yer place," Mcwigik said repeatedly as the howling circled them and the two younger powries appeared as if they would break and run. Every now and then a darker shadow slipped past one or another's field of view, or starlight shining eyes stared at them from not so far away.

"Ye think we've the weapons to beat them?" Bikelbrin asked his friend candidly.

"I got me Prag's axe, and that'll put a dent in a wolf's skull," Mcwigik answered.

Pergwick jumped up suddenly and backed a step, which sent him tumbling over the cairn atop Ruggirs, who similarly scrambled to his feet. Mcwigik was about to scold them, but as he turned he saw the cause of the younger powrie's concern. Not five feet from the cairn, teeth bared, eyes shining, stood a large canine creature.

Mcwigik came past the tumbled two fast and yelled at the wolf, pumping his arm threateningly.

The wolf snapped and barked sharply, and Mcwigik found himself falling back over the other two, who both screamed as the wolf advanced.

But then it yelped as a rock pegged it on the flank, and it ran off.

"I ain't for fighting that!" Pergwick cried.

"So we seen," said Bikelbrin, the rock-thrower.

"Mcwigik fell, too!" Pergwick protested.

"Yach, he just caught me by surprise, he did," Mcwigik said, brushing himself off as if that motion might polish up a bit of his lost dignity. "Ain't fought one in a hundred years and more!"

"A record ye're not to keep for long," Bikelbrin remarked, stepping up beside him, another rock in hand. "The beastie ain't gone far."

More howling ensued, as if on cue.

The four spent many hours on the edge of their wits, jumping at every sound, but no wolves came that close again, though the howls and growls showed that the hungry canines were never far.

And if that wasn't bad enough for the tired and cold group, the rocks cooled long before the night had even reached its midway point, and the wind from the west didn't catch any of Mithranidoon's heated mist.

Gradually, they all drifted off to sleep, but so late into the night that the blazing dawnslight awakened them less than an hour after Pergwick, the last to find slumber, had closed his eyes. Even Bikelbrin, who had been the first to manage sleep, hadn't realized three hours of it.

They all looked to Mcwigik, the chief conspirator in this breakout from Mithranidoon. He certainly didn't appear as boisterous and determined as he had the previous morning when he had led them to the boat and off their island home.

"What're ye thinking?" asked Bikelbrin.

"And how many days're ye saying it's to take us to find the Mirianic?" Pergwick dared interject, drawing a glare from Bikelbrin, though—surprisingly—Mcwigik didn't react at all to the question.

"A month to two, he said," Ruggirs answered. "And each night's to get colder and longer, aye?"

"Not so," Bikelbrin replied. "It ain't like that."

"But generally so," said Pergwick, and Bikelbrin had to concede that point.

"More than a month or two," Ruggirs said.

"But what are ye knowing about it?" Bikelbrin demanded. "Ye never been!"

"But I'm knowing that me toes are hurting, and so're yers," the younger dwarf argued. "And hurtin' toes're meaning slower steps, and slower steps're meaning more steps and more days, and I'm not for thinking . . ."

"We're going back," said Mcwigik, and all three looked at him in surprise.

"We ain't to make it," the chief conspirator said, looking directly at Bikelbrin and shaking his head, his face a mask of disappointment. "We ain't the tools, the weapons, or the clothes. If them wolves don't eat us alive, they'll tear the skin from our frozen bones to be sure."

"The lake's not so bad," said Ruggirs, but no one paid him any heed.

"I'm wanting the smell o' the Mirianic in me nose as much as any powrie alive, don't ye doubt," Mcwigik went on. "But I'm thinking we're dead long before we near the place."

"If we even know where it is," Pergwick dared interject, and so downtrodden was Mcwigik, and so surprised
by the sudden turn was Bikelbrin, that neither argued a
point that would have brought them both to fury only a
day before.

So they gathered their supplies and turned back to the
north, and found their boat shortly after sunset. They returned to the powrie island without any ruckus, without
any questions, but a few of the dwarfs who had known
their plans did offer a superior I-telled-ye-so smirk.

The bitter defeat stayed with Mcwigik for many weeks.

THIRTEEN

Consequences

Brother Giavno grimaced against the line of fiery pain coming from a deep gash across the meat of his upper arm. He had only avoided the brunt of the hurled spear at the last instant, so close a call that it had poignantly reminded Giavno of his mortality, had pulled him from the battle for a few troublesome seconds as he pondered eternity. With great effort and determination, though, the monk had stubbornly held on to the large rock he had carried this far up the chapel's stairs. He stumbled through the upper room's open door and across the small bridge that led to the parapet of the outer wall. Before him monks cried out frantic instructions and scrambled to and fro, trying to avoid the near-constant rain of rocks and spears and other missiles that flew up from below.

Over to the side of the bridge, a pair of brothers worked desperately to dislodge a ladder, the top rung and the tips of its posts visible above the wall. Giavno shuffled as fast as his burden would allow, and didn't even pause to confirm when he arrived, just threw his back against the wall immediately below the ladder posts, then heaved the rock up to his shoulder, and over farther, until it dropped from the wall and tumbled down, guided in its fall by the ladder.

He heard a shout of warning from below, followed by a scream of surprise fast turning to a howl of pain, followed by a crash. Then he dared stand, and turned to look out and regard his work.

A wave of nausea rolled over him, but, as with the pain in his arm, he gritted his teeth and pushed through it. One man lay on the ground, squirming in pain, his legs obviously shattered and his back probably so. He couldn't have been far from the top when Giavno's rock went over, and the more than twenty-foot fall had not been kind.

Kinder than the rock, however, which the lead climber had apparently eluded, but the spotter, or second climber, had not, taking it squarely on the head.

She, too, lay on the ground, but she wasn't squirming, her head split open and her brains splattered about the base of the ladder.

Giavno swallowed hard. This was his first confirmed kill and a woman at that (though Giavno understood that these barbarian women could fight as well as any man he had ever known in the southland). Given the ferocity and determination of the barbarian attack, this first kill would not be Giavno's last.

"Pull it up! Pull it up!" Giavno ordered the other two monks, for the falling rock and falling barbarians had scattered the attackers momentarily. He began to haul, and the others, emboldened by his courage, dared stand up and grab at the sides, hoisting the ladder straight from the ground.

Down below, barbarians rushed back in. One tall man leaped high and managed to grab onto the bottom rungs, and his weight halted the monks' progress.

A fourth brother came to the spot, though, grapnel in hand, and with Giavno's help, they secured it to the third-highest rung. The attached rope strung down to the

small courtyard, feeding into a sturdy cranking mecha-
nism the brothers had constructed to haul large rocks up
from the lower portions of the island. The team down
below went to work immediately, bending their backs
against the poles and methodically walking around the
base, cranking in the rope.

The ladder creaked and groaned in protest, but even
the weight of a second barbarian who had leaped up to
join his companion couldn't suppress the pull. With the
wall acting as a fulcrum, the ladder's top dipped and the
bottom, two men and all, raised up and out from the wall
base. Their feet soon fully ten feet from the ground, the
two barbarians stubbornly held on, with more barbarians
rushing over and leaping up to secure them by the legs
and feet. The sheer human ballast countered the crank
and the ladder held steady, three rungs over the wall top,
the rest suspended outside the chapel.

Only momentarily, however, for the ladder snapped
apart under the awkward strain, dropping the barbarians
in a heap.

"Now!" cried a monk far to Giavno's right, and he
turned to regard the men there on the wall. Using the distraction of the commotion outside, they sprang up as one
and hurled a volley of stones down at the piled barbarians, scoring many solid hits. The Alpinadoran attackers
at the base of the wall withered under the barrage, their
formations breaking apart and many of them retreating.
They had just started to reorganize when a bolt of lightning blasted out of a lower window—Father De Guilbe's
work, no doubt.

That proved enough to shatter the attackers' sensibilities, and they ran off as one, though even under that terrible assault, they did not leave a single barbarian behind,
not even the woman Giavno had killed and another felled
by De Guilbe's lightning bolt.

Brother Giavno spun about and slumped down, putting his back against the cool stone of the parapet. They
had won the day, he knew, but he understood, too, that

this would be only the first of many such days. The brothers did not have near the firepower to break out of their chapel against so large a force, and the barbarians didn't seem to be going anywhere anytime soon. Indeed, the size of their force had confirmed the monks' worst fears: that the many barbarian tribes of Mithranidoon had come together in common cause—something that had been unthinkable only a few hours before.

The brothers and their servants were badly outnumbered here, and every rock and every spear they had thrown at the attackers was one less they'd have at their disposal in the next round.

"Father De Guilbe has asked for you," a monk who appeared at the opening back in the main keep informed Giavno.

The weary brother nodded and hauled himself up from the stone. He glanced back at the distant barbarians to see them setting up large tents down by the beach before the dozens of boats that had brought them here.

From the top of the wall above the main gate to the small chapel compound, Cormack stared out at the bloodstains. Not so far away, he could see the hair and pieces of scalp of one unfortunate Alpinadoran who had caught a rock on the head. A woman, he had been told by one of the other brothers.

He couldn't see in much detail from this distance, but the small tuft of hair blowing in the gentle wind could well have been Milkeila's.

The monk resisted the urge to throw up. She could be lost to him forever. She could lie dead at the beach, her head split apart. Because she had been out there, he was certain, standing strong among her kin, standing determined that the imprisonment of the three men would not hold.

Father De Guilbe was wrong, Cormack knew in his heart and soul. To proselytize in the name of Blessed

Abelle was a good thing, but not like this, not under penalty of a dungeon cell. Even if the men in captivity agreed to recant their own faith and follow the ways of Abelle, even if they came to do so with all their hearts and souls, it would be a hollow gain for the Church, and certainly not worth this fighting.

Cormack put his arm up on the stone railing and rested his chin in the crook of his elbow, staring helplessly at the distant tuft of hair, hoping and praying that it was not Milkeila's.

But even if his prayers were answered, it would do little to mitigate the realization that at least one woman, young and strong and full of pride and certainty to match Giavno's own, had died this day who should not have.

Not over this.

"Brother Cormack!" He knew Giavno's voice all too well these days. He slowly turned to face the man, trying to keep his agitation off his face.

"The fight has ended," Giavno said from the keep's main door, some twenty feet back of the main gate on the surrounding wall. "Be quick to your work. We need water to wash our wounds."

Cormack motioned toward Giavno's torn upper arm. "Have you been tended?"

"I go to Father De Guilbe," the man replied, though his voice softened in response to Cormack's honest and obvious concern. "He will use a soul stone."

"Quickly," Cormack bade him. Giavno nodded and disappeared inside the keep.

He is a good man, Cormack reminded himself. Despite his current anger at Giavno over the barbarian prisoners, despite his rage that it had come to this—a prolonged and lethal battle and siege—Cormack understood that Giavno's heart was good.

But the man's thoughts were misplaced. And if "good" men could precipitate this kind of foolish and worthless slaughter, then . . . The thought made Cormack grimace.

He pulled himself up and noted the commotion inside the courtyard that surrounded the main keep, where brothers ran to and fro to shore up the wall in places where it had been damaged, or where the work on it had never been good enough to begin with. Truly even he had to appreciate the efforts of the Abellican contingent, no matter his feelings regarding their current choices and mission, for the work on this chapel fortress was remarkable to behold. They had built a circular tower keep, easily the tallest structure on the lake at more than thirty feet, and when the battling had begun those two years ago, the brothers had constructed, and so quickly, the surrounding wall, a dozen feet high in places like Cormack's present position, the front gate, but more than twenty feet high in other areas. A series of bridges had been fashioned to traverse to those higher areas from inside the upper stories of the keep, allowing the brothers to bring in reserves quickly and efficiently wherever they might be needed.

This had been the first true battle where the enemy had come against them in such numbers and with such ferocity, and it seemed to Cormack that the fortress had held up amazingly well.

He scrambled down to the ground and went around to the left side of the tower, to a small and square supplementary building. From there, he opened a bulkhead and headed down a natural tunnel that had been widened by the monks, with stairs carved into the slippery and downward-sloping stone. He passed a side tunnel leading to the prisoners' dungeon, and grimaced as he heard the shaman of the trio chanting loudly, in open defiance.

They knew of the fighting, Cormack realized. They knew that their people had come for them.

Cormack pulled a torch from its wall sconce and hustled along, past another corridor and down another descent, at last coming to a heavy door barred on his side with three separate iron poles. He opened two smaller hatchways on the door—one for him to peer through and a second that allowed him to thrust his torch into the cave beyond before going in. The flickering of that torchlight amplified many times over once it had passed through the portal, for this cave sat at the base of the island, just above the water level, and the floor of its lower reaches was the lake itself.

The quick check before opening the door was more a ritual than actual security, for the brothers had done well to secure that cave as well, building a gridwork gate that allowed the fish to enter but kept out anything larger, like the fast-swimming glacial trolls.

The warmth of the misty air washed over Cormack when he opened the door, and the smell in this cave was particularly thick with fish, for the monks had been down here angling extensively in preparation for what they knew to be a siege, and they had cleaned their catch at the water's edge and thrown the scraps back in to attract more fish and the common crabs.

Cormack welcomed that warmth, and the smell, hoping that he would lose himself in the heavy sensations and forget the horrific battle he had just witnessed. If he had been able to do that, he would have lingered for some time down in this sanctuary.

But he filled several waterskins and headed right back out, and in his mind he still heard the screams, and the smell of fish had not replaced the smell of death.

They will come again," Father De Guilbe said to Brother Giavno. "And again after that. Stubborn lot."

"Foolish lot," said Giavno. "Our walls are too strong!"

"I appreciate your confidence, Brother," said De Guilbe, "but we both understand that our enemies will adapt their tactics accordingly. In this first exchange we had several wounded, yourself among them."

"It is just a scratch," Giavno protested. He turned his arm, presenting it to De Guilbe. Soul stone in hand, the father pressed his fingers against the wound and began praying to Blessed Abelle.

The warmth permeated Giavno's body, as comforting as the arms of a lover. In that magical embrace he wondered how these idiot barbarians could not understand the beauty that was Abelle. Why would they, why would anyone, not embrace the power and goodness that could afford such wondrous magic as this? Why would anyone not appreciate such healing and utility, and with the promise of everlasting life beyond this mortal coil?

He closed his eyes and let the warmth flow through his body. He could understand the hesitance of the Samhaists, perhaps, for an embrace of Abelle would rob them of their tyrannical power hold. But not these barbarians of Alpinador—well, other than their shamans. For the average Alpinadoran, Blessed Abelle offered everything. And yet, they had rejected the monks at every turn. The men in the dungeon would rather be killed than accept Abelle! And it wasn't just because one of them was a shaman of some high standing, Giavno knew. The other two were just as stubborn and unyielding.

But why?

"What is troubling you, Brother?" Father De Guilbe said, drawing Giavno from his contemplation.

Giavno opened his eyes and only then realized that the healing session was long over, that he was holding his arm up high before him for no reason at all. He cleared his throat and straightened before the father. "I told you that it was but a minor wound," he said.

"What is it?" De Guilbe pressed. "Does such battle leave an evil taste in your mouth?"

"No, I mean, well, yes, Father," Giavno stuttered. "It seems nonsensical to me that the barbarians would throw themselves against our fortifications over such a matter. Their companions are alive only through our work with the gemstones—they cannot deny that truth. And all that we have asked in return is the acceptance of the source of that healing magic by those three."

Father De Guilbe spent a long moment staring at his second. "You have heard of the Battle of Cordon Roe?"

Giavno nodded numbly at the preposterous question. How could anyone, let alone any Abellican, not know that cursed name? Cordon Roe was a street in Delaval City where the word of Blessed Abelle first came to the great city at the mouth of the river. The first monks of Blessed Abelle in that most populous center had set up their chapel (though it was really no more than a two-story house) on Cordon Roe and preached the words of faith.

"What do you know of Cordon Roe, Brother?"

"I know that the brothers who traveled there were well received by the people of Delaval City," Giavno answered. "Their services quickly came to encompass the entirety of the street, and on some days the surrounding avenues were clogged with onlookers."

"It was a promising start in the early days of our Church, yes?"

"Of course."

"Too promising," said Father De Guilbe. "Blessed Abelle had sent the priests to that largest city in Honce not long after the word of Chapel Abelle had arrived there. They were granted entrance by the Laird Delaval, our current Laird Delaval's grandfather, if memory serves me correctly, and indeed he proved to be their first patient, the first recipient of gemstone magic in the city, as he was afflicted with some minor but aggravating malady. So Laird Delaval granted them access and allowed them their prayers and their practices. And the people responded, as we know most will to Blessed Abelle once they have felt the power of the gemstones."

"And that angered the Samhaists," Giavno said.

Father De Guilbe nodded solemnly. "And threatened Laird Delaval himself," he explained. "And so was the garrison of Delaval City turned upon our brethren, and Cordon Roe became a fortress within that fortress city."

"Every brother knows of this."

"But do you know that the father of Cordon Roe brokered a deal with Laird Delaval to allow the brothers safe egress from the city?"

"I had not heard of that," Giavno admitted.

"It is not common knowledge. The story goes that the Samhaists inspired the mob of the city to descend upon Cordon Roe, and the brothers of Abelle, refusing to use the gemstone magic to kill their attackers, were overrun and murdered."

"Yes, all ten!"

"No, Brother. It did not happen like that. The brothers brokered a deal with Laird Delaval, but as they were preparing to leave he came to them with altered terms. They could leave or they could stay, but they must renounce Blessed Abelle and embrace the Samhaist creed. Under those conditions, no further penalty would be exacted upon them."

Brother Giavno's eyes widened with horror as he considered the awful price. He licked his suddenly dry lips and said, "And they refused, and so Laird Delaval's forces overran them?"

"They refused, and unwilling to kill in the name of Abelle they killed themselves, all ten, and a hundred of their peasant followers committed suicide as well, robbing Laird Delaval and the Samhaists—most importantly, the Samhaists!—from claiming victory at Cordon Roe. Pity their fate not at all, Brother, for their action, their ultimate dedication to their faith, broke Laird Delaval's heart. Within five years another contingent from Blessed Abelle arrived in Delaval City, this one invited by the laird himself, and with promises that they could practice their faith unhindered by him or by the Samhaists."

Brother Giavno swallowed hard, trying to digest it all.

"They killed themselves rather than renounce Blessed

Abelle," Father De Guilbe explained. "And we name them as heroes. Now we face barbarians who do the same, and you would name them as foolish?"

"Your pardon—" Giavno started, but De Guilbe continued over him.

"The three downstairs are not so unlike our long-lost brethren, though of course they are misguided in their faith. Do not begrudge them their stubbornness, Brother, for if the roles were reversed I would expect of myself, and of you, no less dedication. Death is not our master. That is the promise of Abelle. Our . . . guests hold faith in a similar promise, no doubt, as do those who line up against us and throw themselves at our wall. There are many reasons to die, some good and some not so reasonable. This is a good one, I think, and so do the barbarians, and so we know they will come on again and again after that. I respect them for their dedication. I will respect them even as I kill them."

"Of course, Father," said a humbled Giavno, and he lowered his gaze to the floor.

"This is not Cordon Roe," De Guilbe went on, his voice growing stronger and more deliberate. "And we of the Abellican Order have grown stronger and more secure in our faith. We will hold these walls, whatever the cost to our enemies. With the Covenant of God's Year Thirty, there are no restrictions regarding our own defense placed upon us as were upon our lost brethren of Cordon Roe."

"What do you mean?"

"You witnessed my lightning blast?"

"Yes."

"When the barbarians come at us again, we will return their stones and arrows with a barrage of magic that will shake the waters of Mithranidoon!" Father De Guilbe asserted. "If we kill a dozen, a score, a hundred, so be it. Chapel Isle will not fall to the unbelievers. We are here and we are staying, and the men in our dungeon will remain there, will rot there, as the bodies of their kin will rot on the rocks before our walls. No quarter, Brother. Mercy is for the deserving, and unlike our lost brethren of Cordon Roe, we are not docile. We are warriors of Abelle, and woe to our enemies."

Outside of Father De Guilbe's door, Brother Cormack leaned back against the stone wall and put his head in his hands. The rousing speech had Giavno and the attendants in the room cheering, and that applause, that vicious affirmation of the elevation of the Brothers of Abelle above all others, tore a hole in Cormack's heart.

He thought of Milkeila, and pictured her lying dead on the stones.

He left the bucket of water right there outside the door and rushed back to his own tiny room, where he prayed for guidance, all the while almost hoping that a spear would find his heart in the opening moments of the next attack.

FOURTEEN

No Choice to Be Found

After an uneventful and swift sail through the gulf, the growing late-summer westerlies filling her sails, *Lady Dreamer* slid into dock at Pireth Vanguard, the oldest Honce settlement in the land of the same name. Callen, Cadayle, and Bransen stood at the bow, watching the boat glide into place beside the long wharf.

"We'll find him," Bransen whispered quietly, his hand about the soul stone in his small belt pouch, his other hand clutching Cadayle's. In response Cadayle gave a comforting squeeze.

"And you'll get your answers, and some peace," said Callen. "None are more deserving of that."

"We will get off first, ahead of the commotion," Cadayle decided.

"Begging your pardon, good lady . . . ladies and sir, but Captain McKeege would see you in his cabin," came a voice behind them, turning them, all three (for Bransen, in his surprise, swung about, and not awkwardly), to face a young sailor they recognized as *Lady Dreamer*'s cabin boy, nicknamed Dungwalker by the uncouth crew.

"Shouldn't he be out here directing the docking?" Callen asked.

Dungwalker shrugged. "Any on the boat can do it. Captain's in his cabin, and he sent me to find you and tell you."

"Lead on, then," said Cadayle, and to her two companions she offered a dismissive shrug. "Meet with him here or out in the town. It's all the same."

They followed the cabin boy to the captain's quarters, located under the flying bridge at the rear of the top deck. Dawson was alone inside waiting for them with an opened bottle of rum and four metal cups set out on his desk.

"Fair seas," he said in greeting when they came in, the cabin boy taking his leave and closing the door behind them. "As fine a sail as we could have hoped for at any time of the year."

He motioned for them to sit at the three chairs he had placed in front of his desk. As the two women helped Bransen, Cadayle noted a curious-looking smirk on Dawson's face. She wasn't sure what it might portend, but somehow it seemed out of place to her.

"I hoped you would join me for a drink," Dawson explained when they had settled in. He poured some rum in his own cup, which already contained some, Cadayle noticed, and then in Callen's and Cadayle's. He paused, holding the bottle over the cup set before Bransen.

"Better that you don't," Callen remarked. Dawson nodded and pulled the bottle back, then dropped into his chair.

"To good friends," he said, lifting his cup.

"To finding Brother Dynard," Cadayle added before she tapped it.

"Dynard, yes," Dawson agreed after he had sipped. "I'm not sure which chapel, but they'll know at Pellinor."

"A long journey?" asked Callen. "If it is, we should secure a wagon for Bransen."

"A journey of two weeks, and one I'll make with the others. We'll take you three as far as Tanadoon, a small town just a few miles inland. They've many new houses waiting for folks, any folks, to take them. We will be putting the few families of our new soldiers there, too. So you'll have neighbors among some of the folk you've met on our journey, and all of you with your own houses and large plots of land." He gave a little laugh and explained, "Aye, we've got more wood for more houses than we've people to put in them! Here's to hoping you come to love this land as I do. It's a hard life, but one worth living, to be sure, and Vanguard would welcome the addition of such fine folk as yourselves." He lifted his cup again in toast, but he was alone this time.

"I do not know that my husband could manage it," Cadayle said.

"Of course," Dawson replied, and again Cadayle caught a flash of that strange, too-knowing smile. "I should be quick then in my search that we can get you three, and maybe Brother Dynard, back across the gulf before the winter snows."

"That would be good, yes," said Cadayle, drawing a poke from Callen.

"Don't be so ungrateful, daughter," Callen scolded.

"Everyone grows impatient when his grasp nears the goal," Dawson said with a grin. "No steps as desperate as the last three to the gate, eh?"

The procession of more than a hundred people, including most of Dawson's crew and a garrison from Pireth Vanguard, set out later that same day down the road, no more than a flattened trail, to the new town of Tanadoon.

New indeed! The smell of freshly cut wood greeted the caravan as they entered the southeastern gate of the wood-walled village. Neat and tidy houses all in a row greeted them inside, all looking very much the same. A few were occupied by families who had resettled from within Vanguard, but most sat empty and waiting.

"As you were promised," Dawson called out when all of the folk were inside. "Even you men who have no kinfolk with you can claim a home as your own—two men to each, if you've not family, please. Though you'll not be staying beyond this one night. But know in your hearts that you've a place to return to when your debt to Dame Gwydre is paid."

There was no cheer at that, which surprised Cadayle as she surveyed the dour bunch. Most of them were prisoners of Laird Delaval, a few from Laird Ethelbert, and none seemed overly pleased to be here.

The trio found a small home soon enough, settling in under the shadow of the northeastern corner. It was sparsely furnished, but had enough straw for them to make comfortable enough beds, and Dawson's men brought a fair number of supplies—foodstuffs and barrels of water and even a rough map of the area that included directions to a nearby stream.

"It is not so bad," Callen announced later that evening, the three sitting about a single candle, sharing a loaf of sweet cake. "All of it, I mean. The house and the food and the welcome of our hosts. A good and generous man is Dawson McKeege."

"Too much so I fear," said Cadayle, but Callen scoffed at her and waved the suspicions away.

The next morning, the men who had come to serve Dame Gwydre marched out of town for distant battles, a few leaving wives and children behind, totaling a score of folk or so to add to the like number already settled in Tanadoon and the handful of sentries patrolling the town's wall. The village had been built to hold near to three hundred people easily, but there couldn't have been a quarter of that number left after Dawson marched.

"I'll return presently with word of Bran Dynard for

you," Dawson promised Bransen from atop his small chestnut stallion. He tipped his cap to Cadayle, then more assuredly and boldly to Callen (which made Cadayle blink more than once as she regarded her mother!), then cantered out to the head of the military line, and out through the same gate they had entered the afternoon before.

"I hate the waiting," Bransen whispered.

"He'll be back as soon as he can," Callen assured him with surprising confidence, drawing another blink from Cadayle.

"Mother?" she asked.

"He's a good man," Callen answered. With that she spun away and practically skipped into their chosen house.

"She's taken a liking to Vanguard," Bransen said dryly.

"It is a difficult place for the Stork," Cadayle replied, stealing his mirth.

Bransen turned on her. "Every place is difficult for the Stork," he said, trying hard to keep his voice low so that he would not jeopardize his disguise. Clearly agitated, that was no easy chore!

"I know," said Cadayle. "The sooner we are out of the reach of Ethelbert or Delaval or any of them, the better."

"We should have found a way to Behr instead of coming north," Bransen lamented, and turned away, feigning a stumble as a couple of other "townsfolk" walked by.

"We seek answers, so we go where the questions lead us," Cadayle replied. "Now it is Vanguard, but perhaps we are not so far from Behr as you believe. Dawson has been there several times, to a city he called Jacintha. The sail takes the whole of a season, but it is one he's made before and promises to make again."

Bransen quieted at that and seemed to Cadayle to relax quite a bit. She helped him back into the house, where they would spend the next few days anxiously awaiting Dawson's return with the word, as promised.

He came in with little fanfare but great commotion at the end of the next week, surrounded by a score and more of soldiers, including several of the men who had sailed north with Bransen, Cadayle, and Callen. Most of his entourage, though, was of longtime Vanguardsmen, all toughened by years of battle. The way they rode, the way they dismounted, the way their weapons came easily to their hands, spoke volumes of that.

"A fine morning made finer by the sight of you," Dawson said when the trio came out to greet him. He stayed up on his horse, as did the armed and armored warriors flanking him, several to either side.

Bransen stuttered to say something, but lurched suddenly and appeared as if he would have fallen had not Callen and Cadayle grabbed him at the last minute (in a perfectly choreographed maneuver).

"You need not do that," Dawson said.

"Well we're not to let him fall on his face now, are we?" asked Callen.

"I meant that he did not need to do that," Dawson explained, and all three looked at him curiously. "You, Bransen Garibond. There is no need to wear your mask of the cripple here."

Bransen stuttered and drooled, and he wasn't faking, for he had let go of the gemstone.

"Do not mock my husband!" Cadayle retorted.

"Your husband, the Highwayman?" asked Dawson.

"I know not what you mean," Cadayle said, and she straightened Bransen, steadying him on his feet, before taking a resolute step toward Dawson. "Have you come here to mock us? You promised us news of Brother Bran Dynard. . . ."

"He is dead."

That stole Cadayle's momentum, and Bransen let out a little squeal, as if he had been punched in the gut.

"I am sorry—truly," said Dawson, and he seemed sincere despite the confusing atmosphere here. "Bran Dynard died on the road more than twenty years ago on his way to Chapel Abelle. He never made it. The brothers think it was a powrie attack, which seems likely as the Holdings were at relative peace in those times, but powries remained thick about the land."

"Dead?" Bransen mumbled. He thought of the Book of Jhest, his salvation, and it seemed so incongruous to him that the man who had penned that magnificent work could have been killed so senselessly on the road so long ago. *The man who had penned it,* he mused, and he realized that he was referring to his father. He didn't know how to feel, or what to feel; nothing made sense to him at that stunning moment of revelation. He wanted to deny Dawson's claims, but wasn't even sure if his desire to do so was because the man had penned the book and might have some answers for him, or because the man was his father.

His father! Dead! Bransen was not as surprised as he would have guessed. So long, no word. A man he had never known. Would never know.

"How did you discover this?" Cadayle demanded. Suddenly she seemed to be stuttering almost as much as her husband, and that fact alone drew Bransen from his emotional jumble.

"The brothers told me back at Chapel Abelle."

"You lied to us!" said Cadayle. Next to her Callen let out a little shriek, covering her mouth in horror.

"I did and I admit it, but I did it for your own good," Dawson calmly replied. "And stop your lurching and drooling, man! Did you really believe that you could travel the length and breadth of the land in such an obvious guise? Word was run to every chapel in Honce to beware the man they called the Stork, for he slew Laird Prydae and left Pryd Holding in turmoil."

"That is a lie!" said Cadayle.

"Please, good lady, I am not your judge," said Dawson, and now he did dismount, though several of the fearsome guards around him bristled at the movement. "Nor did the brothers of Chapel Abelle wish to pass judgment. But they would have had no choice—indeed, they thought they had no choice. But I offered them one of mutual benefit."

"Liar!"

"And your husband's alive because of it!"

"Enough!" Bransen said, startling them all with the sudden power in his voice.

For a few moments all held quiet, then Dawson bowed low and said, "Welcome, Highwayman. Your reputation precedes you."

Bransen stared at him hard.

"If I had said nothing, if I had left you there, the brothers of Chapel Abelle would have taken you in chains and handed you to the nearest laird faithful to Laird Delaval. They wished no such thing, but they were bound, surely so. You can understand that."

Bransen didn't reply, didn't move at all.

"You were passed on the road by Brother Fatuus from the Chapel of Precious Memories of Palmaristown," Dawson explained. "He arrived bearing news of the Stork, the Highwayman. They watched your approach before you ever neared Weatherguard. I offered them a deal, for your sake, for my dame's benefit, and to relieve the brothers of their regrettable duty."

"To take me here to fight in your dame's war," Bransen reasoned.

Dawson shrugged sheepishly. "We are in desperate need of strong warriors, and as I said, your reputation preceded you. The acting steward of Pryd Holding warned all of your prowess with the blade. You are a deadly sort, I am told."

"I want no part of your war," said Bransen, and Cadayle grabbed his arm tightly.

"There is no choice to be found, I fear," said Dawson. "You have nowhere to go, nor do your beautiful companions."

"You threaten them?" Bransen growled. The soldiers stepped their mounts in closer.

"Our fight is a good one," said Dawson. "Not like the meaningless slaughter in the South. We battle goblins and glacial trolls, evil little brutes, all. And heathen barbarian murderers, who steal in at night and slaughter our children in their sleep. We battle Samhaists, and I have heard you have no love for them, either."

"You seem to hear a lot."

"True enough," Dawson said, and he bowed, turning the sarcasm into a compliment. "I regret my lie, and I humbly apologize. Without it you would be long dead by now, your beautiful wife widowed, but still the need to so lie left a sour taste in my mouth. But that lie is irrelevant now, for the deed is done."

"Just let us leave," said Bransen.

"To go where?"

"Anywhere that is not here."

"Will you swim across the gulf, then? Or run west all the way around it, through wild lands where monsters and hungry hunting cats and bears are thicker than the trees? Be reasonable. There is no choice to be found."

"We will find a boat sailing south to Honce. Or to Behr, even."

"None will leave before the winter's end."

"Then we will wai . . ."

"Enough!" said Dawson, his visage suddenly hardening. He quickly mounted his steed. "Enough, Highwayman. You are fairly caught, and already convicted in the South, where the sentence would be death. I offer you this alternative. You will march with Dame Gwydre's forces—many of the same men who shared your boat ride to Pireth Vanguard—in a goodly campaign. We are desperate here. I am not asking you for this service."

"Meaning?"

"Meaning that if you refuse your life is forfeit."

Bransen narrowed his eyes and squared his shoulders.

"And so are the lives of your companions."

If Dawson had spun his horse about and prompted it

to kick Bransen in the face, the impact would have been no less staggering.

"How dare you!" Bransen demanded, but Dawson tugged his horse around and began walking it away, and the mounted guards pressed in on Bransen and the two women in his wake.

"Say your good-byes to them, Highwayman," Dawson insisted. "We leave now. Serve us well through the winter campaign. If we fight back the Samhaist horde, you will be returned, and all crimes forgiven. I offer you passage anywhere in the world *Lady Dreamer* can take you." He stopped his horse and turned about, locking stares with the fuming Bransen. "That is the best offer you will ever get, Highwayman. I can legally have my soldiers kill you, and them, right now, by order of Dame Gwydre herself. Now gather your things and say your farewells. We've a long ride this night, and a longer one tomorrow."

Not since he had learned of Garibond's execution had Bransen felt such a profound emptiness within him. Lost opportunity, was the only thought he could hear. He didn't know what to feel and then didn't know what to make of that! That confusion brought guilt, and that guilt brought more confusion, and truly, Bransen seemed to be spiraling downward.

Dawson McKeege had duped them so easily! The cage the clever man had built around them, both with soldiers and by simple location, seemed as unbreakable as any Bransen had ever known. He sat in the small house the trio had taken as their own, his back to the door, his soul stone strapped under his black silk bandanna about his forehead.

"We could find our way out through the back window and over the wall," Cadayle said to him as she tied the silk strap about his upper right arm—which was really just an ornament now that his identity was fully revealed. "We'd be gone into the thick forest before Dawson and his men ever knew we'd left."

Bransen shook his head slowly and deliberately. "Gone to where? That forest is without end. Even if you and I could make our way, your mother is not a young woman."

"Then you go out," Cadayle said. "Be gone, Bransen, I beg. You are not for war; your heart is not the heart of a soldier. When you are fighting men—Alpinadorans—who have not wronged you, will you revel in the kill?"

"No choice to be found," Bransen said, echoing Dawson's words.

"Run!" Cadayle begged him.

"And that will leave you and Callen to the mercy of Dame Gwydre. You heard Dawson's warning."

"Dawson will not harm us."

"He will, milady," came Dawson's voice from the doorway. "Regrettably, but certainly."

Bransen narrowed his eyes as he stared at the man. He instinctively grasped the hilt of his fabulous sword at his side. But he could not deny the truth of Dawson's logic, that the monks would have killed him to avoid the wrath of Laird Delaval.

"You do not appreciate our desperation," Dawson went on, walking into the room. "We are pushed to the gulf. Entire villages have been slaughtered by the Samhaist aggressors and their monstrous minions. Entire villages! Women and children and even the animals. I have no love of deceiving you: I feel not clever or happy with the act. But doubt not my words of warning, for your own sake."

He looked at Bransen. "Now," he said. "We go," he announced simply, walking through the door.

Stunned with the sudden turn of events, Cadayle wrapped Bransen in a desperate hug. Callen came over and joined in, the shoulders of both women bobbing with sorrow.

Bransen pushed them back just enough so that he could stand. He kissed Cadayle on the cheek and wiped away her tears, though more were sure to replace them in short order.

"I will return to you," he promised. "Never doubt." With that, Bransen set her back firmly and followed Dawson through the door.

FIFTEEN

Echoes of Cordon Roe

Concentration!" Brother Giavno warned above the tumult of the battle raging again about the chapel's strong walls, which mostly involved crude spears (sharpened sticks) volleying against stones thrown from on high, coupled with a continual exchange of taunts and the incessant thumping of barbarians pounding on the fitted stones with heavy wooden mallets in an amazing attempt to weaken the integrity of the fortification. "It is most important, to your very survival."

The two younger monks looked at each other with obvious concern—and why should they not? For they were about to go into the middle of the barbarian attackers!

"Brother Faldo, you must maintain the power of the serpentine," Giavno repeated yet again. "At all costs! Accept a spear to your chest, but do not allow the magic of that gem to dissipate!"

Faldo rested the huge and surprisingly lightweight shield on one shoulder and nodded sheepishly. Behind him, the other young volunteer, Brother Moorkris, moved closer and took his companion's hand and together they shuffled for the secret door set in the wall, just to the side of the main fighting. Moorkris held out his open palm toward Giavno, as he had been instructed, and Giavno nodded for Faldo to enact the serpentine shield.

A moment later, a blue-white glow encompassed both young monks, and Giavno gave promising Brother Moorkris a ruby, the stone of fire.

"Charge into them," he whispered, and he nodded to the pair working the door.

It opened fast and Giavno shoved the two terrified young brothers out, then fell back through the door quickly and spun about, throwing his back against the stone. He knew they wouldn't long hold their nerve.

And he was right, for the pair had barely moved from the outside of the door before the barbarians took note of them. Faldo did well to keep low behind his shield and to keep his thoughts on the serpentine, maintaining the magical protection. A spear hit the shield, then a second, but this was of barbarian make, woven of thin wood into layers behind a leather front, and those weapons did not get through the clever tangle.

But the Alpinadorans didn't hesitate in the least and charged right in, and Faldo got rammed hard as a shoulder slammed against his shield, sending him lurching back and nearly upending him.

To his credit, he maintained the serpentine barrier, but the jolt broke his grip with his companion just as Moorkris sent his energy through the ruby and conjured a tremendous fireball.

With the connection to Faldo broken, Moorkris had no protection from his own blast, and like the poor barbarians caught in the area of conflagration, he was engulfed in his own flames.

It was all screaming and burning and shouting then, and Brother Faldo, confused and dazed and having no idea of where to turn next, stumbled back through the smoke toward the door. He felt someone punch him in the back, but he managed to stagger through, and Giavno and the others quickly shut and secured the portal behind him.

"I held the barrier," the devastated young brother started to explain, blubbering through his mounting guilt as he came to understand that his failure to hold on had immolated his friend Moorkris. He couldn't finish the thought, though, as he just fell over, for that punch in the back was not a punch at all, but a spear that had driven deep into his kidney.

"Get him to Father De Guilbe," Giavno yelled at the other two, and he rushed for a ladder that would take him up to the parapets. When he got there, he found that his comrades were no longer raining stones on the attackers, and when he peered over the wall, he understood.

For the Alpinadorans were running off, and just below Giavno no less than seven bodies—whether men or women, he could hardly tell—either lay very still or writhed on the ground in mortal agony, their clothing melted to their blistered and bubbling skin. He recognized the monk he had sent out there by the shape of the still-burning robes, and his instinct to run out and retrieve Brother Moorkris lasted only the heartbeat it took him to realize that the young and promising young Abellican was already dead.

With a heavy heart and a heavy sigh, Brother Giavno started for Father De Guilbe's quarters, praying that Brother Faldo, at least, would survive.

He paused at a group of several brothers, all staring hard at the gruesome scene below. "Go out through the secret door and see if any of our enemies can be saved. Be quick about it, and return at first sign that their companions are coming after you."

He thought that an insignificant command, easily followed and without consequence—other than perhaps the notion one or two of their charred enemies might be pulled from the grip of death. But he could not have been more wrong, for as soon as the brothers moved out to the writhing wounded, the barbarian forces from across the way howled and charged with fury beyond anything Giavno could have anticipated. The monks made it safely back inside, with one grievously wounded Alpinadoran warrior in tow, but they had to secure the door fast, and calls for renewed support along the parapets rang out almost immediately thereafter.

For the Alpinadorans came on with abandon, throwing themselves against the stone, smashing at it and seeming not to care about the rain of stones that came down upon them.

"Bolster that portal!" Giavno cried, and nearly as many brothers had to work at piling stones behind the battered secret door as were up on the walls trying to repel the attackers.

Of the three fights so far, that battle was the most lopsided, with another handful of barbarians dead, and several more badly wounded, and not a monk seriously injured.

But for Giavno, that last battle was the most unnerving of all, the one that told him in his heart of hearts that these enemies who had come against Chapel Isle were willing to die to a man and woman to retrieve their brethren.

He had never seen such ferocious dedication.

Nor had Cormack, who had watched it all—the fireball, the retrieval, the second wave of wild assault—with horror. "We cannot win," Cormack muttered many times during and after that second battle, for only then did he understand, truly understand, what "winning" might mean.

He saw Brother Giavno hustling toward De Guilbe's door shortly thereafter, and thought to follow and plead with them to abandon this madness.

But his feet would not move to the commands of his

brain. He had no heart for another round of verbal battle with those two.

The three monks stood in a line, side by side, in De Guilbe's office, facing the father and Brother Giavno, who stood before the first, demanding his report.

"They are not eating," the young monk sheepishly replied to Giavno's question.

At the other end of that short line, Brother Cormack winced at every word. He knew it to be true. Androosis and the others would not eat—not a morsel. The captured shaman had decreed that they would die before acceding to the wishes of their wretched captors.

"Then make them eat," Giavno said to the man, who retreated a step from the sheer intensity of the senior brother's angry tone.

"We have," he stammered in reply. "We held them and forced food and water into their mouths. Most they spit back."

"But they got some," Giavno reasoned. "That is good. Their bodies will likely outlast their determination."

"Likely," Cormack mouthed under his breath.

"When we returned to them the next day, they were covered in vomit," the young monk explained.

Giavno glanced back at Father De Guilbe and gave a disgusted sigh. "Bind them more tightly," he ordered as he turned back to face the young monk. "That they cannot get their fingers down their throats."

"Yes, Brother," the young monk answered, lowering his gaze.

"The fourth has been placed with them?" Father De Guilbe asked, referring to the barbarian who had been caught in Brother Moorkris's fireball. The man would carry horrible scars for the rest of his life, but through the miracle of the gemstone magic, his life had been saved.

"Not yet, Father," the monk replied. "Brother Mn'Ache fears that his wounds will fester if he is laid in the dirt."

"Then put a blanket under him," Giavno intervened, and from Father De Guilbe's nod, Cormack could see that the man was of like mind.

"He recovers well, and should be ready for the dungeon in . . ." the young monk tried to explain, but Giavno cut him short.

"He recovers in the dungeon or he recovers not at all. I will not have a dangerous enemy in our midst when again his people attack. Would you have him climb out of his cot and murder Brother Mn'Ache while he was distracted at tending one of us?"

"He is bound."

"Now, Brother," Giavno ordered. "To the dungeon with him. Be gone!"

The young monk hesitated for just a moment, then whirled about and sprinted away.

"It is an unpleasant business," Father De Guilbe admitted. "Hold faith, all of you. Keep in mind that our Brother Mn'Ache was able to save two lives during the night, that of the burned barbarian and that of Brother Faldo."

"Brother Faldo is not yet awake," Giavno replied. "Nor is Brother Mn'Ache certain that he will recover."

"He will," said De Guilbe with a confident smile, and he motioned for Giavno to move along.

The next monk in the line, the one standing right beside Cormack, offered details on the work at shoring up the walls and cutting stones and the like to hurl down at the barbarians. With confidence he assured, "They will not breach our defenses."

The assertion was ridiculous, of course, and spoken more as a cheer than a proper evaluation, but it seemed to satisfy the inquisitor brothers, for Giavno patted the monk on the shoulder and moved to stand before Brother Cormack.

"The water supply is inexhaustible," Cormack reported

with a shrug before Gaivno could even inquire, as if to ask of Giavno why they bothered to bring him to these meetings. His only oversight was that of supplying water and fish, after all.

"And the fish?"

"The lake is full of them. They come to our hidden pond to feed, and are not so hard to catch."

"Triple the catch," Father De Guilbe unexpectedly interjected.

"Father?" Cormack asked.

"Triple—at least," the man answered. "Our barbarian enemies will not relent, but they will pay too heavy a price to continue throwing themselves at our wall, I am sure. They will look for other ways to strike at us, and if they come to understand that we have this inexhaustible resource at our disposal, they might try to interrupt it. That, we cannot have."

"Yes, Father," Cormack said.

"On your travels to the pond, do you look in on our guests?" De Guilbe asked.

Cormack shrugged noncommittally.

"You are not prohibited from doing so," Father De Guilbe prompted.

"Sometimes," Cormack admitted.

"And it is as was described here?"

"They will not eat," Cormack admitted, and the floodgates opened then. "They grow weak. There is no bend in them, Father. They will not recant their beliefs and embrace ours—not at the price of their very lives—"

"Cordon Roe," Father De Guilbe interrupted, aiming the remark at Brother Giavno, who nodded, and Cormack grimaced at the reference.

If De Guilbe could see that apt analogy, then why would he insist on keeping the Alpinadorans as prisoners? For the end result would be their deaths or continued misery—how could it be otherwise?

Cormack wanted to shout those questions at these

two monks, but the door swung open and the same monk who had just left to fetch the burned Alpinadoran and bring him to the dungeon burst in.

"A messenger!" he cried, clearly out of breath. "At the front gate. A messenger from our enemies approaches."

"Bring him in?" Brother Giavno asked of De Guilbe, who thought about it for a few heartbeats, then shook his head.

"No, he will learn too much of our inner defenses," the leader decided. "Let us go to him and greet him at the wall instead."

He started out immediately, Giavno beside him, and Cormack and the others, having not been ordered to stay behind, swept into their wake.

As soon as he climbed the ladder to the parapet above the chapel's gate, Cormack realized he was looking at one, if not the, leader of the barbarians of Yossunfier. The man was a shaman, obviously, for he wore the same ornamental necklaces as Milkeila, only grander by far, with his loose clothing decorated with shells and other trinkets, so that they rattled with his every step. He was old, well into his sixth decade of life, at least, and Milkeila had told Cormack enough about Alpinadoran society for him to understand that age was no small matter in the hierarchy of the tribes.

"I am Teydru," he said, his voice clear and strong, and Cormack sucked in his breath, for he had indeed heard that name before, and knew then that he was standing before the absolute spiritual leader of Milkeila's people.

"You come uninvited to this place, Teydru," Father De Guilbe replied rather curtly. It seemed even more snappish and stilted due to the man's lack of command of the common Alpinadoran language.

"You have three of my people," Teydru went on, unrattled.

"Four," De Guilbe corrected, and that seemed to shake the man just a bit. "And all of them alive only through the holy gifts of Blessed Abelle. Only through our work and healing powers."

"Better they had died, then," said Teydru, and out of the corner of his eye, Cormack caught De Guilbe's silent sneer.

"Leave this island," De Guilbe said.

"Return to us our brethren and we will be gone."

"Your brethren are alive only through our efforts. They have felt the warmth and love of Abelle."

"They embrace your faith?" Teydru asked, and his tone told the monks that he didn't believe it for a moment.

"They begin to see the truth of Blessed Abelle," De Guilbe countered cryptically.

To Cormack, there was great irony in that statement, for Father De Guilbe had proclaimed it without the slightest recognition that he, himself, would never begin to see the truth of anything other than Blessed Abelle. He was a man of complete intolerance demanding tolerance of others.

"Bring them forth to speak!" Teydru demanded, and De Guilbe crossed his arms over his chest, staring down at the man from on high.

"You are in no position to bargain," the monk reminded the shaman. "You have attacked us three times, and three times you have been repelled. That will not change. Your people die at our walls, but we remain. You cannot win, Teydru."

Unshaken, the shaman replied, "We will not leave. We will not stop attacking you. We will have our brethren."

"Or what? Or you will all lie dead at the base of our walls?"

The chide didn't have quite the effect De Guilbe was trying for, obviously, for Teydru squared his shoulders and proudly lifted his chin.

"If that is what our spirits demand," he answered, not a quiver in his voice. "We will not leave. We will not stop attacking you. We will have our brethren."

Cormack licked his lips and managed to pry his gaze from the imposing barbarian to glance at Father De Guilbe.

"We will kill you all," the monk promised.

"Then we will die with joy," said Teydru, and he turned and slowly walked away.

Father De Guilbe and Brother Giavno lingered for only a very short while before heading back to the father's office.

"They cannot defeat us, so they try to bargain," one young monk said hopefully to a group gathered not far from Cormack. "They will give up and leave soon enough."

"They will not," Cormack corrected him, and many sets of eyes turned his way. "They will fight us to the last."

"They are not that foolish," the man argued.

"But they are that faithful," said Cormack, and he headed for the tunnels and the pond, and this time he paid more attention to the details of the four prisoners and the dungeon holding them as he passed.

Four tense days passed before the next attack, just when some of the brothers were beginning to whisper that the barbarians would besiege the chapel rather than assault it again.

No such luck, and the reason for the delay became apparent very quickly: that the barbarians had been training, and thinking, and better preparing. Nowhere was that more evident than when a pair of brothers went out into the throng, much as Faldo and Moorkris had done. The horde retreated from them at full speed, while others, farther away, launched a barrage of spears and rocks at the brothers that had them scrambling back toward the wall.

Pursuit came swift, and to the credit of the monks, they had maintained their concentration on the serpentine shield throughout, and so they were ready to counter with a dazzling fireball.

But those nearest Alpinadorans, obviously expecting the blast, quickly veered aside, and more impressively, they had come in wrapped in water-soaked blankets! A couple were wounded—only minimally—but suddenly the two poor brothers found themselves under brutal assault.

From the wall, Giavno, Cormack, and the others cried out for them to get back to safety, and run they did. They couldn't outrun the spear volley, though.

Lightning bolts lashed out from the wall, along with a barrage of stones. Several barbarians fell, grievously wounded.

But so too did the brothers fall, side by side.

They would have survived their wounds, likely, had not the monks on the wall continued their barrage at the approaching horde. For the attackers wanted prisoners, that they could exact an exchange. They couldn't get near the fallen brothers, though, in the face of that barrage, so they settled for the next best option.

The Alpinadorans rained another volley of spears at the defenseless duo.

On the far side of the chapel, the western wall, a second wave crept up and then broke into a howling charge, knowing that most of the monks were across to the other side, trying to help their fallen.

"Go! Go! Go!" Giavno yelled at Cormack and some others, and the group leaped down from the wall and rushed across, to see brothers on the opposite parapets already engaging the ferocious enemy. A series of lightning bolts shook the ground beneath their feet as they ran to bolster the defense, and Cormack understood that the immediate threat had been eradicated, though the fighting hardly quieted.

The others ran ahead of Cormack as he slowed to a stop. He glanced back at Brother Giavno and the continuing battle at the eastern wall, wincing almost constantly from the terrible screams.

He went to the side structure of the keep, and to the bulkhead, where he picked up a torch and slipped down into the tunnels.

The sound of the fighting receded behind him, but it would take more than a closed bulkhead door to cleanse poor Cormack's sensibilities. That reality only made him move with more purpose, however, down the side tunnel to the dungeon where the four barbarians sat miserably, side by side. Cormack considered the task ahead of them and wondered if they could possibly succeed. Beyond weary, half-starved by choice, and one still recovering from immolation, Cormack had to wonder if they would even be able to stand up once he freed them of their bonds.

"Your people come on again," he said. "Men and women are dying up there."

Androosis lifted his head toward the monk, and Cormack simply couldn't read the expression on his face. Did he feel betrayed? Was he angry with Cormack? Confused?

"You would have us renounce our faith," the shaman said in a voice parched and dry and so very weak. "We would die first."

"I know."

The simple answer elicited a curious look from both the shaman and Androosis, and that gave Cormack some hope. He set the torch in a sconce and moved around the wooden wall. "We will venture deeper," he said as he loosened Androosis's bonds.

"Because you fear my people will overrun your pathetic castle," said Toniquay the shaman. "You move us away in desperation!"

Cormack hustled fast around the barrier to stand before the still-bound shaman. "Your people will not get through the wall. Not now and not ever. They will be killed to a man and woman at the base of the stones, unless we end this."

"You doubt the power . . ."

"Shut up," said Cormack. "More than twenty of your kin are dead already. More are dying right now. They will not relent and they cannot prevail. Their loyalty to you is commendable—and foolish."

"What would you have us do?" Androosis interjected, and Cormack was glad of that, for Toniquay was about to issue another stubborn retort, and time was too short for such bickering. He moved around the wall again and freed all three, with Toniquay last.

As they were freeing themselves of the rope, and climbing out of the mud and the piss and the feces, Cormack went back to the sconce and retrieved the torch.

"Follow closely, and as fast as you can manage," he instructed.

"And if we do not?"

Cormack swung about with a heavy sigh, drawing out a knife as he turned. "This ends today, now," he said. "I will show you the way out of here, or . . ." He brandished the knife. "It ends today."

"And why are we to believe you?"

"What choice have we?" Androosis asked, and motioned for Cormack to go.

To Cormack's relief, they all followed, with Androosis helping the burned man, even lifting him in his arms and carrying him along. That gave Cormack pause—would they even be able to execute the planned escape?

They went through the door at the tunnel's end, into the chamber where the lake comprised most of the floor.

"You are all strong swimmers, I would expect and hope," Cormack said, placing his torch down and starting to strip off his heavy cloak. He paused, though, and considered the action. "I cannot," he said.

Androosis shot him a concerned look. "We are not going back," he said.

Cormack shook his head, showing the four that such

was not what he was talking about at all. "I cannot go into the water and open the grate, as I had intended," he explained. "If I return to my people with wet hair, they will know of my involvement."

"Grate?" Androosis asked.

"A simple netting, with minor reinforcement," Cormack explained, pointing to the northwestern corner of the underground pool. "Beyond it is a short tunnel—an easy swim to freedom."

Androosis stared long and hard at Cormack. He placed his companion down gently and waded into the dark pool, walking in until the warm water was up to his waist before ducking under. While Canrak, the fourth of the barbarian party, lent an arm of support to the burned man, Toniquay stared unrelentingly at Cormack.

"You are so afraid of my people," he said with a twisted grin.

Cormack brushed him off with a smirk and shake of his head, never taking his eyes off the spot where Androosis had disappeared.

"If it is not true, then why?" the shaman demanded.

"Because my God would expect no less," said Cormack.

Androosis came up with a splash, sucking in a deep breath of air. "The way is clear," he announced. "It is a short swim, with open water beyond."

"What about him?" Cormack asked with sincere concern, and he indicated the barely conscious newest prisoner.

"I will get him through," Androosis promised. He walked over to Cormack then and dropped his hands on the monk's shoulders. "You are a good man," he said simply, and that was all Cormack had to hear to know that he had indeed done the right thing. The cost to him might prove great, but whatever Father De Guilbe might do could not begin to approach the cost to Cormack's sensibilities had he continued to do nothing.

Cormack came out of the side chamber a short while

later, to find the battle still on in full, still loud and chaotic, still, he hoped, providing him the cover he needed.

He went to battle and prayed with all his heart that it would be the last.

S I X T E E N

Mitigating

They called him a multitude of names, and seemed to create a new one whenever he put his sword to work. The Dancing Sword, the Bird of Prey—any and all adjectives and superlatives to toss upon this warrior who stood so clearly above all others. Whenever a new title was bestowed, all knew to whom it referred, for there was only one it fit. All the conversations came back to the name by which they all knew him, the name used in his introduction to the soldiers. The Highwayman, he was called, and more than one sturdy soul shuddered to think of meeting this man on a darkened highway in southern Honce!

True to form, he danced this day, running about the battlefield, leaping and spinning, lashing out with his feet as he soared through the mobs and always striking mortal blows as he landed. Like a small tornado he rushed through the battling throng, and as the enemies—this day they were exclusively the blue-skinned and ugly little trolls—were easily distinguished from his comrades, there wasn't the slightest hesitation in his movements and strikes.

He ran past one man and troll in a death clench and struck fast and hard and true, and the troll howled and thrashed and toppled to the ground.

Its killer was already gone, to another man, fallen, with two trolls standing over him and stabbing down at his supine form as he scrambled desperately and futilely to block.

The Highwayman leaped between the two surprised trolls, his feet kicking out to either side. He connected squarely on both, snapping their heads back. One went flying to the ground, while the other somehow managed to stay on its feet.

The standing one died first.

The Highwayman charged at another, and as soon as it recognized him, his black mask and outfit, it shrieked and threw up its hands in a pitiful defense.

Feeling another troll rushing at his back, he leaped high and spun, coming around to circle-kick the defending troll with a sweeping strike that spun it out to the right. In midair, he flipped his blade from his right hand to his left, and allowed the momentum of his turn to guide the strike as that fabulous and decorated sword of wrapped metal plunged into the troll's chest. The Highwayman retracted immediately and flipped the blade back to his right in a reverse grip, and stabbed out with a backhand as he came fully around, timing it just right to slash across the chest of one pursuing troll, and send the second pursuer stumbling backward.

He flipped his sword to right his grip as he rushed past the bleeding troll, launching a heavy left-hand blow to lay the dying creature low as he pursued its backpedaling companion. That one, shield and small sword in hand, brought both up to block, but the man drove on, smashing away with abandon, his sword too fine for the meager defenses. A piece of shield went flying away, a piece of troll arm following. The blade of the troll's

sword fell free to the ground, the head of the troll fast
following.

The warrior known as the Highwayman skidded to a
stop to catch his breath and survey the field. Only one
concentration of trolls remained intact, a group of about
twenty formed into a tight wedge on the far side of the
fighting.

Behind the black mask, the man narrowed his eyes.

Twenty trolls.

He yelled and charged.

And he kept yelling, demanding their attention. A
spear flew at him and he snapped his sword across,
knocking it harmlessly aside. He caught a second hurled
spear with his free hand and threw it down. He turned
sideways, still moving forward, and leaned back, letting a third slip past, then angled and dove into a roll,
under a fourth, and came up in a leap, above the fifth
missile.

The volley grew more concentrated and coordinated,
a barrage of rocks flying out at him.

He yelled in rage, in glee, in sheer ferocity, his sword
and free hand working wildly as he turned and ducked
and leaned, and he came right through the volley, showing not a scratch.

The troll wedge formation, appearing so formidable
just a few heartbeats before, broke apart, the creatures
running away from this madman they also knew by
many names, all inspiring terror.

The closest one, then second, then third, fell in rapid
succession to his flashing, marvelous blade, and he
continued the chase for a long while, though he only
scored one more kill, to drive the group far from the
field.

He was angry at being out here, angry at being tricked,
angry at being away from his beloved, but Bransen
couldn't deny the elation of this furious fight against an
irredeemable enemy.

All of that anger flowed into his arms, bringing them strength and speed.

And no amount of troll blood would satiate him.

Y ou did well in tricking that one," Brother Jond Du- molnay said to Dawson McKeege as they watched Bransen dance away in pursuit of the fleeing monsters. The monk continued his work on one of the wounded Vanguardsmen as he spoke, pulling open the man's tunic to reveal a gaping hole in his chest, blood gushing forth. Jond took a deep breath at the imposing, horrible sight and went to work with his soul stone, summoning its healing powers to try to stem the flow.

"It was for his own good, as much as our own," McKeege replied, more than a little defensively. "Your church would have turned the man over to Laird Delaval, and he'd have been sacked with a snake, to be sure."

Brother Jond continued his prayers, paused and looked at the continuing flow, then went back to his prayers—but only momentarily, for he saw the bleeding stem and nodded in relief that the man was now somewhat stable. Jond sighed and rocked back on his knees, dropping his bloody hands on his thighs.

"They would have sacked him?" he answered McKeege, and both of them knew the conversation to be a necessary and very welcome diversion. "Not if they understood his skill with the blade! They would have sent him posthaste to the south to do battle with Laird Ethelbert, I'd wager."

"The whispers have it that this Highwayman rained particular embarrassment upon Prince Yeslnik, one of Laird Delaval's favored nephews. No, if Delaval had gotten his hands on that one, Bransen would not have had the chance to prove his worth—and I doubt he'd have battled for Delaval. He had a bit of a run-in with the Laird of Pryd—word's that he killed the man."

"Laird Pryd himself?"

"His son, Prydae. You're knowing them?"

"I know—or knew—the father," Brother Jond explained.

"And?"

"Probably deserved it," Brother Jond admitted with a helpless chuckle. "If the son was much like the father, I mean."

Dawson McKeege gave a laugh at that, hardly one to disagree. By his estimation, most of the lairds of Honce, titles handed down through generations, weren't of much worth, which of course only made him appreciate his beloved Dame Gwydre, that notable exception, even more.

"Here comes your new champion," Jond said, indicating the returning Bransen. "It will take the Masur Delaval itself to wash the blood from his blade, I fear."

"Bloodier with every battle," Dawson agreed.

"A dozen huzzahs for Dawson's wit," said Brother Jond.

Bransen approached, looking at Jond. When he took note of Dawson, though, he veered suddenly, his face growing very tight.

"It is appropriate for a returning fighter to report his findings to his commander," Dawson reminded.

Bransen stopped and stood very still for a few heartbeats, composing himself.

"In fact, you should consider it required," Dawson pressed.

Bransen slowly turned to regard him. "The beasts are in full disarray and retreat," he said. "They'll not return anytime soon."

"Good enough, then," Brother Jond interjected lightly, his favorable relationship with both men serving to diffuse the obvious tension. "Myself and my Abellican brethren near the limit of our magical energies. Another assault would see less magical tending of the wounded, I fear."

"Curious," said a voice from the side, and all three

turned and nearly gasped to find Dame Gwydre sitting astride her roan mare. "From all that I have heard of Brother Jond, I would be certain that he would find more energy within himself, somehow, some way, if a man lay wounded before him."

"Milady," said Dawson, stumbling to his feet. "When did you arrive on the field?"

"Be at ease, my friend," she replied, waving him back.

"You are much too kind, Dame Gwydre," Brother Jond said, lowering his gaze.

"I only hear the whispers, good brother," she replied. "I do not create them. Your reputation overrides your humility, and all of Vanguard is blessed and pleased that you are among us."

Despite himself and his sincere humility, Brother Jond couldn't suppress a wisp of a smile at that.

"And you," Gwydre said, addressing Bransen. "The Dancing Sword, is it?"

"That is not my name."

"It is Bransen Garibond," Dawson said, shooting a scolding glance at the impudent young warrior. "Or perhaps he prefers the Highwayman, the name attached to him for his misdeeds in the South, the name for which he would have been sacked or hanged by the neck."

Bransen smiled at the man, more than willing to take that bait. "The Highwayman will do, indeed."

"Your exploits are not unnoticed . . . Bransen," said Gwydre. "When this is ended, should you choose to leave Vanguard, I promise that my note of appreciation and pardon will accompany you, though whether the Southern lairds would honor such, I cannot say."

"Should I choose?" Bransen quipped. "What prisoner would willingly remain in his dungeon?"

"A bit of respect!" Dawson warned, but Gwydre motioned for him to be quiet.

"Vanguard is no dungeon, Bransen Garibond," Dame

Gwydre said. "She is home. Home to many, many good people. You are free to view it in any manner you choose, of course—never would I deign to take that choice from any man."

"Yet I must fight for her, whatever my feelings."

"Fight for yourself, then," Dame Gwydre retorted. "For your freedom, such as it may be, and for the benefit of your young and beautiful wife, who does not deserve to see her husband put in a sack with venomous snakes. I care not why you fight, but I insist that you do. And while you may not see the good your fine blade is doing, we surely do. And while you may not care for those families given a chance to live in peace and security because of your actions against the Samhaist-inspired hordes, we surely do."

With that, she turned her roan mare and walked it away.

Dawson wore a pitying smirk as he shook his head, regarding Bransen. "One day you'll lose that stubborn pride," he predicted. "And you'll see the truth of Dame Gwydre, the truth of all of this, and you'll be shamed to have spoken to her such."

Then Dawson, too, walked away.

Bransen stared at him as he left, unblinking, his eyes boring holes into the man's back.

"You fought brilliantly today," Brother Jond said to him. "I had thought the line lost and expected that we would be the ones driven from the field."

Bransen looked at Jond, a man he had found it difficult to hate, despite his anger and his general feelings for Abellicans.

"That may mean little to you," Jond went on. "What field is worth the effort, of course, and you care not if Gwydre wins or Gwydre falls." He looked at the man lying before him. "But had we been driven from the field, this man would not have survived his wounds, and a woman not so unlike your wife would grieve forever."

"Dame Gwydre does not care why I fight," Bransen answered him, holding stubbornly to his anger. "Why would you?"

"Dame Gwydre has bigger things to care about than a single man's heart and soul, perhaps."

"And Brother Jond does not?"

The monk shrugged. "My victories are smaller, no doubt, but no less consequential, and no less satisfying."

Bransen started to snipe back, but held his tongue and just waved his free hand in defeat, then walked off to be alone.

Brother Jond watched him go with a knowing smile. Bransen's anger was real, but so was his compassion.

And in the end, Jond held faith that the compassion would prevail, because he had seen more than Bransen the warrior, this Sworddancer or Highwayman, as he was alternately known. After the previous battles, Bransen had helped Brother Jond and the others in tending the wounded, and his prowess in such matters was no less than his fighting ability.

Indeed, later that very night, Bransen and Jond worked side by side on the wounded.

"You hate them," Jond remarked.

"Them?"

"McKeege and Dame Gwydre, for a start," Jond explained. "My brethren in the South, as well. You are a young man too full of anger."

Bransen regarded him curiously, in no small part because this wizened monk wasn't much his elder, and to hear Jond calling him a "young man" seemed a bit strange.

"I am not as angry as you believe."

"It pleases me to hear that," Jond said, sincerely.

"But I have seen more dishonesty and evil than I ever expected," Bransen went on. He paused and bent low over a severely wounded woman, placing his hand on her belly and closing his eyes. He felt his hand grow warm, and the woman's soft moan told him that his effort was having some effect—though he couldn't begin to guess whether it would be sufficient balm to get her through the tearing and twisting a spear had caused in her bowels.

After a short while, Bransen opened his eyes and leaned back to see Brother Jond staring at him.

"What do you do?" Jond asked. "To heal them, I mean. You have no gemstones, and yet I cannot deny what my eyes show to me. Your work has a positive effect on their wounds, almost as much so as a skilled brother with a soul stone."

"My mother was Jhesta Tu," said Bransen, and Brother Jond crinkled his face. "Do you know what that means?"

The monk shook his head, and Bransen snickered and said, "I did not expect anything different."

"Jhesta Tu is a . . . religion?"

"A way of life," said Bransen. "A philosophy. A religion? Yes. And since it is one not of Honce, but of Behr, I would hope that the Abellican Order has no reason to hate it. But of course they do. Why control people's lives only a bit of the way, after all?"

"There is no end to your sarcasm."

"None that you'll ever see," Bransen promised, but he was smiling as he spoke, despite himself, and Brother Jond got a laugh out of that, too.

"I know that your journey here was the result of a lie," Jond said a long while later, as the two finally neared the end of the line of wounded. "But I cannot deny that I am glad you have come. As are they," he added, sweeping his arm and his gaze out over the injured.

Bransen wanted to offer a stinging retort, but in the face of the suffering laid out before him, he found that he could not.

"As am I," came a voice from behind, and the pair turned to see Dame Gwydre, stepping into one of Brother Jond's conversations for the second time that day.

Bransen stared at her and did not otherwise respond.

"Greetings again, Lady," Brother Jond said. "Your presence will surely uplift the spirits of these poor wounded warriors."

"Soon," she promised. "For the moment, though, I would speak with your companion."

She matched Bransen's stare, and motioned for him to join her outside the tent.

"Your anger is understandable," she said when he joined her outside. She led the way, walking across the encampment through a light rain that had come up.

"I will sleep easier knowing that you approve," he said, taking some solace in being able to so casually and impudently address this imposing and powerful figure. He felt as if he had scored a little victory in that retort, though he quickly scolded himself silently for such a petulant and childish need, particularly when Gwydre took it all in stride, as if it was deserved or at least understandable.

"The wind has a bit of winter's bite in it this evening," she said. "The season is not so far away, I fear. Our enemies will not relent—glacial trolls feel the cold not at all. But my own forces will be more miserable by far."

"A fact that little concerns you, I expect," Bransen said, and this time he did elicit a glower from the Dame of Vanguard. "Other than how it might affect your holding, I mean."

"Do you understand and accept why Dawson brought you here?" Gwydre asked quietly.

"I understand that I was deceived."

"For your own good."

"And for yours." Bransen stopped as he spoke the accusation, and turned to face the lady as she similarly swung about to regard him.

"Yes, I admit it," she said. "And though I knew not of Bransen Garibond, this Highwayman legend, when Dawson left Pireth Vanguard, and though I had no idea that he would so coerce you to come, I admit openly that I approve of his tactics and of the result."

"You would say that standing out here alone with me?"

Gwydre laughed at him. "Openly," she reiterated. "I know enough of Bransen to recognize that he is no murderer."

"Yet my anger is justified."

"Justified does not mean that it is not misplaced," said Gwydre. "I see that you have forged a friendship with Brother Jond and some others."

Bransen shrugged.

"If I granted you your freedom right now, with no recourse should you decide to leave, would you?" she asked. "Would you collect your wife and her mother and be gone from Vanguard?"

"Yes," Bransen said without hesitation and with as much conviction as he could flood into his voice.

"Would you really?" Dame Gwydre pressed. "You would leave Brother Jond and the others? You would allow the troll hordes of the Samhaists to overrun Vanguard and slaughter innocent men, women, and children?"

"This is not my fight!" Bransen retorted, somewhat less convincingly.

"It is now."

"By deception alone!"

Gwydre paused, and held up her hand to silence the agitated Bransen. "As you will," she conceded.

"You will let me leave?"

"No, I cannot, though surely I would like to—for you and for all of the soldiers," she said. "There is too much at stake, and so I insist that you remain."

"Dawson McKeege would be proud of you," Bransen replied, his sarcasm unrelenting.

"I do not wish to allow this war to go through the winter," Dame Gwydre said and turned and started off yet again, Bransen in tow. "The cold favors my enemies."

"Please, end it."

"I am considering creating a select team of warriors to strike deep into our enemy's ranks, perhaps to decapitate the beast. The hordes are held together by the sheer will and maliciousness of Ancient Badden, a most unpleasant Samhaist."

"A redundant description, from what I have seen."

"Indeed," Dame Gwydre agreed. "Do you agree with my reasoning?"

"You're asking me to join your attack force."

"I am tasking you with exactly that."

Bransen stopped, and Gwydre did as well, glancing back and allowing him all the time he needed to think it through.

"How far and how long?" he asked.

"Somewhere in the North," she replied. "Probably a journey of more than two weeks—and that if the enemy is oblivious to your passing."

"If I go, and if this beast, Ancient Badden, is killed, I would have my freedom," Bransen said. "Even if this assault does not end your war, as you hope. I would have my freedom with your blessing and imprimatur to return unhindered to the lands of southern Honce? And you will provide a ship to sail my family home."

"You are in no position to bargain," she said.

"And yet, bargain I do. Even if killing Ancient Badden does nothing to end this war, I will have my freedom."

"You will not walk away," Dame Gwydre said.

"If you believe that, then you have nothing to lose."

"Agreed, then," she said. "Bring me the head of Badden and I will have Dawson McKeege take you back to Chapel Abelle, along with my insistence that you be forgiven your past indiscretions, though I cannot guarantee that the Southern lairds and Church will heed that imprimatur."

"Allow me to worry about that."

Dame Gwydre stared at him a moment longer as she gathered her cloak up tight against her neck, and with a slight nod, she walked away.

Bransen stood there for a long while watching her go,

and thinking that at least he had a direction before him now, a place to go with the hope that it might indeed end in the near future.

It did not occur to him that Ancient Badden would prove to be the most formidable foe he had ever faced.

SEVENTEEN

The Cost of Conscience

They repelled the assault but not without cost, for this last attack by the determined Alpinadorans had left several brothers seriously wounded, one critically. The cost to the Alpinadorans had been even more grievous, with many carried from the field.

"Fools, all!" Father De Guilbe scolded, shaking his fist at the departing horde. None of the monks around him dared utter a word in response, for never had they seen their leader so obviously flummoxed. "Will we kill you all? Is this the choice you force upon us, fool Teydru? If you are concerned for your flock, why do you throw it to the hungry wolves?"

By that point, almost all of the Alpinadorans were back at their beachfront encampment, and though De Guilbe was yelling at the top of his lungs, it was fairly obvious that they could not hear him well enough to make out his words. Still, he ranted for several minutes, his diatribe turning mostly against Teydru, before he at last turned to face his own brethren.

"Idiots!" he said with a snarl, and many brothers nodded their heads in agreement, and one whispered, "They will not break through our walls," in support of the father's general thesis.

Father De Guilbe took a deep breath then and settled back against the stone parapet, letting the tension drain from his battle-weary body. "We will be working the soul stones long into the night," he said, mostly to Giavno. "Determine a rotation and be certain that our wounded brethren are tended dusk to dawn."

"Of course," Brother Giavno replied with a respectful bow.

"And if they come on again this day, conserve your magical powers," De Guilbe told them all. "Let us ensure that we have the energy to heal our wounded. Repel the fools with stones and hot water."

With that he took his leave, moving to the ladder that would take him to the courtyard. He had just started down when one of the brothers up high on the main keep yelled out, "They break camp!"

Father De Guilbe stood there for a moment looking up at the man, as did all the others, before they rushed wholesale to the wall to view the spectacle.

As the lookout had reported, they watched tents being struck, the distant barbarian encampment bustling with activity.

"Where are they moving their supplies?" Father De Guilbe yelled up to the lookout.

"To the boats!" he yelled back excitedly. "To the boats! They are taking to their boats!"

Father De Guilbe paused for a moment, then spun back to the wall to stare out at the distant camp. "Did we break their will at long last?" he quietly asked, and all of those around him murmured their hopeful agreement.

Soon after, all the brothers of Chapel Isle, save those already working the soul-stone magic on the wounded, gathered at the highest points on the southern battlements, staring out hopefully. Within an hour of the battle's end, the first sails rose up on the Alpinadoran boats and the first paddles hit the warm waters of Mithranidoon, and a great cheer erupted across the chapel.

"Perhaps they are not as foolish as we believed," Father De Guilbe said to Brother Giavno, both men smiling with the expectation that they had come through their dark trials.

That sense of victory was soon enough shattered, however, when a breathless young monk rushed into Father De Guilbe's audience chambers.

"They are gone!" he stammered.

"They?" Brother Giavno asked before De Guilbe could.

"The barbarians!" the young man explained.

"Yes, we watched them break camp," Giavno said.

"No, no," the man stuttered, trying to catch his breath long enough to explain. "The barbarians in our dungeon. They are gone!"

"Gone?" This time it was Father De Guilbe asking.

"Out of their chamber and down the tunnel. The door to the pond was open and the grate has been dislodged," the monk reported. "They are gone! Through the water and out, I am sure."

De Guilbe and Giavno exchanged concerned looks.

"Now we understand why our enemies broke camp and departed," Brother Giavno said.

Father De Guilbe was already moving, out to the hall and down the stairs. As they came out of the keep, rushing around to the entryway to the lower levels, Giavno spotted Brother Cormack and waved at him to join them.

"This is my fault," Cormack said unexpectedly when they entered the now-empty dungeon.

The others turned to regard him.

"I should have recognized their ruse," Cormack improvised. "Their unwillingness to eat."

"What do you know of this?" Brother Giavno demanded.

"It was an enchantment, do you not see?" Cormack asked. "They were not starving themselves in protest, to die before converting to our ways. At their shaman's instruction, they were starving themselves that he, or one of the others, could thin himself appropriately so that he could slip his bonds. Oh, but we should have guessed!"

"You babble!" Giavno said.

"Let him continue," bade Father De Guilbe.

Cormack held up his arms and shook his head. "Their magic is tied to the natural way," he tried to explain. "Perhaps—yes, I think it likely—their imposed starvation was merely so that they, their shaman, could enact some spell to further thin his wrists and hands."

"Those bindings were tight," another monk protested. "I tied them myself."

"That was many days ago," Cormack reminded. "The captives were far heavier then—all of them."

"You cannot know," Giavno said.

"Agreed," said Cormack. "But somehow they managed to slip their bonds. It all makes sense now, I fear— their starvation, their confidence, their impudence. When first we encountered these people, before the lincs of intransigence and battle were etched, I learned much of their ways, and I know their magic is tied to the natural. Their shamans have spells to make their warriors appear taller, to strike fear into their enemies. It is said that their greatest spiritualists can shape change into animal form, much like the great Samhaists of legend."

"So you believe that their refusal to eat was a design to allow them escape?" Father De Guilbe asked.

To Cormack's ears, the large man didn't sound very convinced. Nor did Giavno, scowling at him from the side of the small dungeon, appear overly enthusiastic for Cormack's improvised lie. But now Cormack had to carry it through, of course. "It makes sense in the context of what I know about their type of magic," he said. "I should have guessed this ruse."

He shook his head and moved aside, hoping to take their scrutiny off of him before more holes could be shot into his theory. To his great relief, Father De Guilbe merely said, "Perhaps your assessment is correct. Clever fools, though fools they remain." He turned his attention to the other two lesser brothers in the room. "Search the whole of the keep, of the tunnels and the compound," he ordered. "Likely they went out to the open lake—that would explain the departure of their stubborn kin. But if they remain, find them posthaste."

The pair started right out, sweeping Cormack up with them as they began their exhaustive search.

"And doubly secure that grate," Father De Guilbe called after them, and he paused to listen to the receding footsteps. "Brother Cormack thinks he has sorted out the mystery," he said to Giavno when they were securely alone.

"Perhaps he has," said Giavno as he moved around the wooden wall that had served to hold the bindings of the prisoners. "Though I wonder," he said when he got to the back, "if the shaman reduced his wrist and hand enough to slip his bonds, then why are all four of the binding ropes cut?"

Father De Guilbe gave a noncommittal shrug as if it did not matter—and at that, it really didn't seem to. The Alpinadorans were gone, escaped, and the men and women of Yossunfier had left Chapel Isle, bringing the whole ordeal to an end. That Cormack would be proven right or wrong seemed of little consequence. With a wave of his hand, a dejected Father De Guilbe left the dungeon.

Brother Giavno certainly understood that malaise. What had they been fighting for, after all? The souls of four men had been taken from them, somehow, some way, whether through Alpinadoran magic, or simple stubbornness, or . . .

A slight smile creased Giavno's face as he considered the torn bindings, as he considered the explanation offered by Brother Cormack.

The unsolicited explanation.

I should never have doubted you," Milkeila said breathlessly as she stood on the sandbar in Cormack's arms under a brilliant, starry sky.

"Speak not of it," Cormack bade her.

"But Androosis has already written songs to Corma—"

"I beg of you," said Cormack, hushing her with finger pressed to her lips. "That battle, that siege, all of it, is nothing I wish to relive or remember at all."

"It was painful to you to see the truth of your Church brothers," Milkeila reasoned. "And to betray them."

"And to see the truth of your people, no less stubborn."

Milkeila moved back to arm's length, scrutinizing Cormack sternly. "We did not hold prisoners," she reminded him. "We did not invade your lands insisting that you convert to our ways!"

Cormack hushed her again, and tried to kiss her, but she avoided him. "I know," he said. "And you know how I feel about it." She started to argue, but he wouldn't let her get a word in at that point. "And you know what I just did. Have you forgotten so quickly?"

"Of course I've not!"

"Then kiss me!" Cormack said playfully, trying desperately to turn this conversation to a lighter place.

Milkeila recognized that and smiled, and did indeed kiss Cormack, surrendering to him as they slid down together to the sandbar. As they fumbled with their clothing, Cormack paused and brought forth the gemstone necklace. Milkeila didn't argue with him as he placed it over her head.

Sitting idly and alone in a small boat out on the lake, Brother Giavno listened to their lovemaking as he had listened to their conversation, marveling at how well sound traveled across the dark waters on a night so clear.

He wasn't really surprised that Cormack had been the one to betray them, of course, but it stung him profoundly nonetheless. The young and handsome brother, so full of fire and potential, strong of arm and strong with the gemstones, simply did not understand the meaning of what it was to be an Abellican brother as they moved toward completion of the first century of their Church. Cormack's way was the art of exhaustive compromise, and that in a world full of enemies who would accept such Abellican concessions only as a pretense for their continued road to dominance.

For the Abellicans were at that time involved in a great struggle with the Samhaists, who would not forsake their old and brutal ways. Were it not for that ancient cult, Cormack's overly abundant tolerance of others—even of powries—might itself be tolerated within the Church.

But that was not the case. Not now. Not with all of Honce aflame as laird battled laird and both churches, Abellican and Samhaist, struggled mightily for supremacy. The other races, human and otherwise, had no choice but to pick sides. Neutrality was not an option.

Nor was tolerance for barbarians who would not see the truth and beauty of Blessed Abelle.

Brother Giavno had always liked Cormack, but hearing the man fornicating with a barbarian, a shaman no less, was more than his sensibilities could handle.

Cormack glided his craft easily onto the sand, lightly scrambling out and dragging the boat the rest of the way out of the water. Another boat rested nearby, flipped over, and the two handlers, whose job it was to make sure that all the craft were properly stored and secured whenever they were not in use, rested aside the paddles of the first returned craft and hustled over to help Cormack.

"Father De Guilbe wishes to speak with you," one of them told the returning sailor monk. "And what did you catch for us this day?"

Cormack held up a pair of trout strung on a line—fish that Milkeila had given to him, as was their custom whenever they met on the sandbar.

"You always do better when you're out alone," the other boathandler said. "They should put you out there every day!"

Cormack grinned and nodded, thinking that meeting Milkeila at their special place daily wouldn't be so bad a thing. None of the three on the beach understood the prophetic nature of the remarks, however.

With a noticeably lighter step, Cormack trotted back up from the beach to the chapel, and indeed all of Chapel Isle seemed as if a great weight had been lifted from it, as if perpetual storm clouds had at last parted. The three-week siege had taxed the brothers greatly, and though they were not all thrilled that their prisoners had escaped, and less thrilled that four of their ranks had been lost to battle and several others would be a long time in recovering, life got back to somewhat normal fairly quickly.

It occurred to Cormack that the work on the walls hadn't been this frenetic since the early days of construction. Frenetic and with true zeal, he realized, for the brothers were going at their labors with a renewed sense of purpose, as if they were finally, finally, doing much more than the simple tasks necessary for day-to-day survival. They had built the chapel for defense and as a celebration of Blessed Abelle. Now they had seen it through its former purpose firsthand. They had witnessed what had worked and what hadn't; already many plans had been drawn up for strengthening the walls and giving the brothers more and better options for repelling any future attackers. Mingled in with those practical plans were the requisite glorious design features, the marks of pride and gratitude to their patron.

"Purpose," Cormack whispered as he crossed into the courtyard. He wondered then if that need to find meaning wasn't in some twisted way responsible for the continuing warfare among the various peoples and powries of the Mithranidoon islands. Without the ever-present enemies, could the folk of the islands find meaning in their lives?

It was a truly chilling thought for the gentlehearted man, but he didn't let it weight the spring in his step.

Brother Giavno's look at him as he entered Father De Guilbe's office did exactly that, however, a withering gaze that immediately sent Cormack's thoughts back to the beach, to the second, overturned boat, which had obviously been recently returned.

"Fa . . . Father De Guilbe, I was told that you wished to speak to me," Cormack managed to stutter, though his eyes never left Giavno as he spoke.

"Where have you been?" the leader of Chapel Isle replied, and Cormack couldn't miss the undertone of his voice, so full of disappointment.

He turned to regard the man, and paused just a few moments to collect his thoughts and to try and sort all this out before answering, "Fishing. I go often, and with Brother Giavno's blessing. I landed two this day—one of good size—"

"You fish from your boat or from another island?"

"The boat, of course—"

"Then why were you on an island?" Father De Guilbe demanded. "It was an island, was it not? Where you met with the barbarian woman?"

Stunned, Cormack shook his head. "Father, I . . ."

This time De Guilbe did not interrupt, but the stammering Cormack couldn't find a response anyway.

"You freed them," Father De Guilbe accused. "During the frenzy of battle you slipped into the tunnels and freed our four prisoners."

"No, Father."

De Guilbe's sigh profoundly wounded the young monk. "Do not compound your crime with lies, Brother." He paused and sighed again, shaking his head, before finishing, simply, "Cormack."

"Four souls for Blessed Abelle released to pursue heathen ways that will surely damn them for eternity," Brother Giavno put in harshly. "How will you reconcile your conscience with that, I wonder?"

"No," Cormack said, still shaking his head. "We thought they were not eating in protest, but it was an enchantment, perhaps. Or . . ."

"Brother Giavno followed you out onto the lake, Cormack," said Father De Guilbe, and again, his omission of Cormack's Abellican title struck hard at the young monk's sensibilities. "He heard you with the woman—all of it. And while your lust could be rather easily forgiven and atoned for—brothers often surrender to such urges—the action which precipitated your tryst is a different matter."

Cormack stared at him blankly, and indeed, that was exactly how he felt. He replayed his conversation with Milkeila in his head, and quickly recognized that an eavesdropping Giavno had heard more than enough to erase any doubt, or to defeat any protests coming forth from him. So he stood there and took Father De Guilbe's stream of anger, and he felt an empty vessel through it all, though he would not let that venom fill him.

"How could you betray us like that?" De Guilbe demanded. "Men died to protect that treasure: the souls of four Alpinadoran barbarians. Four of your brethren are dead, and a fifth might soon join them! What would you say to their families? Their parents? How would you explain to them that their sons died for nothing?"

"Too many were dying," Cormack said, his voice barely above a whisper, but the room went absolutely silent as he started to speak and all heard him well enough. "Too many were still to die."

"We would have held them!" Brother Giavno insisted.

"Then we would have murdered them all," Cormack retorted. "Surely there is nothing holy in that action. Surely Blessed Abelle—"

The name had barely escaped his lips when a bolt of lightning erupted from Father De Guilbe's hand and threw Cormack back hard to slam into the doorjamb. He crumpled to the floor, disoriented and writhing in pain.

"Strip him down and tie him in the open courtyard," Father De Guilbe instructed, and Giavno waved a couple of monks over to collect the fallen man.

As Cormack was dragged away, Brother Giavno faced Father De Guilbe directly. "Twenty hard lashes," De Guilbe started to say, but he stopped and corrected himself. "Fifty. And with barbs."

"That will almost surely kill him."

"Then he will be dead. He betrayed us beyond redemption. Administer the beating without remorse or amelioration. Beat him until you are weary, then hand the whip off to the strongest brother in the chapel. Fifty—no less, though I care not if you exceed the mandate. If he is dead at forty, administer the last ten to his corpse."

Brother Giavno felt the deep remorse in Father De Guilbe's voice, and he sympathized completely. This business was neither pleasant nor pleasurable, but it was certainly necessary. The fool Cormack had made his choice, and he had betrayed his brethren for the sake of barbarians—barbarians who were assailing Chapel Isle at the time of Cormack's treachery.

That could not stand.

Brother Giavno nodded solemnly to his superior and turned to leave. Before he got to the door, De Guilbe said to him, "Should he somehow survive the beating, or should he not, put him in a small boat and tow him out onto the lake. Leave him for the trolls or the fish or the carrion birds. Brother Cormack is already dead to us."

More than two hours later, the semiconscious Cormack was unceremoniously dropped into the smallest and worst boat in Chapel Isle's small fleet as it bobbed on the low surf at the island's edge.

"Is he already dead?" one of the monks asked to the group congregating around the craft.

"Who's to care?" another answered with a disgusted snort—which pretty well summed up the mood. Many of these men had been friends of Cormack's, some had even looked up to him. But his betrayal was a raw wound to them all, and too fresh a revelation for any to take a step back and see any perspective on this other than the harsh sentence imposed by Father De Guilbe.

For other friends of theirs, like Brother Moorkris, had died in protecting the prisoners and the chapel. Arguing about whether or not Father De Guilbe's decision to keep their prisoners and accept the siege and battle was not their prerogative, nor had any found the time to do so. Their jobs had focused simply on survival, on beating back the enemy whatever the reasons for the enemy being there.

On a logical level, some might come to understand and accept Cormack's treacherous actions. On a visceral level, the fallen brother had gotten exactly what he had deserved.

"If he's still alive, he's not long for it," another brother said.

Giavno stepped forward and tossed a red beret, Cormack's powrie cap, into the boat atop the prostrate, bleeding man. "It is a wound to every heart on Chapel Isle," he said. "Cast him out that the currents might take him to a cove where the beasts will feast, and when he is gone we will speak no more of fallen Brother Cormack."

Giavno turned and walked away and a group took hold of the small craft, guiding it toward the water. One man paused long enough to take the beret and set it upon Cormack's head, and when he looked at the curious stares coming at him for the action, he merely shrugged. "Seems fitting."

They all laughed—it was either that or cry—and brought the boat out onto the lake, giving it a strong shove to get it away from the island far enough so that one or another of the many crisscrossing currents caused by the underground hot streams that fed the lake would catch it.

"If it washes back in, I'll tie it to another and tow it far out," one brother volunteered, but that wasn't necessary. As a brilliant orange sunset graced the western sky, the stark, low silhouette of Cormack's funereal boat at last moved out of sight.

EIGHTEEN

Dame Gwydre's Trump

He walked with a sure and determined stride that mocked time itself, for he had seen seven decades of life and could pace men one-third his age. He stood tall and broad-shouldered, but his thick muscles had slackened, and his skin, so weathered in the northern sun, had sagged a bit. Still, no one doubted that the large fist of this man, Jameston Sequin, could flatten a nose and take both cheekbones with it!

His hair was long and gray, his beard not so long and still showing hints of the darker colors of his earlier years, and his great and thick mustache stood out most of all. He wore a tri-cornered cap, one he had fashioned, one that had been considered unique when he had fashioned it. Long and narrow, it trailed back from a round-pointed front to a flattened back that was just a bit wider than his head, and he kept a black feather along its right side, bent low to follow the line of the hat.

At one of Vanguard's archery contests half a century before, one won by young Jameston, of course, the man had received more than a bit of teasing regarding his rather unusual cap—until, of course, he had explained that the pointed front allowed him to properly line up his shots. Within a few months, and to this day, the Jameston, as the hat was called, was quite common among Vanguard's hunters, thereby adding to a legend that needed no enhancement.

It was said that he was of Alpinadoran descent, or mixed blood at least, but his long nose and protruding brow spoke of ancestors along the southeastern coast of Honce. His eyes were green, and his smile, though a bit snaggletoothed now, was infectious and strangely disarming, given the man's imposing stature and often withering glare.

He was smiling now, as much out of curiosity as anything else. "This far north?" he asked himself (a not unusual occurrence) as he moved far enough down the side of one mountain to better view the combatants in the dell below, which included men, apparently Vanguardsmen.

Now more interested in the fight, which he had presumed to be another skirmish between the various troll or goblin tribes, Jameston quick-stepped closer, but to a higher perch with a better view.

His first instinct at that point was to charge right in, for a quick glance made him realize that the small group seemed sorely outnumbered and sure to be overwhelmed. Before he had taken a step, though, he understood that such impressions didn't begin to tell this tale. The goblins, with a dozen lying dead already, were the ones in need of support.

Jameston drew Banewarren from his shoulder and set an arrow on its resting string as he watched the play. One man in particular, dressed in black from bandanna to boot, had the old scout nodding with approval. The man raced the length of the line, leaping and spinning, his thin sword cutting graceful and precise lines through the air and through the goblins alike. Wherever that man passed, goblins fell dead, and though an Abellican monk stood back from the action, ready to heal this man or any others who needed his magical services, Jameston doubted he'd expend much of his healing energy on this one.

A second, burlier figure crossed the black-clothed man's wake as he rushed out to the far left of the human defensive formation, and Jameston smiled even wider. For this one, Vaughna por Lolone, he surely knew. "Crazy V," he whispered, her nickname, and he laughed aloud as she lived up to it yet again, throwing herself with abandon into the midst of the goblins.

Jameston moved to find a better vantage point, testing the pull of Banewarren with every long stride.

Vaughna carried two iron hand axes as solidly as if they were extensions of her living arms. She punched out with her left, lifting the angle of the blow to clip a goblin forehead and jerk the creature's head back. Her second hand came in fast at the exposed neck, but she had flipped her axe into the air, hitting the goblin's exposed throat with her stiffened fingers instead.

As it staggered back gasping, Crazy V put her face right in front of the beast's, opened wide her eyes and mouth, and screamed wildly. As she did, she blindly caught her descending axe, dropped her shoulders back, and delivered a chop into the goblin's side, bending it over in pain.

Crazy V drove across with her left but brought it up short, evading the wounded creature's flimsy defense. For she stepped out with her left as she swung and pivoted on that foot, bringing a trailing right-hand backhand all the way about to chop the goblin almost exactly across from the first serious wound.

Then she spun away as if to leave but turned about suddenly and unloaded a barrage of chops, left and right, on the creature, melting it into a pile of torn muck.

Blood-spattered and unbothered, Crazy V twirled about and sought her next target, and even took a step that way before an unusual, red-feathered arrow whipped into the goblin and sent it flying into a tree, where the arrow drove through and pinned the dead thing upright.

Crazy V's face erupted in a gleeful look of recognition and she yelled again, just because. Only one man in this region was known for such fletching. She rushed off to find something to hit, because she knew that between this Highwayman and his sword and their newest arrival, there soon would be few remaining targets!

Bransen was careful that his dance did not venture too close to the ferocious Vaughna; he always took pains to avoid that one. It had nothing to do with his personal feelings, though the crass and crude woman often left him shaking his head. Rather, it was because her fighting style was so unpredictable, so out-of-control, it could interrupt the flow of his own, meticulous motions.

He stayed nearest to Brother Jond, both to ensure that the monk was free to continue his gemstone healing and the occasional magical offensive strike and because of the friendship they had forged in previous battles.

The remaining two members of the strike force, a middle-aged crusty old warrior named Crait and a red-headed young bull named Olconna, fell somewhere on the spectrum between Bransen and Vaughna. Neither could match his grace or her ferocity, but both performed an effective enough combination of the two.

Bransen, out of targets now that Vaughna had charged into the middle of the goblin line and had, predictably, broken it, sending goblins running every which way, paused and managed to glance over at Crait and Olconna, fighting side by side behind Brother Jond.

Crait dodged one blow coming in at his right, and moved so far to the left that it appeared as if he had opened himself up to a devastating spear thrust. But when the goblin took that opening, it found only Olconna's shield, and the creature's failure allowed Crait to fast-step forward behind his partner's block and plunge his bronze short sword into the goblin's chest.

Crait rolled to the left after the kill, sliding right in front of Olconna, his sword and shield slashing and bashing, but only as a ruse.

For he kept going and Olconna rushed into the void as he passed, and the goblin couldn't refocus its attention fast enough.

Bransen nodded his admiration. These two had been fighting together for a long time now, and had made quite a name for themselves farther to the east and north, where the battles along the coast had been more scattered but no less fierce.

This one was over, at least, or soon to be, and Bransen leaped past Brother Jond and charged off Olconna's right flank in fast pursuit of the now-fleeing monsters, hoping to get at least one more kill.

He managed two, and fast closed on a third when a red-fletched arrow beat him to the mark, throwing the goblin to the ground. Bransen looked around to spy the archer, but no one was in sight, and none of his friends, still back in the dell some twenty paces behind him, held any bows.

He finished the squirming goblin with a stroke to its neck, then rolled it enough so that he could push the beautifully crafted arrow right through. When he arrived back with his friends to present it, he found Brother Jond holding a similar one.

"Our day's gone brighter," Vaughna explained, in that voice of hers that always seemed to be on the edge of hysterical laughter.

"It is him?" Olconna asked, his voice thick with unabashed awe.

"Aye, that'd be the mark of Jameston," Crait answered.

"Jameston Sequin," Brother Jond explained to the obviously confused Bransen. "A hunter of great renown, who splits his time between Vanguard and Alpinador. It is said he knows the trails better than any man alive, and it will prove a fortunate turn for us if he is indeed about."

"There is the greatest understatement I've ever heard," Vaughna chimed in, and her tone made it clear that she was talking about more than a blessing for their mission. She nearly swooned (which seemed almost comical to Bransen, given her fire-spitting demeanor) as she pointed across a small lea, jumping up and down like a little girl getting her first view of a king. "It is him! It is him!"

"He's worth all that?" Olconna snickered.

The approaching man's legs seemed just a bit too long for his frame, giving him as determined and force-ful a stride as one could imagine. His face, weathered and creased, showed nothing but strength and a com-manding pragmatism. Bransen could see simply from the set of the man's jaw that this one, Jameston, wasn't loose with his words.

"You're a long way north of Dame Gwydre's lines, and you don't look like Samhaists to me," Jameston said when he neared the group. "Especially not you," he added, nod-ding his gray-bearded chin at Brother Jond.

"Hardly that," the monk agreed.

Jameston's gaze fell over Bransen, his face crinkling in a strange manner. For the first time since he had donned his mother's black silk suit, Bransen felt a bit self-conscious about his unusual dress.

"We did not come north just to find Jameston," Vaughna volunteered. "But we're glad to see you."

Jameston glanced at her for just a moment before of-fering a wink of familiarity, his face brightening. "Crazy V," he said. "Been a lot of years."

"Too many."

"And you, too, Crait," Jameston went on.

"I'm surprised you remember me," the old warrior replied.

"Not so hard a thing to do," Jameston answered. "How many might be living who have seen the fights you and I can claim as experience?"

Crait thought it over for a few heartbeats, then answered with a laugh, "Two?"

"Might be," said Jameston. "Might be." He stepped over to accept Crait's extended hand, the two clasping wrists with the respect old warriors often reserved for other old warriors.

Brother Jond cleared his throat, and after a curious glance at him, Crait began the introductions, though Vaughna interrupted him as soon as he had named Olconna and presented Bransen and Brother Jond.

"You wandered lost?" Jameston asked.

"Here on purpose," Vaughna corrected. "The fighting has been terrible in the South. Entire villages are gone."

Jameston nodded solemnly. "I've seen Badden's charges march out and figured as much."

"The Samhaists know no moral boundaries," Brother Jond put in, but Jameston's sudden grin silenced him, for it showed the grizzled old hunter to be far beyond the influences of proselytizing Abellicans and Samhaists alike in their unending struggle to collect every man's soul.

"You are a scouting band?" Jameston presumed.

"Half right," said Vaughna, and Brother Jond cleared his throat as if to remind her not to speak too openly. But this was Jameston Sequin, after all, and the woman just cast the monk a dismissive glance. "Dame Gwydre sees that we have to stop this war."

"And negotiating with the Samhaists won't get you far," Jameston reasoned, and let his knowing gaze encompass them all, and Bransen found it hard not to be naked under that man's imposing stare.

"You've come to kill Badden himself," the old hunter said, and the undercurrent of humor in his voice had the five exchanging worried glances.

That was all the confirmation Jameston needed.

"We will find him, and we will kill him, yes," Bransen announced unexpectedly, and stepped forward beside Vaughna. "He has earned the sentence."

"A hundred times over before you were ever born, boy," Jameston replied.

Bransen tried to recover fast from the response, which was both easy agreement and somewhat condescending—maybe. He just couldn't be certain, for this man, this apparently legendary hunter, had him in a continually un-balanced state.

"Never been enamored of that one," Jameston went on, beating Bransen to the dialogue. "Only thing I've found stupider than men who claim to speak for the gods are the people who listen to them. My apologies, Brother," he added to Jond.

Jond half shrugged, half nodded, seeming at least as off-balanced as Bransen.

"Help us kill him," Vaughna blurted on impulse.

"Never been one to pick sides," Jameston replied.

"But you have been helping Dame Gwydre," Vaughna protested. "You have been sending reports south, so it's said."

"Counts of goblins and trolls and the like," Jameston agreed. "And the second count I made of them, after I left them, was always less than the initial."

"So you've already chosen your side, then," Vaughna laughed.

"Killing goblins and trolls isn't a side," Jameston deadpanned. "It's a religion. Might be the only religion worth fighting for."

"Well, since Ancient Badden has thrown in with the beasts, he has chosen sides contrary to your . . . religion," Brother Jond reasoned.

Jameston gave him a sidelong glance and a snicker. "Ten days of marching east of here would get you to a hot lake called Mithranidoon. Taking the trails west of that, into the mountains, will bring you Cold'rin, the glacier the hot waters hold back. Atop that is where

you'll find Badden and his high priests. I'll take you to
him—what you do once you get there's your own choice
to decide."

He ended with a nod that brooked no debate, took his
arrows from Bransen and Brother Jond, and threw one
more wink Vaughna's way before hiking off to the east.

The party of five just shrugged and followed. What
else was there for them to do?

A fter they made their camp that night, Vaughna and
Jameston sat together, chatting and laughing like
old friends.

"They were once lovers," Olconna remarked to Crait,
the two of them on the far side of the encampment, clean-
ing and sharpening their weapons.

Crait laughed heartily. "More than once, if I'm
knowin' Crazy V!"

Olconna shot him a curious glance, and his face crinkled. "You as well?"

Crait laughed again. "And I'm knowin' Crazy V!" he
said.

Olconna looked back at the sturdy woman, shaking
his head.

"That a problem for you?" Crait asked bluntly. "Make
you think less of me, does it?"

"She's not so pretty," Olconna said.

"Bah!" Crait retorted without the slightest hesitation,
and he, too, turned to regard the woman. "She's the most
beautiful woman I ever seen."

Olconna put on a most incredulous expression.

"And if she's e'er to offer you a ride, you'd be a wise
man to take it!" Crait added with a wink.

"Like everyone else?" the younger man asked sarcas-
tically.

"Oh, but don't be going to that place," Crait replied.
"You spend your days killing people and you're to judge
one who takes a ride now and then?"

"But . . ."

"Ain't nothing to 'but' about," Crait cut him short. "Look at her, boy, and look at her well. Crazy V. She's living every moment with fire and filling her soul with memories and experiences most folk will never begin to imagine. She can outfight, outspit, outswear, and outfornicate almost any man alive and any woman I ever heard of. She'll go to her grave without regret. How many of us can say that?"

Olconna started to reply—several times—but he fumbled with the words, and all the while he stared at Vaughna.

Crait sat quietly, staring at the young warrior who had become his protégé of sorts and thinking that he had just given Olconna one of the most valuable lessons of all.

PART THREE

Part of Something Bigger

I resist.

I do not know where it comes from, what deep-seated instinct or subconscious component of my being precipitates the apathy, but for all the truth and truthful desperation of Dame Gwydre's plea I resist her call to arms. She is correct in everything she said. I do not doubt that, had I stayed in Honce proper, the Church or the lairds would have caught up with me and brought me to an untimely and painful end. I do not doubt Dawson's words that the brothers of Chapel Abelle knew the truth of the Highwayman and were prepared to capture or kill me. I have seen Abellican justice before.

I do not doubt that the Dame of Vanguard is desperate or that her people are suffering terribly under the weight of encroaching hordes, bounded (as they are Samhaist driven) by no moral constraints.

And still I resist.

I have seen the result of the troll raids, a town burned to the ground, every soul slaughtered. I am revolted and repulsed and angered to my heart and soul. I feel Dame Gwydre's outrage and her desperation and know that if she felt anything different she would be a lesser person. I see her trembling with outrage, not because of the tentative nature of her survival and title, but because she truly feels for those people who look to her for leadership—that alone, I know, elevates her high above the average laird of Honce proper.

And still I resist.

Who am I? I thought I knew, for all my life the answer was so self-evident that I never bothered to ask the question. At least not in this manner.

The Book of Jhest and the gemstones freed me from my infirmities and redefined me in a physical sense. That much is obvious. But now I come to know that the blessing of the inner healing is forcing upon me a second remaking, or at the very least, a very basic questioning of this man I am, this man I have become.

Who am I?

And what am I beyond the confines of my strengthened flesh?

Quite contrary to my expectations, this strengthening, this healing, has led me to a more uncomfortable place. It has forced upon me a sense of obligation and responsibility for others.

For others. . . .

For all of my youth and into early adulthood there were few others, and those—Garibond, some few brothers of Chapel Pryd, Cadayle on those occasions when I was graced with her presence—were important to me almost exclusively because of what they could do for me. They were in the life of Bransen Garibond because Bransen Garibond needed them.

It is difficult for me to admit that there was something comfortable and comforting in my infirmities. While the other young men were competing in this game we call life, whether simply running against each other, or seeing who could throw a rock the farthest, or in the more formal competitions to gain a position in the Church or in the court of the laird, I was excluded. It wasn't even an option.

There was pain in that exclusion to be sure, but I would be a liar if I didn't admit that there was also a measure of comfort. I did not have to compete in the endless battles to determine the hierarchy of the boys my age. I did not have to suffer the embarrassment of being honestly beaten, because no one could beat the Stork honestly!

My infirmity was no dodge, of course, but I cannot be certain that I would have eschewed a dodge had I needed one. I cannot make that claim because I never had to face that choice.

Then, suddenly, I was freed of that infirmity. Suddenly I became the Highwayman. Even in that identity I cannot claim purity of intent or righteousness of motive.

Who did the Highwayman truly serve in his battle with the powers that were in Pryd Holding? The people? Or did he serve the Highwayman?

The world of the Highwayman is not as simple as that of the Stork.

—BRANSEN GARIBOND

N I N E T E E N

Uncomfortable Riddles

A splash of water brought a cough. With that convulsion Cormack slid back from the deep darkness of unconsciousness. He felt wet along one side and sensed that his lower legs were floating.

The first image that registered to him was that of a glacial troll face, not far from his own, the creature hanging on the side of a (of his, apparently!) small boat and forcing its edge under the water to swamp it.

Cormack reacted purely on instinct. He rolled up to his elbow, facing the troll, reached across with his left hand, and grabbed the creature by its scraggly hair. He kept rolling, using his weight to push that ugly head back, then turned under, rolling his shoulder and hopping to his knees, thus driving the troll's head forward and down. It cracked its chin on the side rail but slid over so that Cormack's weight had it pinned on the rail by its neck.

Up leaped the man. The quick movement freed him enough to lift one leg and stomp down hard on the troll, eliciting a sickening crackle of bone. Cormack nearly overbalanced in the process and tumbled overboard.

Overboard? How had he gotten on a boat, out in the middle of the lake? Burning pain from his back reminded him of his last awful conscious moments, and the rest began to fall in place even as he tried to sort out his present dilemma.

They had cast him out, set him adrift, and now the trolls had found him.

The boat rocked, and Cormack had to work hard to hold his balance. The aft was almost underwater, lifting the prow into the air. Cormack started to turn back that way when he noted a troll scrambling over the prow and coming down at him.

He feigned obliviousness until the last second, then jammed his elbow back, cracking it into the creature's ugly face, crunching its long and skinny nose over to one cheek and tearing its upper lip on its own jagged teeth. The monk retracted and slammed his elbow back again, then a third time, for the troll's weight wouldn't allow it to simply fall away on the steep incline.

Cormack turned and knifed his free hand into the troll's throat, clamping tight. The troll scratched at his forearm, drawing lines of blood, but he held fast, choking the life from it. Or he would have had another of the creatures come over the aft, further tipping the boat.

Cormack turned fast but didn't let go, dragging the diminutive creature along to launch it at its companion. As the two trolls tumbled, Cormack leaped forward and stomped his foot hard on the newcomer's exposed head. He grabbed the second in both hands, by the throat again and the groin, and lifted it up over his head, then slammed it down on its companion.

He stomped and kicked desperately until one went completely still, but Cormack was out of time and he knew it, for yet another troll appeared at the low-riding aft. When the creature pushed up onto that rail the rear of the boat submerged, water flooding in.

Cormack turned and scrambled to the high-riding prow, trying to counteract the weight and lift the rear.

He was too late, so he went to the very tip of the prow, glanced around quickly, and dove away. He counted on surprise, for though he was a strong swimmer he certainly couldn't outdistance glacial trolls in the water!

But he had to try.

M ilkeila sat on the sandbar that she often shared with her Abellican lover, remembering fondly their last moments together. She didn't know why Cormack hadn't come out to see her after that encounter. It really wasn't unexpected that time would pass between their trysts, for, given both of their responsibilities to their warring peoples, they more often than not sat alone on the sandbar.

But something nagged at the woman this day, some deep feeling that things were amiss, that something was wrong.

She rose and walked to the eastern end of the sandbar, the point nearest to Chapel Isle, and peered into the mist as if expecting some revelation or maybe to see Cormack gliding toward her in his small boat.

All she saw was mist. All she heard were tiny waves lapping the sand and stones of the bar.

Her gut told her that something was wrong. She had nothing else.

H e swam for his life, legs and arms pumping furiously. Cormack had shed his heavy robe as soon as he hit the water and wore only the knee-length white pants and sleeveless shirt typical for his order. That and the stubborn powrie cap, which clung to his head as if by magic. Whether he dove under or kept his head up in the splashing water, that bloodred beret moved not at all from its secure perch.

Cormack knew that he had put about fifteen long strides between himself and the troll and its companions. He tried to do logical estimates of the remaining distance to the small island he had spotted. He could only pray that his dive had surprised the vile creatures, and that he would find the island quickly.

Good fortune showed him that the island wasn't as far as he had believed—not nearly—but on the flip side of that revelation was the knowledge that what he had taken to be an island was really no more than a couple of large rocks protruding above the water.

He could get to them—he did get to them—but what sanctuary might they provide? The highest point of the largest rock sat no more than four feet above the waterline, and the whole of that "island" proved no more than a dozen strides across its diameter.

Cormack crawled up onto it anyway, having little choice, for the trolls were not far behind. He had no desire to do battle with them in the water where they could dive and climb and maneuver with the grace of a fish compared to the lumbering human. He had barely set himself when a splash alerted him to the first of the pursuing beasts.

The monk moved to the highest point, crawling on all fours, and found a loose rock on his way. He pivoted and threw with all his strength, smacking a troll right in the face. The creature shrieked and began flailing wildly as its thin blood streamed over its nose and jaw.

Cormack seized the opportunity, skipping down and launching a barrage of punches and kicks on the troll. He had it turning, spinning, and hooked its arms behind its back and bore it down hard. With frightening viciousness, the man grabbed the troll's hair and began lifting its head, smashing it repeatedly on the rock.

He had to break away, though, as another exited the

water. It slashed at him with clawlike fingers, but the monk was too quick, leaning out of range as he squared up.

Another troll broke the water, closing in savagely.

Cormack kept his focus on the first, trading harmless slaps and parries, but all the while he watched the second out of the corner of his eye. That troll leaped in with typical recklessness, but Cormack had set himself appropriately.

He dropped his weight fully on his right leg, then threw himself forward onto his left, closing the distance with the charging troll. Pivoting as he landed, he lifted his right foot into a well-aimed circle-kick that connected solidly with the troll's face, snapping its head back.

Cormack held the pose, leg up, and snapped off a couple of more kicks, though the troll was already beyond consciousness. As he did, he worked his arms frantically to fend off the first troll, which was trying to take advantage of his distraction.

Brother Cormack had been trained by the finest fighters in the Abellican Church, an order that had grown increasingly militant in recent years and had learned well to defend itself.

As the second troll slumped down to the stone, Cormack settled once more into a defensive posture against its furious companion. He didn't hold the defense for long, though. He outweighed the troll by fifty pounds at least, and as this flight and frenzy had settled more rationally into his consciousness, a stark reality became obvious to the man.

He had nothing left to lose.

So he waded right into the troll, oblivious of its swinging arms. In close, he unloaded a series of heavy punches, left and right, accepting a couple of hits in response. But while the troll was scratching and stinging him, he was inflicting real damage, and the clutch lasted only a matter of a few seconds before the troll crumpled before him, where he summarily smashed it into oblivion.

More trolls came from the water to battle him, but there was no coordination to any of it, just a line of victims. Cormack took them on, punching until his knuckles had become one mass of blood, until his feet bled from nicks caused by smashing troll teeth, until his arms felt as if they weighed a hundred pounds each, so great a weariness came over him.

But good luck and sheer rage drove his fury just long enough. When the last of the trolls, the seventh to crawl from the lake, fell limp before him, Cormack slumped to his knees on the stone.

Gasping for breath, Cormack tried to take a survey of his wounds, which included many deep cuts from claws and teeth. He knew that he had to get down to the water to cleanse them—troll bites were notorious for becoming pussy and sore—but he simply didn't have the strength at that moment. He was certain that if just one more troll crawled out of the lake he would surely be doomed.

The sun climbed higher in the eastern sky. The minutes became an hour, then two. The hot waters of Mithranidoon fought back the cold chill of Alpinador. At last Cormack managed to get down to the water and cleaned his wounds and drank deeply. He knelt there, letting his mind whirl through the events that had brought him to this desolate place. The memories of his last hours at Chapel Isle flooded back to him, and he looked again upon the deep disappointment etched into the face of Father De Guilbe, and even the regret evident in Giavno's voice.

Even as the man had scourged him senseless.

There was no going back. His banishment was not a trial or a penance; it represented finality and not forgiveness.

There was no going back.

Cormack was alone, in the middle of a lake full of monsters and trolls, surrounded by enemies. He looked at the steamy waters, and for a few moments he hoped that a group of trolls would rise up from the depths and overwhelm him. For in those dark hours Cormack's future loomed before him, empty, uninviting, terrifying.

He had all that he could drink, obviously, and he might even catch a fish, but to what end?

He peered out into the direction from which he had come, hoping against all logic that he'd see his boat out there, capsized but floating. He knew it would not be so; trolls were expert at destroying craft when they put their minds to it, and the best he could reasonably hope for would be a splinter or a plank washing up against his empty little piece of rock.

Cormack thought back to his fateful decision to free Androosis and the others, the choice that had landed him here, battered and sure to die. For a moment, he regretted his choice, but only for a moment.

"I did the right thing," he said aloud, needing to hear the words. "Father De Guilbe was wrong—they were all wrong." He paused and put his hands on his hips, looking around in an attempt to discern this portion of the lake. It was simply too steamy, though Cormack got the distinct feeling that he was farther to the north. So he turned south and a bit to the east (or so he believed) that he might be somewhat facing Chapel Isle.

"You were wrong!" he shouted out across the waves. "You *are* wrong! Faith is not coerced! It cannot be! It blossoms within—truth revealed in the heart and soul. You are wrong!" Cormack sat down upon the stones, though he felt energized by his outburst, by his proclamation, by the verbal reinforcement of his moral choice.

A slight splash to the side turned his attention that way, where he saw his Abellican robe bobbing in the water against the stones. He retrieved it and laid it out on the stones to dry, and in doing so took note of his powrie beret still set firmly on his head. He put his hand up to touch it. There was, indeed, some magic within that cap.

Cormack looked to the troll bite on one arm to find that it was well on the way to healing, showing no signs of infection. He considered the deep wounds on his back from the whipping. He should not have survived those without tending and yet he had come through them, floating alone in a boat.

The beret, Cormack knew in his heart. The powrie beret somehow acted in a manner to the soul stone and was possessed of magic.

The fallen monk chuckled helplessly. There lay a common thread here, he knew. From the powries to the Alpinadoran shamans to the Abellicans and even the Samhaists there lay a common magic, a bonding of purpose and power.

A singular God for all?

Were the names the various peoples tagged upon their gods really important distinctions? At that moment of epiphany on an empty island, staring certain mortality in the face, Cormack realized that they were not.

But what did it matter? He had nowhere to go, and his plight was only confirmed a short while later when a plank of wood from his boat washed up against the rocks. He retrieved it as the sun sank in the west behind him.

His stomach roared with hunger when he awoke the next morning. He gulped down lake water to try to quell the emptiness. Facedown near the water, hands cupping it and bringing it up to his dry lips, Cormack nearly fell over when he saw the troll right beside him. He fell back, scrambling to find some defensive posture, and cut his elbows and knees in his desperate thrashing before he finally realized that it was one of the dead ones from the day before, bobbing high in the water.

Cormack splashed in to his waist and came beside the troll. He dared to push down on it to try to force it under the waves and was amazed at its buoyancy.

He glanced back at his empty island, certain to be his grave site. He looked out to Mithranidoon and saw another dead and floating troll. Cormack blew a long sigh. Was it possible?

TWENTY

The Gathering

They came in through a variety of means, either running with steps magically lightened and lengthened, or in the form of a fast cat, or even, in the case of the older and more powerful, in the form of birds, flying across the mountain updrafts. They came from their respective parishes, their "Circles," to the call of their leader.

From Devongel Ancient Badden watched each approach, his magical attunement with the land informing him whenever a brother Samhaist crossed into his domain. Their number swelled to twenty, to thirty, and finally, to thirty-two, meaning that all but one of the Samhaists of Vanguard had survived the last months of war, and that one dead priest had died gloriously in the first battle of Chapel Pellinor.

Ancient Badden was pleased.

When they were all together he gave them a complete tour of the grand—now grander—ice palace he had constructed. He even took them to his room of power at the top of the highest tower, where a well reached deep through the castle floor, deep through the glacier, and deep into the energy of the hot springs far below.

"Bask in it," he bade them, and they did, many nearly swooning in the orgy of earth power of this near-perfect conduit to the Rift of Samhain, the holy lake of Mithranidoon.

Ancient Badden led the procession out of Devongel and onto Cold'rin Glacier. He showed them the work at the chasm, where the white worm god continued its destructive work, where the misting blood of trolls prevented the natural repairs. He even sacrificed a pair of prisoners so that his brethren could hear the feasting of the worm.

From their smiles Badden knew that he had been wise to summon them. Morale demanded it. What could be more pleasing to his fellow Samhaists than the strength of Devongel and the fearsome power of D'no?

"Gwydre reinforces from the south," one of the younger Samhaists, whose domain was near to the Gulf of Corona, reported when the group gathered north of the chasm. Badden bade them to share their knowledge. "Nothing substantial as yet, but . . ."

"It will remain nothing substantial," another insisted. "I have been south to Honce proper. The fighting between Laird Delaval and Laird Ethelbert does not abate. Indeed, it is more furious than ever. I had thought Delaval to be gaining the advantage, but Ethelbert has unleashed legions of Behr barbarians. They have cut a fine line across the northern foothills of the Belt-and-Buckle Mountains, moving so near to Delaval's throne that he was forced to bring back most of his frontline forces who were pressing the city of Ethelbert dos Entel."

"That does not bode well," yet another interjected. "Delaval will not be pushed from his city—he will win out in the end, but now that end seems more distant."

"Why do you think that ill?" Ancient Badden asked.

"It prolongs the war."

"And . . . ?" Badden pressed.

"The pain of war is not unnecessary," another Samhaist reminded. "Everyone dies. That some will have their lives shortened is not our concern."

"Easy, friend," Badden said, and he looked back to the other. "And . . . ?" he repeated.

"I only fear that the followers of Abelle grow stronger with every passing year of war," the younger man admitted. "Their gemstones are greatly coveted by the lairds—all the lairds—and every man they heal moves them deeper into the heart of the people."

A couple of the others gasped that the young one would speak so boldly to Ancient Badden, but to their surprise Badden seemed unconcerned and far from angry.

"You think in terms of years, young one," he said, and more gently than anyone expected. "Consider the decades before us. The centuries. Fear not the followers of Abelle.

"We will win in the end because we are right," he continued. "We will win because the order of society depends upon it. There can be no lasting victory for the followers of that fool Abelle, because any gains they make unwind the order. They are gentle—they do not inspire fear in the people. Absent that, anarchy ensues. History tells us as much again and again. As the people begin to lose their fear of the severity of honest justice, they will become lax in their morals. Every woman a whore, every man a fornicator and adulterer. Promises of eternal paradise will not stop a wife from cuckolding her husband! Declarations of a merciful god invite sin and, ultimately, anarchy.

"The monks of Abelle will have their day in Honce," Ancient Badden predicted solemnly, and almost all of the gathering gasped in unison at the admission they had all feared. "They will win, my brothers, but only until the structures of Honce society fall away. It will take a generation, perhaps a few, but the cuckolds and other victims will call out for us. Do not doubt it. Let the fighting rage south of the Gulf of Honce. What you perceive as victory for the monks is also the distraction that will prevent Gwydre from gaining help from the lairds. Let them have Honce proper while we secure ourselves forever in Vanguard. We will always be ready, be assured, to answer the pleas of the victims of the concept of a merciful god and the false promises of sweet eternity.

"Because, my brethren, in the end, it is order that holds civilization together," Badden concluded. "And because, my brethren, that order needs severity."

A cheer went up around the Ancient, one heartfelt and full of awe. Badden knew that he had yet again reaffirmed his position in his order. He was the Ancient, and none would challenge him.

"Go," he bade them all. "Return to your Circles and observe. The trolls and goblins who sweep the land do so because the people of Vanguard deny us. When, in any of your Circles, they stop denying us, when they deny Gwydre and her lover, we will redirect our attacks to another Circle."

All around him, Samhaists began to bow repeatedly.

"We cannot tell the common folk the truth of the monks and their false mercy because they are too stupid to properly recognize the greater truth," said Badden, "that severe justice to the criminal is mercy to the goodly man. We are the merciful ones. They, the followers of the fool Abelle, invite chaos and ruin."

He returned the bow to his minions, then walked through them back toward his house. Behind him, several raced off on magical legs, several cracked and reformed their bones to become swift-running animals, and the greatest became as birds and flew away.

TWENTY-ONE

A Heroic Mistake

"Badden surrounds himself with formidable allies," Jameston Sequin tried to explain to the group of five road-weary heroes. "You should have come north with an army to properly execute your plan."

"We could not have supplied such a force," said the pragmatic and experienced Crait. "And the attraction it would have wrought would have had us fighting trolls and goblins and barbarians every step of the way."

"By the time we reached our goal, if ever we did, we'd be lucky to have even this many remaining," Brother Jond added.

"Then it seems as if your goal was never really in reach," said Jameston. "You do not appreciate the power of your enemy. He is Badden, Ancient Badden, the Ancient of all the Samhaists. They regard him as a god, and not without cause. His powers are extreme."

"Ever see that monk use his gemstones?" Crait interrupted. "Or that one swing that sword of his?" he added, nodding his chin toward Bransen.

"I have and was impressed—at both!" Jameston ad-

mitted. "But have you ever witnessed a dragon of despair?"

"A dragon?" Bransen asked.

"Ancient Badden is near to a god among the Samhaists,
and not without cause," Jameston said. "Have you ever
battled a giant? Not a big man, but a true giant? You will if
you deign to approach Badden. Creatures thrice the height
of a tall man and several times his weight, with power to
snap your spine with the ease that one of us might snap the
shaft of an old arrow."

"We could not bring an army," Brother Jond said with
finality. "Nor can Dame Gwydre's people continue under the duress of Badden's pressing hordes. We know
the desperation of our plan—and to a man and woman
we accepted it. Why can't you?"

Jameston started to respond, but thought better and bit
it back, offering a conciliatory, helpless laugh. "We
should stay to the populated lands as much as possible,"
he said instead. He crouched and drew his dagger, then
etched a rough map on the ground. "We can get right into
southern Alpinador along a fairly defined road, here, just
east of the mountains. There are a couple of villages—
reasonable Alpinadoran tribes—where we can resupply."

"How do we know that they won't send word of us to
Badden?" asked Vaughna.

"If they even know of Badden," Jameston replied,
"they owe him no allegiance. Do not make the mistake
of believing that the Samhaist has captured the hearts of
the Alpinadorans. They are a proud collection of tribes
with their own histories, beliefs, and practices. I know
of no Alpinadoran Samhaists, not one."

"Yet barbarians have been known among Badden's
invading hordes," Brother Jond pointed out.

"Opportunism more than loyalty, I am certain," said
Jameston.

"It is too great a risk," Brother Jond decided. "Let us
keep to the shadows."

"The glacier where Ancient Badden has made his home is a long and difficult trek, through wild lands that are already beginning to feel the chill of winter."

Brother Jond nodded, and Jameston shrugged his agreement.

They set off soon after, heading generally north. They came under the shadows of a range of towering mountains on their west. Though Jameston heeded the demands of Brother Jond, over the next couple of days they often came in sight of a rudimentary road, and on several occasions, they saw the rising smoke from Alpinadoran campfires.

"Grace or muscle?" Vaughna remarked to Crait on one such occasion, when Jameston and Brother Jond had moved down to better view a village, leaving Bransen and Olconna in full view on the back edge of a bluff.

Crait snickered.

"Ah, but I like the way that Highwayman moves," Vaughna added. "It's all like a dance, like the wind under a moon."

"But the redheaded one . . ." Crait prompted, understanding where Crazy V would go.

"Arms to hold a lover aloft," she said. "A determined swing that's not to be blocked or parried. . . ."

Crait laughed aloud, and the two men at the bluff turned to regard him.

"Good thing for you I'm not the type to blush," Vaughna whispered.

"To make others blush, though."

"Aye, that's the fun of life," said Vaughna. "Grace or muscle?"

"The Highwayman's got himself a wife, a new one, and a beloved one," Crait reminded.

Vaughna sighed, clearly disappointed. "Muscle'll do," she said, and Crait laughed again.

Jameston and Jond returned, and the half-dozen moved along as always and set camp as always—except that night Olconna found an unexpected visitor.

His step was lighter the next day.

One afternoon as they passed through a stretch of pines and rocks, just below the snow line and in air cold enough so that they could see their breaths, Jameston whispered to the group that they were being watched.

"The P'noss Tribe," he explained. "Small in number but very fierce. They range from the road below to the passes above. This is their territory."

Bransen put a hand on his sword hilt, a movement Jameston did not miss. The scout shook his head. "We would be foolish to tarry, but they will let us pass through as long as we keep going. They trust in my respect of them."

The group continued along, single-file, and the five unfamiliar with the land kept glancing left and right, as if expecting to see painted barbarian warriors hiding behind every tree, spear in hand.

"Try not to look so terrified," Jameston chided them. "You will just make our hosts nervous."

The rest of the day passed without incident. Jameston kept them up high in the mountains that night, and the cold winds howled at them, and a few snowflakes even drifted about. But Jameston Sequin knew this place as well as the Alpinadorans who called it home. He had a blazing fire going and warmed rocks for the five to keep them comfortable as they slept.

Bransen watched the man carefully long into the night and marveled at the simple serenity on Jameston's face. He seemed fully at peace out here, like a man who had long left behind the trivial troubles of feuding lairds and Churches and petty human squabbles. As Jameston sat upon a boulder and stared up at the night sky, Bransen got a sense of a man truly at peace, of a man who had found his place in the universe and who seemed truly comfortable in that place. It occurred to Bransen that there was something Jhesta Tu about Jameston Sequin.

A thought crossed Bransen's mind. For a fleeting moment he considered the notion that Jameston Sequin might be his father. Was it possible that McKeege was wrong, that Bran Dynard had survived the road and had used his training from the Walk of Clouds to become this legend in the northland?

Bransen gave a little snort at his own absurdity, wondering how in the world that notion had infiltrated his mind. Wishful thinking. . . . He wanted Jameston Sequin to be his father. He wanted *someone* to be his father, particularly someone he could admire. Bransen had tried to dismiss the notion that Dawson McKeege's proclamation regarding Bran Dynard's fate had hurt him profoundly.

Jameston walked over and stirred the flames of the low-burning fire. The orange light danced across his weathered face, shadowing his deep wrinkles and reflecting off his thick mustache.

Bransen saw experience there, and competence and wisdom, and it only confirmed Bransen's earlier recognition of serenity. This wasn't Bran Dynard, though Bransen wished that it could be true.

He would settle for being spiritual companions, if indeed they were.

Over the course of the next few days the road all but disappeared, and no more villages spotted the landscape. Jameston's temperament sobered considerably. Taking that lead, the other five began to feel the gravity of their situation.

They were getting close, they all believed, though none asked Jameston openly about it. They just did as the scout suggested, moving along in a straight line to the north, a few hundred feet up in the foothills of the seemingly endless mountain range. Jameston had to give them the di-

rections far in advance for he was increasingly absent
from their line, moving all about to scout the region and
pick their course. On one such afternoon, with Bransen
leading the five through more rows of tall and dark ever-
greens, the quiet emptiness was lost to a sudden sharp
sound. Bransen pulled up and slid low behind some brush
staring out.

"The crack of a whip," Brother Jond whispered, moving in beside him.

Bransen resisted the urge to say that he would expect
an Abellican to recognize such a sound but decided
against it. He had come to like Jond. In any case, what
was to be gained by creating tension among the tight-knit
group?

A motion to the side turned them both to the right
where Vaughna crouched behind a stump. She looked at
them and pointed down and farther to the right. Following her finger, the pair did note some movement among
the lower trees, though they couldn't make out anything
definite.

"Stay here," Bransen whispered to Jond. He waved to
Vaughna, and then to Olconna and Crait, who were similarly crouching in some brush up above the woman, to
do the same.

Bransen reached inside himself, to his Jhesta Tu training. He surveyed the landscape, falling away before him,
and potential paths appeared to him as clearly as if he
were drawing it all out on a map. He belly-crawled out
from the brush, popped up into a crouch, and darted to a
tree some ten feet from Brother Jond. He paused only
briefly before rushing out again, to the left this time, then
down again to a pile of stones before belly-crawling his
way to a lower stand of trees.

Soon he was out of sight of the others, sliding from
shadow to shadow, for it was darker down here with the
sun beginning to dip behind the mountains.

A long while passed.

Movement alerted the four to Bransen's return—so

they thought. For the form that emerged from some trees in a running crouch was that of Jameston, not Bransen. He moved to the pair highest up, and Jond and Vaughna joined him there.

Jameston's sharp eyes instantly assessed. "Where is Bransen?"

Brother Jond motioned to the valley in the east. "Scouting."

A concerned look crossed the scout's face.

"What is it, then?" Crait asked.

"Trolls, mostly," the scout answered. "Many of them, escorting a line of captured men and women to the north."

Four sets of concerned eyes turned east immediately.

"How many trolls?" Vaughna and Olconna said together, both voices full of eagerness.

Crait couldn't help but grin as he considered Olconna's tone. Play hard, fight hard, he thought, for that was always the way he had regarded Crazy V. She was rubbing off on his young companion already, apparently.

"Too many," Jameston argued. "A score at least, though the line is too long for me to get an accurate count. I dared not tarry, fearing that you five would run down heroically to intervene."

"Are you saying that we should not?" Vaughna protested. "If there are men and women down there . . ."

"The Highwayman returns," Olconna announced. They turned as one to see Bransen picking a careful path back up the mountainside. He rushed in and skidded down in the midst of the group.

"Trolls with prisoners," he breathlessly announced.

"So we've been told," Vaughna replied. "Too many trolls, so says Jameston." She eyed the scout out of the corner of her eye as she spoke, as if in challenge.

But Jameston wasn't taking that bait. "You wish to get to Ancient Badden, and we are only a couple of days from his glacial home. If you engage this group here and now you risk being killed or captured. You also risk having some escape to carry a warning to that most dangerous Samhaist. You have no chance of succeeding if Badden knows you are coming, of course, and little even if he does not. How many trolls are too many trolls, in that case?"

"One troll's too many," Crait grumbled, but the helpless shake of his head accompanying the statement showed that he had no practical answer to Jameston.

"For the greater good you would ask us to let the prisoners be tortured and murdered?" Brother Jond reasoned.

"I'm not envying your choices," said Jameston, and he turned to Bransen as he spoke, for the Highwayman was shaking his head. Jameston knew well where this was leading.

The snap of a whip crackled through the air.

"If we hit them hard and fast, we might have them all dead or fleeing in short order," Bransen offered.

"We've got the high ground to start our attack," Olconna added.

"But if any are getting away—" warned Crait.

"Then they'll think we came from the south to rescue the captives," finished Bransen. "And will they even report the disaster to the Ancient? Would they dare face him with such failure?"

"A score—at least," said Jameston.

"Then you need only kill three or four to do your share," Vaughna interjected. She hoisted her two axes onto her shoulders. "We can't let them walk right past us."

"There is the greater good to consider," Brother Jond protested.

"Spoken like an Abellican, to be sure," Vaughna replied with a snicker.

Brother Jond sighed and looked to Bransen.

"We cannot just let them pass," Bransen agreed. "I'd not sleep well on hard ground or soft bed alike for the rest of my days."

"True enough and more," said Vaughna. "We're arguing as if we've got a choice, and none of us here is thinking that."

Jameston's eyes narrowed. "Do not underestimate trolls," he warned.

"Killed a score of the ugly things already," Vaughna retorted. "More than that. Let's hit them and hit them hard."

All heads nodded. Jameston just gave a resigned sigh and started to lay out a plan, but Bransen beat him to it, sending the scout down north of the group to pick off any trolls who would flee that way.

With Olconna and Crait moving farthest to the south, Bransen, Vaughna, and Brother Jond traveled straight down the hill. Bransen took the lead, directing the movements of the other two so that they remained out of sight until they were right above the path, the line of monsters and miserable captives rapidly approaching.

"You're not too worn out to give a good fight, are you?" Crait whispered to Olconna as they settled into position.

Olconna looked at him curiously, even incredulously.

Crait's smile nearly took in his ears. "Told you it was a ride worth taking," he whispered.

Olconna's cheeks turned as red as his hair.

With grace and speed and perfectly silently, Jameston moved undetected into position behind a clutch of boulders a dozen feet up from the trail and just ahead of the lead troll drivers.

One in particular caught his eye, a nasty-looking beast with half of its face torn away. It swung a whip easily, with practiced efficiency, and the way the others—trolls, and not just the miserable prisoners—cowered against its every word told Jameston that this was likely the leader of the group.

He drew out his finest arrow and set it to his bowstring. With steady arm, he drew back and settled perfectly. He didn't want to shoot prematurely and ruin the surprise, but the moment the trolls became aware of the attack that ugly beast would die.

Jamestone nodded to himself. He still didn't agree with the decision to engage, but he couldn't deny that it would be great sport.

"Thirty or more," Brother Jond whispered breathlessly as he slid in between Bransen and Vaughan just above the road.

Neither could disagree with his assessment. Trolls milled all about the line of a dozen or so prisoners. The estimate of a score seemed inadequate indeed.

"Call it off," Brother Jond whispered, grabbing Bransen by the arm.

For a moment Bransen seemed as if he would agree. But how? To their right Olconna and Crait were already settled, and too far away to be called back. And now the troll line had advanced and was right below them, barely a dozen strides away. There was no chance that they could sneak back up the hill unseen.

Bransen motioned farther back along the troll line to a cluster of the brutes about two-thirds of the way to the end. "Hit them harder," he whispered. Vaughna nodded, and even Brother Jond had to concede that they truly had no options here.

They had committed. They had made their choice up on the hill. The trolls and prisoners flowed before them. They took up their weapons and set their feet under them. The first strike would be crucial.

Olconna and Crait had already surmised the higher-than-expected count and the challenges it would bring. They crouched low behind some brush, glancing over to their left, the north, waiting for the trio to begin the assault.

When that delayed longer than expected, the pair wondered if perhaps the added numbers had turned them about, but it was a brief consideration and nothing more, for as the largest cluster of trolls, nearly a dozen, moved under the trio's position, Bransen and Vaughna leaped down on them, axes and that fabulous sword swinging hard.

"Cut the back!" Crait growled, echoing their earlier conversation, when they had decided their best action to be swinging around the rear of the troll line and driving the creatures forward in to a confused muddle. The toughened old warrior leaped up and started down, but paused as soon as he realized that Olconna wasn't moving with him. He looked at his partner, and saw that Olconna was looking past him, was looking to the south.

"By Abelle's skinny arse," Crait swore when he glanced that way, when he realized that this group of trolls and prisoners was merely the lead, and that many, many more trolls were approaching from the south.

"Be quick, for we've got no choice!" the old warrior yelled, and tugged at Olconna's arm, and the two charged down at the surprised creatures below.

The first few frenzied moments of that attack played out exactly as Bransen had hoped. He and Vaughna cut deep into the troll ranks, slashing and chopping the group apart. Any cohesion the trolls might have found in mounting a defense seemed scattered. Another troll fell before Bransen's slashing sword.

To the north a squeal of agony told the attackers that Jameston would not disappoint, and for a few moments all three believed that whether it was twenty or thirty or a hundred trolls the day would be fast won!

Brother Jond's cry brought them back to reality, though, followed as it was by shouts from Olconna and Crait.

Bransen managed a moment's reprieve to look that

way, and his heart surely sank. Olconna was in full flight, running toward him with a look of utter desperation. Behind him, straddling a dead troll, Crait stood with his back to Bransen, his arms up to ward off a barrage of flying spears. And beyond those came the trolls, so many more trolls, running and hooting.

"Free the prisoners!" Bransen yelled. "Give them troll weapons—anything!" He leaped toward the nearest humans as he shouted, but they shied away from him. Broken by days, weeks even, of tortured capture, not one of them appeared to be in any condition to fight. Those nearest fell to the ground, cowering, whimpering as Bransen approached.

A pair of trolls came in hard at him, but Bransen, too full of rage at that moment, turned aside both their spears with a single downward slash of his blade. He stepped in behind it, stiffening the fingers of his left hand and thrusting them into the throat of the troll on his left while retracting his blade from the double parry and slashing it back across, sending the troll on his right spinning to the ground.

He turned toward the south. Crait was down and squirming. Though it seemed as if he would make it, Olconna lurched suddenly and grabbed at his calf, where a spear had hit home. He stumbled down to one knee. Another spear clipped him across the side of his neck, and a fountain of red exploded about him. He fell facedown to the ground, curled and covered, groaning with pain.

Bransen rushed back to Vaughna and Brother Jond, pressed on two sides by trolls. Hope surged in him again as he marveled at Vaughna's prowess, at the accuracy and power of her strokes. Behind her, Brother Jond lifted his fist and sent forth a bolt of bluish lightning, cutting the air above Crait and Olconna, meeting the troll charge head-on. As he let fly the bolt, so the mob of trolls let fly a volley of rocks, filling the air with missiles. Vaughna grunted and cursed as more than one smacked her hard.

Bransen had better luck—at first—twisting and dodging and snapping off a series of precise parries that deflected one rock, two, and then a third. With the third, though, the rock clipped aside but kept coming at him, right at his head. Bransen ducked it.

Almost.

It clipped him on the forehead and rebounded away. He staggered for just a moment before shaking it off. "Jameston, cover our backs!" he shouted, and started forward, going right by Vaughna. He ripped off a series of slashes and stabs that overwhelmed the nearest troll and kept on moving, determined to drive back the mob, to protect his two fallen companions.

Another lightning bolt reached past him, slamming the lead trolls, but another rock soared in for Bransen's head. He ducked fast to the side and came right back up.

His bandanna and gemstone fell free.

He took a couple more strides, more on inertia than conscious thought, and by the end of the second, he stepped awkwardly, badly twisting his ankle and knee. "What?" he tried to cry in surprise, but he only got out, "Whaaaa. . . ."

He knew. The Stork knew.

Bransen staggered and stumbled. The trolls closed in on him, and he tried to lift his sword to strike. He thought of the Book of Jhest, tried to recall his lessons, tried to fight through the sudden disconnect between his body and his mind. It was too sudden, too unexpected.

Bransen stumbled and fumbled. He dropped his sword and didn't even know it, swinging his arm across as if he still held the blade. A rock smacked him in the face. The nearest trolls, both carrying clubs, ran to flank him, either side, and whacked him hard, driving him to the ground. One flew away, though, a hand axe stuck deep into its forehead.

Vaughna and Brother Jond came forward in a rush, protecting Bransen. Hardly slowing as she neared, Vaughna bent and scooped up his sword and waded into the trolls, axe and sword. She scored a kill, and wounded two others.

"Net!" Brother Jond yelled, but before the word even truly registered to Vaughna she saw the trap, a huge net thrown by a trio of trolls. Instinctively she slashed at it. Bransen's fine sword sliced through one of its thick strands. But more nets were already airborne. The trolls pressed in from in front and from behind.

If it had been twenty, they might have won.

If it had been thirty, they might have won.

TWENTY-TWO

Fed to the Fishes

The arm crackled in protest as Cormack bent it over the torso of another dead troll. He tried to find some levity in this gruesome task. In truth, the monk couldn't believe what he was doing here: tying together the bodies of several trolls he had slain into a makeshift raft. So he laughed because he wanted to scream, because the whole world had suddenly become surreal and ridiculous.

"What have you reduced me to, Brother Giavno?" he asked aloud. He paused, surprised by the name he had put to his lament. Giavno hadn't passed judgment upon him, after all. That had fallen to Father De Guilbe, so why had he just used Giavno's name?

Because Brother Giavno represented to him all the promise and all the failure of the Abellican Church. So much potential and such shortsightedness all wrapped into one complex package. Just thinking of the man made Cormack's back ache, and yet, strangely, he found that he bore the man no ill will. He couldn't agree with the premise of his missionary brothers, and certainly not with their coercive and borderline evil methods, but he understood their perspective. He understood it all.

So he would stand against it. Out here, on a barren lump of rock in the middle of a steamy lake, tying trolls together into a macabre raft. Cormack laughed for real this time. It was that or cry, and he preferred to laugh.

Using strands of dead plants washed up against the rocks and contorting the stiffening troll bodies to complement each other, he soon enough had his bobbing craft constructed. He waded out with it to where the water was waist-deep, then pressed down on it to test its ballast. Dead trolls proved surprisingly buoyant—much more than a human, he thought, though of course he had no idea of how long his craft might last. Wouldn't it be fitting for him to float out into the middle of Mithranidoon only to discover that troll buoyancy lasted only a short while? He chuckled again.

To stay here was to die. That much he knew. Either trolls would come out of the water to attack him, or he'd waste away with little to nothing to eat, or he'd parch under the sun. Or a great storm would come up and wash him into the water—winter was closing in on Alpinador, after all, and even the warm waters of Mithranidoon were not immune to terrible storms.

So he had his raft. He had no other chances to take. Cormack gathered up the plank of his destroyed boat to use as a paddle and pushed off, drifting into the mist on a squishy pillow of flesh. He had no true idea of where he was on the lake, no idea of which way lay Chapel Isle, or Yossunfier, so he played his hunch and paddled out generally in the direction he considered south.

The plank wasn't much of an oar. Mithranidoon's strong crossing currents, brought on by the many hot springs that fed the lake and the constant battles between the colder surface water sinking into the heated depths, had Cormack swirling all over the place. The mist proved especially heavy this day, and the man couldn't see more than a few feet in any direction. Eventually, he just surrendered to the whims of the lake and reclined on the troll raft.

Sometime later, a slight twitch beneath him surprised him. He moved up to his elbows. The raft twitched again, then again more insistently. Cormack moved to the edge and peered into the dark waters, expecting to see a troll tugging at the raft. He fell back, swallowed hard, and knew he was horribly doomed, for a great fish had glided by just beneath him, a fish longer than he was tall.

Breathing hard, the man knelt on the center of the macabre raft and took up his paddle. He had to get out of here, had to get anywhere that was not open water. The raft jerked one way then shuddered as something large bumped it from below. Suddenly it began moving sidelong against all of Cormack's efforts, caught not by a current but by the gigantic fish!

He scrambled to the edge; his face blanched as he saw the beast just below him, its large mouth clamped about a dangling troll leg. Cormack took up the plank in both hands and stabbed hard at the fish. The whole raft bobbed under the water suddenly then popped back up, its integrity beginning to fail. Cormack saw the fish swim off with the troll leg in its mouth.

He rubbed his face. The raft continued to spasm as more and more of the huge fish nibbled, bit, and bumped it. He grabbed the plank and repeatedly smashed it down hard upon the water, trying to frighten the beasts away. For a few moments things did calm. Cormack held his breath, hoping he had escaped. But the raft was falling apart around him, and when he moved to hold it together he saw them, the great fish, circling and waiting.

"Oh, Giavno, what have you reduced me to?" the

distraught monk asked into the stifling Mithranidoon fog.

Y ach, pull 'er left, ye fool!" Kriminig chastised the four dwarves rowing the boat. Cranky old Kriminig, all gray beard and wrinkled face, stood at the prow, clutching his bloodstained beret, which was the shiniest among the powries of Mithranidoon. For none had seen more battles and none had scored more kills than Kriminig.

He closed his eyes as the boat began its turn and let his thoughts flow through his beret. All powrie caps shared the magic of bestowing toughness; wounds healed faster for the wearer, and the brighter a beret, the more cushion it would offer to its wearer. A few of those berets gained added benefits, as the layers of blood on the fabric and wisdom of experience for the wearer brought added insight.

For dwarves like Kriminig, the berets could serve almost as beacons, though weak lights in a thick fog, where he could sense the magic of another powrie cap. An injured dwarf would spark the magic, and that magic resonated.

Out on the lake fishing this day, Kriminig had felt such a pang, and though curious that it was coming from a direction opposite to their home island and far distant, and though he was confident that no dwarves other than the eight on his boat were off the island, he was certain of the feeling.

"A powrie's in trouble," he declared, leaving no room for debate.

"But our kin're all back at the home," another had argued.

"Then more've come to the lake," said a third, and so the debate went, round and round, and only one on the boat knew that he had an answer to the curious riddle.

But Mcwigik, sitting in the back with the fishing net, thought it best to keep his suspicions to himself. A couple of the others, though, had heard rumors about Pragganag's cap, and cast curious glances Mcwigik's way.

"Just ye keep rowing," he said to them. "There might be something interesting to find."

"Too much left!" Kriminig grumbled. "Ease her back to starboard!"

Mcwigik rubbed his ruddy face, wondering if they'd come upon a fight between the monks and the barbarians.

He looked around frantically, lifting his head as much as possible, though he didn't dare stand or even kneel on the rocking troll raft. Even if he spotted another island, Cormack knew that he was doomed: there was no way he could outswim these giant fish even if he managed to surprise them and get a good lead as he had done with the powries.

One came up right before him and bit at a troll hand protruding in the air. Cormack saw those fish teeth all too clearly as they tore the fingers apart. If only he had an enchanted amber! He could use its magic and run across the water, barely disturbing the surface.

If only . . . !

This surely wasn't how the young monk had pictured he would die. He had always recognized that he might not live to a ripe old age. When he had signed on to the mission in Alpinador, Cormack had known well that several other brothers had been killed by the barbarians. He wasn't afraid to die, particularly if it happened in service to Blessed Abelle. Better to live life with a purpose, even with the risks, than to hide in a hole and hope for old age.

But he didn't want to die like this, anonymously, and for no better reason than to feed some fish.

One came up and bit him on the side of his calf, tearing his skin. He swung about fast and slammed his fist into the side of the fish. While that action did send the thing back under the water, the movement also further diminished the integrity of the raft. Another troll body broke free, leaving Cormack on only three remaining ragged things.

He felt his robes weighing him down as he often bobbed into the water, and he thought to take them off. To what point?

All the fear and the anger went away then, suddenly. Resigned to his fate, Cormack stopped himself from removing the soaked and heavy robes. He would let them drag him down to the depths. Better to surrender to it and get it over with.

He hoped he would lose consciousness quickly, that the pain wouldn't be so intense.

He took a deep breath, then blew it all out and set himself to plunge into the water, thinking he would just keep swimming down.

Just as he was about to go, though, he heard a splash that he recognized as an oar dipping into the lake.

"Here! Here!" he yelled, and he began smacking at the fish again with renewed urgency. "Here!"

A fish as long as Cormack was tall leaped up before him, coming for his face, but the agile monk reacted with fury and speed, smashing it in the side of the head with a right cross that turned it aside. He hit it again several times as it thumped onto his raft and rolled into the water.

But now he was in the water, the troll bodies all floating apart. His robes pulled him down as he worked his weary arms furiously to try to tread water. He tilted his head back as far as he could, gasping for breath. He got a mouthful of water instead and felt himself submerging.

A strong hand grabbed his shoulder, though, and hauled him back up. A giant fish brushed against his leg, and he slammed his head as he went up over the side of a boat. Then he was lying on the wood, eyes closed, only semiconscious, and curled defensively. He coughed and felt water pouring from his mouth.

"Well, what d'we got here?" he heard in that distinctive powrie dialect and the typical dwarf voice, which sounded somewhat like a receding wave rattling a beach of small stones.

"Name's Cormack," said another, a voice the monk recognized. "Won the cap fair and square."

"So take the cap and throw the fool back to the Mith trout," said the first, the last thing Cormack heard.

TWENTY-THREE

Captives

"Don't let him fall," Brother Jond implored Vaughna as she struggled to keep Bransen marching in the line of prisoners. They knew well what would happen if that occurred, for one of the other prisoners had tumbled from exhaustion and the cold and the thin air earlier that day up high on a mountain pass. The trolls had descended on that poor soul immediately, whipping and kicking, and when the woman hadn't been able to get up (they prevented anyone from helping her), they had beaten her, laughing at and mocking her all the while, then left her for dead.

"What is wrong with him?" Vaughna asked, for she had never seen anything like Bransen's awkward, stork-like gait.

"He got hit too hard in the head," Brother Jond replied. It was the eighth time he had answered that same question to Vaughna and to Olconna, whom he was now helping along the march. Olconna had taken a few fairly serious hits, and Jond initially feared that he would not survive. Most of those wounds had proven superficial, though, and Olconna's growing reputation for toughness had proven well earned. Now, though in pain and needing support, he moved along without a whimper of complaint.

Bransen listened to the conversations very distantly. He had thought to slur out some rudimentary explanation early on in the march, but had forgone the effort, realizing that there was nothing his companions could do. Brother Jond had retrieved the bandanna, but the soul stone was not to be found, and the trolls had stripped the monk of all of his possessions, particularly the magical gemstones.

Crait lay dead back at the scene of the battle. All of the four surviving heroes sent by Dame Gwydre had been hurt, Bransen the least of all, Olconna by far the worst. But without the gemstone, Bransen couldn't count himself as fortunate. He stayed within himself, focused on his Jhesta Tu training, and forced his *chi* somewhat in line. He didn't exhaust the process, though, understanding that there were limits to his concentration and that after a while his stork affliction would win out.

But he had to keep going, had to keep his focus intense enough so that he would keep putting one foot in front of the other. And he and his three remaining companions had to hope that the trolls would make a critical mistake, and in that event, Bransen was ready to fully immerse himself in Jhesta Tu and try to find at least a few moments of effective fighting.

Their hopes for such an error had waned throughout the remainder of that day and long into the night, for this group of jailers proved quite skilled, and the troll numbers overwhelming. At camp, the prisoners were separated into small groups, and every one lay facedown on the cold ground, a spear poised at the back of his or her neck.

Their only hope was Jameston. Only Jameston Sequin could get them out of this, though Bransen had to wonder what in the world a single man might do against the awful power of Badden and his minions. He tried not to think of that, tried not to succumb to the reality that he would never see his beloved Cadayle and Callen again.

The next day the line of prisoners was marched through a long, descending, barren pass overlooking a river of blue-white ice. As they neared the base of that path the ground became more slippery, and no matter how hard he focused or how hard Vaughna tried to help him Bransen fell repeatedly. The first time he thought his long trial would end with the trolls descending upon him to whip him to death. But many of the weary humans were slipping and falling. Unbeknownst to Bransen and the others they were too close to their destination for the trolls to allow any to die.

They moved out of the rocky mountain pass and onto the glacial sheet, and surprisingly, the footing was actually better there and far more consistent than on the ice-speckled mountain trail.

They had trudged on for nearly an hour when a gasp from in front brought all eyes up the slope to the southeast where a large castle appeared as if made completely of ice. Glistening minarets and towers reached up from foreboding bluish, nearly translucent walls. More dread-filled gasps issued throughout the group as they neared, both from the scope and aura of sheer power emanating from the castle and because this was the first time that any of them had actually looked upon a giant.

These were giants, as Jameston had warned, and not simply large humans. Thrice Bransen's height, the behemoth humanoid creatures mocked his warrior pride. No matter how fine he became with his weapon, no matter how strong he honed his muscles, no matter how fine and precise his reactions, how could he ever hope to do battle against such a behemoth?

Bransen shook his head and mumbled, "N . . . N . . . N . . . No," throwing the negative and distracting thoughts aside. For before him lay the ultimate challenge, the final pinnacle, perhaps. He had no doubt that this was the abode of Ancient Badden, the key to his freedom, or more likely by far, he now understood, the gateway to the afterlife.

Jameston Sequin had survived for so long in hostile lands because he knew when to run away. He had put six arrows into the air at the beginning of the battle and had scored three hits he knew to be mortal, sending a fourth troll spinning down to the ground in agony.

The frenzy had grown too confused after that, however, with human prisoners and trolls scrambling all over each other, and of course, his companions in the mix. Then had come the reinforcements, and all hope washed away.

Bitterness filling his heart, Jameston had found few options: charge in and die or be captured, or flee. He ran. He took little heart in noting that most of the group was still alive when the prisoner caravan passed beneath his perch a short while later, for he knew their destination.

He watched the second group of trolls moving across soon after and cursed under his breath repeatedly for his foolishness in not at least demanding a wider scouting of the area before the impulsive attack. He couldn't have stopped the stubborn would-be heroes, but perhaps he could have delayed them!

The scout shadowed that caravan the rest of the day and tried repeatedly to find some way into the troll encampment that night. But this was no novice group, and no openings presented themselves to the skilled hunter. He couldn't get near to his companions.

The next day proved even worse, for the two troll groups tightened up as they hit the more difficult and broken mountain trails that led high above Toonruc's Glacier. He watched helplessly as one woman stumbled

and fell out of line to the ground. The trolls fell over her,
beating and whipping, taunting and kicking, leaving her
bloody form heaped on the ground.

As soon as they had moved out, Jameston rushed to
her and was surprised indeed to find her still alive,
though barely. He used his waterskin to clean the gashes,
then pulled off his small pack and pulled out some ban-
dages and herb salves and went to work on her many
wounds.

She survived that ordeal with many groans and whim-
pers, but never opened her eyes. Jameston feared she
never would open them again. He looked along the trail
to where the trolls and their prisoners had disappeared
and heaved a great sigh. Then he tenderly lifted the battered woman in his arms and moved off the way he had
come.

It would be a long journey back to Vanguard, he
knew, but that was this poor soul's only chance, and he
had to inform Dame Gwydre that her team of assassins
had failed. The prospect of a Vanguard ruled by Ancient
Badden did not sit well with Jameston.

B ound, dirty, cold, and bone-weary, the prisoners
were forced into a side-by-side line out in the middle of the glacier, just south of the enormous ice castle
that graced the mountainside on the eastern edge of the
ice river, and just before an enormous chasm in the glacial ice. Not far away, a pair of giants pounded wedges
deep into the ice, but even their brute force could not in-
timidate the prisoners more than the old, but hardly feeble, man who stood before them.

Bransen knew it to be Ancient Badden, for he, who
had slain the vile Samhaist Bernivvigar, surely recognized the Samhaist robes of station. The sheer power
exuded by the old man, a commanding presence that
seemed to mock any who stood near to him, reminded

Bransen clearly of his long-ago encounter with the imposing Bernivvigar.

Only this one was stronger, he understood. Much stronger.

Ancient Badden let a long, long time slide past silently. The trolls stepped nervously from foot to foot, occasionally tittering, though not one dared speak. The prisoners tried hard not to meet Badden's withering gaze, but whenever one did he or she knew true hopelessness.

"Him first," the Samhaist instructed, pointing to Olconna, who was doing much better than his friends had anticipated. "Take the rest away. Keep them alive and keep them miserable that they will more welcome their deaths."

A trio of trolls grabbed Olconna and hustled him forward. When he tried to resist they tripped him facedown to the ice, his hands bound behind his back. He landed with a sharp crack. Olconna only groaned, but when he rolled to his side he left a stream of bright-red blood on the blue-white surface.

Bransen glanced at Ancient Badden to gauge his response; if the man had even noted Olconna's fall he didn't show it. Instead, his gaze had locked on a troll off to the side, the one that carried Bransen's sword strapped diagonally across its back. The Samhaist stared at it curiously for just a moment, then reached out his hand and grasped suddenly, as if he were grabbing the troll by the throat.

And indeed, magically, he had done just that from the way the creature suddenly stiffened and reached up with its own hands. Ancient Badden retracted his hand, and the troll stumbled toward him at such an angle that it obviously would have fallen over had not the Samhaist's magic been holding it on its feet.

As the troll came in Badden grabbed it by the throat with his real hand and with surprisingly little effort lifted the squirming creature into the air and turned it about. He regarded the decorated sword for only a moment before pulling it free, then dropped the troll back to the ground.

Ancient Badden's eyes sparkled as he studied the magnificent weapon. He said something to the troll that Bransen and the others couldn't hear. The troll responded more loudly, but in a language that none of them understood. Badden pushed the troll away and took up the sword in both hands, waving it before his eyes, his expression that of someone who had just realized a great treasure.

That expression changed abruptly. Ancient Badden sniffed at the air, eyes narrowing. Bransen managed to keep from throwing himself off balance as he glanced back to note Badden's souring expression, to see the Samhaist bring the sword blade up horizontally under his nose and sniff it, as a hunting dog might sniff.

Unaware of the changing mood, the trolls began herding the prisoners away from the gorge. Bransen and the rest started away, but Ancient Badden called a command for them to wait. As they all, troll and prisoner alike, turned to regard the man, he again took up his conversation with the troll who had delivered the sword. That creature whirled about and pointed in the direction of the prisoners, in the general area of Bransen.

Ancient Badden calmly walked over and spoke not to Bransen but to Vaughna at his side. "I am told you wielded this blade in the fight," he said.

Vaughna glanced nervously at Brother Jond and Bransen. "I did," she said, not knowing what else to say.

Badden motioned, and the trolls dragged her forward. "This blade," Ancient Badden announced, "has the scent of the blood of a Samhaist elder on it." His glower fell squarely over Vaughna. "This blade killed a friend of mine."

Vaughna seemed to shrink at the remark. She turned

her head as if to look back at her friends for support. Bransen tried to call out that the sword was his, but the Stork was unable to make his cry any more than an undecipherable keen.

"I only acquired it recently," Vaughna stammered, seeming to shrink next to the Ancient one. "I never met a Samhaist elder."

"You have now," Ancient Badden replied. Without warning he stabbed the sword into Vaughna's belly. Her eyes registered shock briefly before she doubled over, howling and holding her spilling guts, and sank to one knee. Her companions recoiled in disbelief.

Ancient Badden motioned to the trolls, then to Olconna and to another group, followed by a nod of his chin toward Vaughna. His well-trained charges knew what to do. As one group moved to lift Olconna to his feet and shove him back to the others, a second group fell over Vaughna, dragging her forward trailing blood and bile.

She fought as well as she could which wasn't much, given her condition and the odds. The gutsy woman did manage to squirm about to regard Olconna as he was dragged the other way. "Every moment precious," she gasped to him, despite the pain, despite her imminent demise.

One troll ran to retrieve a rope, looped over a pulley at the end of a beam that was hanging out over the chasm. Bransen and the others watched in horror as the trolls tied the rope about Vaughna's ankle and dragged her to the edge of the chasm and left her there as Ancient Badden strolled over, sword still in hand.

The trolls around the prisoners began herding them again, but Badden stopped them. "Let them watch," he said with a wicked edge to his voice.

Hot with horror and revulsion, Bransen fell within himself. He fought to find his Jhesta Tu edge to cry out that it was his sword. The second the sound escaped his lips something smashed hard into the side of his head, dropping him to the ground. He looked up in surprise to see that it was Brother Jond's fist and not that of a troll.

"Do not insult her sacrifice," the monk whispered harshly.

It took the dazed Bransen a few moments to reorient himself. He looked back at Ancient Badden and the chasm where Vaughna hung upside down by one leg, trying to curl up, to grab her bleeding stomach. Bransen's heart sank, every fiber in his body tense with disbelief and shock. Brother Jond pulled the transfixed Bransen back to his feet.

Ancient Badden stood on the ledge before Vaughna, his arms upraised. He began a chant, calling forth the power of the "great worm of the ice."

"What is he doing?" the thoroughly shaken Olconna asked, or started to, for before he finished, a thundering, rumbling roar shook the ice beneath their feet.

Hanging over the chasm, Vaughna looked down, and her face drained of all color, despite being upside down. She began sputtering and tried to swing herself toward the edge while the trolls began to turn a crank, lowering her from sight. From somewhere below a great beast roared again with obvious excitement. Vaughna began to scream beneath the lip of the chasm, beyond sight. The trolls kept turning the crank, easing the woman a long, long way down. More screams, more roars, and then suddenly it went very quiet.

Suddenly the rope jerked so forcefully that the heavy beam bent and seemed as if it would break. It held, and the trolls began hauling up the rope—no need for the crank anymore.

"Justice is done," Ancient Badden pronounced, turning about to the gathering, a supreme and contented smile on his old face. He motioned to the trolls to begin herding the remaining prisoners away.

Suddenly another squeal from the chasm turned the stunned prisoners about yet again, this time to see the end of the rope. Vaughna's leg dangled from it, the flesh of her mid-thigh ripped and shredded where some nightmarish monster had swallowed the rest of her.

"By Abelle," Brother Jond muttered fervently, head bowed.

TWENTY-FOUR

The Anvil over Their Heads

"They're wanting ye to use yer long legs and wade out for better fishing," Mcwigik explained to Cormack.

The man sat on a large rock on the northeastern side of the powries' nearly barren island, staring at the misty waters.

"We're not going to kill ye," Mcwigik assured him, handing him a weighted net. "Not unless ye do something asking us to kill ye."

"I do appreciate the rescue, and your generosity in allowing me to live."

Mcwigik shrugged. "I'm thinking that the bosses are wanting Prag's son to get old enough to see if the boy can win his dead father's cap back."

"The bosses? Aren't you one of the bosses?"

"Yeah, but I'm wanting to keep ye alive just because."

"Just because."

"Yeah."

Despite his troubling situation Cormack managed a little grin at that cryptic admission from the rough powrie. He had grown somewhat fond of the dwarf.

"Ye don't give us any reason to kill ye, and we won't

kill ye," Mcwigik reiterated. "Now go get us some fish." The dwarf hocked and spat on the rocks and turned and started away.

"And what happens when you go to battle?" Cormack asked, stopping the dwarf in his tracks. Hands on hips, Mcwigik slowly turned about. "When the powries row out to do battle with the monks or the Alpinadorans, what am I to do?"

"Ye're a long way from getting us to let you go along," Mcwigik replied, completely missing the point.

Cormack gave a little laugh. "I could never go to such a fight, and you know it well."

"Yach, but ye fought them barbarians all the time."

"Not by my choice," said Cormack. "Never by my choice. Not against them and not against you powries."

Mcwigik hocked another large ball of spit, this time landing it near Cormack's feet. "I'm knowing ye better than to think ye're afraid of a fight," he said.

"There is no point to the fighting!"

"No? How about the trolls, then? Would ye—"

Cormack cut in. "I'll help you kill all the trolls you can find."

Mcwigik smiled approvingly. "Yeah, we seen what was left of yer boat. Durndest boat any of us e'er seen. Might be a big part of why th'others're letting ye stay."

"But I cannot stay," said Cormack.

"Up for a long swim, are ye?"

"I cannot remain here for long, anyway," the fallen monk went on, ignoring the sarcasm. "This is no place for me."

"Ye wanting us to put ye back with the monks?" asked Mcwigik. "Aye, might that we can, but that ye'll have to earn. So go get the fish, and keep getting the fish—"

"I can never go back there," Cormack interrupted. "They would not have me, and I would not have them. They set me adrift, thinking they had left me for dead, but somehow I didn't die."

"Not somehow, ye dolt," said Mcwigik. "Was the cap on yer head." Cormack reached up to adjust his beret in acknowledgment.

"So ye're not wanting to go back there, and ye're saying ye can't stay here . . ."

"Yossunfier," said Cormack.

"The barbarians?"

"Yes," the monk replied. "I would have you drop me there."

"They'll kill ye."

Cormack pursed his lips. "Nevertheless, that is where I would like to go."

"Well, ye ain't for going there with us," said the dwarf. "Not a place we go near. Those folk ain't like yer monk friends. They know the water and know when anything's near their island. They been there a hundred years, ye know. And more, lots more. They're not using stones to throw lightning like yer own. Nah, their magic's quieter but worse for us if we venture near."

"Then give me a boat so I can go there alone."

Mcwigik spat again, this time hitting Cormack in the foot. "Ye're daft. Boats're worth more than yerself."

"I will return it in short order."

"Then how're ye getting back to their island after ye drop it back here?"

"I'm not going back to that island or any island," Cormack said, half under his breath, and it surprised him to see Mcwigik stiffen at that remark, a look of intrigue suddenly upon his face.

"This has never been my place."

"What're ye saying, boy? Say it plain."

"I have a friend—several, perhaps—on Yossunfier who wishes to be gone from this lake. Lend me a boat so I can retrieve her."

"Her? Haha, but that's telling me a lot."

"We'll come right back with the boat. Then, with your agreement, you can take us to the shore and never think of us again."

Mcwigik started to respond in several different directions. Cormack gathered this by the way the dwarf's mouth worked in weird circles with no real sounds coming out.

"Yach, just catch the durned fish!" he finally blurted, waving a hand at Cormack dismissively as he stormed away.

Cormack had no idea what all that might be about, so he took up the net and waded into the warm lake waters.

You keep looking out to the south," Androosis remarked, walking up beside Milkeila. "You fear that something has happened to him."

It was a statement, not a question, and an observation that Milkeila could not dispute.

"We took care to make it appear as if our escape had been of our doing," Androosis tried to assure her. "I doubt that our friend's complicity is known to the monks."

"And yet he does not signal . . . in any way," said Milkeila.

Androosis put a hand on her shoulder to comfort her. Barely had his hand touched her when Toniquay yelled, "Your duties!" They broke away from each other and turned as one to regard the shaman, who was striding their way. "You spend far too much time seeking an Abellican," Toniquay scolded.

"An Abellican who saved us," said Androosis. He shrank back as soon as he uttered the words, surprised by his own outburst at this powerful figure.

"It is true then, what they say," Toniquay said to Milkeila. "You have fallen for this Abellican named Cormack." He snapped a glare at Androosis, too, daring the young man to say again that Cormack had saved their lives.

"He is a friend," Milkeila replied coolly. "A loyal one."

"Friend," Toniquay spat derisively. "A mere friend does not betray his own brethren. Nay, there is more at work here than friendship. His betrayal bespeaks fires in his loins."

Milkeila didn't respond at all, didn't blink or sneer or speak.

"Your duties await," Toniquay reminded her, adding as she walked by, "You would do well to prove yourself."

"I am shaman—"

"For now."

The warning did indeed shake the woman, visibly so, and she turned and hurried away.

Toniquay turned his withering gaze back to Androosis. "And you," the shaman said, "would do well to learn and accept your place. My patience nears its end for Androosis. I took you to dangerous waters. Men of honor paid with their lives!" Androosis's stunned expression spoke volumes, clearly arguing that the disaster on the boat was hardly his fault.

But Toniquay wasn't hearing any of it. "We went out of our way to try to save you, young and spirited one. But no more. Prove yourself or you will be banished—if you are fortunate and the elders are feeling generous."

"Yes, Toniquay," Androosis replied obediently, hanging his head in humility.

The shaman walked away, eyeing the young man's every step sternly.

A somber mood accompanied Brother Giavno and the rest as they went to work collecting the larger stones from the area of the island they had come to regard as their quarry. Giavno winced and couldn't help but recall the last time he had been down here, when powries had arrived and Cormack had battled them so magnificently, so bravely.

The loss of Cormack was no small thing to the brothers

of Chapel Isle. The manner in which it had occurred had left them all, particularly Giavno, tasked with delivering the very likely fatal beating, feeling empty and desolate. No one had spoken the fallen brother's name since he had been pushed out adrift in the small boat. No one had to.

It was written on all of their faces, Giavno clearly saw. To a one they had been shaken. To a one Cormack's betrayal had asked primary and devastating questions about their purpose and place in this foreign land and among these foreign societies.

Why had Cormack done it? Why had the man betrayed them, betrayed the very tenets of their mission, according to Father De Guilbe's interpretation?

Giavno thought he had the answer to that, echoed in the sounds of Cormack's lovemaking to the barbarian woman. Love was the strongest of human emotions, Blessed Abelle had taught, and more people had been brought down by love than by hate. While there was no specific prohibition of marriage in the Order of Blessed Abelle, such relationships were scorned among the brotherhood. If you gave yourself to the Church, it was to be wholly so. Worse still, to foster a love affair with a heathen, with a barbarian shaman, was far beyond the bounds of acceptability.

Cormack had earned his beating, Giavno believed, and had told himself a million times since that awful day. He could still feel the tug of the whip as its barbed ends dug into and hooked on the flesh of Cormack's back.

He shuddered, and only then realized that one of the brothers had been asking him a question, and probably for some time.

"Yes, Brother?" he replied.

"The stone?" the younger man inquired.

"Stone?"

The monk offered a curious stare at Giavno for just a

moment, then nodded as if he completely understood (which he likely did, for the cause of distraction was quite common at that time) and motioned toward one large rock that had been set off to the side.

"Is it too large, do you think?" the monk asked.

Giavno looked at him curiously. "No, of course not."

"I cannot carry it alone," the monk replied.

"Then get someone to help you."

"They are all busy, Brother Giavno. I thought that perhaps you could help, either with your arms or through use of the malachite stone in lessening the weight."

Giavno was about to reprimand the brother for being so foolish; Giavno was overseeing the work detail and not participating. But then he caught something in the young brother's eye, a look of both hopefulness and sympathy, and when he glanced out at the wider scene, he realized that more than one of the other workers had taken a subtle, covert interest in this distant conversation.

Brother Giavno smiled as it hit him fully: They were trying to distract him. As the work was keeping their minds off of the tragedy of Brother Cormack, so they had thought to include Brother Giavno in that blessed busyness.

"Yes, Brother," Giavno addressed the young monk. "Come. Together we two will carry the stone to the chapel, and what a fine addition to the wall it will be."

Together, he thought, for all that the brothers of Blessed Abelle had was each other. So far from home, so far from kin, without that mutual bond they would all surely lose their minds.

That was what had made Cormack's betrayal so particularly difficult.

Ye might remember Bikelbrin, and these are me friends, Ruggirs and Pergwick," Mcwigik said, splashing at the water's edge behind Cormack.

Cormack nodded to each in turn, wondering uneasily what this unexpected meeting might be all about.

"We'll take ye to her," Mcwigik announced, and the fishing spear fell out of Cormack's hand. "Not sure how we'll do it, but we'll find a way. But we got a price."

Cormack held up his arms, fully displaying his now-ragged brown robe. "I have little, but what I have—"

"Ye know yer way about out there," Mcwigik interrupted. "That's the price."

Cormack looked at him curiously.

"The four of us're done with this rock, and have been for a long time," the dwarf explained. "We're wanting to be gone from the lake, but we're not for knowing the land about. Been a hundred years since I walked those paths, but for yourself, it's not so long. So we'll help ye get yer girl, and in exchange, ye'll take us along."

"My road will be south, no doubt, out of Alpinador and into the Honce land of Vanguard—maybe even across the gulf and into Honce proper, itself. I'm not sure how well-received a powrie might be . . ."

"Ye'll take care of it," Mcwigik said. "So start thinking on how we might get ye to yer girl, and then we're off this rock, all six—or five, if she's not to come."

"Or nine or ten, perhaps even twelve," said Cormack, "if her friends decide that they, too, wish to see the wider world."

"Bring a hundred," said Mcwigik. "A thousand! Long as me and me boys get to get out o' here and to places more interesting."

Cormack settled back on his heels. He could hardly believe the sudden turn of events. One moment, he was floating on a raft of tied troll carcasses, about to be eaten by fish, and now he was looking at escape, at what he and Milkeila had dreamed of for a long, long time.

He nodded—stupidly, he figured.

"We can find Yossunfier at night," Mcwigik said. "And we're thinking to go in one of the next few."

Cormack nodded again, no less stupidly. Mcwigik thumped his hands on his hips and walked off.

Cormack retrieved his fishing spear. Oddly, he couldn't hit another thing the rest of the afternoon.

TWENTY-FIVE

For the Enjoyment of the Ancient

They huddled in the cold on the glacial ice with little or nothing to eat or drink, growing weaker by the day.

The fortunate ones continued to huddle in misery, for every couple of days one was grabbed from their midst and dragged to the crevice, to be wounded and lowered into the gorge as food for the beast that lay below.

Ancient Badden presided over those ceremonies of sacrifice, and he seemed to truly enjoy it. How much like Bernivvigar he appeared to Bransen. The same feral look consumed him in those moments of inflicting agony upon others.

The only other time they saw the old wretch was during the daily troll sacrifice. This was done differently, with several trolls hanged over the gorge with slit wrists so that their blood rained into the dark chasm.

"They hang them in different places every day," one of the human prisoners observed. "Like they're trying to make sure that the whole chasm gets coated in troll blood."

"Thin blood, that," another of the prisoners chimed in. "Mix it with water, and the water won't freeze."

None of them had the wherewithal to put it together from there, because, really, what did it matter to the doomed prisoners?

Bransen, however, noted every detail. His entire existence at that point centered around his mental acuity, as his physical limitations had only increased with the brutal conditions. He tried to put all his Jhesta Tu training and discipline to the side for the time being, as if he was storing it for one furious moment. That was his only hope. He had to find exactly the right time and hope that such an opportunity would present itself.

One gray morning Bransen knew that his last chance had come.

Only Brother Jond fought for him when the troll guards came to drag Bransen away. Even Olconna mitigated Jond's protests, quietly telling the monk that maybe it was for the better that Bransen's misery be ended. Whether they fought for him or not wouldn't have mattered in a practical sense, but Olconna's attitude stung Bransen profoundly. He had more important things to think about, however, as the trolls dragged him to the edge of the chasm. He lay helpless as Ancient Badden approached, carrying Bransen's sword.

This was his moment, Bransen realized. He had to somehow call upon the powers of his training, had to strike fast and sure, get that sword and finish Badden as he had done with Bernivvigar. But he had possessed a soul stone on that long-ago occasion; every step and movement wasn't a battle for him then as it was now. Still, he had to try!

"This one?" Ancient Badden asked. His incredulous tone allowed the prisoner to ease back from his shining moment of fury. "Hmm," Badden mumbled, glancing from Bransen to the gorge. "No," he decided.

Bransen breathed a sigh of relief, though he knew

any reprieve could only be temporary. Every one of the prisoners was being kept alive for one purpose. "No, if we feed him to the worm, he will likely infect the beast with . . . with whatever malady it is that so wrenched his limbs. Bring him south."

Ancient Badden started off in that same direction, crossing an ice bridge to the southern rim of the chasm, then walking off the hundred strides or so to the glacier's cliff edge. The trolls dragged Bransen behind.

Bransen knew he had avoided being sacrificed but not escaped execution. His resistance was not a conscious decision; it came from pure instinct, simple and unafraid, as only a man who realizes death is both imminent and unavoidable might discover. All of his muscles twitched in magnificent harmony, moving together for the first time since he had lost the soul stone, lifting him suddenly to his feet, his wrists and ankles breaking free of the hold of the four escorting trolls as he twisted and then hopped upright.

He snapped a circle-kick against the side of a troll's knee and slugged the creature in the jaw as he came around, launching it away. He leaped straight up as the other three closed on him and kicked out to both sides with perfect balance and stunning power—literally stunning, as the kicks sent two trolls staggering and stumbling to the ground.

The remaining escort leaped onto Bransen's back and began clawing, but the man executed a high somersault and stretched out to full extension as he came over, ending his turn so that he landed flat on his back atop the troll. He wrenched the creature's arms from his chest and throat and twisted them at the wrist as he rolled off the creature. When he hopped back up to his feet, he gave sudden jerks that broke both of those wrists cleanly.

Bransen spun about as two of the first three came in at him. The leading enemy was right upon him as he turned, and got its hands about his throat, choking him. Bransen hooked his thumbs under those of the troll and tugged out and down, then folded his legs under him so that he fell to his knees, taking the troll down with him. He used the suddenness of that impact to viciously drive the troll's thumbs over and down, breaking both.

Bransen hopped right back up, but he felt the pangs of the Stork within, the moment of Jhesta Tu–inspired coordination fast fading. He barely slapped aside the clawing strikes of the last of that group, and worse, several more were fast heading his way. Worst of all for Bransen, Ancient Badden had taken note of the fight.

The ice under Bransen's feet suddenly turned to water, and he plunged down, and only avoided continuing deep into the glacier by throwing himself to the side. Instinctively, Bransen rolled himself out of the water— and a good thing that was, for it froze again almost immediately.

Across the way, Ancient Badden cackled with enjoyment. Trolls fell over Bransen, beating and clawing him. His glorious moment of concentration was lost, falling to the curse of the Stork once more. He still tried to flail, for what it was worth, but the four trolls now bearing him held him tightly and a pair of others walked alongside, punching him hard every time he moved.

They dropped the nearly unconscious man at Ancient Badden's feet near the edge of the glacier and moved fearfully away.

"Do you see it?" Ancient Badden asked him. Lying helpless, Bransen saw only the sky and the tall man towering over him. Badden reached down and took him by the front of his shirt and with surprising and terrifying strength hoisted him upright. Bransen looked out on a long, long drop, hundreds of feet and more, to a wide and long lake that was almost completely blanketed by fog.

"Mithranidoon," Ancient Badden explained. "It's called that even by the Alpinadoran barbarians. A Samhaist name in this northern land. Do you know why that is?"

Bransen didn't even try to respond, for he wasn't even sure what he was seeing or feeling or hearing. He had all he could handle to merely keep himself from falling into a deep and dark place. He could not allow that to happen. Not now.

"Because the magic of this place cannot be denied—not even by the barbarians," Ancient Badden proclaimed. "Even they understand that our name for it—Mithranidoon—is the most fitting. Even they accept that this is, as it long ago was, a Samhaist holy place. And yet it is not under my dominion. Not yet. Not until I wash away the vermin who have deceitfully come to call Mithranidoon their home, as if any but the Ancient of the Samhaists holds any claim on Mithranidoon!"

Bransen tried to commit Badden's words to memory, though he expected that they would mean nothing to him in short order, since he would be dead. Still, that part in him that would never surrender kept working, kept plotting, kept trying.

"The great worm does its burrowing work," Ancient Badden said, and it was obvious to Bransen that he wasn't talking to him anymore, was just speaking out loud to hear the glory of his words. "The blood of trolls ensures that the god-beast's work is not reversed by the cold. And soon Mithranidoon will be cleansed."

Ancient Badden's voice had risen with each word, in glorious proclamation, and he ended with a self-deprecating chuckle, as if a bit embarrassed by his outburst. "I cannot allow you to participate," Badden said to Bransen. "I am sorry, but you will not share in the glory of my victory. My god-beast is too precious to me to allow it to eat you.

"Of course, none of this matters to you," Ancient Badden said, his voice lowering as he threw Bransen from the cliff.

In all me days, I ain't seen anything as stupid," Mcwigik grumbled, and pulled on the oar to complement Bikelbrin, who was sitting beside him. "Ye're taking us to get cold so we won't be getting cold?"

"It is called acclimating," Cormack explained.

"It's called stupid."

"You said you want to get off the island and the lake."

"Get off and stay off! But not to sleep against the ice."

"We might have to," said Cormack. "Winter hasn't come in yet, but it's drawing near, and even this time of year can bring freezing winds and deep snows to the higher passes."

"Then we won't go to the higher passes," Mcwigik argued.

Cormack exhaled and tried to relax. He knew that part of the dwarf's agitation was due to the dramatic adventure they might soon be undertaking. He and these four powries, along with Milkeila, he prayed, and perhaps some of her friends, were bound to leave Mithranidoon. This was not the best time to undertake such a journey, but the thought of spending another several months on the lake surrounded by nothing but powries was more than Cormack's sensibilities could handle. It hadn't taken him long to decipher that Mcwigik and his fellows felt the same way, either. They all wanted out—now.

"Shouldn't yer lady friend be with us?" Mcwigik asked.

"Shouldn't you take me to her so that I can find out?" came the sarcastic reply.

"In good time—when others' eyes ain't on ye so much."

"The more we get to the cold, the better. It will thicken your blood."

"Yeah, acclimating," said Bikelbrin. Behind him Pergwick chuckled.

"Stupid," muttered Mcwigik under his breath, but he let it go at that. For all his complaining, everyone there knew well that he wanted to get away from Mithranidoon as much or more than anyone else.

In fact, Mcwigik picked up his rowing pace as soon as the conversation ended, nudging Bikelbrin to match him.

Instinct replaced conscious thought as Bransen plummeted from the ledge. Arms flailing, body twisting, the man's sensibilities were too consumed by sudden terror to consider his Stork limitations. The Book of Jhest resonated in his thoughts, and he reflexively twisted to get his arms nearer the sheer ice wall.

Then those arms worked desperately, frantically, catching, grabbing, pulling, scraping—never enough to jolt him or send him tumbling, for that would have been a fatal mistake, but enough to continually jerk against the fall. It took him a couple of heartbeats to align his sight properly below and put his arms in synch, reacting to the edges and bumps as he registered them. But once he found that balance and timing he began to literally pick his path below him and devise the best strategies.

He manipulated by the angle of his grabs and slaps and the constant twists of his waist, and his handwork became more intrusive and stronger. He spotted one bigger ledge just below, and reacted fast enough to hook his fingers a dozen feet above it—not to break his fall as much as to give him the leverage to turn vertical. His feet hit the ledge hard; his legs bent to absorb the blow, and he did not resist as he fell right over backward, having somewhat slowed his descent.

Then his hands went back to work, and he kicked his feet against every possible jag as well, working furiously to counter the force of his fall. Some two dozen feet from the ground, though, the glacial wall sloped in and away, and the already plummeting Bransen could only free-fall that last expanse. He knew that he was going too fast to attempt to roll out of it as he hit, so he flattened himself out horizontally and spread his arms and his legs.

He slammed into the muddy ground, and the bright sky winked out.

Ha! Looks like yer eyes seen right," Mcwigik said when the group of four dwarves and Cormack came around an ice and boulder jag at the base of the glacier to see a man lying flat out on his back, driven more than halfway into the muddy ground.

"I'm guessing that hurt," Ruggirs said, and all four of the powries chuckled. Cormack, though, saw nothing funny in the tragic fall, and rushed to the man, though in looking up at the towering glacial cliff face, he knew that this one was certainly dead.

The man's strange black clothing made him even more curious, and when Cormack got beside him, the lightweight nature of the smooth fabric had him scratching his head, as it was totally unfamiliar to him.

Cormack nearly leaped out of his shoes when the man stirred.

"Yach, but he's a tough one," remarked Mcwigik, coming up behind Cormack.

After the shock wore off Cormack immediately went back to the man, bringing his ear close to the fallen one's mouth to see if he could detect any sounds of breath.

"He is alive," Cormack announced.

"Not for long," Mcwigik chortled. "Better for him that the fall had snuffed out his lights for good."

"Aye, that had to hurt," Ruggirs said again.

Cormack continued to inspect the man, to try to determine the extent of his injuries. In truth, he was thinking that the most merciful thing he could do would be to smother this one and end his pain, but the more he looked, the more his estimate of injuries lessened. He pulled off his powrie cap and set it over the man's head.

"It's to take more than that," Mcwigik grumbled, but Cormack ignored him and kept moving the fallen man, one leg or one arm, or rolling him up to a near-sitting position. Through it all, the injured man made not a sound.

"I don't think he fell all the way," Cormack announced.

"Yach, but he buried himself half into the mud!" Mcwigik argued.

"He could live," Cormack replied. "His wounds are not as bad as we expected."

"Ye're not for knowing any such thing."

"Nor are you for knowing that I'm wrong," Cormack shot back. "This man can live. If I had a gemstone . . . We have to get him to Yossunfier. Help me now, without delay." The powries all looked at Cormack incredulously, and none made a move.

"We cannot just let him die!" Cormack yelled at them, and all four burst into laughter.

Cormack took a deep breath to calm himself. Screaming at the powries now would likely just get him stranded here or worse and would do nothing to help this poor fellow. "Please," he said quietly. "There is a chance I can save him. We humans don't just bury hearts and pop out of the ground again."

"Ye'd be smart to watch yer words," Pergwick warned, but Cormack waved him away.

"I know, I know," he said. "But it is important to me to try to save him."

"Ye know him?" Mcwigik asked.

"No, of course not."

"Then what do ye care?"

"I just do," the increasingly impatient Cormack retorted. "Please, just get me to Yossunfier that I can at least try to save him."

"Yach, but ye're just wanting to take yer girl along with us—again," Mcwigik argued.

"She already is coming with us by our agreement."

"Then ye're wanting her with us sooner, and we already told ye . . ."

"She will be of great help to us," Cormack admitted.

"All of her people will. Save this man and help ourselves, I say."

"We get near to Yossunfier, and we're to see the sky full o' barbarian barbs," Mcwigik grumbled. "Ye think it's an easy thing, but ye're a blind fool. Them barbarians see us coming, and we'll all be dead before we step on their beach. Now, are ye thinking that'd be a good thing for your flat friend there?"

Cormack took another deep and steadying breath, and looked all around, feeling as if the answer was right there before him, waiting to be unveiled.

He smiled. "There may be another way."

You wonder why I have allowed you to live this long," Ancient Badden said to Brother Jond after having the monk beaten and dragged to him in the ice castle.

Brother Jond looked up at him blankly, trying to appear as impassive as possible. He was terrified, of course, but he didn't want to give the wretched Samhaist the pleasure of seeing him squirm.

Ancient Badden stared at him for many heartbeats and nodded his chin as if prompting the man to respond, which Brother Jond would not do.

Badden's visage melted into a profound scowl. "You would think that an Abellican monk would be my first victim, of course, since your Church has been the scourge of the land these last seven decades." In fighting off the urge to respond, Brother Jond couldn't suppress a slight smile, and that only made Badden scowl all the more.

The Ancient broke into a sudden giggle, cackled through a quick chant, and waggled his necklace at the monk. The floor beneath Brother Jond's feet turned from ice to water suddenly, plunging him in.

But not deeply, for Ancient Badden cut the spell short and reversed it, freezing the floor around Brother

Jond's legs, up to mid-thigh. The contraction of the ice squeezed him so hard that he could feel the blood rushing up from his legs. He felt suddenly sick to his stomach and light-headed at the same time. His eyes bulged as if the rush of blood would simply launch them from their sockets. He tried to remain silent, but a soft groan escaped his lips. The ice tightened some more.

Now Ancient Badden towered over him. "Ah, but I would so love to tear your limbs from your torso." He brought the side of Bransen's sword against Jond's cheek with a stinging slap, then turned the blade as he flashed it past, just enough to draw a deep cut across the monk's face. "Or to open your belly, side to side, and slowly draw out your entrails. Have you ever seen the face of a man so tortured? It is the most exquisite mask of agony."

"And you declare yourself a man of God!" Brother Jond blurted before he could reconsider his reaction.

"Ah, so he speaks," Ancient Badden laughed at him. "I had thought you a mute, which would be an improvement for any Abellican, of course. I am not a man of your childish and benign creation, fool. I am a man of the Ancient Ones, of the truths of life and death. You are too cowardly to face those truths, so you cannot begin to comprehend the way of the Samhaist! I almost pity you and all the others born after Abelle, who were raised in the echoes of his lies and false hopes."

Brother Jond narrowed his eyes, but his threat was so impotent as to be laughable, which of course, Ancient Badden did.

"I said 'almost,'" Ancient Badden reminded. He waggled his necklace, and the ice gripped on Jond's legs even more tightly.

"I keep you alive because you may be of use to me," the Samhaist offered. "As my armies press—"

"Your hordes of monsters, you mean."

Badden shrugged as if that hardly mattered. "They serve a greater purpose."

"They are—"

Brother Jond stopped suddenly as Ancient Badden kicked him squarely in the face. His head snapped back and forward, and a couple of teeth flew from his mouth along with a gush of blood and spittle.

"If you interrupt me again I will hurt you more profoundly than you have ever experienced, more so than anything you could ever have imagined," Ancient Badden warned.

Dazed, temples throbbing, legs aching, Brother Jond could not even bring a defiant stare to his face.

"As my armies press into Vanguard and drive Dame Gwydre to Pireth Vanguard, she will seek parlay," Ancient Badden explained. "As her principal consort is one of your feeble Abellican associates, your presence among my prisoners will grant me a greater ante." The Samhaist bent low and stared into Brother Jond's face, and when Jond tried to turn away, Badden punched him hard, grabbed him by the chin, and forced him to lock stares.

"Does that please you? To know that you will help facilitate the downfall of your religion in the region of Vanguard? Nor will it end there, I promise. When the war in the southland is ended, so too will be the tricks of your kin that so enrapture the dueling lairds. The reality of the conflict will weigh heavily upon the grieving people, and we will be there. For the Samhaists know Death, while the Abellicans deny it. The Samhaists understand the inevitability, while the Abellicans offer false promises. That will be your downfall."

Brother Jond's face became a mask of apathy.

"What is your name?" Ancient Badden asked. No answer.

"It is a simple question, one carrying great importance," said Badden. "For if you do not answer, I will bring in one of the prisoners and torture him to death before your eyes. It will be an hour of screams that will echo in your mind for the rest of your days, short though they will be."

Brother Jond glared at him as he started to motion to the troll attendants. "Brother Jond Dumolnay," he said.

"Dumolnay? A Vanguard name, or of the Mantis Arm, perhaps."

Brother Jond didn't answer.

"Mantis Arm," Ancient Badden decided. "If you had been raised in Vanguard you would better know the Samhaist way and would never have fallen for the lies of the fool Abelle."

"Blessed Abelle!" Brother Jond corrected, spitting blood with every syllable. "The Truth and the Hope of the world! Who mocks the Samhaist death cult and your use of terror to control the people you claim to serve!"

"Claim to serve?" Ancient Badden said, and laughed loudly.

"Then you do not even pretend!"

"We show them the truth, and they may do of that truth what they choose," the Samhaist growled back. "We bring order and justice to rabble who would eat each other if they were not instructed not to!"

Brother Jond couldn't suppress a grin, glad, despite the beating, that he had irked the Samhaist enough to garner such a rise of emotion. "Justice?" he said with a sarcastic laugh.

Ancient Badden went silent suddenly and stood up straight, staring down at the ice-trapped monk.

Brother Jond took a deep breath to steady his nerves, guessing that he had gone too far here. But it was too late for any retraction, he understood, too late to bring the Samhaist back to a level of calm. So he followed his heart and put his fears behind him.

"I will see your demise, Ancient Badden," he declared. "I will see the victory of Blessed Abelle in Vanguard and throughout Honce!"

"Indeed," the Ancient replied calmly—too calmly. His arm swept across, slashing Bransen's sword, drawing a line in Brother Jond's face and taking both his eyes and the bridge of his nose in the process.

The monk howled and screamed, thrashing in agony.

"I doubt you will 'see' anything," Ancient Badden said to him, and walked away.

TWENTY-SIX

Well Found in a Dark Place

Milkeila wasn't consciously thinking of anything as she walked on the beach one dark and breezy night. Resignation filled her thoughts and filled her heart, so much so that she had abandoned her hopes of what might have been, in full knowledge that her reality simply could never approach those hopes and dreams.

She didn't know how many days had passed since she had last seen her beloved Cormack. Too many, though, for her to ever expect to see him again. Either he had been found out as a traitor and imprisoned or put to death, or he had buried himself in guilt over his stark actions and had abandoned his wayward course—a course that included Milkeila.

For several days, the woman had tried to concoct some mental scenario in which she could lead her people to go and rescue Cormack; she had allowed herself to fantasize about again besieging Chapel Isle and forcing the monks to relinquish their unfaithful brother.

That could never happen, of course, and she didn't even know if such was Cormack's condition. So, for the sake of her own survival, Milkeila had let it all go, had exhaled and exorcised Cormack from her heart and mind.

And always, Toniquay was there, looking over her shoulder, reading her emotions and reminding her, ever reminding her, of her responsibilities to the traditions. She was shaman, and among the Alpinadoran tribes that was no small thing.

She walked the beach this night, the wind blowing aside the mists enough to afford her a wonderful view of the starry canopy above, the water gently lapping the rocks and the black volcanic sand of Yossunfier's beach, and she was at peace. Until she saw a single light in the southeast.

Milkeila's heart skipped a beat. She thought it must be Chapel Isle—perhaps a lantern at the top of their ever-growing tower. But no, she realized, it could not be. The light was not far enough away.

A boat, perhaps, she silently cautioned, and she stood perfectly still and tried to not allow the movement of the small waves to distort her perception. After many heart-wrenching moments, she realized that the light was not moving. It was on the sandbar.

Milkeila had to consciously breathe and steady herself. She started for the boats immediately, but her swift stride slowed as it occurred to her that the light could be a trap. Perhaps Cormack had been discovered as a traitor and had been tortured into revealing all! Perhaps a group of monks had lit her and Cormack's private signal beacon to lure her to the sandbar and capture her.

Those thoughts continued to swirl in Milkeila's head even after she had appropriated one of the smallest Yossunfier boats and had started quietly paddling out from the shore.

Her heart raced as she came to confirm that the light was indeed coming from the sandbar, or near to it, but she was a bit concerned that Cormack would burn such a light for so long on so clear a night. Certainly it could be seen from Red Cap or Chapel Isle, and after so many minutes, perhaps even some of Milkeila's own people would decide to go and investigate. Of course, all of this was based on the presumption that it was indeed Cormack.

Milkeila gave one long and powerful pull with her paddle, then put it up and bent low in the small boat so that her silhouette wouldn't stand out against the horizon as she glided toward the sandbar. Peering through the thin mist, she saw a form, and the way the tall man paced left no doubt in her that it was indeed her beloved Cormack. She started to sit up, even to call out, but she bit back the call as she noted another form on the sandbar, short and thick. A powrie.

Milkeila sat up and speared her paddle into the water to create drag and slow the boat. She was still drifting, the current and her momentum bringing her very slowly toward the sandbar. She didn't know what to do! She wanted to see Cormack—more than anything in the world, Milkeila wanted to be certain that her lover was all right, wanted to feel his strong arms about her again.

But what was this? Why would Cormack bring a bloody-cap dwarf to their private place? A groan from the far side of the sandbar made her realize that there were others, as well, and soon she was close enough to see another powrie over there, kneeling over something—a man, perhaps?

Despite her caution, Milkeila couldn't turn away from this. Cormack's movements showed her that she had been seen, and the man rushed to the point on the sandbar nearest to her and softly called out her name, waving frantically for her to come ashore. And she did, and Cormack wrapped her in as tight a hug as she had ever known.

"Powries," she said, her voice as shaken as her sensibilities.

"Quickly, here," Cormack said, taking her by the wrist and dragging her along to the back side of the sandbar, where an injured man lay on the ground, a second powrie beside him. As if that wasn't distressing enough, a third powrie sat in their boat, just a short distance away.

"Cormack, what are you doing?" Milkeila asked, and when the monk didn't answer, she just stated, rather severely, "Cormack!"

He stopped and swung about to face her. "We found him. You have the gemstones? He will die."

"Who?"

Cormack dragged her over. "This man."

"Who is he?"

Cormack shook his head. "We found him at the base of the glacier, half-buried in the mud."

"We? You and the powries?"

"Yes."

"Cormack?"

The monk paused and took a deep breath. "I was expelled from Chapel Isle, beaten and left for dead. This powrie—"

"Mcwigik's the name," the dwarf interjected.

"Mcwigik saved my life," Cormack explained. "They've taken me in."

"Every dwarf needs a dog," Mcwigik mumbled.

"We were going to come and get you," Cormack continued. "We're leaving the lake."

"You and the powries?"

"A few, yes. But we found this man, and he will surely die . . ." As he finished, Cormack reached for Milkeila's tooth-and-claw necklace, and twisted it out of the way to reveal the string of gemstones he had given to her. "Help me, I beg," he said, and reached to remove the magical necklace.

Milkeila instinctively bent and helped him do so, following Cormack as he rushed to the supine man, fumbling with the gems to find the powerful soul stone. He went to work immediately, pressing the stone against one egregious wound, where the man's leg was swollen and possibly broken. Milkeila put her hand atop Cormack's and began a prayer of her own, using the soul stone connection to the wounded man to impart her energy into the gem to heighten Cormack's work. The man groaned and stirred a bit.

They went to the next wound and then the next after that, and with each application of gemstone magic their bond tightened. They shared smiles after every victory, though they had no idea of whether or not these little bits of mending would win the largest battle of all and keep this stranger alive.

"He's wearing your cap," Milkeila remarked.

"Magic in a powrie beret," Mcwigik said from the side.

If either Milkeila or Cormack heard the dwarf, neither showed it, for they had locked stares and hearts and to them at that moment, the outside world didn't exist.

"He fell from the glacier?"

"And somehow he is not dead," Cormack answered. "The mud, I guess, for the ground at the glacier's base is soft."

"It is a long fall," the woman replied, obviously doubting.

"And yet he lives," said Cormack with a shrug, as if nothing else really mattered.

They had worked their way up over the most obvious wounds by that point, and Cormack put the soul stone on top of an area of swelling on the battered man's forehead. Again he sent the gemstone's magical energy flowing into the stranger, and again Milkeila put her hand atop his to help.

But then the supine man did likewise, his hand snapping up to grab Cormack by the wrist. His eyes popped open wide and Cormack instinctively tugged away.

"No!" the stranger started to say, but the monk and Milkeila had moved too forcefully for him to prevent them from pulling the stone from his forehead, and as soon as that happened, he lost all strength and the two healers fell back, staring at him.

"Gemmm . . . gem . . . ge . . . ge . . . ge," the wounded man pleaded, his jaw shaking and drool sliding from the side of his mouth.

"I think ye forgot to put his brains back in," Mcwigik quipped, seeming very amused by the man's sudden and pathetic attempts to sit up or even to communicate.

"Ge . . . Ge . . . Gemmmm," the man cried, reaching out at the recoiling duo.

"I'm thinking he lived by landing on his head," Mcwigik said, and his two powrie companions chuckled.

"He wants the soul stone," Cormack surmised.

"The poor man," said Milkeila.

The stranger kept stuttering and drooling and shaking so badly that he seemed as if he would just collapse.

"Give it to him," Milkeila said.

Cormack looked at her incredulously.

"He cannot run away with it," the woman reminded.

Cormack reached out and put his fist, clenched over the soul stone, in the stranger's shaking palm. As soon as the man tightened his grip about Cormack's fist, Cormack relaxed his grasp and let the gemstone fall to the wounded man.

Shaking fingers immediately stilled and closed over the gemstone, and with a great and collected exhale, the wounded man lay easily on the sandbar. Many heartbeats passed.

"I think it killed him to death," Mcwigik said, but then the man reached his hand up and pressed the gemstone against his forehead.

"Or not," muttered the dwarf, and his voice reeked of disappointment.

Many more heartbeats slipped past and the stranger remained motionless on the ground, his hand pressed against his forehead. Then—with hardly an effort, it seemed!—he sat up, still holding the gemstone to his forehead, and said in an accent that was obviously from south of the Gulf of Corona, "Well found in a dark place and know that you have my eternal gratitude. I am Bransen."

They hadn't hit anything vital, he believed; the wound was not mortal. It hurt, though. How it hurt, and it was all poor Olconna could do to turn his focus to his surroundings and not the cut in his belly.

He had managed to secure a knife; he surely would have preferred a sword, but the knife he had hidden away in his boot would have to suffice.

He couldn't deny his fear as the giants lowered him head-down into the ice chasm, a thick rope tied tightly about his ankle. But Olconna had spent the better part of his adolescence and all of his adulthood in battle, and had faced tremendous odds again and again. Always he had found his answer, his way to victory or at least to escape, and he had no reason to believe that this time would be any different. Ancient Badden had erred, Olconna believed, because he had allowed the man to greatly recover from the wounds he had received in the fight when he had been captured.

He brandished the knife. He forced himself to extend downward and stretch the wound, as he couldn't hope to battle whatever beast might be down here while doubled over.

It was darker now, for he was well over a hundred feet down from the ledge, but not pitch-black. Olconna forced himself into a slow turn, taking in the myriad edges and jags of the chasm walls, trying to pick out a shape among them that foretold something else.

"Faster," he muttered under his breath, wanting to be on the floor and free of the rope before this beast appeared. In the back of his head, Vaughna's last words, "every moment precious," played over and over like a constant echo of regret. For the man, cautious in everything but battle, hadn't lived that way—until he had encountered Crazy V. The notion weighed on him for a short moment, but Ol-

conna turned that fear that he had lost his chance into determination that he wouldn't let it end now, that he would
find a way to gain some years where Vaughna's words
would guide him as sound advice.

But a moment later Olconna heard a low rumble, like
a huge rock rolling down a hill. The beast smelled his
blood, just as that old wretch Badden had predicted before he had stabbed Olconna in the belly.

Olconna slowly turned at the end of the rope, his gaze
passing the long and open stretch of corridor. He noted a
movement down there, a quick glimpse of something
large, something awful. He tried to battle his momentum,
to stop and face the beast, but he kept going around. He
managed to twist about, eliciting terrific pain from his
torn belly, to catch a few quick views of the approaching
monster. It looked like a gigantic worm, or more accurately a caterpillar, for the many small legs scrabbling at
its sides. Giant mandibles arched out in semicircles before its black, round maw—the type of toothy orifice often found on sea creatures, which seemed to pucker as
much as open.

"Faster!" Olconna said again, cursing the giants who
were lowering him, but as if on cue, the rope stopped.

He hung there, twenty feet from the ground, too high
to try to free himself, for the fall would surely leave him
helpless in the face of the monster. But too far, he believed, for the approaching beast to get at him. He managed to steady his turn properly so that he could face the
crawling nightmare.

They'll let me bleed out up here, above it, he reasoned, and he decided then that if the worm came under
him he would cut free his ankle and drop upon it, all
caution be damned!

That thought rang as a beacon of hope in his mind,
turned his fear into action, into violence, as he had trained
to do for all of his life.

But the worm reared up like a cobra, and before Olconna even appreciated that fact it lashed out.

Olconna tried to respond with the dagger, but so shocked was he that he didn't even realize that his weapon arm was gone until he saw it disappearing into the awful beast's mouth!

Now he screamed. There was nothing else. Just the pain and the helplessness—that was the worst of it for a man like Olconna.

No, not the worst. The worst of it were Vaughna's echoing words, a creed for her, a lament for him: Every moment precious.

The worm took its time, lashing and tearing, and Olconna felt no less than six more stabbing and slashing bites before he finally slipped into that deepest darkness.

Cormack sat on the rail of the beached boat, his shoulders slumped as if all of the air had been sucked out of his lean body. Before him, Milkeila paced nervously back and forth, continually glancing at the surprising man in the black suit.

The man who had just informed them that their entire world was soon to be washed away.

"Are you to let him keep the soul stone?" Milkeila asked, pacing.

"It is your stone."

The shaman stopped and turned on her lover curiously.

"I would counsel that you let him keep it," Cormack decided. "It is the most important of gems, I agree, but if what Bransen says is true, then he is all but helpless without it."

"And with it, he walks with the grace of a warrior," Milkeila added as both watched the young man, who stood across the sandbar going through a series of movements and turns, the practice of a warrior, as brilliant and precise as anything either of them had ever seen. Cormack in particular appreciated Bransen's movements, for his training in the arts martial as a young brother of the Order of Abelle had been extensive and complete.

Or so he had thought, but in watching Bransen, Cormack recognized an even deeper level of concentration than he had ever achieved, and by far.

"I believe his every word," Milkeila admitted, and she seemed surprised by that statement. She turned to see Cormack nodding his agreement.

"It is too outrageous a story to not be true."

"We have to tell them—all of them," said Milkeila. "Your people and mine."

"And even Mcwigik's," Cormack added. "At the very least, Mithranidoon must be abandoned."

Milkeila lamented, "A wall of falling ice to wash us all away."

TWENTY-SEVEN

Three Perspectives

"On pain of death!" Brother Giavno said again, becoming dangerously animated. Out on rock-collection detail, Giavno and his two companions had been the first to note the approach of Cormack and the strange-looking man in the black suit of some exotic material—Giavno thought it was called "silk," but as he had seen the stuff only once in his life, and many years before, he couldn't be certain. The stranger wore a typical farmer's hat, but Giavno noted some black fabric under that as well.

"Greetings to you, too," Cormack replied.

"How can you be alive?" one of the other brothers asked, and Cormack tapped his beret.

"God's will and good luck, I would say," the fallen monk replied.

"You know nothing of God," Giavno growled.

"Says the man who whipped him nearly to death," Bransen, at Cormack's side, quipped. "A godly act, indeed—at least, according to the mores of many Abellicans I have known. It is strange to me how much like Samhaists they seem."

Giavno trembled and seemed about to explode. Behind him, over the rocky ridge, some other monks called out and soon a swarm of brothers was fast running toward the rocky beach.

"Why did you come here, Cormack?" Giavno asked, seeming as much concerned as outraged—a poignant reminder to Cormack that he and this man had once been friends. "You know the consequences."

"You thought me already dead."

"A death you earned with your treachery."

"Your definition, not mine. I followed that which was in my heart, and many of the brothers here, I would wager, were glad of it. I find it difficult to comprehend that I was alone in my distaste for our imprisoning of the Alpinadorans."

"What you find difficult to comprehend is that you make no rules here, or anywhere in the Church. If Father De Guilbe wished for your opinion on the matter, he would have asked. And he did not."

"Ever the dutiful one, aren't you?" Cormack replied, and Giavno narrowed his eyes.

"Alive?" came a shout from behind, and Father De Guilbe, surrounded by an armed entourage, appeared over the crest of the hill. "Are you mad to come back here?"

"How would I know differently?" Cormack asked. "I remember little beyond the sting of your mercy."

"Play not coy with me, traitor," said De Guilbe, and unlike Giavno, there wasn't a hint of compassion or mercy in his tone. He turned to the nearest guards and said, "Take him."

"I would not," said the man standing beside Cormack.

Father De Guilbe dropped a withering gaze over him—except he did not shrink back in the least. "And who are you?"

"My name is Bransen, though that is of no consequence to you," Bransen replied. "I am a man here not of my will, but of misfortune, and I come to you only to repay the debt that I owe to this man, and to the people of some of the other islands."

De Guilbe shook his head as if not comprehending any of it, and Bransen let it go, for it was of no consequence.

"I bring a grave warning that your world is about to be washed away," Bransen said. "It is my duty to tell you that, I suppose, but whether you choose to act upon it or not is of little consequence to me."

A couple of the monks bristled, obviously focusing on the last part of his quip and not the more important announcement. Of the group, now twenty brothers, only a few raised their eyebrows in alarm, and even that became a past thought almost immediately, as one of Father De Guilbe's entourage announced, pointing at Bransen, "He has a gemstone!"

Cormack glanced at Bransen in alarm, but the man from Pryd Town seemed bothered not at all.

"Is this true?" asked Father De Guilbe.

"If it is, it is none of your affair."

"You walk a dangerous—"

"I walk where I choose to walk and how I choose to walk," Bransen interrupted. "Feign no dominion over me, disingenuous old fool. My father was of your order, a brother of great accomplishment. No, not any accomplishment that you would understand or appreciate," he answered De Guilbe's curious look. "And more to your pity."

"From Entel?" Father De Guilbe asked. "Your swarthy appearance bespeaks a Southern heritage."

Bransen grinned knowingly at the obvious ploy.

"It matters not," De Guilbe said. "You are here with a criminal and carrying contraband."

"Contraband?" Bransen said with a mocking chuckle. "You presume to know how I came about this gemstone. You presume that I have a gemstone. You do not understand Jhesta Tu philosophy, yet pretend that you have any understanding of me, or of what I will do to your guards if you send them forth, or of how I will come back in the dark of night and easily defeat any defenses you construct, that you and I will speak more directly at your own bedside."

It took a while for all of that to digest, and Giavno at last broke the uncomfortable silence by berating Cormack, "What have you brought to us?"

"A man to deliver a message, and then we are gone from here."

"The glacier north of your lake is home to a Samhaist," Bransen announced. "The Ancient himself. Ancient Badden, who wars with Dame Gwydre of Vanguard."

"How do you know?"

"Because I was there, just yesterday," Bransen answered. "Badden claims dominion over this lake and works to ensure that all here, yourselves included—and especially, if he should ever learn that Abellicans reside on this most holy of Samhaist places—will be washed away on a great wave of his murderous wrath. If he executes his plan there is for you no escape. If he is not stopped this place you name as Chapel Isle will become a washed stone on an uninhabited hot lake."

"Preposterous!" said Giavno, while the monks around him whispered and shuffled nervously, and looked all around for someone to settle their fears from the sudden shock.

Bransen shrugged, as if unconcerned.

"We are to believe you?" Father De Guilbe asked skeptically. "You come to us beside a traitor. . . ."

"A man I hardly know, but one possessed of more sense than you it would seem. I have come to deliver a message as repayment to this man you name as traitor and yet who feels obligated to you still. Whether you act upon that message or not is not my concern. I hold no love for your Church. Indeed, from what I have seen you are more than deserving of my contempt. But I am

Jhesta Tu, and so such feelings as contempt have no place in my world."

He turned to Cormack, but before he could address the man, Giavno assailed him, "Jhesta Tu? What is Jhesta Tu?"

Bransen eyed the fiery man out of the corner of his eye. "Something you could never begin to comprehend."

"Take them!" Giavno yelled, and immediately a pair of guards, brandishing short swords, leaped at Bransen and Cormack.

They never got close. Bransen, expecting it, even coaxing it, leaped at the first, kicking his right foot out to the man's right side, then sweeping it across. It posed no real threat to the monk, but had him distracted so that that the real attack, a snap-kick from Bransen's left foot, caught him right in the chest, blasting out his breath in a great gasp. Bransen landed lightly back on his right foot and propelled himself forward and left, beside the staggering monk's awkward thrust. He snatched the man by the wrist with his right hand, drove his left hand brutally against the monk's straightened elbow, then quickly covered the man's sword hand with his own, bending the monk's wrist over painfully and stealing his strength—and his grip on the sword.

The blade didn't fall an inch before Bransen snapped it out of the air, and he spun away, back-kicking the wounded monk in the side to ensure that there would be no pursuit, and also to shift his own momentum, driving him to intercept the second approaching guard.

The short swords collided repeatedly in a series of arm-numbing parries that ended with Bransen looping his blade over that of the confused monk. A twist and jerk sent the short sword to the ground, and left the tip of Bransen's sword at the stunned monk's throat. And it all happened in the space of a few heartbeats.

Bransen laughed and straightened, moving his blade back from the terrified man. He hooked the fallen sword with his own and deftly flipped it into his left hand, then turned to Giavno and flung both swords, spinning end over end, to stick into the ground right before the monk.

"You have been warned," Bransen announced. "Ancient Badden will destroy you."

He turned and walked away.

Cormack lingered a short while longer, looking mostly to Father De Guilbe. His expression was one of apology, perhaps, but mostly it was filled with pleading. But there was no more to say, so he followed Bransen back to the boat.

Both Cormack and Milkeila accompanied Bransen onto the forested island of Yossunfier. Many more people came out to greet them before they even got their boat ashore. The whole of Milkeila's tribe, it seemed, came down to the waterfront, shielding their eyes from the morning glare, whispering among themselves at this surprising group approaching their island home.

Many scowls focused on Cormack and his obvious Abellican attire, but Androosis was there, along with Toniquay and Canrak, instructing his kin that this particular monk was no enemy of Yossunfier.

As the trio glided in near the beach, strong hands grabbed the craft and ushered it up onto the beach. Toniquay stepped front and center before Milkeila as she exited the boat, the higher-ranking shamans deferring to him because of his intimate knowledge of this situation and these participants.

He stared at Milkeila for just a few moments, then scrutinized Cormack, his expression giving the man no indication of how much his actions had ingratiated him to the barbarians. Then Toniquay's gaze fell over Bransen, but only for a moment.

"What do you presume?" Toniquay asked Milkeila. He waited just a short while of uncomfortable silence before adding, "Do you believe that your friend has earned the right to step onto our land simply because he, unlike so many of his kin, took a moral road? Do you think that all past wrongs will be simply forgotten?"

"It was at great personal cost!" Milkeila replied, instinctively defending her lover, who put a hand on her arm to calm her. "But that is not why we have come. Cormack signaled to me and I answered his call."

"Signaled?" Toniquay said suspiciously. "And how did he know a way in which he might signal you, Milkeila? And how did you know to answ . . ." He stopped and waved his hand and shook his head. His point had been made that the woman would surely have to answer for her apparent secret relationship with this Abellican, but Toniquay was more interested in hearing Milkeila's tale at that time.

"Why is he here?" the shaman asked.

"Cormack found this man, Bransen," Milkeila replied, and she put her hand on Bransen's shoulder. The man in the black suit nodded, though he obviously understood little of the conversation.

"Bransen fell from the glacier," said Milkeila.

Toniquay looked at her skeptically, and doubting murmurs grew all about them. "Then he would be dead," Toniquay said.

"But he is not," said Milkeila. "Whether through simple luck and soft mud, or his extraordinary powers— and he is truly blessed—I know not. But he is here, and he was up there, and he comes to us with a dire warning. The Ancient of the Samhaists has taken the glacier as his home, and plots now to destroy all of us who dwell upon Mithranidoon."

"Samhaists?" Toniquay echoed. He had heard the name before, in the private discussions among the shamans about people who lived beyond Mithranidoon's warm waters. The Samhaists, so it was rumored, had given this place its name, though that had been centuries before. In the lore of Yan Ossum, shamans had gone south to teach their magic to the men of Honce, long before the many battles and wars between the two peoples. In Alpinadoran mythology, Samhaist magic was a direct offshoot of the Alpinadoran Ancient Gods, though in Samhaist lore, the order, and who taught whom, was of course reversed.

"This stranger is from outside of Mithranidoon?" Toniquay asked. "Strange then that he arrives just a few years after the Abellicans. Before them, none had come to us from the outside since the powries, before my father's father was born." Even as he denied the possibility, though, Toniquay had to admit that the man's clothing was fairly convincing, and unlike anything he had ever seen.

"He is an Abellican spy," someone from the side yelled, a sentiment that was echoed through the crowd.

"He is not of my former comrades," Cormack answered. "He is no Abellican, and has only been to Chapel Isle on one occasion—yesterday—to deliver the same message there that we deliver here. This is no trick, Toniquay. On my word, for what that is worth to you. I found this man in the mud on the northern bank of Mithranidoon, injured. He came to us with a tale that you must hear, that my people must hear, that the powries must hear. For if he speaks truly, and I believe that he does, then all of us are in dire peril, and will soon be washed from our homes."

Toniquay stared hard at Cormack for just a few moments and then motioned to some of his nearby tribesmen. Soon the trio found themselves surrounded by armed Alpinadoran warriors.

Cormack immediately turned to Bransen and grabbed the man by the arm. "They are honorable, but careful," he said in the common language of Honce.

"I insist that you remain with us while we investigate your claims," Toniquay explained.

"Be fast, for all our sakes," Milkeila answered.

Toniquay nodded his agreement and motioned to the warriors, who escorted Bransen and Cormack to a nearby hut, while Milkeila stayed with Toniquay and the other shamans.

She knew what they would do, and was not surprised when several of the more powerful shamans called down high-flying birds. Weaving spells, they each bound their sight to that of an individual bird, then sent the winged creatures on their way, and for the next several minutes, the powerful elders saw through the eyes of their familiars. Unlike Ancient Badden's heightened powers, though, these shamans couldn't control their familiars, and so they were at the whims of the aerial creatures.

Still, it didn't take very long for more than one of the birds to climb above the glacial rim, and the ice castle gleamed in the midday light.

To her surprise, a most pleasant one, Milkeila was allowed to leave Yossunfier with her two companions. She had not been forgiven, Toniquay assured her, and would ultimately have to answer the many questions her arrival with the men of Honce had raised, beyond the worries of some strange "Ancient" plotting atop the glacier.

Now, though, given the revelations, they all had more important issues before them, so Milkeila, Bransen, and Cormack paddled off for Red Cap Island, while Toniquay and the others plotted as to how they would best bring all the Alpinadoran tribes of the islands together again in an even more urgent cause.

Father De Guilbe rubbed his face and leaned back in his seat, breathing hard.

"It cannot be," Brother Giavno said, shaking his head in denial.

"Exactly as the stranger said," De Guilbe confirmed. He tossed a soul stone back onto his desk, the same stone that had just allowed him an out-of-body journey, where he had willed his spirit to fly up to the great glacier looming over Mithranidoon.

"They are boring a chasm that will collapse the front edge of the glacier into our lake," he explained.

"Ancient Badden?"

"It can only be. The castle of ice has the Samhaist tree design."

"Then Cormack was not lying, and the stranger is . . . ?"

"Of no concern to us at this time," Father De Guilbe answered. "We must be gone from this place posthaste. Our time here was not profitable—we claimed not a single soul—and so we will continue our mission elsewhere."

"We will allow Ancient Badden to destroy the lake and all who live upon it?"

"What choice have we, Brother?"

Brother Giavno trembled and lifted his hands several times, as if about to divulge some plan. But alas, he had no answers.

"Prepare the brothers, prepare the boats," Father De Guilbe instructed.

The differences between the reactions of the three peoples were not lost on the foursome of Bransen, Cormack, Milkeila, and Mcwigik. In fact, the reaction of the supposedly vile powries as compared to that of the humans proved startling to the two men and Milkeila—startling and embarrassing.

"Yach, but ye done good!" Kriminig the powrie leader congratulated Mcwigik after he had led Bransen and the others to his boss so that the stranger could tell his tale. "That beast up there's thinking to be dumping on us when we're not knowing, but now that we're knowing, we're the ones to be doing the dumping!"

"You know of Ancient Badden?" Cormack dared interject.

"Ye just told me of him," Kriminig replied, as if he

didn't understand the point of the question, and while the dwarf leader began barking commands at his charges, readying them for a fight, the three humans found a moment of quiet discussion.

"He believed us without reservation," Cormack whispered, his tone clearly marking the distinction of that reaction to those of the monks and the Alpinadorans.

"Or maybe he is just happy for a fight," Milkeila said, and she swung about to the wider commotion going on around them, the many excited discussions springing up among the powries.

"Bah, but I'm sad to hear this killer's surrounded himself with trolls," one said. "Their blood's not much for shining me beret."

"Aye, but he's got a swarm o' them, they're saying," another piped in. "We'll get a glow out of it. The folks of the other islands won't be needing their share, don't ye know?"

"Yach, and there'll be bunches o' them folks about, too, won't there?" the first replied with a wink. "More than a few're going to be bleeding bright red."

"And who's to say they won't be turning on us when this killer's chopped down?" asked a third.

"A few hundred trolls and a few hundred men, and only two score of us," the first said with a sigh. "It'll take me all the day to collect the blood!"

"Ha ha!" the others laughed, and they swatted each other on sturdy shoulders and rolled along their way, as only powries could.

That last comment had brought a look of alarm to both Milkeila and Cormack, though—until Mcwigik and Bikelbrin shuffled over.

"Bah, but don't ye be thinking me kin're to start any trouble up there, other than the trouble that . . . what did ye call him? That Ancient?" said Mcwigik. "No trouble, I tell ye, other than finishing the trouble that one's already started."

"They are willing to fight beside the monks and the Alpinadorans, then?" asked Cormack.

"Ye heard Kriminig say just that," said Bikelbrin.

"Sure, and a fine row it'll be, we're all for hoping," Mcwigik added. "Though we're not even knowing if yer monks're coming along for the play. Did ye hear them say that?"

Cormack's lips grew very tight, all the confirmation anyone there needed to understand that he was filled with doubts about whether his brethren would march alongside the rest or not.

"Yach, but it's not to matter," Mcwigik said generously, and he slapped Cormack on the back. "That Ancient up there's made himself an angry swarm o' powries, and we're meaning to show him that doing so wasn't the smartest thing he's ever done!"

"Hope he's not too old and withered," said Bikelbrin. "Me beret's needing a bit of a gloss."

TWENTY-EIGHT

The Meaning of Home

Brother Giavno stepped out of the small boat onto the shore of Lake Mithranidoon for the first time in more than a year. He glanced back in the direction of Chapel Isle, the place that had been his home for these last few years. Not much of a home, and not much of an island, Giavno knew, but still there was in his heart a great lament, a profound sense of loss. Nothing more than a cursory glance at his dour companions told him that he was not alone in these feelings.

He let his gaze drift north along this, the western coastline of Mithranidoon. Cormack was up there, he knew, along with his strange collection of friends and perhaps with more allies culled from the various islands. He meant to go against Ancient Badden, and that was a noble cause, whatever the reason.

A splash behind him turned Giavno back to the lake, where the last boat, bearing Father De Guilbe and a foursome of Chapel Isle's best warriors, neared the shore. As the five debarked, Giavno was left wondering how many years, decades, centuries even, might pass before the construction at Chapel Isle was once more inhabited by disciples of Blessed Abelle. Their monument would stand against the wave should it come, Giavno believed, and even if someone else, powrie or Alpinadoran, happened upon the island, they would more likely use the sturdy chapel fortress than tear it down. So maybe, someday long in the future, the Abellicans would return and continue the work done by Giavno and De Guilbe and the others.

"Form them up at once and let us be far away from this place," Father De Guilbe instructed Giavno as he walked past. "I would find Dame Gwydre before the onset of winter, and that will be no easy road."

"Of course, Father," Giavno replied, and a part of him agreed. Another part, though, had him looking to the north yet again, and wondering about Cormack and the others. He recognized the expediency of De Guilbe's decision to abandon their mission and return where they were likely needed, but that didn't stop him from feeling as if he and his brethren were, perhaps, abandoning their neighbors in this time of dire need. For despite all of their fighting, even the deadly siege put upon Chapel Isle by the Alpinadorans, Brother Giavno did think of them, and of the powries, as neighbors.

That was the surprising paradox that dominated his mind and his heart.

"Brother Giavno!" Father De Guilbe shouted, shaking the man from his contemplations. He nodded and rushed off to rouse the brothers.

He was glad that it was not his place to make these decisions.

They glided out of the mists of Mithranidoon like the ghosts of their warrior ancestors, painted with berry dyes of red and yellow and blue, carrying spears and clubs, and decorated with trinkets and necklaces of teeth and claws and paws and beaks and feathers—so many feathers. Their flotilla numbered boats in the hundreds, each boat carrying as few as one or as many as a half-dozen of the proud Alpinadorans. Most stood up as the boats reached the shore, as if in defiance to the task and enemy that awaited them.

Even Milkeila, intimately familiar with her people, even Bransen, who had seen the armies of southern Honce, even Mcwigik, who was never much impressed with anything human, gasped at the spectacle of the many diverse tribes of Mithranidoon coming together as one. And for Cormack, this marvelous sight served to reinforce his understanding that proselytizing these people, with their traditions, heritage, and pride, was no more than a fool's errand, and a condescending one at that.

For Milkeila, though, another emotion accompanied it all, based on her certainty that she was looking upon her people for the last time, likely forever. Even if she managed to survive the coming battle, she knew that it was over for her. Her small group of friends, co-conspirators dreaming of leaving Mithranidoon only two years before, had been split apart from her in more ways than physical. She stood with the man she had come to love, but inside, Milkeila had never felt more alone.

Still, the spectacle before her made her proud to be, or to have been, of Yan Ossum.

At the center of the Alpinadoran force came the shamans, Teydru and Toniquay prominent among their ranks. More than just spiritual leaders, Alpinadoran shamans were considered the wise men of their respective tribes, the advisors on all matters important.

"They will direct the attack," Milkeila explained to her companions, indicating the select group.

"They will likely wish to speak more with Bransen then," said Cormack, "as he has seen the passes and the glacial structures." He was about to add that he would help Milkeila in translating the exchange, but the woman just shook her head.

"They have seen them," she explained. "Both the way to Badden and his defenses. If we were to be a part of their execution, they would have summoned us as they debarked their boats."

"What's that to mean?" Mcwigik demanded. "Got all me boys together just to be a part of it."

Milkeila calmed him with an upraised hand, and cautiously made her way along the beach to speak with Toniquay.

"The powries wish to help," she said to her superior. "They have brought the whole of their force to join in our march."

"Our march?" Toniquay quipped, his expression sour. "You have plotted to leave us, and conspired of late to expedite your journey. Because you brought us this information, Shaman Teydru has seen fit to grant you your wish without prejudice or punishment. You have paid your worth to us and are free to go."

While those words might have once sounded as welcome to the young woman, in this time and place they hit her as mightily as a bolt of lightning. She had known it was coming, indeed, but still, to hear the declaration spoken so clearly and directly unnerved the poor young woman. The black wings of panic fluttered up all around her, threatening to drown her sensibilities in their confused jumble of flapping. She felt alone, suddenly. Homeless and without family, stranded on the beach of a hostile world, all security stolen.

She looked over to her tribesmen, trying to sort through the jumble to spot Androosis, or some other friend who had expressed similar desires of leaving Mithranidoon.

"Your young friends will not be joining you," said Toniquay, as if he had read her mind (and indeed, that was not beyond his power). "They have offered no compensation for the freedom they desire—not even Androosis, though there was debate about whether or not he, too, should be given free leave."

Milkeila stood there for a long while, trying to find her breath.

"I would have thought this news exciting and welcome to you," Toniquay teased, for of course he had anticipated exactly this.

Milkeila regained her composure, albeit with great difficulty. "Of course," she said, for what choice did she have? A decision so rendered by the shaman council was not an invitation to debate.

"The powries have come in whole to join in your battle with Ancient Badden," she restated. "They are fierce allies and ferocious enemies, as you are well aware. They would know their place in this, among a force so many times their size."

"How generous of them," Toniquay remarked, contempt thickening his voice. "Better than the cowardly monks, at least, who debark far to the south and run down the road of the same direction. They stand strong only behind thick walls of stone, it would seem."

"Their place?" Milkeila pressed, knowing well that Toniquay could launch into a diatribe of many minutes, and one that left him far from her original question, if he was not quickly reined.

"They have no place among us," Toniquay answered bluntly. "If they wish a place in the battle, then it is to the side, and out of our way."

Milkeila started to argue, but Toniquay was hearing none of it. "We do not train beside powries, nor are we to expect our warriors to trust any of them. The same is true of the monk and the stranger."

"And of Milkeila?"

"You trained beside us once."

"But the trust?"

Toniquay paused and let the question slide away before reiterating, "Their place is not among us. They, you, all of you, would do well to stay far to the side of our march."

Milkeila couldn't help it as her misty eyes were

drawn out to the lake, toward Yossunfier, which had once been her home.

Once and always and nevermore.

They were not properly outfitted to survive the climate off of Mithranidoon, even now before the onset of winter, so the Alpinadorans, led by their shamans, who had used the views of eagles and hawks and crows to spy out and map the passes, wasted no time in their march. Long and swift strides carried their formations up the mountain passes beside the glacier; shamans and other leaders shouted encouragement and bolstered the warriors with magic and herb-treated waters to hold their spirit and their strength. There would be no camp, no respite. Their swift pace would end when they met the enemy.

Behind them came the powries, and among them Bransen and his two now-homeless companions, still trying to figure out where they would fit into this upcoming battle.

Before they had even reached the glacier, sounds of fighting erupted far ahead, at the front of the Alpinadoran line. The ranks tightened, powries eagerly adjusting their berets. But those ranks quickly loosened up again, and when the trailing group crossed the battlefield they discovered that the army had happened upon, and had summarily overrun, an encampment of no more than a dozen trolls.

"Here's for hoping that one or more got away to warn their friends and set them all about us," Mcwigik grumbled. "Sure to be the only way we're to find any fightin' this day!"

"Aye, the tall ones'll run all the way through Badden's door," Bikelbrin, at Mcwigik's side, lamented.

Bransen glanced at Milkeila and Cormack, the three of them understanding that they were the only ones among this group who hoped the prediction would prove true.

And Bransen, who had been at Badden's camp, who had seen the hundreds of trolls and the giants there, knew it to be an unrealistic hope, and one that would soon enough be destroyed.

They ran over another group of trolls soon after. A volley of Alpinadoran spears flew out to the east soon after that, taking down a pair of scouts.

The barbarian horde didn't even slow to retrieve the missiles.

Good fortune gave Bransen and his companions a fine vantage point as the real battle commenced. The path wound down and around a huge outcropping before spilling onto the glacier, and the powrie contingent, Bransen's trio among them, was up high and still back of the stone when the leading Alpindorans swept onto the ice like a breaking wave, washing over those nearest trolls before smashing into a more coordinated defensive formation. Spears crisscrossed in midair, with the trolls taking the brunt of it, as their spears were too small and light to get through the Alpinadoran wicker and leather shields.

The Alpinadoran warriors poured over the front troll ranks, their towering line of broad-shouldered men and women, most well over six feet in height, dwarfing the diminutive, light-featured trolls.

But the trolls did not break and flee, and those in the back scrambled all over each other trying to get to the front ranks and into the fight. Like a horde of rats, they leaped and bit and scratched and kicked, flailing so wildly that they were as likely to strike their own as they were to hit their enemies.

More barbarians swept onto the glacier, lengthening the line and filling in the holes as some of their kin fell away.

In the back, watching from on high, Milkeila chewed her bottom lip, her knuckles whitening about the handle of the stone axe she carried.

"They are winning," Cormack pointed out to her, and draped an arm across her sturdy shoulder.

"Yach, but we're not to even get to the ice afore the fight's done," Mcwigik complained.

"Aye, and all that fine spilled blood'll seep into the cracks by then," added Pergwick, he and the young Ruggirs hopping over to join Mcwigik and Bikelbrin and the humans. "Or mixed with the scraped and melted ice to be even thinner!"

"Come on, ye bleating sheep," another dwarf called, and as they turned to regard the shouter, he waved them his way. Apparently they weren't the only ones concerned that the fight would end before their arrival, for before that yelling dwarf, a line of powries was going over the ledge and out of sight, picking their way, the group learned when they got to the spot, down a steep but climbable descent that would get them out onto the glacier just to the south of the Alpinadoran position.

Glancing over the ledge and following the line of powries climbing down (with amazing deftness, he thought, given their short limbs), Bransen could pick out the point of demarcation. Few trolls stood in that area of the glacier, focused far more heavily to the north and the barbarians.

For a brief moment, Bransen's eyes flashed wickedly, wondering if the enemy had left open a flank they might exploit.

But as the leading powrie dropped down the last few feet to land upon the ice, Bransen's excitement turned to dread.

A rain of heavy, large stones complemented the dwarf's arrival. The northern, left flank, far from open, had been charged to the giants, half a dozen of the behemoths, standing tall now behind a wall of ice blocks that had obscured their position. With their light, bluish skin, white hair, and wrappings of white fur, they blended well with their shiny and eye-stinging environment, but that camouflage did nothing to diminish their overwhelming aura of strength now that they had been spotted.

Bransen started to call the dwarves back up, but

stopped, stunned, as they seemed more excited and eager to get down than they had before the giants had risen up.

"Giants!" Bransen pleaded with those dwarves around him, a call seconded by Cormack.

"Bah, them ain't giants," Mcwigik said with a howl.

"Not like the giants we got on the Julianthes," Bikelbrin added, using the powrie name for the Weathered Isles, their Mirianic Ocean homeland.

"Not half," Mcwigik agreed, "but I'm betting their blood runs thick!"

That was all the others had to hear, and Pergwick and Ruggirs nearly tumbled from the ledge as they fought and scrambled over each other to get to the descent. After the dwarfish tumble rolled away, the three humans stepped up to the ledge.

"You do not seem convinced of your course," Cormack remarked to Bransen, and the Highwayman smiled at his own inability to keep his emotions from his face.

"I came here to buy freedom for myself and my family," he replied honestly. "Badden's head for a journey south."

"We'll make sure that you get the foul one's head, then," Milkeila assured him.

Bransen snickered. "All who came north with me are lost. Either dead or trapped in that castle. Dame Gwydre would not refuse me my reward even should I return now, before the task is complete."

"But Badden must be stopped," Cormack said.

Bransen looked at him skeptically.

"Do you deny his evilness?" said Cormack.

"Not his, not that of your Church. Not of the lairds—not one of them," said Bransen.

Cormack stiffened at that poignant reminder of the lack of familiarity between them.

"Then you agree that he, Badden, is worth killing," said Milkeila, her voice taking on a distinctively sharper edge.

Bransen looked at her carefully, his expression measured, and caught somewhere between amusement and condescension. "That is not the question. The question is: Is Badden worth dying over?"

Below them, the powries encountered a group of trolls and the fight was on. "He is," said Cormack, and he started over the ledge, moving swiftly down the steep decline. Milkeila shot a disappointed look Bransen's way and followed.

Bransen passed them easily, using his Jhesta Tu training and his marvelous control of his body to run down the cliff.

TWENTY-NINE

Despoilment, Inevitability, and Questionable Triumph

By the time Bransen got down to the ice shelf, most of the trolls were either down or scattering and more than half of the powrie contingent was already in a full sprint to the edge of the chasm just south of their position. Both their courage and commitment stunned Bransen, for not only were they charging headlong into the waiting giants, but they were putting themselves into a position where they would be afforded one less avenue of retreat, where, if the battle went badly, they would find no escape.

It wasn't stupidity, or ignorance of battle techniques, that launched them to the chasm, Bransen knew. They weren't going to retreat. They were either taking the fight right to Badden's castle across the way, or they were going to die trying.

His surprise and confusion over their level of commitment nearly cost Bransen his life, as a troll spear flew in for his side. At the last moment, and with the prompting of a cry from Milkeila, the Highwayman half turned and snapped a backhand against the spear, just below its stone head. The force of the blow flipped the light spear into a near-right-angled turn, and the nimble Bransen flipped his hand and snatched it from the air, his legs moving perfectly to catch up to his shifting shoulders.

He sent the missile back out at the nearest troll, though he didn't know if that was the missile-thrower or not. The creature flailed wildly and tried to fall away, and indeed did fall away, though not as it had intended, embedded as it was on the end of the spear.

Bransen thought to yank that spear back out of the squirming troll as he ran past. But he shook his head, confident that his hands and feet would prove to be all the weaponry he needed at that time. He skied into a pair of trolls, spinning a circle-kick as he came in. That one foot turned both their spears aside, and as he came around fully, Bransen quick-stepped forward, snapping off quick left and right jabs into the faces of the respective trolls. He pressed forward, staying inside the optimum reach of their weapons. He spun to face the one on his left and drove his elbow back behind him to further smash the face of the other.

A fast left-right-left combination knocked the troll facing him back and to the ground; then Bransen similarly dropped, turning sidelong and coiling his legs as he did. The troll behind him, now below his prostrated form, had just begun to recover from the elbow to the face when Bransen swept his lower, left leg across, hooking the troll behind the ankle and sliding its foot forward, while Bransen's right leg straight-kicked for that same knee.

Legs weren't supposed to bend like that, as the troll's howl of agony proved.

Bransen thrust his left arm down below him, driving his upper torso up from the ice. He tucked his legs again and spun with the momentum, right into a standing, turning position that allowed him to circle-kick the descending troll right in the face.

Its head snapped over backward with such force that its neck bones shattered.

A roar from behind turned Bransen around just in time to see a giant topple over, grasping both its knees. The powries wasted no time, swarming over the behemoth with glee, stabbing it and slashing it and wiping their berets across the wounds.

Bransen's jaw dropped open in disbelief as he lifted his gaze to view the fight beyond the fallen giant, to where a group of powries was rushing to and fro and back again, in and around the legs of a futilely swatting giant who never got close to hitting any of them.

Oh, but they were hitting the giant! Great, reverberating smacks, and always about the knee. They looked like wild lumberjacks chasing animated trees. The giant danced and tried to keep ahead of them, but they'd only reverse direction, dart between its legs, and whomp it yet again. They howled with excitement and sheer enjoyment, and that only infuriated the beast more, it seemed, and its swings became more frantic, and more futile. Other powries joined in the dance, chopping, always chopping, at the giant's legs. Down it went, to be swarmed and finished.

Bransen remembered his feelings upon first seeing the giants. How puny and helpless he had thought himself. But the powries had long ago found the answer to the imposing, seemingly impregnable behemoths. One after another, the giants fell. And the powries rolled along, berets glowing in the afternoon sun.

Cormack and Milkeila collected the stunned Bransen as they rushed to catch up. "We'll be at the ice castle within the hour!" Cormack predicted.

Accurately, Bransen knew.

Toniquay sang great songs of rousing tenor, heroic deeds, captured and amplified and now enhanced magically to provide more than a morale boost, but an actual physical boost to the listener. And the warriors of Alpinador, the brave men and women of the many tribes that inhabited Mithranidoon, lived up to their heroic heritage. With coordination and fury, their line drove deep into troll ranks; whenever one group broke through and spearheaded out in front, those to either flank appropriately stretched behind them, so that instead of having any group get caught out alone and surrounded, the length of the barbarian line surged forward in a series of small wedge formations. One-against-one, there was no contest to be found. The larger, stronger, better-armed Alpinadorans stabbed ahead with impunity, skewering troll after troll.

And yet, Toniquay and the other leaders observed, their progress proved painfully slow. Waves of trolls came against them. Mobs of the monsters rushed in, leading with a barrage of flying spears that set the barbarians back on their heels and forced them to pause and cover with their wicker and leather shields.

Toniquay looked to the distant ice castle, their goal, and then to the west, toward the dipping sun. They would not get to the castle in daylight, he surmised to his dismay, and the night would not be kind.

A cheer in the southern end of the Alpinadoran line turned Toniquay that way, and when he noted the fierce fighting there, he did not at first understand. As he focused, though, he heard the bolstering cry "Another giant is down!"

He swept his gaze out farther to the south, to the powries, the fallen monk, the stranger, and Milkeila. The shaman's tight old face crinkled with confusion and consternation; were these to be the saviors of Mithranidoon?

All he had for weapons were his hands and feet, and Bransen really didn't see how either would do any damage to the giant battling the powries before him. But he had to try.

A dwarf rolled right around the behemoth's treelike leg, ending with a solid, two-handed wallop of his heavy club against the front of the giant's knee. As the behemoth lurched and howled, Bransen closed the last dozen running strides and leaped high. Good luck was with him, for even as he lifted, the dwarf, having gone around to the back of the giant's leg, drove in a dagger, then smacked it hard with his club. The giant lurched backward this time, distracted and overbalancing just as Bransen crashed in and began launching a series of heavy punches. Over went the giant, crashing down to its back on the ice, and Bransen hopped up to a crouch, sprang into a forward somersault, and double-stomped his heels into the giant's eyes.

The giant howled and swatted him, launching him away, and only good fortune and a beam of wood prevented Bransen from going over the lip of the chasm. As soon as he had steadied himself, his legs dangling over the ledge, he looked back in fear, expecting the behemoth to rush over and finish him, but the damage had been done, and now powries swarmed over the supine giant, hacking with abandon.

Cormack slid down low and clamped his hands on Bransen's shoulders, desperately steadying him. Bransen started to assure the man that he was all right, but a shriek from the north, a supernatural, preternatural piercing screech, cut him short.

When he looked at the small dragon swooping across the lines of cowering barbarians, Bransen knew at once that it was Ancient Badden. Leathery wings propelled the beast with great speed, its long hind legs and talon-tipped feet snapping down to keep the warriors ducking and diving aside.

It screeched again, and there was magic behind that powerful wail, for many men fell to their knees, screaming in pain and grabbing at their ears. A dragon claw caught a woman by the shoulder and jerked her from the ground with such force that one of her boots was left behind! With that one foot holding her tight, the dragon's other foot raked at her, talons tearing clothing and skin with ease.

The creature banked and rolled back under, and with a sudden halt of its momentum, hurled the broken woman like a missile through the throng of barbarians. The dragon breathed forth a line of fire, immolating some and creating an obscuring fog.

Spears reached up at it but they seemed to bother the beast not at all, for they did not penetrate its armored body, or what seemed like a magical barrier encompassing that body. The defiant dragon issued that deafening, earsplitting screech again, sending more warriors to their knees in pain.

"We have to help them!" Cormack cried, tugging Bransen back from the ledge. He scrambled to his feet, as Bransen did behind him, and started for the Alpinadorans.

"That is Badden," Milkeila mouthed in horror-filled understanding.

Bransen grabbed Cormack by the shoulder, tugging him about. "The castle," he said.

"We have to help them!" Cormack implored.

"We help them by taking the castle," Bransen replied. "It is the source, the conduit, of Badden's power."

Cormack glanced back at the desperate fight to the north, but desperate acquiescence was in his eyes as he turned back to Bransen.

"Go on! Go on!" Bransen shouted to the powries, for he saw that the way was clear. "To the castle doors, for all our sakes!"

But few powries heeded that call, entranced by the allure of bright giant blood, and with still more behemoths to be tripped up and slaughtered. And the hesitancy of the behemoths—obviously they had fought the tough little powries before—only made the dwarves hungrier.

"Mcwigik!" Cormack called, and the dwarf skidded

to a stop and turned to face the humans. "To the castle!" Cormack yelled, pointing emphatically that way.

Mcwigik put on a sour look, but he did stab out his arm to stop Pergwick from running by. Cormack nodded and started off, Milkeila and Bransen close behind. By the time they crossed the glacier to the ice ramp leading into the castle, Mcwigik and his three cohorts trailed in close pursuit.

A strange sense of urgency came over Bransen, then, and he overtook Cormack, moving from a trot to a sprint for the front of the large castle. He looked all about as he ran, though his path was straight. Were Brother Jond and Olconna still alive?

How much he suddenly cared about the pair and the other prisoners surprised Bransen, and he silently cursed himself for his hesitance back on the path. How could he have considered turning aside? He lowered his head and ran on faster, right to the base of the ice ramp that led up through the carved towerlike guardhouses that flanked the opening to the castle's bailey. But there, right at the base of the ramp, he skidded to a stop, and he quickly put his arm out to block Cormack from running by him.

"It is warded," he explained.

"How do you know?"

Bransen shook his head, but did not otherwise answer. He fell within himself, finding the line of his *chi* and willfully extending that life energy down to the ground beneath him. He felt the power there, clearly, and discordant with the teeming magic that had constructed and now maintained this castle.

"He says that it is trapped," Cormack said to Milkeila when she came up beside them, the four dwarves huffing and puffing close behind.

Milkeila nodded her agreement almost immediately. Her magic was quite similar to that of the Samhaists, both drawing their energies from the power of the world beneath their feet. She stepped up tentatively and began chanting and rattling her claw and tooth necklace.

She nodded again and looked back to Cormack. "Our adversary has collected the muted countering energies to his construction together in this one place," she explained. "It is a powerful ward."

"Can you defeat it?" Cormack asked.

"Or can ye bleed it?" asked Mcwigik, and Cormack looked at him curiously, and all the more curiously when he noted Milkcila nodding and smiling.

The shaman tentatively walked up the ramp, rattling her necklace before her as if it served as a guard to the release of Samhaist magic. As she neared the opening to the castle bailey, she began to softly chant while jiggling her necklace with one hand and running her other hand in the air right near the doorjamb without touching it. Immediately the gleaming ice began to sweat and drip, and little flames seemed to dance within the ice itself.

Bransen felt it all profoundly. He understood Milkeila's counter; she was calling to the ward in measured volume, bringing it forth in bits and pieces to release the pressure. He nodded as he came to understand the trapped flames in the doorjamb, designed to burst forth with tremendous energy if any crossed through without the appropriate magical commands.

As his understanding of both the ward and Milkeila's apparent answer to it crystallized, Bransen joined in the effort, channeling his *chi* to tease out pieces of the warding magic. Now the jamb was sweating all about so profusely that a steady drip fell from the overhead ice beam like a moderate rain.

"Yach, but ye're to drop the whole thing!" Mcwigik grumbled.

"Exactly what the trap was designed to do," Bransen explained. "But Milkeila and I have diffused it enough so that . . ." With a grin back at the dwarf, the Highwayman darted ahead past Milkeila through the opening.

Flames burst forth all around him, a sudden and sharp release of energy, but nowhere near what it would have been initially.

"The explosion would have taken down the front wall," Milkeila explained, leading the others through the puddles and the portal to join Bransen. And not a moment too soon, for they found their friend already engaged with another contingent of the stubborn and pesky trolls.

The first spear thrown his way had become Bransen's weapon as he sprinted right into the midst of the creatures, who quickly formed a semicircle about him. Holding the light spear in his left hand only, Bransen thrust it out to the left, and as he did, he hooked its back end behind his hip. Using that leverage, he swept the spear across in front of him, catching it in a reverse grip with his right hand. He kept the spear head moving left to right, as if he meant to put the thing right around his back, but instead rolled it in his fingers, deftly flipping it to a forehand grip with his right before stabbing it out that way. The troll on that flank, taking the bait that the spear would fast disappear behind the man, had just lifted its club and begun its charge when the thrusting spear pierced its chest.

Bransen bent his arm at the elbow powerfully, sending his hand straight up, and he flipped the spear back across his shoulders. He caught it with an underhand grip with his left and subtly altered the angle of momentum, rolling it completely around to stab out in front of him, again left to right. He loosened his grip, letting the spear slide forth as if in a throw, but caught it firmly lower on the handle with his left and grasped it at midpoint with his right, then stabbed diagonally out to his right more powerfully, retracted, reangled and stabbed straight ahead, then again, turning his hips to put it out right of his position in three short and devastating thrusts.

Three trolls fell away. The others of the group fell back on their heels, confused and frightened, and just as Bransen's friends rushed past him, overwhelming the lot of the trolls. Only an unlucky turn, a broken spear hooking at a bad angle, caused a wound on any of the companions, catching Pergwick painfully in the hip.

The dwarf shrugged off any attention, though, and matched the pace of the others as they charged across the courtyard to the castle's inner door. Again Bransen took the lead, and again he thought to filter out his sensitivity to magic to seek out wards. But the door slid aside and out jumped a man dressed in Samhaist robes and holding a short bronze sword. For a brief instant, Bransen thought it to be Ancient Badden, and he instinctively pulled up.

That proved a fortunate delay, as the Samhaist sent a gout of flames out through his hand to engulf his sword blade and came forward with a series of mighty sweeps, extending those flames out before him.

Mcwigik ambled by Bransen and nearly right into them, before finally stopping with a shout of surprise. He shouted again when Bransen leaped atop him, then sprang from the dwarf's sturdy frame, soaring high and far, lifting his *chi* as he went to carry him far above the expected mortal boundaries. He threw his spear at the man as he went, but the Samhaist was appropriately warded against such missiles and it did not penetrate.

It was no more than a diversion, anyway, and Bransen soared up and over. The surprised Samhaist turned his blade upward to try to intercept, but Bransen was too high. He landed behind the Samhaist, turning as he descended, and as the man tried to turn, Bransen shot his arm through the gap in the man's bended elbow, then knifed his hand up behind the Samhaist's neck, catching a firm grip. He turned with the Samhaist, staying right behind him and up against him, and as soon as the man tried to reverse back the other way, throwing back his shoulder and arm instinctively to break his momentum, Bransen similarly knifed his other arm in the same manner as the first. Now with both of his hands clamped behind the Samhaist's neck, "chicken-winging" his opponent's arms out behind him in the process, Bransen easily turned the man and tripped him up.

They fell together, the Samhaist facedown and with no way to free up his arms to break his fall. Bransen added to the impact by shoving out with his hands just before the Samhaist's face hit the ice.

Bransen sprang up, running right over the man to grab the fallen sword. He was content to leave it at that, but of course, the powries were not. They came in stabbing and slicing, pounding the poor fool back to the ice in short order, so they could dip their berets in his spilling blood.

Through the open door went Bransen. Milkeila came in right behind. "We need to find Badden's place of power," she said. "There must be one greater than all the others."

Before Bransen could agree, Cormack rushed past and shouted, "Brother!" Both Bransen and Milkeila turned his way. The pair then followed Cormack's gaze to the side where a group of miserable prisoners huddled, most prominent among them a man wearing Abellican robes.

"Jond," Bransen breathed, and he thought again of his hesitation back on the ledge, and his serious considerations of just turning around and going south to find Cadayle and Callen.

The Highwayman's face flushed with shame, and even more when Brother Jond called out, "Bransen Garibond, have you come to save us, friend?"

Friend. The word bounced around Bransen's mind, an indictment made all the more damning because Brother Jond didn't even understand that it was one. Cormack had reached him by then, working the ropes to free the man and the others around him.

"Not one will be able to aid us in this battle," Milkeila was saying when Bransen finally joined the couple at the prisoners' side.

"Well found, friend," Bransen said to Jond, and he couldn't suppress his horror at seeing the man's maimed face, scarred slits where his eyeballs once were.

The blind monk followed the voice perfectly and fell over Bransen, wrapping him in a hug, sobbing with joy and appreciation.

"No time," Milkeila said. "That beast is outside, killing my people! I am certain that his power is concentrated in here through some conduit to the magical emanations beneath this glacier."

"A dragon is he!" one of the other miserable prisoners proclaimed.

"Horror of horrors!" another chimed in.

"Whenever Ancient Badden appears to us, he comes down the ramp across the foyer," Brother Jond blurted, shaking his head and pushing Bransen back to arm's length, as if trying to sort it all out.

Bransen recognized the desperation on his face, the need to help here, to try to repay Badden for the injustice that had taken his sight.

"Please! Help me!" came a cry from behind, and all turned to see the Samhaist Bransen had clobbered, crawling on his elbows toward them, the four powries close behind. "Help me!" he said again, reaching plaintively toward the human intruders. As he spoke, Bikelbrin came up beside him, spat in both his hands, and took up a heavy club, lifting it for what was sure to be a killing blow.

"Hold!" Cormack yelled at the dwarf, and he rushed back. "He can tell us."

The warriors of the tribes increased the number and ferocity of their attacks on the dragon. As one, they dismissed their fear and threw their spears, or rushed to engage the beast whenever it swooped low enough for them to reach. They hardly cared for the trolls, then, for next to this monster, those creatures seemed no more than a nuisance.

But the dragon seemed unbothered by it all, seemed pleased by it all. Toniquay and the other shamans, chanting more fiercely to inspire and protect and strengthen their charges, throwing whatever offensive magics they could conjure at the beast, understood better than their noble and ferocious warriors.

And in that understanding, they trembled with fear.

For the dragon not only seemed impervious, but seemed to grow, in size and in strength. No spear penetrated its scaled armor, and no warrior stood against it for more than a few heartbeats. Tearing claws and snapping maw, thunderously beating wings and snapping, clubbing tail drew a line across the Alpinadoran ranks, laying men and women low with impunity.

"How do we even hurt it?" Toniquay heard himself asking. Hoping to answer just that, the shaman completed his spell, bringing forth a bird sculpture he had just magically fashioned from the ice. He held it up before his lips and blew life into the small, crystalline golem, then thrust out his arm, launching it away at the dragon.

The gleaming ice bird flashed overhead, gaining tremendous speed before crashing hard into the dragon.

If the great beast even noticed the animated missile, it did not show it, and the ice bird exploded into a million tiny and harmless droplets of water.

Toniquay winced, and then did so again as he saw another man lifted into the air in the dragon's rear talons. Those mighty feet squeezed powerfully and with such force that the poor warrior's eyeballs popped from their sockets, blood and tissue flushing out behind.

Toniquay could only suck in his breath in horror.

They hustled up the ice ramp, Brother Jond leaning heavily on Bransen and the four dwarves bringing up the back of the line, carrying the captured and battered Samhaist by the wrists and ankles.

The ascending corridor wrapped around to the right as it rose, crossing over one landing and then another, both circular and both centered by the same wide icy beam that seemed the main support for this part of the castle structure.

"I'm not thinking he's long for living," Mcwigik said, and the people in front paused and considered the poor fellow, and winced as one as the dwarves just let him drop face down on the floor.

"Don't ye even be thinking of it," Mcwigik warned them, and Bransen laughed at the accuracy of the dwarf's guess, for he too could clearly see the silent debate between the two over whether or not they would use their healing magic to help the man.

"We cannot just let a fellow human die," Milkeila remarked, as much to her fellow humans as to the dwarves.

Ruggirs walked up beside Mcwigik, stared hard at the humans, then stomped on the back of the Samhaist's neck. Neck bones shattered with a sickening crunch and the Samhaist twitched violently once or twice before lying very still.

"Yer magic's for meself and me boys, and don't ye even think o' using it on one of them that we're fighting when there's fighting afore us," Ruggirs explained.

"Yach, but it's not looking like he was hurt that bad after all," Pergwick said from behind the angry Ruggirs, and Bransen understood the statement to be for the sake of the humans and nothing more, a way to accentuate Ruggirs's point.

"But ye was right, Mcwigik," Pergwick went on. "He weren't long for living."

Mcwigik waved his hand at the humans, bidding them to move along.

They wore expressions of shock (even outrage, in the case of Milkeila and Brother Jond), but they did indeed move along, for they hadn't the time to discuss the powries' tactics.

At the top of the ramp, they came into another circular room, and recognized that they were in the highest tower of the many-turreted castle. Here, too, the support beam ended, but at floor level and not at the ceiling, for it was no support beam in the conventional sense at all.

It was the base of a fountain, one that sprayed a fine and warm mist into this room. That mist contained power, Bransen recognized immediately, and so did Milkeila. That mist was the stuff of Samhaist and shaman earth magic, the exact conduit Milkeila had sought.

The water stream lifted about six feet into the air, before collapsing back in on itself and splashing down into a two-tiered bowl, and though that base was also made of ice, it seemed impervious to the warm flow.

"This is his source of power," Milkeila stated, moving closer and lifting her hand to feel the splash and spray. "This is where Ancient Badden connects to his earthly power."

"You can feel it?" Cormack asked, and Milkeila's expression showed clearly that she was surprised that he could not.

"I can, as well," Bransen said. "It is not so unlike the emanations of your gemstones. It teems with energy, with *ki-chi-kree*."

Cormack rubbed his face and looked over at Brother Jond, who sat silent and expressionless. What Bransen had just said, the comparison of Samhaist magic to Abellican, would be considered heretical to the leaders of the Abellican Church, but Jond seemed not to mind, nor to disagree.

And Cormack certainly didn't. Adding the fact that Bransen had also included his own mystical powers, this strange concept of *chi,* only reinforced to Cormack that he was right in this, that all the Churches and magical powers were in fact pieces of the same god and same godly magic.

As he considered that, he felt an acute sting, a memory of his whipping, across his torn back.

Bransen closed his eyes and stepped up to the fountain, then washed his bare arm through it.

"If that is Badden's source of power, can we, too, use it?" Cormack asked. "Perhaps to counter the Ancient?"

"We cannot use it as he uses it," Milkeila replied. "The powers he garners from it are . . . beyond me."

"This magic is not focused and stable, as with the Abellican gemstones," said Bransen. "It is fluid and ever-changing, and we cannot access it as Badden does— certainly not in the time we have."

"What, then?" Cormack asked.

"Despoil it," both Jond and Milkeila suggested together.

"I will weave spells into it, to divert it from whatever course Badden has fashioned," the barbarian shaman explained, and she stepped right up and began softly chanting, singing, an ancient rhythm of an ancient blessing.

Similarly, Bransen held his arm in the flow and sent his *chi* into it, trying to stagger the infusions and twist them in a wild attempt to somehow alter the magic within the water.

And most straightforward of all came the powries, all four. "Ye heard her, boys," said Mcwigik. "Put a bit o' the dwarf into it!" They lined up around the bowl, unbuckled their heavy belts and dropped their britches, and began their own special and to-the-point method of despoiling the magical water.

"Hope he's not drinking it," Bikelbrin noted with a snicker.

"Yach, but I hope he is," Pergwick added. "We'll give him a taste o' the powries he's not to forget, what!"

He soared over their line with impunity, roaring and breathing forth lines of fire, ignoring their feeble spears thrown by their weak, mortal muscles. He was

Badden, Ancient of the Samhaists, the voice of the ancient gods, who blessed him with the power of immortals, in this case, the strength of a true dragon.

He pondered that if he killed enough of them up here, he might not even need to drop the front off of the glacier and flood the lake. It was a fleeting thought, though, for after the contamination these heathens had brought, the lake would be better off for the purification, in any event! Besides, he would *enjoy* it. As he enjoyed this slaughter of unbelievers. He raked the line; he roared with divine joy.

A spear dug deep into his side.

Ancient Badden's roar changed in timbre. More spears reached up and stung him profoundly. He answered with another gout of fiery breath, and indeed, those nearest barbarians shied away from the flames. But those flames were not nearly as intense as the previous.

Badden's serpentine neck swiveled to offer him a view of his distant castle. Something was wrong here, he knew. Something was interrupting the flow and strength of his magic. Another spear pierced him, shooting lines of hot pain. The dragon roared and beat his long and leathery wings, propelling him across the barbarian ranks and beyond.

The barbarians cheered behind him and threw more spears and clubs and rocks—anything to sting the defeated beast. Then they threw taunts, and more than one noted that the dragon seemed as if it had diminished in actual size.

Feeling the painful sting of a dozen wounds, and feeling even more acutely a sudden distance to the power that fed his draconian form, Badden knew those observations to be more than illusion.

There was little for Cormack to do as the other six, in their own special ways, despoiled Badden's fountain conduit. Too late, he thought to take the gemstone necklace from Milkeila, for now he did not dare interrupt her concentrated efforts.

Nor did he want the gemstones at that time, the former Abellican monk had to admit, to himself at least. The sense of betrayal was too raw and too sharp. His communion with the gemstones had always before elicited a feeling of kinship to Blessed Abelle, the man who had founded the Church less than a century before. But now, clearly, the representatives of that dead prophet considered Cormack's worldview as heretical.

If he used the gemstones in this tremendous battle, would he feel the consternation of the spirit of Abelle?

He considered that perhaps he was making too much of it all, was allowing his anger and disappointment to overrule his judgment. He looked over at Milkeila and could see the strain on her face from her continuing efforts. The magic she battled was tangible, and formidable.

With a sharp inhale, Cormack steadied himself and took a step toward her, determined to dismiss his excuses and offer whatever help he could. But he stopped before he had really even started, for through the translucent wall above and behind Milkeila came such a blossom of orange and yellow that Cormack instinctively pondered that he was seeing the birth of the colors themselves. He watched, mouth agape, unable to even call out a warning, as those colors, the fires of dragon breath, turned the icy wall to water and steam, and through the glowing cloud came the beast itself, framed in hot-glowing mist that made it seem as if it were entering through some extradimensional portal!

The powries cried out and scrambled to pull up their pants; Bransen reacted with snakelike speed and precision, diving to the side, out of the way and collecting Milkeila as he went, still deep in her trance.

Cormack could only stand there and gape as the dragon's serpentine neck swept down and the beast rolled right over it, tucking its wings. As it came around, it was not the lower torso of a reptilian dragon that showed, but the legs of a man, feet adorned with painted toenails and vine-tied sandals. Badden continued his transformation as he completed the somersault and it was a man and not a dragon that landed on the floor before the fountain.

But not just any man; it was the Ancient of the Samhaists come calling.

He landed with such a thud that it seemed as if he must be many times his apparent weight, and the same magic that perpetuated that strange perception reached out from Badden and into his magical ice floor. Huge ripples rolled out from the man, waves of ice, as if the floor had been caught somewhere between the state of a solid and of a liquid. Those ripples rose like waves and crested sharply and with tremendous energy, throwing dwarves and humans alike into the air violently. They crashed into the walls and bounced off the fountain, handheld weapons flying wildly. Milkeila splashed down into the fountain, and with the rumbling all about her, it took her a long while to sort out which way was up and get her head above water.

She fared the best, however, for the only place in the room, other than at Badden's feet, that was not violently rolling and crashing was within that very pool. The shaman grimaced as Mcwigik and Bikelbrin flew past her, grabbing at each other for support until they were split apart from each other by the intervening fountain tower, both ricocheting, spinning out toward the walls. She cried out in pain as her beloved Cormack flew straight up into the air, more than a dozen feet—and only his considerable training allowed him to sort himself out enough in his descent to prevent landing on his head.

She winced at watching Bransen, not flying about, but maneuvering over the solid waves as a boat might defy heavy surf, and she gasped in shock to see one wave break right over poor Ruggirs, smashing down on the dwarf with tremendous force, blowing out his breath in a great and profound groan. The ice wave blended right over him, burying him in the floor.

Not far from her, Ancient Badden cackled with enjoyment, and stamped his foot again, giving rise to another series of waves, ones that crashed into the rebounding first set and sent the whole of the room into frenzy. Even the walls began to ripple and buckle! Now all of Milkeila's friends flopped and bounced about uncontrollably, except for buried Ruggirs and one other.

To the Jhesta Tu, Bransen's posture was known as *doan-chi-kree,* the "stance of the mountain," a place of complete balance and perfect calm, where the straight-standing mystic reached his line of life energy, his *chi,* below his *ki,* his groin, and down to *doan,* the floor beneath his feet. That line of life energy became the mystic's roots, his stability, and in such a state, a Jhesta Tu could not be moved by a charging giant.

The floor rolled to Badden's command beneath Bransen's feet, but Bransen moved with it, his legs bending and straightening accordingly and so perfectly that his upper body remained perfectly still. He locked stares with Badden. The Ancient stomped his foot again. But Bransen would not be thrown.

Milkeila drew courage from that image and shook herself from her stupor. She reached into her magic again and thrust it into Badden's fountain, demanding that the violence end.

She felt as if she was trying to hold back the great Mirianic Ocean itself! But she shook away her despair and pressed on, blocking out all the distractions, focusing solely on the task at hand.

The room began to quiet.

Ancient Badden broke off his stare and looked over his shoulder at the woman, feeling her intrusion into his magic as keenly as if she was reaching into his stomach and tugging at his entrails. The Samhaist roared, as much the voice of a dragon as that of a man, and stabbed his hands out to the fountain's centering geyser. The roiling waters froze solid suddenly, encasing Milkeila's hands and forearms in a crushing grip.

Badden whipped his arm in a sudden circle, and the icicle responded likewise, turning over itself as it rushed around, twisting Milkeila right over.

She felt her shoulders pop from their sockets, then wrenched her back as the ice stopped its swing abruptly, locking her top half fast in place while her lower body whipped around.

Waves of nausea and dizziness and floating black spots filled her gut and head and eyes, and when the ice returned again to its liquid fountain form, the helpless woman dropped into and under the water, with no sense of direction or awareness at all.

Badden chuckled as he felt his magic flow more fully once more, but he knew that the diversion of this foolish woman had cost him. For in the moment of calm, the humans and dwarves had closed.

The Ancient snapped the fabulous sword off of his back, took the hilt in both hands and sent it out to arm's length. With a maniacal cackle, the man went up onto the ball of one foot, hooked that balance point into his magical energy and began to spin. Not to spin like a young girl at play, but to truly whirl about, gaining speed and momentum with every turn. His form blurred; he altered the angle of his blade so that there was no possible approach.

Pergwick howled in sudden pain and fell away, desperately clutching at his head to hold his scalp in place. He went down to the floor, looking frantically for his lost beret.

Mcwigik and Cormack, side by side, fell away without getting stung, but Cormack shouted anyway, in frustrated outrage and not in physical pain, for he found himself separated from his fallen Milkeila, and he couldn't see her above the rim of the fountain bowl. He tried to maneuver around the side, but got all tangled up with the ducking and retreating Mcwigik.

"What whirlpool's he swimming in?" the dwarf barked in absolute surprise.

Bransen, too, slipped out of reach, but in a more controlled manner, taking a full measure of his adversary, and Bikelbrin dove over the side of the fountain, splashing down into the water. He had just regained his footing when Badden suddenly extended his reach, using the narrow sword as a focus for the release of his magical energy.

The prone Pergwick skidded across the room. Cormack and Mcwigik went flying away in a confused tumble, and Bikelbrin flew back into the center pole of the fountain with such force that his sensibilities kept right on flying.

Dazed and hardly conscious as he hit the water once more, the dwarf flopped over the drowning Milkeila. On pure instinct, he hooked his arm under the woman's head and rolled himself onto his back, atop her back, using her bulk to keep his own head above the water. He kept his arm hooked to hold himself steady, and that alone saved the gasping Milkeila, for the weight of the dwarf rolled him back and his arm brought her head out of the water.

Ancient Badden had never felt a purer release of magical energy, as satisfying as any release any man might know. He stomped his foot to accentuate the magic, sending the room into a series of crashing ice waves once again.

Before he could congratulate himself, however, Ancient Badden looked into the face of one who had not been moved by his magical thrust, and who seemed not bothered in the least by the current rocking.

Bransen Garibond held his ground. "You have my sword," the Highwayman calmly explained, and Badden looked at him in abject disbelief.

"It is you!" the Samhaist replied. "I threw you from the glacier!"

"Highwaymen bounce," Bransen replied.

"You were a babbling fool—an idiot who could hardly stand!"

"Or I was a clever scout, taking a measure of Ancient Badden and his forces before bringing doom upon them."

Badden stood up straight and shook his head—or started to, for faster than a striking serpent the Highwayman struck. He sprang forward and snapped off a left and right jab for the old man's face, connecting solidly both times.

He leaped back immediately, throwing back his hips and keeping his belly just an inch ahead of the thrusting sword. As he bent double with the move, Bransen drove down his forearm to knock the blade downward.

But Badden had anticipated that, and he cunningly turned the sword so that Bransen's arm hit the razor edge.

Bransen did grimace, but simply rolled his hand down lower, changing the angle and driving the blade out wide. Then he rushed back in, slamming against Badden, one hand holding the man's sword arm, the other hand grasping the old man's face.

And Badden responded by snapping his free arm up behind Bransen. First he crushed the man into him, and with strength beyond anything Bransen could ever have believed possible!

Badden grabbed the back of Bransen's hair and bandanna and tugged back violently, and Bransen growled in pain and in the sudden horror that he might again lose that precious gemstone. He raked his hand straight down, fingernails drawing lines of blood on Badden's face, then reversed and hit the old man with a series of short and devastating uppercuts, crunching bone beneath his pounding fist.

Badden reflexively let go of Bransen's hair to bring

his free hand in to stop the barrage, but the moment he did Bransen shot out to the side, going after Badden's sword arm, going after the sword, furiously.

But even though he got the leverage, the proper angle, he couldn't pry the weapon free, and he realized his error, realized how vulnerable he had left himself, right before Badden's fist smashed him in the back, driving his breath from his body. This was no mortal he faced, but some magical monstrosity! He needed the sword, but he couldn't hope to get it. Badden pounded him again, and Bransen's legs went weak.

"Fool!" the old Samhaist chided.

Bransen fell within himself as yet another explosive and thundering punch crashed against his back. He found his line of *chi,* found his center. . . . He thought of Cadayle. He centered all of his fleeting thoughts on her, using her image as a focal point for holding on to his fast-flying consciousness. Something flew past him, and he was jerked backward. Another form rushed by— Cormack. He heard the slap of punches; he managed to glance over his shoulder to see Mcwigik tight about Badden's leg, biting the man hard on the thigh, and to see Cormack facing Badden straight up, raining a rapid barrage of punches against the man's face. That one was no novice to fighting.

But neither was he— were they—a match for Ancient Badden.

Bransen guessed Badden's move—to pull free the sword and be done quickly with all three—so as soon as the Ancient started, Bransen reacted with sudden fury and all the power of his training behind him. He lunged for Badden's sword hand, grasping the wrist and cupping his other hand over the Ancient's clenched fist, snapping with all his strength, with all of his leverage, with every ounce of Jhesta Tu and gemstone magic he could possibly muster. One chance, he knew. One moment of focused power.

Ancient Badden's hand bent back over his wrist, his

wrist-bone shattering. Bransen drove his own hand up over Badden's fist, catching the serpent hilt of his mother's sword and pulling it free.

He got slugged one more time but anticipated it and was diving into a forward roll even as Badden's fist hit him, thus absorbing much of the blow. He rolled head over, coming numbly back to his feet, and he spun about just in time to see Cormack launched in a sidelong somersault by a vicious backhand.

Staring at Bransen with hate-filled eyes, clutching his broken hand in close at his side, the Ancient clawed his free hand down on the stubborn, gnawing powrie, and with frightening strength plucked Mcwigik free.

He lifted the dwarf to throw him at Bransen, but the Highwayman was already there, coming under the would-be sentient missile. He stabbed, and quickly slashed upward, cutting under Badden's arm. The Ancient still managed to throw Mcwigik, but suddenly he had so little strength behind it that the dwarf bounced and turned and roared right back in. Or would have, if there had been a need.

Bransen worked like a dancer, spinning, swinging his arm, changing the angle of his deadly blade with such skill and precision that Ancient Badden never once blocked or turned effectively enough to prevent the Highwayman from hitting him exactly where Bransen had wanted to.

The sword slashed across Badden's belly, came around and poked him hard in the biceps, and as he lurched, his arm lowering, slashed him across the chin, drawing a sizable line across half his throat in the process. Over and over, Bransen rolled the blade, diagonal down, left and right, and lines of bright blood erupted all across the Samhaist's light green robes.

Now Badden wore a mask of fear, and he stumbled backward, trying pitifully to get his arms up. Bransen kept hitting him, slashing him, even lifting a foot to kick him. Back went the Ancient, who suddenly seemed little more than an old man, to fall into an awkward sitting position against the wall. And Bransen was there, suddenly, sword edge against Badden's already bleeding neck. Ancient Badden laughed at him, blood dripping out with every chortle.

"You seem happy for a man about to die," said Bransen. Behind him, Cormack cried out for Milkeila, and Bransen heard splashing.

"We all die, fool," Badden replied. "You will not likely see near the years I have known."

"Or the failure," said Bransen.

"Ah yes, the triumph of your Abellican Church," Badden retorted, and indeed, Bransen's face did crinkle at that.

"My Church?" he asked incredulously.

"You have thrown in with them!"

Bransen snickered at the absurdity of the remark.

"Do you think them any better?" Badden asked, his words becoming more labored. "Oh, they find their shining moment now, when their baubles so impress the young and strong lairds. But where will they be when those lairds are old and lie dying, and those baubles offer nothing?

"We Samhaists know the truth, the inevitability," he went on. "There is no escape from the darkness. Their promises are hollow!" He laughed, a bloody and bitter sound.

"A truth you are about to realize intimately," Bransen reminded him.

But Badden's laugh mocked him. "And as these Abellican fools rise ascendant, buoyed by their empty promises of forever, do you think they will be any better?"

But now Bransen was back on level emotional ground. "Do you think that I care?" he chided right back, and that brought a curious look from the old man.

"Then why are you here?"

Bransen laughed at him and stood straight. "Because they paid me," he said with a cold and casual tone, "and because I hate everything for which you stand."

His sword came across, and Badden's puzzled expression remained on his face as his head rolled across the floor.

EPILOGUE

The six survivors and Brother Jond collected the rest of the prisoners and led them out of Ancient Badden's ice castle.

Outside, the battle had ended; with the dragon chased off, the troll lines had broken, and now both barbarian and dwarf lined the chasm, throwing stones and blocks of ice and spears down at the monster that prowled its depths. From the roars that rose, it seemed as if many were hitting the mark. For the great white worm would not flee into one of its burrows to escape the barrage. It would not back down from the threat, though it had no way of scaling the chasm wall to get at its attackers.

Its mighty bulk and power could not protect it from its own lack of brains.

Mcwigik and Bikelbrin rushed off to join in the fun, and even Pergwick, holding his cap against his head, and his cap holding his scalp in place, followed.

"You are from Vanguard?" Brother Jond asked Cormack, who supported him as they moved across the ice.

"Years ago," Cormack explained. "And Chapel Abelle

before that. I was a member of Father De Guilbe's expedition."

That sparked recognition in Jond, and a great smile creased his face. "I had thought the feel of your clothing to be that of an Abellican robe!"

"I am not Abellican anymore, Brother."

Jond stopped and faced Cormack, though of course he couldn't actually see the man.

"I was cast out," Cormack admitted. "I questioned the limitations."

"Limitations?"

"The Abellican Church's refusal to explore those traditions and magic outside the domain of the Church and the gemstones," Cormack honestly offered. "There is more beauty to be found in this world, a wider truth than that which we have come to represent." Brother Jond gave a curious "hmm," and Cormack had no idea if he was offending or intriguing the man. "The woman who accompanied us into the castle is a shaman of an Alpinadoran tribe," Cormack explained.

"I gathered as much."

"I love her."

"Hmm."

"And I see in her true and divine beauty—I see it in our other friend as well, this man named Bransen."

"Ah, the Highwayman, yes," said Jond. "He is a unique one."

"And possessed of godly powers."

Brother Jond shook his head, unwilling to make that jump.

"Powers akin to those of our gemstones," Cormack clarified, and Jond now nodded.

"I witnessed his healing hands," Jond said. "And his grace is rather amazing. But he is no man of God. Not yet, though I suspect that his nature compels him to look that way. For all his life, our friend Bransen cared only for Bransen, and absent in him is a sense of community and greater good. No, not absent," he quickly corrected.

"Simply not yet developed. I hold out great hopes for that one, if he doesn't get himself killed too soon."

As Jond put forth those observations, Cormack looked out at Bransen, who was paralleling the powries toward the chasm. The monk's words, so very much like his own to Milkeila regarding the Highwayman, rang true indeed.

"We will get you back to Chapel Pellinor and Dame Gwydre," Cormack promised.

"Perhaps I might put in a good word for Brother Cormack."

Cormack winced at the title Jond had used, both because he doubted that any good word would do any good, and because he wasn't sure that he wanted it back.

"They ran, you know," he said. "Father De Guilbe and the others of Chapel Isle—our chapel here in Alpinador— did not join in the greater cause with the Alpinadorans and the powries. Instead, they fled south, bound for Vanguard."

Brother Jond started to reply—to offer some justification, Cormack knew. But instead he just sighed and shook his head, and Cormack realized that this wasn't the first time this man had been disappointed by the actions of fellow Abellicans.

Cormack didn't press him on it, though. He hooked his arm under Jond's shoulder to support the man, and led him away.

Ye been wanting this for a long time, mate," Mcwigik said.

Pergwick, a thick white bandage running about his head, chin to top, and under his replaced beret, lowered his eyes and kicked a stone. "Ruggirs was me brother," he said. "We slapped blood together that if either got killed to death, th'other would watch over the Sepulcher and care for the kid. It'll be me brother, too, ye know."

"Aye, there's that," Mcwigik agreed. "But I'm not for

waiting the years ye're to need. The lake's made me batzy already, I tell ye!"

"Not asking ye to wait, and I'm thinking that yerself and Bik are to open things up for the rest," Pergwick replied, looking up and seeming much more at ease. "Kriminig and the others've said as much—that we'll all go south when word comes back from Mcwigik that there's a place for us. I'm guessing that more'n ourselves have had too much o' Mithranidoon."

Mcwigik nodded and clapped Pergwick on the shoulder. "Good enough, then, and I'll be smiling when I see ye again."

Pergwick grinned and began to nod, but Mcwigik cautioned him with an upraised hand.

"Don't ye go shaking yer head too rough!" the dwarf said.

"Aye, we're not wanting yer brains to go flying out. Ye're not for much to spare," added Bikelbrin, walking over and carrying a large sack full of supplies.

"What do ye know?" Mcwigik asked, and Bikelbrin motioned to the side, where Cormack, Bransen, Milkeila, and Brother Jond stood in a group, all carrying sacks.

"Where'd they get the goods?" asked Mcwigik.

"The barbarians," Bikelbrin replied. "They ain't too happy with the girl, but they know she just saved their homes."

"An easier road for us all, then," Mcwigik reasoned.

"More food to start, at least. As for the rest, we'll be seein'."

They both patted Pergwick on the shoulder, then moved to join the others. The group of six was off the glacier that same night, moving determinedly south. The weather stayed warm over the next couple of days, and they encountered no trolls, and so they made great progress, despite the soreness from their fight with Badden and the more serious wounds, which Milkeila's people had treated very well. Even Brother Jond, sightless though he was, walked with a spring in his step and took up hearty and spirited conversations with the two powries.

"You will return to your wife?" Milkeila asked Bransen a couple of days out.

"The moment I deliver this"—he jostled the small pack tied to the side of his pouch, one that contained the head of Ancient Badden—"and she grants me the passage, as promised."

"You will sail far away?"

"As far as I can."

"To where?"

That question seemed to startle Bransen.

"Are you running to something or away from something?" Milkeila asked, as Cormack walked over.

"The two are not mutually exclusive," Bransen replied.

"But the distinction is important."

Bransen shrugged as if he didn't agree.

"You are a man of marvelous skills—important skills in this trying time," Cormack added.

"All times are trying."

"Then all times call for heroes, else all will be lost," Milkeila said.

Bransen snorted. "The way of the world is the way of the world and beyond any one man."

"That seems a pointless outlook," said Cormack.

"It is one I have come by through bitter experience."

Milkeila quickly added, "You have been given a great gift and have never thought to turn it to the benefit of all?"

Bransen considered his time in Pryd Holding, when he first earned the title of the Highwayman, when he spent his days stealing from the laird and distributing the booty to the unfortunate peasants, crushed under the weight of his heel, and he could not help but laugh. That laugh quickly soured, though, for he could not help but admit that even then, the good of the people was more a vehicle for his own ego than truly for the good of his people.

"We just saved the people of Mithranidoon," Milkeila reminded.

"And with positive ramifications that will spread throughout the whole of Vanguard, no doubt," Cormack added. "You cannot deny that we did indeed just changed the world for the better. The bloody head you hold in your belt pouch is no small matter—perhaps it is in the measure of the centuries, but it certainly is not a small matter to the people of this day and age and region."

Bransen snickered and waved them away. His road was to his beloved Cadayle and to Callen. His responsibilities were to them, and to himself. The idea that he owed anyone else anything seemed on its surface preposterous—how many people in the world had ever shown the young Stork compassion and service?

As the two walked off, Bransen looked around at his fellow heroes and poor Brother Jond, the only other survivor of the band that had come north on the command of Dame Gwydre. He thought of Crait and Olconna and couldn't help but grin as he considered Crazy V.

He tried to deny it but could not. He had found a strange comfort and warmth in being a part of that lost group. And as much as Bransen told himself that he was only along on the mission for the sake of Cadayle and his family . . . He had hesitated at the bluff overlooking the glacier, yes, but in the end, he had gone down to do battle with Badden.

And in the process, he had formed a new bond with this competent group. He couldn't deny the warmth.

He felt like he belonged.

Visit **www.panmacmillan.com** to read more about all our books and to buy them. You will also find features, author interviews and news of any author events, and you can sign up for e-newsletters so that you're always first to hear about our new releases.